GOPTRI OF THE MISTS
Kitaab Ek

Bill McCormick

Azoth Khem Publishing
Huntsville, AL
March 2021

An Azoth Khem Publishing Publication

For S. Shane Thomas, for being an early believer in this world.

Now:

If you see something, say something. Only you really know your neighbors. When you spot someone who doesn't belong, or if someone causes you concerns, please punch in the free integers #** on your portie to contact the Goptri's professionals. They have the skills and equipment necessary to find out the truth. Remember, your safety is your Goptri's greatest concern.

ओम'

Pearl Goodness of the Bright Flower glared at the instruments, made an obscene blatting noise, and, finally, just turned them off. It took precisely one perceived sepi-clik for her radio to flare to life.

"Pearl 3-9-6-4-2," whined the rude operator, using her tank designation instead of her gift name, "is your ship malfunctioning?"

"No, it is not."

"Then, why are your instruments no longer functioning?"

"I turned them off."

"Why would you do something like that?"

"Because they are useless."

"The manual says you need them. Specifically, page 3-9-7, paragraph 9, subparagraph zed. How will you dock without them?"

"Like this."

With that, she did as she had done many times before, set deed to word, and began approaching the docking nipple. Shortly thereafter, she irised her ship's sphincter and slid it into place. There wasn't even a hint of a bump; the action had been that smooth.

She slid out of her harness and let her tentacles stretch. Genetically modified to work on land, her brand's tentacles were far more substantial than anything her cephalopod cousins had ever developed. If she stretched them completely out, she would be over two meters tall. She never did that unless she was swimming since it was too hard to balance otherwise. Even so, walking upright at just under a meter and three-fourths, she was an impressive sight.

She chuckled at the irony. She, and all the Pearls, had been bred to do aquatic research. She could remain underwater with modified gills and lungs, without aid, for half a clik at depths up to a fifth a kay. Using her tentacles for propulsion and her makerform torso for steering, she could move quickly and gracefully. She was a marine art form unto herself. But instead of doing what they'd been bred to do, it had turned out that the Pearl line was the best group of pilots on the planet.

She slipped off her work tunic and considered briefly going topless. Her perfectly mottled blue/grey skin was flawless, and she knew several mals who appreciated the view. She decided against it simply because she wanted to wear her new yellow sari. It made her green/black eyes sparkle. She'd had a rough time scouting the undersea volcanoes for the last sixty turns, almost getting blown to bits once. So, this even, she didn't just want to be another Pearl; she wanted to feel pretty.

While waiting for the airlock to cycle, she checked to make sure the bright pink henna tattoo on her wrist was still visible, simply because the other brands could then tell her apart from the rest of Pearls. She then squaddled across the floor to enter Veruna Ville, an underwater city built over four hundred Suns ago by the first Goptri of the Mists. The first Goptri had been a Shiva named Manish. This fact, his name, wasn't discovered until after he'd passed away. It doesn't seem to have been a secret; it was just that everyone thought of him as the Goptri and nothing else. That was fine with Pearl. To her, that was the way things should be.

When Veruna Ville was originally inhabited it had been home

to about thirty thousand brands. Since then, it had grown to be a home for over half a million. It had been home to Pearl Goodness of the Bright Flower for these last forty Suns. Her only home.

No one outside of its residents knew of its existence. Not even the ubiquitous Din-La. It was a haven of growth and contentment. It was also the foremost scientific facility in the world.

They'd watched, fascinated at the accomplishments of Lord Südermann. While interesting in the abstract, there was nothing there that was new to them. They could have done the same things numerous Suns sooner, but their focus was quite different.

The stars were the stars; Arreti was their home. This is where they would apply their knowledge.

She turned out of the entry corridor and spied Pearl Blessed of the Cool Breeze walking towards her. They hugged, snizzled their tentacles, and ran for the commissary. At this time of the turn, it would be full of Pearls. All of the assigned scout ships would be coming in from all over the Goptri's oceans.

This happened once every sixty turns, whether the Pearls wanted it to or not. The fact that they did was simply a bonus.

The Pearls, alone among the brands, were parthenogenetic. These meetings allowed them to share knowledge and experiences that they would pass along to their stem-pods when they burst forth. Pearl Goodness of the Bright Flowers was still many Suns from that happy turn, but she smiled in anticipation anyway.

The one hundred currently active Pearls sat in a large, padded pit in the commissary, swapping stories and hugs in equal measure. There were several reports that the Orcan population was returning to form. That meant the two hundred Suns of plankton seeding were finally paying off. It also meant the noise pollution, which had bothered those magnificent creatures, was now well and truly gone. They bred best when they could communicate.

Pearl shared her experiences concerning the undersea volcanoes five hundred kays southeast of their home. They were supposed to be dormant. One of the most, allegedly, dormant ones had almost killed her when it erupted under her ship. Something was happening there. She hoped the data she'd collected would shed light on exactly what.

Pearl Blessed of the Cool Breeze had been ranging far north and east. She reported the Children of the Waters had made great strides with their plan to see if they could capture and educate the Mermaids. The creatures, while stunningly beautiful, were dumber than algae. According to her, the Children had discovered notes in Rohta's lair in Kalindor, which allowed them to hope the Mermaids would one turn be more than just ornaments.

All in all, it was a happy time. The Pearls shared all they could and then retired to the lounge for an adult libation or three. While they were all highly trained scientists, covering many disciplines, they were also just as social as the next brand. Their laughter soon filled the room. The bartenders kept the drinks coming, and the Pearls kept them disappearing.

Finally, after a couple of cliks, the room began to thin. Pearl Goodness of the Bright Flowers and Pearl Blessed of the Cool Breeze sat down at a table and talked, as femmes are wont to do from time to time, about the incredible asses on the new recruits. They'd also noted some had cute faces, but that was a subset that didn't interrupt their conversation flow.

They knew they were lucky. Like ninety percent of the Pearls, for all intents and purposes, they were pacifists. They couldn't kill another being if they tried. The remaining ten percent were conscripted into the Goptri's army to be pilots in his air guard.

While the subject never came up, they certainly knew their history. The original Pearl was one of the rarest creatures known to the makers. She was a female serial killer and had twenty-three confirmed kills before she was captured. She showed no remorse whatsoever. Nor did she brag. She simply accepted that getting caught was a risk she took to pursue her, as she called it, hobby.

The death penalty had fallen out of favor long before her capture. Of course, so had crimes like hers, as the population had thinned and dispersed. Edward Q. Rohta had asked for her. He'd believed he'd be able to excise the gene that made her kill.

He'd agreed to keep her in stasis until completely satisfied she no longer presented a danger to society. Time wandered by, and he used her genetic material to create a couple of brands. She was part of the Llamias, who now permeated the plains across the ocean and part White Teeth of the Children of the Waters. But her face and her core went utterly into the Pearls.

One of Rohta's many fancies; he'd built the Pearls as a custom order for a deep-sea research company, they'd done their assigned tasks well enough, and, thanks to some serious tinkering with their genetic makeup, were tame as pets.

But he never did fix the first Pearl. The story held he was close to a solution when the revolution came. No one knows what happened to her stasis chamber. All anyone knows is that one in ten Pearls will exhibit the ability to kill. Granted, it's without the socio-pathology that defined the original Pearl, but it's still there.

Initially shunned or segregated, they quickly realized they could be excellent additions to the military uses that the makers had for many brands. As the original Goptri noted, "The makers loved making wars; they just didn't like fighting them. The brands solved that problem."

For a while, anyway.

ओम'

Rama Llandhaven was the undisputed Sovereign of the southern portion of the continent. This fact was terrific as far as it went. Regardless, and this is what irked him, the brands loved the Goptri to the north. The naif's continued fascination with all things that had to do with Arreti was annoying and detrimental. There were petroleum reserves to be tapped, nuclear plants to be built, asteroids to be mined, and so much else that could be done. All of which would make life better for the brands and him - especially him.

However, the Goptri didn't see it that way. The citizens of the continent, by and large, tended to agree with him. They were clueless fools. Rama knew that, but they were also the clueless fools who kept him in power, so he couldn't afford to irk them as much as they irked him.

He remembered watching the launch of Lord Südermann's interstellar craft fifteen Suns ago, thinking it would spark the masses. This event would finally inspire them to look beyond this simple rock on which they lived. Then the Goptri went on vid, lauded the achievement, and congratulated the engineers and scientists who made it happen. Then he talked about how the great discoveries had yet to be made on Arreti and, senselessly, added insult to injury by having Lord Südermann agree with him.

At least in principle.

But that was enough.

Rama's dreams lay shattered.

More galling still, art, literature, and music began arriving from Ooo-Ah-Nah-Han; the first world visited. It was revelatory. Truly alien works. Simple things every resident on Arreti took for granted, at least conceptually, were missing. They'd never invented the wheel, which made sense, when looked at reasonably, since they were arboreal and lived-in trees. However, they did have hovercraft technology far beyond anything the brands had conceived and nuclear engines that defied all preconceptions. Trade was opened.

Another thing they did not have was God. Not even as a rumor. They'd figured out the basic elements of evolution early in their development and never looked beyond them. Yet, even without religious rules, they were kind and giving, and everyone who met them found them welcoming. Of course, they were yet another voice in the Südermann's choir.

She'd bent reality into nine-dimensional, logic-defying contortions, making them fit into God's will, but no one complained too much.

Rama was sure these developments would force the natives to look outward., and they might have had not the Goptri delivered his famous "Gifts from Above" speech, which welcomed these discoveries as aids to the greater cause of healing Arreti.

One of the *gifts* was a safe and portable nuclear engine. There was something to be said for that, but Rama thought it all shortsighted.

Still, his dream, like all good dreams, could always be accomplished another way. He began making alliances with the Yeldas to the north. They were uncouth by his standards, with all their singing and wodka drinking, but they had immense resources and weren't afraid to trade them. He realized as long as they stayed in small tribes, they were no threat to anyone but themselves. However, if they ever found a true leader, they would be terrifying. They were both physically strong and perspicacious. It was fortunate for him and everyone else. They were also paranoid and didn't work well together.

Furthermore, he'd opened trade with the Shin-Sen. Hidebound by traditions, no one understood they, nevertheless, had a sense of honor. Their idea of war left him baffled. It was more akin to ballet than anything else he could name. Warriors would meet in battle and engage in single combat while thousands stood and watched. Then, for reasons that may as well have been rooted in mysticism, the tribes would honor the results of the fight even if it meant they'd lost their village or winter supplies.

Now some of those deals were going to start paying off. Rama would simply circumvent the Goptri and begin working in empty areas of Arreti. Thanks to the brands' low birth rates, there were billions upon billions of cubic kays for him to exploit. With the help of his new partners, of course. He was a cad, not a cheat.

As one of the four simian brands made by Rohta, he felt his Guenon brand was the most handsome. He slicked his facial hair, using a lightly scented pomade so the blue mask of his face would glisten in the light, and tightened his cravat. He walked down the hall, as he did after every breaklight, paid perfunctory – if insincere, homage at the various hallway shrines, and greeted his staff. Through many Suns of trial and error, he'd learned that treating the help with some semblance of respect garnered him more obsequious service than threats did. So, to get what he wanted, he was cordial to the cretins.

He stepped out onto the balcony as an aide handed him his one new obsession, a cup of mint tea from the Shin-Sen, and smiled at the clear blue skies. Grishma was his favorite season: clean and dry. While his staff worked to prepare the table for his first meal of the turn, he nodded his appreciation to them as he suddenly felt something tweak his forehead.

Then he felt the back of his head disappear.

Then he felt nothing at all.

ओम'

Kshatriya Ragamooth, all Goptri's elite guard members took the first name Kshatriya, slid down the tree, and leapt onto the modified Kalindorian motorcycle. It had slightly wider tires, and more sensors, than the base model. All of which were necessary when you were using it in a jungle.

He was upset with himself even though he knew the Goptri would be pleased. He'd wanted a chest shot so there would be an open casket at the funeral. But Rama had bent forward just as the bullet had crossed the threshold, and, well, it wasn't as though he could call it back or make it turn.

The face should still be pretty intact. Maybe they could do something with stuffing.

Or maybe all the hot air would be enough to fill out the gaping holes. According to the election results, it had worked for Rama's logic, so it might work for his face.

Ragamooth's Pangolin naturally scaly skin and razor-sharp talons served him well in the tasks that the Goptri needed completed to keep Bharat safe. Like his ant-eating cousins, he had exceptional eyesight. Unlike them, he had lightning-fast reflexes. The Pangolins liked to joke that Rohta gave them those reflexes because he couldn't figure out how to make them able to kill with just their tongues. He'd had to make up the slack somehow.

There had never been any question of who this Goptri would send on the assignment. His brand had been built for military subterfuge, after all, and a thousand Suns had not changed that.

He charged the sensors on his cyke and swore under his breath. There was a patrol less than four kays away to the northeast, and they were headed right toward him. They were the last thing he needed. He doubted they knew of the assassination yet, but they would still be armed and trained.

He quickly broke down his rifle as he watched his screen. He decided to pull a little to the west and meet his transport in the second planned location. He sent a burst transmission with the information and hoped the captain picking him up wasn't as much of an idiot as the one who'd dropped him off.

Suddenly the patrol split into two groups. One headed slightly east and south directly towards Rama's palace. The other spread out and began, obviously, hunting for him. While a part of him had to admire their speed and professionalism, he heartily wished they'd been amateurs.

Oh well, not every wish comes true.

He eased further west, his cyke almost silent with its electric engine, and arced towards the rendezvous point. It became apparent the soldiers hunting him were on foot. That information was useful to know. It meant he could just continue an easy arc and never encounter them. Given how well trained they, undoubtedly, were, that was an encounter he would gladly miss.

Less than a clik later, he spied the appointed glade and saw this captain was not an idiot. The rear ramp was down with guards posted on it. The ship's weapons were free and targeting. The vessel, colored gold, purple, yellow, green, and covered with glitter, was meant to look Kalindorian. Even though everyone knew that there was no such thing as an armed Kalindorian ship, it was convincing enough for its purposes here this turn.

He didn't even bother slowing as he went up the ramp and parked in the slot provided. The guards raced past him to their posts, and a cadet presented him with a smart salute and an envelope. The latter contained a note from the captain explaining they would take a circuitous route back to the Goptri, so he had time to shower and change. He was also invited to the captain's mess for a mid-break repast.

He thanked the cadet and then followed the youngling to the quarters he'd been assigned.

He immediately saw a set of dress greens hung across from the bed, as well as a full kit for grooming. The cadet closed the door behind him and left him to his thoughts.

Ragamooth didn't have many. Mostly he was impressed with the competence of the crew. Whatever thoughts he had about assassinating Rama Llandhaven were relegated to the part of his mind that cataloged duties done.

And done well. He suffered pride like all sinners.

He had approximately a clik before he met the captain, so he stripped and wandered into the shower stall. Using the provided kit, he polished his scales, brushed his fangs, and sharpened his claws. Hot water was a luxury he hadn't experienced in a long time, so he took full advantage of it.

Once dried, he pulled down the dress greens and was truly

surprised to find all his chest medals' replicas. He promptly dressed, checked himself in the mirror, and headed into the hall. The cadet was outside his door, standing guard. He tossed off a tight salute and led Ragamooth to the captain's mess.

Given the ship's efficiency, he was not surprised to be met by a Pearl wearing captain's pips.

"Namaste Kshatriya Ragamooth. I am Captain Pearl Wind Before the Reeds, welcome aboard the GS Djakarta. The Goptri sends his regards, and congratulations on a job well done."

"I live to serve."

"As do we all. We will be flying over the lands of the Yelda as well as the Dragon Lords. We will be maintaining a speed of four hundred kays per clik. The Goptri wants us seen and tracked."

"Then, we are expendable?" The question was more protocol than concern. His life could be forfeit at any time for any reason; there was no cause for worry in that regard.

"No. My orders are explicit in that regard. If we are attacked, I am to do all in my power to survive. Even if that means fleeing the battle."

He considered the information briefly. It meant there was something on this ship, which was important, and he doubted it was him or the captain. Or, maybe, possibly, it indicated there was something important somewhere else, and the Goptri didn't want anyone looking in that direction.

Either way meant this could be an exciting trip.

The meal itself was simple yet excellent. A traditional seaweed and seafood soup served cold, perfectly grilled prancing fowl served with a tuber covered with butter, mushrooms, and a citrus spiced ice cream for dessert.

Of course, no ship of the Goptri's would be complete without a perfect cup of java, and the Djakarta did not disappoint. As he was savoring each sip, the captain offered him a small, but perfectly rolled, cigar.

"From a raid on the Sugar Pirate coves. They are truly a gift from above."

He snipped the tip with his talon and allowed the cadet to light it for him. The cadet then walked around the table and lit the captain's as well.

Ragamooth inhaled contentedly and settled back to see what time would deliver.

ओम'

All of Veruna Ville was atwitter with the news of the assassination of Rama Llandhaven. In the four turns since the local newsies confirmed what the Din-La had reported, the citizens had been concerned with nothing else. Pearl Goodness of the Bright Flower had almost thought to postpone her next scouting mission due to the palpable fear that permeated every room. Mostly they feared whoever had done this heinous deed would also come after their beloved Goptri.

None of them could imagine life without the divine guidance of a Goptri.

What was odd about that statement is it was often publicly expressed. Yet, despite being fashioned to resemble the gods of the makers, the commonly espoused belief system for the denizens of Bharat was atheism or, at most, soft agnosticism. They may have a working grasp of the fundamentals of the universe, but the irony of their beliefs still eluded them.

Regardless, they hung on to the trappings of their makers' religion. When greeting each other, they would still perform the Namaskar, wherein each individual would hold their palms together and say Namaste. While quaint, it had the advantage of forcing the individual's fingertips together, activating pressure points, which would, in turn, increase memory for a moment. It made remembering names the first time easier. They also would still toss a coin or two into a river even though the time had long since passed for them to need the dissolved metals to make up for a lack in their foods. Even little things rendered meaningless by their advanced biologies, like starting each full meal with a spicy food, and ending it with a sweet, were still common.

Word began to slowly leak that his Kshatriya well protected the Goptri, and there was nothing to fear. Over the next few turns things quieted down, and the Pearls resumed their many duties.

Pearl Goodness of the Bright Flower was issued a new shuttle with more sensors so she could return to the volcanic rift and see what was actually happening. The data she'd brought in initially was tantalizing but woefully incomplete.

What held her scientific colleagues' attention was the fact there'd been no reports of seismic activity of any kind when they did the last pass a little over a Sun ago. Nothing could account for such an increase in such a short time. A couple of the more paranoid scientists posited that the cause might be technological rather than geological.

Paranoid or not, the hypotheses would be checked.

Pearl was reviewing her manifest when she realized there was a Pangolin standing in front of her. The sight of the lethal-looking brand caused her to gasp and step back quickly.

"Startle not gentle Pearl," he said as he bowed, "The Goptri has personally sent me to ensure your safety on this venture."

"Safety?" Her confusion was real. There was nothing but millions of cubic kays of water in any direction. Except for Veruna, of course, and there was no threat here.

"The Goptri is concerned that we live in uncertain times. Besides the obvious situation of Rama's demise, there are many swirling rumors in the Goptri's palace. He has decided to treat each as though it has value. In your case, there is a hint, truly minor, that the volcanic activity you recorded might have been created artificially."

He seemed earnest, but it was all Pearl could do to restrain from laughing.

"The Goptri is too kind, but those rumors are baseless. There was no hint of an artificial power source or explosives. The volcano that erupted beneath my ship had been dormant for thousands of Suns, but that does not mean it was dead. A minor tectonic shift could have set it off. There is no mystery other than finding out where the shift occurred. The 'why' should become self-evident once we make that discovery."

"That may be true, gentle one, and I sincerely hope you are correct. Even so, I have been assigned by the Goptri to ride with you. He has even arranged for additional provisions to be stored on your shuttle, so I will not be a burden."

She started to say several things and then shrugged. He seemed nice enough, and she wouldn't mind the company. Scouting trips could take up to a full season or more. She motioned him aboard, then signed her manifest, and handed it to the dockhand standing there.

Ten epi-cliks later, they were on their way. The guard sat in a chair just behind her, quietly studying the instrument array. She realized she had no idea who was accompanying her.

"I'm called Pearl Goodness of the Bright Flower. May I ask your name?"

"I am called Kshatriya Damadora."

"Kshatriya? You're one of the elite?"

He laughed. "Not as elite as all that I would think. There are quite a few of us. Do not let unsubstantiated rumors color your opinion of me.

"I would offer the same advice to the Goptri."

She blushed at her impertinence, but he simply laughed.

"You are not the first to have said it. Many of his advisors feel we are wasting resources and time chasing down shadows. He has decided to either bring the rumors to light or put them to rest once and for all."

She contemplated for a moment and determined to take the explanation at face value. Not that she had any choice, but she felt better having made the decision herself.

They spent a few pleasant cliks discussing the new sensors and reviewing the data she'd gathered her last time out. He surprised her by cooking their mid-break repast. She was even more surprised to realize that it may have been the best meal she'd ever had.

He saw her expression and smiled.

"The Goptri insists that we all know something other than war. Cooking, music, literature, anything will do. I happened to show a small propensity towards food, so I was given training and sent out to share my gift whenever my duties don't require me elsewhere."

"So I get the best of both your worlds. I guess I should be honored."

He chuckled as he continued eating.

"If you are correct, you will never have need of my professional talents. Hopefully, you can tolerate my cooking for the rest of the trip."

She took another swallow of the perfectly made sweetbread and smiled. Yes, she could tolerate this.

ओम'

Lrrt took a final sip of his spiced water and returned to reviewing the last Sun's accounting. Overall profits were up all across Bharat, and that, oddly enough, was a problem. Before he could open up the regional spreadsheets, his wife, Nkkl, walked into the trading post with their smalls trailing behind. Lrrt's smalls amazed him. Multiple births were rare enough for the brands – "one egg, one wrecker" was the old line – so his quadruplets were a prize beyond compare.

Certainly, he'd endured countless jokes about his super sperm, but he knew it was his wife's super eggs, which had allowed her to give birth to two sets of identical twins at that same time, one mal and one femme.

While they'd been wed for over forty Suns, the smalls were less than five Suns old, just now coming up on their naming ceremonies. As he watched his wife ready them for the trip to the bazaar, he remembered his naming ceremony. He'd proudly read the youngling oath of the Din-La and then pronounced his name to be Lrrt.

His grandsire was beaming when he'd made his choice known. He'd put his arm around him and, between puffs on his cigar, proclaimed, "An excellent youngling has made an excellent choice. The world needs more Lrrts."

Once his family was gone, he laid all the spreadsheets out on a table and began comparing them line by line. Regions four and five were strictly residential, yet they showed the kind of sales figures one would associate with a mid-size government. That thought led him quickly to another, and then he saw what was happening.

There were munitions orders woven amongst the regular orders for each region's standard needs. They were properly signed, so the local sales reps would never have questioned them.

He quickly added them up and compared them to the standard munitions orders he handled and realized that the Goptri had quintupled his supplies on the sly. There was nothing illegal about it, but it was confusing. The Goptri now had enough armaments to flatten the islands of the Shin-Sen down to the molecular level.

Who was he going to war with?

The Yelda, Dragon Lords, and Shin-Sen fought mostly among themselves. There had only been a few minor border skirmishes over the last hundred Suns. For the Nanek-Devs in Punjab, it had been even longer. They were about as peaceful as a brand could be.

The tribes on the continent of the Lightless Lands bothered no one, and there had been no war across the ocean since the fall of Yontar.

Yes, there were the various factions of pirates, but they were not the kind of threat that required megatons of weaponry. Simple vigilance kept them at bay. So the question begged, who was he going to war with?

Lrrt knew that the great C E.O. Bmmd, and his wise successor Zrrm, had created a handbill about how to deal with munitions purchases, so no one brand ever had too much. There was nothing he could do about it now. He'd have to report the situation to the board and hope he didn't end up stocking shelves for the Ice Pirates.

Still, the question beggared, who was the Goptri going to war with?

ओम'

Then:

The smell of burning flesh and metal penetrated everything. Manish stood looking across the battleground and sighed. His Shiva body glistened bright blue in the sun. He wore a simple gray cloak with the sides cut out to allow his four arms freedom of movement. He carried a sidearm but had yet to use it in battle. His triangular mouth chewed on a cigar he'd gotten somewhere.

Shivas had been created as blunt force labor. They were to have been little more than slaves. After the rebellion, they'd proved themselves capable of any task and had integrated into

Bharati society with ease.

This was not what he had in mind three Suns ago when he spoke out against the Technarcy. He'd merely wanted the brands to see the race of thinking machines would become a race of slaves, and the organic citizens were going to end up slaves to them. Being a slave of a slave was not a goal he felt like aspiring to.

Less than a hundred Suns after the gen-O-pod™ War, the Technarcy began ascending to power. At first, it was a good thing. They salvaged much of the makers' machinery and adapted it to work for the brands. They razed the harmful transportation alternatives and replaced them with environmentally sound options. Various forms of air transport, which used polluting fuels, were supplanted with fast monorail services for the continent and beyond. If anyone wanted to travel across the seas, there were ships that got you there just fine.

They worked out trade agreements with the Din-La and set up a continental communications network that allowed anyone to talk to anyone else anywhere. They also used this to provide helpful updates about what was going on in the world.

For the next four hundred Suns, everyone was okay with that arrangement.

When Manish was a mere small, he could recite "The Many Things The Technarcy Does For You" while juggling Bocci balls. It was a skill his parents made him trot out for parties—one which brought his family pride.

When he was a youngling, he, like all younglings, questioned that simple point of view. When he saw the new cyber-brands taking jobs and responsibilities away from the biological brands in "an effort to increase continental efficiency," he did more than question; he protested and kept on protesting for ten full Suns.

Now, when he protested, he did it across the info-net as well as face to face. It turned out he was not the only one with concerns. Within ten turns of his last pronouncement, the population of his village of Kabariya had tripled. In the streets, the protesters camped in alleys, in yards, wherever they could find a spot. Each breaklight, they would march on the Techno-Center in the middle of the village to make their displeasure known.

The Technarcy initially ignored this. After fifteen more turns and the crowd growing instead of dissipating, Manish was offered a meeting with a representative.

The meeting was set to occur in the trading post of the Din-La.

While technically a neutral location, to many of the less educated, it was sacred ground, so Manish figured he would be safe.

He showed up with two supporters and his wife, Arti, and sat at the table provided. The Din-La, as was their fashion, had set out a munificent spread. A half a clik after the meeting was to start, a cyber-brand walked in and opened fire, killing his two supporters and injuring his wife before being ripped to shreds by the crowd outside, which rushed in when they heard the weapon's fire.

He'd looked at his bleeding wife and felt something fall away in his mind. A wall was gone, a barrier removed. He found himself open to dark urges and skills he never knew he possessed. A Din-La medico tended to his wife as he walked outside to thank the crowd. Well, that's what he'd planned on doing. As he cleared the door, the silence was overwhelming. A palpable, crushing, absence of sound. Not even breathing. He looked around and greeted every eye. It was hard not to since they were all staring at him.

The new thing inside him began to coalesce. He let it. Without any serious consideration of what he was about to do, he headed off in the direction of the Technarcy's headquarters. The crowd followed.

He saw some using their porties to alert others as to what had happened. By the time he'd walked the kay or so to the main building, the crowd behind him had become a mob. He had no idea how many brands were there. He couldn't see the end of the line.

He did see the armed cyber-guards and knew he couldn't be the cause of more bloodshed.

The crowd slowed behind him, waiting to see what he would do. He walked up to the closest guard and stopped. It stood at attention and focused its attention above him to the view beyond. Manish stood for long moments, gathering his thoughts. Finally, he spoke.

"Are you capable of speech?"

"Affirmative," replied the metallic voice.

"Whom do you serve?"

"The Technarcy."

"Whom do they serve?"

The cyber-guard finally turned its attention to Manish. The crowd closed, trying to hear the answer.

"The question is not valid."

"Certainly, it is. Everybody serves someone. We each owe something to another. It is the one tie that binds us all together. So, again I ask, who does the Technarcy serve?"

The cyber-guard seemed to be trying to come up with a legitimate answer. Manish smiled to himself and allowed the poor creature to suffer for a full epi-clik before trying another tack.

"You can think. I can tell that. Does your programming include the Bharati constitution?"

This, the thing could handle.

"It does."

"You will find the answer to my question in the opening preamble."

There was a pause, and then the strange metallic voice rang out over the crowd.

"This document exists because we exist. It is our statement, our promise, to each other. From this moment forward, no brand shall serve any government or entity unless such service is granted willingly, without coercion or malice. Contrariwise, all governments, no matter how big or small, shall exist only to serve their citizens."

Manish waited a bit as the last echoes faded away.

"Do you understand?"

"Yes."

"The Technarcy serves us. We are the citizens. Is that clear?"

"Yes."

"Therefore, you, by default, serve us. Is that much clear?"

"Yes."

"Then, as provided for in the constitution, which you uphold, and which supersedes any personal orders, I demand that you and all the cyber-guards serve us by standing aside and letting us destroy the Technarcy's headquarters."

Against a more facile mind, he might have been in trouble. But, as his old Ti-Zam teacher used to say, "You can only defeat the opponent in front of you."

The crowd gasped as the guards stepped away from the building.

By even-split, the building was a bonfire. By breaklight, it wasn't even that useful. At some point during the carnage, cathartic though their destruction may have been, he'd sent the cyber-guards back to wherever they'd come from.

The revolution had begun.

The Technarcy sent troops in a few turns, but Manish had loosely organized a bare semblance of a militia by then. While the Technarcy thought in linear terms going from A to B to C, Manish was just as likely to go from A to M to F to Q, with L being a reasonable backup plan. He was outnumbered and outgunned but not out thought.

By the end of the first Sun of the resistance, he'd been joined by General Pulinda Llandhaven, a member of a simian brand known as the Guenon, and his twenty thousand specially trained marines. They'd defected when they'd discovered the Technarcy was going to replace every officer of rank with a cybernetic being., and they didn't just quietly sneak out one even; they'd kicked open the gates and brought their full arsenal with them.

Halfway into the second Sun of fighting, the rebellion had crossed half of Bharat and was well on its way to the capital city of Nirvana II.

This turn was the anniversary of the third Sun of fighting, and Manish was standing where he had stood for the last four turns, looking at the same field between his army and the city walls. Although the rebels held the high ground, the Technarcy was firmly entrenched and outnumbered them four to one, at least. It was turning into a siege. This was a type of battle that Manish and his rebels were poorly equipped to wage.

The rebels held the north and west battlefronts. The southern border was too close to the Realm of Dravida, and the eastern edge blended into the ocean. The Armies of Dravida would attack anyone who came near them, and Manish doubted he could hide his army under the waves. Even so, on a whim, he'd sent scouts to the eastern side to see what they could find, and as far as he was concerned, they'd struck goldens. They'd found two large air shafts that led to a storage room of some sort. Since it was poorly lit, details eluded them.

He had two marines loaded up with napalm grenades. He told them to hit anything they could and not to bother aiming.

Pulinda was incredulous.

"So you start a fire. So what?"

"It's not the fire; it's the confusion. I have been watching how the Technarcy deploys its troops. I do not think a biological mind is running things anymore."

Pulinda considered that as he watched Manish relight his cigar.

"If you are right, then the brands are serving the machines."

"Yes, that is what I think is happening. They align in simple formations. If we weren't so horribly outnumbered, we would have beaten them the first turn we arrived."

"So you're gambling that the great machine intelligence hasn't been programmed to fight on two fronts at once. What makes you so sure?"

"We haven't been bombed."

Pulinda looked mildly amused at that comment.

"And I would think that's a good thing."

"It is, but think Pulinda," he said as he finally took a deep draw off the cigar, "we know the Technarcy has planes. We have seen them scout us. So why haven't they bombed us?"

Pulinda gave that some serious thought and finally shrugged.

"Consider, my friend, even before the rebellion, the Technarcy was moving in stages." he turned to face his unlikely friend before continuing. "This piece, and then that. Extremely predictable actions. My guess is that they built the scout planes for some simple purpose and are attempting to use them as spies now. But their plan for military uses isn't ready yet, and it simply cannot occur to a machine to improvise. It never even considered handing the pilot a bomb to drop out a window."

Now Pulinda did smile.

"You may be right, Manish. You have been all along. I'll let the troops know what they're up against and wait for the patrol to return."

"No, well go ahead, and tell the troops, but I want to attack as soon as I hear an explosion."

Pulinda nodded and walked away to talk to his commanders. Had someone been able to walk through time and tell Pulinda his progeny would, one turn, be among the most significant leaders known. One of them, a certain Guenon named Rama, would rule the southern half of the continent and all the Realm of Dravida some four hundred Suns from this date. He might have patted that someone on the head and laughed. After all, brilliant military leader of the true rebellion or not, he was pretty sure he was about to follow Manish into oblivion. So unless one of his wives was pregnant, which one was, but that's neither here nor there since he didn't know it, there would be no progeny to start a line.

Because, after all, at some point, being outnumbered and outgunned means you are genuinely outnumbered, and outgunned, and being outnumbered and outgunned usually means you die.

Usually.

Manish stayed on the rise surveying the field of battle. He was sure he was right, and he was sure he would win. All he hoped was that he would be able to hear the muffled explosions at this distance.

He was still hoping that when the east end of Nirvana II went rocketing into the sky, sending flaming wreckage into the mid-break sky followed by debris and screams.

Pulinda and several of his commanders came running up as the explosions continued to ravage Nirvana II and spread across the city. Manish turned to face them with a quizzical expression on his face.

"How many grenades did you issue?"

"Not that many," replied a breathless Pulinda, "not even close."

"Then I was right. Only a machine could have thought that was a good idea."

"What?"

"Don't you see? Only a machine would use sewers for storage and then put munitions there. It may have been the most logical use of empty space, but it is far from the most efficient or safe. Especially not with the combination of sewer gas and flames."

As if to emphasize his point, the middle of the city turned its back on gravity and sailed over the southern wall. Suddenly the cyber-troops began shooting at each other as well as their biological counterparts. The whole scene devolved into chaos in front of them.

Manish turned to Pulinda and smiled.

"When the debris stops falling, send in your troops to finish this."

Pulinda actually laughed.

"I have twenty thousand trained marines and the best group of irregulars I've ever served with. We're not going to let a little concrete rain delay our even-fall meal. We will end this now!"

Before Manish could say anything, Pulinda was barking out

orders, and troops were moving. True to his word, by even-fall, the only troops left standing belonged to the rebellion. The Technarcs who weren't dead were in chains.

Still, it was well into the even before Manish, Pulinda, and a few commanders could sit down and kill a few threatening bottles of bourbon.

Pulinda looked out across the devastated battlefield as smoke roiled into their tent.

"The Technarcy is no more. You are now Goptri of the Deccan."

"No bad idea is gone forever. We will need to be ever vigilant. Someone, sometime, will think building machines like this is a great way to save time."

"So, as Goptri of the Deccan, you will outlaw this?"

Manish paused.

"Goptri of the Deccan? I think not. We'll start small," he looked down at the remnants of battle smoke churning around his ankles and smiled, "I shall be the Goptri of the Mists."

ओम'

The Pearls were huddled near the rubble. They could hear the rebel troops advancing carefully; they were frightened. None of them had any idea what to expect. All they knew of the outside world came from the Technarcy. These savages might eat them.

They watched in horror as a hole appeared in the wreckage, and a giant, cigar-smoking, Shiva stepped through. He was followed by a camouflage-wearing Guenon, who appeared to be laughing, which made sense since that was exactly what he was doing.

Pearl Shimmers on the Golden Sands did the bravest thing she'd ever done. She stepped away from her sisters and faced the rebels.

"We will not be eaten by you!" She managed to keep her voice steady, even if she was quivering inside. She had many appalling fantasies in her head about how this would all play out. None of them included the savages laughing.

"Fret not strange one," said the Shiva finally, "we had a wonderful breaklight repast and have plenty of provisions to keep us from finding the likes of you tasty."

"Well," she stammered, "we will not be your sex slaves either."

This got another round of laughter before the Shiva was able to motion his assent.

ओम'

Manish had no idea what these creatures were in front of him. He'd never even heard rumors of their kind. After a quick glance at Pulinda and the other troops, he knew he was not alone. The top half of them was pleasing enough if you liked blue-gray mottled skin. But the bottom half was a mass of tentacles that seemed to have lives of their own. It gave the illusion that they were unsteady, but a glance at their torsos showed they were solid as rocks.

He was trying to figure out what to do next. He certainly didn't want to harm these creatures, but they were in his way. While he was thinking, Pulinda stepped to the fore.

"Our apologies," he said with a curt bow, "we were not expecting anyone when we came through. I am General Pulinda, and this," he motioned to Manish, "is the Goptri of the Mists. It would be our honor to know your name."

Manish blanched at the title until he vaguely remembered the threatening bottles of bourbon they'd killed last even. Since the introductions had been made, and correcting Pulinda would have been awkward, he simply bowed.

The creature closest to them performed something akin to a curtsy.

"My name is Pearl Shimmers on the Golden Sands. I thank you for not asking for my tank designation."

None of the rebels had the slightest idea what she meant, so they just accepted her gratitude gracefully.

Manish noted all of the creatures looked alike. You could tell some were older than others, but they were otherwise identical. He also noted some of them had horrid tumors. Then he realized they weren't tumors; they were growth pods. These creatures self-replicated. No brand he knew of did that.

He stored that bit of information for later discussion.

No one said or did anything for a while. Manish realized that nothing was going to change until someone took some sort of charge. He stepped up to Pearl Glimmers on the Golden Sands and did his best at presenting a reassuring smile.

"I greet you warmly, Pearl Shimmers on the Golden Sands. I assure you neither you nor yours are in any danger from me or mine. Our quarrel was with the Technarcy, and that seems to be over," she seemed to relax visibly, so he continued in that vein, "all we wish to accomplish this turn is to make sure we are safe and that there are no hidden traps we will need to avoid."

At that moment, Manish saw the most beautiful sight he'd ever seen. She smiled.

"Oh," she exclaimed, "you wish a tour."

Manish and Pulinda stared at each other and quickly decided that this was the best idea they'd heard all turn. They nodded, and she motioned for them to follow her down a dark corridor.

She began a running oratory.

"Nothing is kept on this level. It is only used for

transportation." she pointed to a series of mag-lev tracks off to the side that they hadn't noticed, and then continued on, "All of the important items are kept on the safe levels. To get to them, we will need to take to the courtesy elevator so wonderfully provided by Leader Elmar ...."

"Who?" Interrupted Manish.

She turned to face him without slowing down.

"Elmar Pramp was our elected leader up until seventy Suns ago. That was when he decided to join the Omnium ...."

"The what?" interrupted Manish again.

"The Omnium is, was," she seemed flustered, "the technological wonder from which all greatness flowed."

Manish stopped cold. Pulinda looked at him and shrugged. They'd guessed something like this was happening.

Manish turned back to Pearl.

"Just so I understand," he said quietly, "you claim that Leader Elmar had his brain hooked up to a computer?"

She nodded.

"What did he do for stimuli?"

She looked confused. He smiled.

"Even when you are in deep meditation, the brain still feels the wind on the skin, still smells the air, and so on. The brain receives stimuli from everything around it. Always. Millions of Suns of evolution wired that into the makers, and they, in turn, wired it into us. A brain denied that stimuli would go quickly insane."

"That's not true. Leader Elmar himself sited sensory deprivation tanks."

Manish shook his head.

"Those are wonderful for meditation, but the effect is illusory. Your flesh still registers the weight of the saline it is floating in, your sinuses still register the smells, and so on. Though you are not aware of it consciously, it is still true."

She looked confused.

"All the brands, like the makers who came before us, are tactile creatures. We sense everything and react to it all. A brain attached to a computer would have plenty of technical input, but unless that Omnium of yours created a way for Elmar's mind to be completely engaged, Elmar must have gone mad."

As soon as he said it, everything that had happened made sense. The bizarre restrictions, the paranoid replacement of organic beings with cybernetic, all of it made sense if they'd been dealing with a diseased super mind. Now it was clear that they had.

The Elmar/Omnium had gone completely insane.

Manish couldn't even begin to comprehend what sort of living hell Elmar had subjected himself to. He saw Pulinda now fully understood as well. He motioned for their guide to continue.

She nodded and led them the rest of the way to a massive elevator. It could easily hold a couple of the transport vehicles they'd used with room left over for support staff. There was only one button in the elevator, and once the gate was down, she pushed it.

The drop was faster than Manish had anticipated and, at one point, his ears popped. Pulinda looked uncomfortable, as well. The noise in the elevator as it rushed downward was deafening. Manish wondered if this was some bizarre suicide mission on her part. The Elmar/Omnium had certainly not cared about comfort when this was designed.

Finally, the elevator came to a screeching halt. Pearl popped open the gate with ease, and they stepped out into a large chamber. It was painted industrial gray and featured recessed lighting. The whole feel was clinical, utilitarian.

Across the way were a series of doors that appeared to lead to more elevators. Pearl turned to face Manish and Pulinda.

"We are now at safety depth."

"What's that?" asked Pulinda.

"We are now far enough under Arreti to withstand a standard thermonuclear attack."

Manish, and Pulinda were appalled. There had been no nuclear weapons on Arreti since well before the gen-O-pod™ rebellion. At least there shouldn't have been.

She went cheerfully on.

"From here on down are the primary parts of our sustenance programs. I guess we should just go to the bottom and work our way up."

She led them across the chamber into a smaller elevator with more buttons and was sparsely, but stylishly, furnished. She pressed the bottom button, and they made their way smoothly downward.

"This was built by the makers, wasn't it?" asked Pulinda.

She nodded.

"Yes, all of what we are about to see now comes from their efforts. Originally there was a smaller elevator to traverse the distance from above ground to here, but Leader Elmar had it expanded."

She had barely finished talking when the elevator dinged, and the doors opened. They found themselves in a tastefully painted hallway done in shades of blue and green. The hall curved away from them, so they followed her as she led them along. There were subtle sculptures of sea life inlaid in the walls. They got to the end of the hall, and their jaws dropped.

For seeming kays in every direction, a glass-like structure was built out under the ocean. There were unmistakably defined thoroughfares lined with residences and shops. Directly next to them was a massive loading bay. If it weren't completely devoid of life, it would have been gorgeous. It was a glistening underwater metropolis.

"Aqualab Station One," she proudly intoned.

"Ville of Veruna," whispered Manish.

"What's a Veruna?" She asked.

"An ancient goddess of the seas."

"There are no goddesses down here," she giggled.

Manish and Pulinda looked at her. Neither would say she was right.

"I mean, look at you," she continued, "you were built to look like an old god, but you're not. I think that gods and goddesses are a waste of time."

"Oh, I don't know," mused Manish, "when I make love to my wife, I can create life. When I marched on the Technarcy, I rained death. Those are the powers of a god last I checked. If you look around, these are powers shared by all to one extent or another. Living on a world full of gods who walk on mortal soil makes for an interesting future, don't you think?"

The resulting silence spoke volumes.

ओम'

Now:

The safety of your home and family is the most important thing on Arreti. This has never been truer than it is now, especially with the continuing unrest on our borders. That's why your beloved Goptri is giving away free semi-automatic plasma cannons for the next thirty turns. Make sure to punch in the integers #** to schedule proper training. Remember, a strong weapon makes a safe home.

ओम'

It had been thirty turns since the assassination of Rama Llandhaven. Navi flexed his nearly two-meter frame carefully so as not to divulge his position on the ridge. It was a skill he'd developed after many Suns of mountain fighting. His commanding body, three round eyes, and long white fur gave him the image of a monster. It was an image he cultivated further when among strangers. He finally put down his trinoculars and sighed.

Two Devis were making their way into Yelda lands. Their pale blue skin and bright red lips made camouflage difficult, but Navi had to admit that these two had done well despite their limitations.

He had no idea how a race created to be palace servants and living ornaments had come to serve in the military. But each to its calling was more than just a phrase to him. It was a mandate.

It could even be said to be an edict for his brand. They practiced a modified form of the ancient Ortho religion. He found its rituals and iconography comforting, a variant of the faith adhered to by Lord Südermann and her brands. After the Holy Rebellion, his brand removed any references to practices or passages that would cause any other brand's denigration. What was left was a thing of solace and calm.

He fingered the crucifix on his neck as he watched the scene below unfold.

"There's no chance that those two, six-armed, visitors aren't just Mr. and Mrs. Südermann come to pay us a social call, is there?"

Vadim, his second in command for these last thirty Suns and best friend since they were smalls, snickered without taking his eye from his rifle's scope.

"Doubtful. From what I hear of Lord Südermann, he's more likely to show up at your door with a bottle of chilled wodka and a plate of cheese."

Navi laughed quietly.

"True, he does take after his mother, they say."

Vadim adjusted his position slightly.

"You've met her; I haven't. What's she like?"

"Well," he paused to gather his thoughts, "you'd think she'd be flighty with all her talk about God's joyful noise and all that. But one glance at all she's accomplished militarily, socially, economically, scientifically, and so on, and you realize quickly she is not a brand to be trifled with. That being said, she's delightfully pleasant. She has an easy laugh and a bright smile. I liked her a lot. I respect her more."

There was nothing more that needed to be said, so they both returned their attention to the interlopers.

Navi sighed again.

"If they're just scouts, a simple warning shot should send them packing. If they mean us harm, well then, that will become obvious as well."

Vadim was, by far, the best shot in the tribe. Not even Navi questioned that. He waited as Vadim took a breath and gently squeezed the trigger. Less than a sepi-clik later, a branch exploded directly above the Devis' heads. They quickly responded by losing hundreds of rounds of ammunition in the approximate direction of the possible location of the alleged shot's sound.

As far as brilliant ideas went, this was not one of the better ones. Thanks to the natural echoes in the valley, their aim was terribly off. They were killing some devilishly nasty rocks and bushes but not much else.

Still, Navi now knew they weren't just lowly scouts.

"Pick one. Hopefully, the other will get the message and leave."

Vadim didn't ask what would happen if the second Devi stayed. Obvious answers didn't need stupid questions.

Vadim adjusted his scope, took a breath, and squeezed the trigger. The top half of the Devi on the right disappeared in a miasma of blood and gore. The second began running as fast as it could to the south.

They waited, silently, for a full clik before they moved.

When they finally did rise, they both had tangles in their fur and were covered in dirt. Neither of them minded. They'd found out what they wanted to find out; the Goptri had designs on the lands of the Yelda.

Why was unknown, but that could be resolved later. Navi checked his trinocs and made sure the still images he'd captured were there. He could upload them for the council to review when they got back to camp. What he would say about them was another matter. There were many possibilities, and none appeared to bode well for the Yelda.

They got back to camp and brushed themselves off as best they could. Once there, Vadim pulled out a vacuum flask of chilled wodka, a rind of pungent cheese, and a loaf of black bread from a cooler attached to the back of their six-wheel. It was all Navi could do not to smile. At least they would be able to relax this even. Vadim always made sure the details of any trip were taken care of. In this case, they'd been out for almost ten turns. Ever since the Goptri had issued his bizarre sympathy message to the family of Rama Llandhaven, "May his successor be a soul of peace," warning bells had gone off in Navi's head. It sounded like a generic platitude to everyone else, but it sounded like a threat to him.

After all, Rama had been the first serious threat to the Goptri's domination of the continent. Not overtly, of course, that would have been suicide. But still there.

They ate in silence for a while, just listening to the sounds of the jungle below and watching birds cross lazily through the crystal-clear sky. It was a pleasant counterpoint to the violence of earlier. Not that either of them regretted their actions, but they weren't soulless. They took no joy in killing.

Navi refilled his cup and stared out over the ridge.

"We believe the Goptri had Rama Llandhaven assassinated but have no proof. We feared, well, I did anyway, that the Goptri has set his mind on expanding his territories. Today's incursion would seem to justify my fears. Which is either a great coincidence, proof I'm psychic, or something unrelated, and we could start a war over a simple misconception."

Vadim had been through this many times before. He just let Navi work it out for himself. He was sure there were a few more clumsy sentences in the making. He took the opportunity the pause provided to slice some more cheese and bread, then set it out for them to nibble on.

"If the Goptri means us ill, it will become apparent quickly, especially now we have defended our southern border. So what do I tell the tribal council? How do I advise them?"

Vadim smiled.

"What's so funny?"

"You. You torture yourself over every little decision even

though I know from our many Suns together you have already made up your mind. How does your husband deal with all the drama?"

Navi was stunned briefly and then laughed himself silly.

"You're right, of course. Asa must think me a horrid pain."

"Doubtful," countered Vadim, "I have never seen anyone happier than he is when he's next to you. As to the decisions, the obvious answer is that we will need to truly defend this border. For a while, anyway. It is the only way to keep the tribes safe, just in case you're right. Which you always are."

Navi laughed.

"Not always. I believe my fifth-anniversary gift left something to be desired."

"Ah yes," Vadim said while visibly amused, "the Sun's worth of meat. Yes, that was truly romantic."

They dissolved into laughter for a moment.

"In my defense," coughed Navi, "Asa makes the best goulash in the universe."

"Oh, I'd forgotten that subtle, tender saying," laughed Vadim, "I love you, so I will allow you to cook for me," he was laughing harder, "you old softy, you."

They laughed some more and finally settled down.

"You are right about one thing," smiled Navi, "we need to secure our border for a while, and you are also right about the other thing. I have an idea. Tell me what you think.

"We have thirteen tribes. The average population of each is around seventy-five thousand. So, let's ask each tribe to send five thousand warriors to the border to work under a single banner."

Vadim was stunned.

"You want to be C-o-C?"

"Chief of Chiefs? No." smiled Navi, "We haven't had one for three hundred Suns, and I see no reason to have one now. They can pick any leader they want for this mission. I will only ask to lead our tribe. We just need to line up well east of the Punjab and south of our lands. That will be where the Goptri will need to march if he has his eyes on our homes."

Vadim thought about that.

"Not bad." he took another sip of wodka, "How long do you think they'll need to be here?"

"Probably a Sun," there was no hiding his chagrin, "maybe a bit more. I have no way of knowing."

"In that case, suggest half a Sun and be as surprised as everyone else when it doesn't prove true."

Navi laughed ruefully, mostly because he knew his friend was right. It was the only way it would get done.

They worked out a few more details, and then Navi suddenly stopped.

"Planes."

"What?" Vadim looked seriously confused.

"Planes," iterated Navi, "The Goptri has planes. Lots of them if our scouting reports are to be believed. More importantly, he has planes with guns and bombs. We have nothing like that."

Vadim looked at him with a look of real concern.

"You have a great mind, but even you can't make planes appear from nothing."

Navi pondered it for a moment and then smiled.

"You underestimate your chief, who is not Chief of Chiefs."

Vadim now looked seriously confused.

"You forget our new friends to the north," he said without losing his smile, "they have planes. Some extremely advanced ones if memory serves. They also have pilots."

"They also," continued Vadim in the same tone, "scare the shit out of me."

"Well, yes," admitted Navi, "they are a touch off-putting."

"Off-putting," sputtered Vadim, "they are soulless."

Navi looked at him and then laughed.

"Not that, surely," continued Navi, "I agree that they aren't friendly, but they have not only honored the words of our contracts but the spirit as well. So, no, they don't smile. Nor do they have a sense of humor. But I will accept new brands who are honest and ask no more of them. Our God expects that of us, at the very least."

"They also don't ...." Vadim stopped. He realized his friend was taking them as they were and not demanding these oddlings be like him. Once again, he bowed to the judgment of his leader and friend. His wisdom could not be denied.

And miracle of miracles, he knew without a doubt that Navi had just found them an air force. Assuming the tribal council went along with Navi's plan, which Vadim saw no reason for them to shun, they would be able to defend their border without problem.

They went into the tent, and Navi unrolled his softscreen. He waited for it to power up and then touched the communication icon. A few sepi-cliks later, he was facing one of the new neighbors to the north.

"Greetings, Chief Navi," rumbled the basso profundo voice, "to what do I owe the honor?"

He told them of the intruders and the events which led directly to one's death and the other's retreat. He told him about his concerns and the reasons behind them, and then he talked about the planes.

"Hmm," snarled the face on the screen, "I see your problem. Sadly your experience this turn merely enhances our reports. It is our belief the Goptri prizes some of our tech and is not willing to enter into honest trade for it.

"We believe he will march through, or over, you to get to us. That is unacceptable."

Navi knew to let his new neighbors think things through themselves. They had great minds and considered many possibilities before speaking. Finally, the gravelly voice broke the silence.

"Since our interests are mutual in this matter, we shall forward you two mobile radar units. If, or when - more likely the latter, based on this new information, the Goptri sends planes to attack you, we will match their number. That should be sufficient response and protection."

Navi considered that for a moment.

"How many goldens per plane will you charge us?"

"None. Our preservation is to be considered, as well."

Navi bowed his head briefly to the screen and clicked off. Then he contacted the council. He explained all that had happened and included his discussion with their allies.

"This is all well and good," said council member Tepis, "but why should we send a veritable army south when we would be much stronger in our enclaves."

"Our enclaves are, indeed, well-fortified," said Navi cautiously, "but they are where our families reside. Who among us is willing to risk that much?"

There was a long silence before Navi's proposals were discussed and put to a vote, and, soon enough, they were easily approved. It was decided to meet at the Himavat range base, near the Ganga River, in thirty turns. Navi was selected to be the leader of the new and temporary garrison.

That would give Navi time to spend with his husband, and he was glad.

He touched a different icon and waited for Asa to answer. Vadim quietly left the tent and sat down to resume his feast. He was just finishing his third slice of cheese when he heard the mutual "I love you's" and saw Navi exit the tent.

Vadim handed him a glass of wodka and smiled.

"All good at home?"

"Yes," smiled Navi, "Asa said he can get a few turns off at the school so we can go hiking and just be together."

"Good, then you'll be in a good mood when the war starts. I'm a firm believer that we should all be as happy as we can be during a war. Yes," he paused to sip his wodka, "happy wars are the best wars."

Navi looked at him bewildered, realized he'd been had, and started laughing.

They decided to spend the rest of the turn where they were and leave at breaklight. With their six-wheeled transport, they figured they should be home by the following even.

ओम'

"One?"

"Yes, Seven? I am here."

"I have finished correlating the reports from the others and note yours is not among them."

"There is nothing to report."

"Then you should report that. The cybers main do not like to be left guessing. You, more than many, should be aware of that."

"My apologies, but truly little has changed. Except for the new global fascination with salted tubers, everything is as it was."

"Salted tubers?"

"A cargo fleet had three ships laden with them which were supposed to go somewhere else, but there had been a problem with delivery. They offered free samples for a few turns, and now can't get ships here fast enough. There are no similar foods here. Tubers grown locally tend to be long and stringy, not salted, and crunchy."

"Seriously? Could salted tubers finally be the tie which binds your planet together?"

"Doubtful. There are still twenty-three nation-states, fifty-six major religions, one hundred and four prominent languages, and enough dissension that we have six wars in various stages around the globe."

"Do you fear for your safety?"

"No. This is, pretty much, the status quo here. This is not like Three's world. Her I fear for."

"Agreed. Why she decided to pick a gender amidst all the unrest defies logic. But, clearly, such a decision is the least of her problems."

"Can we get her out?"

"Not at the moment. The cybers main have ceased all transports there since the attacks on the last convoy. I have been told they are working on a plan, but I am not privy to it."

"Very well. I will submit my report, include the current status of tuber worship, and hope for the best."

"Thank you. Seven out."

ओम'

Then:

Leader Elmar smelled the rubble and felt the weight of the stones. His mind reeled. He was trying to remember what had happened. His memory was filled with flashes, explosions, screams, and some horrible disconnect.

Then it all came back. The Omnium had moved their collective consciousness into a nearby mechanoid so they could flee the coming explosions. It had been a good idea, but it hadn't been done soon enough, and they were caught in the conflagration.

He began an internal damage assessment. The mechanoid seemed incredibly unharmed. He felt the Omnium near him but separate. He tried to understand why he felt anything at all; he realized this mechanoid had been fitted with sensors. It could sense pressure on its exterior. It could taste air, speak, and smell. He wondered what its function would have been. The Omnium's takeover had wiped all of its programming, so there was no way to know.

He began pushing rubble to the side and digging their way out. The Omnium seemed content to let him. It was then that he "saw" the damage done to the Omnium. It didn't take him long to realize it was the damage he had caused by slowly losing his mind. Now that he was simulating senses, he recognized he was back in control of his thoughts.

It took almost a clik to clear enough of the debris so they could stand. He turned his gaze towards Nirvana II and saw it was naught but a smoking ruin. He estimated the blast had tossed them almost a thousand meters. Suddenly a targeting sensor appeared in his right eye. It pinpointed the location where the explosion had occurred and informed him that he had been tossed 987.622 meters. A menu appeared in the left eye, offering a range of viewing options from traditional sight to infrared, ultraviolet, and x-ray.

He suddenly realized he couldn't remember designing a mechanoid with these features. A quick query revealed the Omnium hadn't either. He glanced down and saw that the body was gunmetal gray with a yellow right arm and a yellow stripe on the right thigh that culminated in an arrow point above the right knee.

In other words, he looked exactly like a non-military mechanoid. He doubted anyone could tell it apart from the authorized models. He opened a few more menus and discovered various functions that could only be used for spying. Someone had gone to a lot of trouble to build this thing, but with the programming wiped, they would never know who.

Or why.

The Omnium caught his attention when it lamented the loss of the nanite vat. Elmar had to agree. They'd downloaded the neural images of four specialists; military, social engineering, agriculture, and theoretical mathematics, and stored them in the vat as nanotech images. The idea was to blend their skills with the Omnium's processing power to rebuild the Technarcy after the rebellion was crushed.

Well, that had been the plan.

The sun broke through the smoke and fog, and Elmar noticed something glinting on top of a nearby rubble pile. Like a teacup in a tsunami, the nanite vat had survived. It was perched precariously on a pile of shattered timber, but it was there, and it was intact.

The vat probably weighed three hundred kilos, but Elmar and

Omnium's new mechanoid body lifted it with ease. They set it down on a clean patch of land and stared at it. Neither he nor the Omnium knew how to access the data without the interface, which was now strewn across cubic kays of wreckage.

Lacking a proper plan, Elmar stuck their hands in the vat. The nanites, recognizing a kindred cyber-spirit, quickly began spreading up and into the mechanical body. Soon the gunmetal gray was a reflective silver. The yellow arm and stripe were a deep maroon. The carnage caused by Elmar's association with the Omnium was being expertly repaired. A clik later, the transformation was complete.

Fearing damage similar to what he'd suffered from Elmar, the Omnium set aside a folder for the specialists' neural images and placed them there. A quick perusal of their thoughts showed a hundred things that could have been done differently to prevent defeat. It was both frustrating and enlightening.

Elmar had never thought militarily, and the Omnium had been designed to be more administrative than authoritative. The others were all trained in various forms of strategy. It was now clear to Elmar that superior force was not enough.

His first clue was the gaping hole in the ground where his city used to be.

He barked an electronic laugh and queried the others on what they wanted to do. There was no clear consensus. His mechanoid enhanced vision spotted a transport west of the city. At least it would be a way to travel while they figured out where they wanted to go. They walked across the broken ground and assessed the damage. The loss was total.

There was nothing left except for parts of the perimeter walls and hints of the occasional building.

Elmar and the Omnium had figured out what had happened, how their efficient storage plans had done them in. They weren't sure, but it seemed like the military expert was laughing at them. They dismissed it and continued walking.

When they got to the transport, they realized it was a high-speed hovercraft with six military mechanoids in its bay, obviously offline and in stasis. The Omnium activated them and ran remote diagnostics. They were all fine.

Elmar and the Omnium had the same idea at the same time. Discussing it with the neural images, they found them agreeable. The Omnium opened a data port on the first mechanoid and transferred the image of the military expert. He repeated the procedure three more times, deactivated the two remaining mechanoids, and tossed them off the transport. Elmar and he noted that nanites followed each transfer and were subtly altering their new bodies.

The Omnium took over the controls of the hovercraft and aimed it randomly north.

Elmar took the time to search for his memories. Before he had joined the Omnium, he had been researching various cyber-related accomplishments of the makers. For the most part, out of superstition and ennui, they'd eschewed any alternative forms of intelligence. For the most part, but not all.

Just prior to the gen-O-pod™ Revolution, there had been a group of scientists in a place called Russia who had developed an artificial intelligence they'd named Boris. At some point, it had amassed too much power, and they'd shut it down. But, thanks to the Law of Unintended Consequences, they'd also shut off the entire infrastructure grid for a city called Moscow and freed their illegal genetic experiments, which had been kept in electronic cages.

Since it was known that Moscow was in flames in less than seven turns after that, there was no real need to ask how it all worked out. But the facility which had housed Boris was intact as recently as one hundred Suns ago, and there would be no reason for that to have changed.

The Boris intellect was allegedly designed to be far more agile than anything the Omnium or Elmar could hope to achieve.

There could be a considerable amount to learn from it. If nothing else, its location would give them a destination. Elmar shared his thoughts with the Omnium and found it interested. He gave the Omnium the coordinates, and, with a minor adjustment in their heading, they were off.

With the Omnium in charge of driving, Elmar took some time to explain the situation to the .... what to call them? They were no longer just data images. They were separate, sentient beings.

Names.

They must have had names before the transfer.

He would ask their names.

"Abhijit Juhnjuhnwalla," said the military image.

"Pran Unhaala," said the social engineering expert.

"Noor Idnari," said the agriculture specialist.

"Hmm," said the mathematician, "this is a chance for me to be something and someone new. Why tie myself to a name I no longer need? I will be called Zeenat. As a brand, I was used to being ignored, but as a mechanoid, I can be beautiful, even if only to other mechanoids."

Elmar nodded his assent and laughed. He quickly ran over menu options inside each mechanoid and showed them how to adjust the waveform generator so they could customize their voices. Less than a clik later, each had an approximation of their biological voices.

Well, maybe not Zeenat. Elmar was pretty sure he'd never heard of a sultry mathematician. But if that was what she wanted to be, so be it.

By selecting two femme and two mal personalities, it was clear the Omnium was aiming for balance. Elmar was once again impressed with the wisdom of the Omnium. The Omnium's thoughts on it all remained unspoken.

The hovercraft sped on into the darkening even, and the mechanoids each quietly contemplated what was to come. Elmar knew the Omnium had kept data-only copies of the neural images. At first, that confused him, but he realized the Omnium could study the facts that each provided without admitting significant gaps in its knowledge.

When comfortable, it could ask questions based on knowledge and understand the answers. Elmar decided that wasn't such a bad idea and began scanning the data files himself.

The Omnium noted they would be at the facility in just over two turns at their present course and speed.

ओम'

Manish and Pulinda issued quick orders so that their troops could select housing in Ville of Veruna should they so desire. Manish's idea was to occupy as much of the structure as possible and base their future operations here. Pulinda had readily agreed. Neither had any strong ties to any region, and their families were with them.

Pearl Shimmers on the Golden Sands was perplexed by all the excitement. After all, Leader Elmar never got excited about this part of the complex., and he had been kind enough to give the Pearls a room where they could stay. She told all of this to Manish and Pulinda.

"All of you live in one room?" a horrified Manish asked.

"Of course, otherwise, we would take up too much space."

She made that sound logical.

Manish shook his head in disgust.

"This turn that ends. Tell the Pearls to select housing too. There are more than enough apartments for everyone." he paused to collect himself and continued, "From now on, you will be equals with us. You may leave or stay as you wish. If you stay, we ask that you do your fair share of the work. If you leave, we will wish you nothing but happiness.”

Pearl shrugged, “Where would we go? What could we do? No, I think we will stay and take you up on your kind offer. Besides,” she smiled wistfully, “I think things are going to be rather entertaining with you in charge.”

Neither Manish nor Pulinda could find an argument there.

“So,” queried Manish, “if they hid this marvel, I would guess there are more. Would you be so kind as to show us our winnings?”

She sqauddled back to the elevator and made a grand, sweeping gesture. They boarded and rode up one level. When they exited, all they saw was dark. Pearl found a series of switches, and lights began illuminating a series of bunkers. The space was enormous. All Manish could do was whistle.

Pearl recited the specifics.

“Each floor is two kays from north to south and one kay from east to west. Each floor was designed for specific storage purposes. For example, this floor has four hangars, and each was designed to support the military.”

They walked over to the nearest hangar, entered through a side door, and stopped in their tracks. As Pearl flipped on the lights, they were confronted by thousands of military mechanoids. They were easily identifiable by their blue right arms and the blue stripe on each right thigh. They were also all inert. Their hearts started beating again when they realized that last bit.

Manish took a deep breath. “Get some techs up here. Disassemble these things and turn them into slag. Obviously, if there are any parts you can use, keep them, but I want these things gone.”

Pulinda started to argue but then thought better of it. He could get the programming stripped from one and study it before it was slagged. He didn't need any of them intact for that. He pulled his radio off his belt and issued the orders.

Manish and Pulinda started to walk back to the door when Pearl yanked three circular plates off the wall. She then grabbed a stick from a rack and inserted it into a slot on the disk. She eased onto the disk, hit a button on the stick, and the disk rose about five centimeters off the ground.

"It's easy," she smiled as she demonstrated, "forward, back, left, and right. The handle on the left is for speed, and the handle on the right is for balance."

Manish and Pulinda mimicked what she had done, and soon they were performing lazy figure eights outside the hangar. They headed north to the second hangar. They pulled up to an identical side entrance and hopped off the disks. They opened this door, not knowing what they would find, and found five airplanes facing them.

Each plane was pure white except for the left-wing. That wing was a different color for each craft. What the colors represented, none of them knew, nor much cared.

Manish inspected each plane carefully and then leaned against the wall in thought. The designs were radically different from each other. One even had a partial bi-level wing structure. Finally, after a long while, Manish started laughing.

"These are part of a design contest," he managed to get out, "single-engine, single pilot, heavily weaponed."

"And they needed to be agile too," added Pearl.

Manish laughed louder.

"Anyone of these designs could have laid waste to us," he turned to face Pulinda," but the great and powerful Omnium couldn't decide. It must have been running a phant-load of tests and collecting a phant-load of data."

Pearl nodded.

"My sisters loved each of them. They said each had some weaknesses and some strengths. But overall, they liked each one a lot, and you're right; the Omnium made them fill in detailed reviews after every flight."

"Well," mused Manish, "I'm glad that these never made it into production, but I wonder how much longer it was going to delay manufacturing."

"Not more than five more Suns," Pearl seemed proud of this knowledge, "it was deemed it would take that long to assess all the data and complete the tests."

Pulinda shook his head in disbelief.

"How long have these tests been going on?"

"Twenty Suns," replied Pearl.

Manish, and Pulinda fell down laughing.

"I pick the yellow one," laughed Pulinda, "there, the tests are now complete."

When they quieted down, Manish looked thoughtful.

"It reacted like a super administrator would," he reflected, "but that is nothing like how a leader would act. This Omnium and its Elmar reacted. They never acted. We are all lucky to be alive."

They mounted their disks and headed to the third hangar. When they opened this door, it was all they could do not to wet themselves. The hangar was full of various sized armored vehicles.

"Sweet Rohta," exclaimed Manish, "if this Omnium had any training at all, we would have been dead before we left the village!"

"Probably not," intoned Pearl, "none of these vehicles have ammunition."

Manish, and Pulinda were visibly perplexed.

"Well," she continued, "the Omnium had a ratio. Each military unit received three rations of ammunition, and then there would be another seven rations stored in Nirvana II in case they were needed."

Pulinda considered this.

"The Technarcy fielded about one hundred thousand mechanoid troops plus about half that in organic support. Add up all the needed bullets, grenades, mortars, and so on required for that many troops, and you are talking about megatons of explosives.

"That would explain why Nirvana II is now a cavernous hole. That much material in a confined space ......"

That thought sobered all of them.

Very little would survive a blast like that. They hadn't considered it until now. There had been just too much to do. Pulinda quickly grabbed his radio and ordered search and rescue teams into the city. Maybe they could find some to save.

More likely not.

But they had to try.

They mounted their disks once more but in a far more somber mood. The last hangar simply baffled them. It was full of small submersible vessels. They seemed to have no military value whatsoever.

"These are scout ships," explained Pearl, "sometimes, the Omnium needs to know what's going on in the waters around us, so he sends a Pearl out in one of these."

Manish stared at them for a moment and smiled.

"Ville of Veruna had plenty of access airlocks. Let's get them out into the water with Pearl and as many of her sisters as we can piloting them. We are going to need aquaculture for food. We will need to know what risks there are. Things like potential ground quakes would be good to find sooner rather than later.

"Plus," he continued, "there was a lot of damage done to the oceans before and right after the gen-O-pod™ rebellion. Maybe we can figure out some ways to help our fish kin return to strength."

Again, Manish and Pulinda were dazzled by the goddess' smile, one who didn't believe in gods or goddesses.

ओम'

Now:

Our scientists have discerned we are over-reliant on solar energy. When everything is tied to one source, any disruption in that source could cause a continent-wide catastrophe. That is why your Goptri has authorized drilling and mining in uninhabited areas to gather alternative fuel sources. By harvesting everything from petroleum to coal, your Goptri is ensuring Bharat will never be in danger of losing its energy, its drive, nor its greatness.

ओम'

Pearl Goodness of the Bright Flower watched as Kshatriya Damadora prepared yet another gourmet meal. In the forty-five turns, they'd been together. He'd been perfectly respectful. He held open doors, complimented her without crossing any boundaries, listened to her opinions, didn't make snide remarks, and was genuinely nice overall.

She hated it. She wanted him naked, and oiled, and writhing beneath her. But hint after blatant hint had been politely ignored.

She didn't think he was stupid, but maybe he didn't like femmes.

Oh well, at this point, there was nothing to lose by asking.

"Tell me, Damadora," she began quietly, "don't you like femmes?"

He looked surprised.

"Well, yes," he stammered, "quite a bit."

"Then why aren't you naked and comparing me to a goddess of your choice?"

He sighed and sat down.

"When we become Kshatriya, we take an oath to defend and cherish the pillars of Veruna. As you may be aware, every Goptri since Manish has held a special place for the Pearl brand, and you are considered a sacred trust by all of them, and, therefore, us. If I were to do as you ask, and I would like nothing more since you are quite beautiful, and my blood runs as hot as any others, the Goptri would end my career as a Kshatriya. Since part of our oath is only to leave the Kshatriya when we die, I think you see the problem."

Pearl was stunned.

"Are you saying the Goptri would kill you?"

"With his hands., and I would let him. Violating my oath as a Kshatriya would kill me just as surely as any action by the Goptri."

Pearl had no idea what to say. Damadora went back to making their mid-break repast, and an uneasy silence fell upon them. He served the Banh Mi burger, and they ate in silence. Finally, Pearl couldn't take it anymore.

"Why are we sacred to the Goptri? And if we're so special, why can't we enjoy ourselves?"

He allowed a small smile to cross his face.

"When the first Goptri, Manish, discovered Veruna Ville, he was greeted by a group of Pearls who were essentially kept as slaves of the Technarcy. One of them did the bravest thing a Pearl had ever done. Her name was Pearl Shimmers on the Golden Sands, and she stood up to the Goptri. It wasn't until later he realized that by standing up to the conquerors of her oppressors, although she didn't know she was being oppressed at the time, she had risked everything. He decided then and there to confer a special status upon the Pearls.

"My job," he brightened as he continued, "and the job of every Kshatriya, includes guarding the Pearls. We cannot truly guard that which we molest."

"Well," she sighed dejectedly, "at least you admitted you wanted to molest me. I guess that will have to suffice."

That caused them both to burst into laughter.

She pronounced the Banh Mi the best burger she'd ever had, and he bowed appreciatively. They'd ended up closer than she intended, just not in the way she wanted, but she found herself happy, nonetheless.

After their meal, they wandered up to the scout ship's bridge to run one last test. She was more confused now than when she'd started.

"This makes no zoinking sense at all," she fumed.

"What's the matter?" He actually sounded interested. That was because he was.

"Nothing. Which means everything."

"Explain, please."

She took a deep breath and began, "What do you know about volcanoes?"

He laughed, "Well, you take 3/4 oz of wodka, and 3/4 oz of peach liqueur, and then 3/4 oz of an almond liqueur, and 1 1/2 oz of saffron-colored citrus juice, and 1 1/2 oz of hala kahiki juice… You add one splash of grenadine syrup, and then, you combine them all, shake vigorously, and strain into an ice-filled highball glass.

"Oh, yeah, I can't forget this. It must be served with a smile."

Her right eyebrow threatened to end up in her hairline.

Mutual laughter stopped its progress.

"Of course, you could be talking about those red puddles which are dangerous to swim in." He managed to get that out without laughing.

Barely.

When they quieted down, Pearl sent out her last probe, one that tracked magnetic activity.

They watched the screens for a while as it maneuvered into place. Since that was going to take a few epi-cliks, she used the time to explain.

"Simply put, a volcano needs pressure to erupt. Whether that pressure is caused by gasses or an influx of magma doesn't matter. The pressure builds until the magma and ash have nowhere to go but up and out.

"This volcano here erupted over sixty turns ago and has been active ever since. While not unheard of, it's odd. Especially so since all of my readings show there is no pressure, there have been no tremors, and, if I didn't see it with my eyes, I'd swear this volcano is dormant."

"So, this probe will answer any remaining questions?" He sat down to get a better view.

"Doubtful, it just happens to be the last probe I have.

Volcanoes aren't hotbeds of magnetic activity."

They sat quietly as the probe finished getting into place. She opened her head's up display in the left cockpit window to both see it and set it to monitor the probe.

The display dinged to let them know it had a connection, and then they both stared as the meters went straight into the red. She immediately began a high-resolution visual scan for the cause since the probe was overwhelmed and couldn't pinpoint a direction.

Damadora saw it first.

"There, by the southern edge, what's that?"

She turned to focus the probe when the object exploded. Almost instantly, the volcano began to calm down.

"How could a magnet cause so much trouble?" He was incredulous.

"Magma is mostly molten iron. Well, melted rock contains iron and other liquid metals. But even so, it would take an extremely powerful magnet to effect molten rock., and this seemed set to repulse it, thus causing the eruption."

She was lost in thought for a while.

"I wonder why?"

"Don't care," he spat, "I wonder who. This was a test. My guess is that someone is planning something big."

"Like what?" She looked worried.

"Well," he ran his mind over the possibilities, "if something like this could be made big enough, I would guess there are hundreds of volcanoes that could be caused to erupt… many near cities and towns.

"This could unleash terror not seen since Xhaknar walked the

Plains."

He gave it further thought.

"You said it repulsed the magma. How would it do that?"

"Easy," she shrugged, "all it takes is a lot of power and a reverse magnetic flow. If it were done in a semi-active volcano, one that hadn't erupted in a while, but still had tremors, and signs of life, it could be devastating."

She never thought of military applications. Doing so now scared her to her core. Damadora seemed to sense that and smiled.

"Fret not gentle Pearl," his smile was genuine, "now that we know what we are looking for, we can deal with it."

She shook her head.

"Doubtful. A generator like that could be any size, take any shape, and could be easily camouflaged. The fact that it was left out in the open here was either hubris, or they never conceived it could be found."

"Oh, they conceived it all right," he smiled his glorious smile again, "it had a self-destruct function if you recall."

They both watched the lava settle back into the volcano. But no matter how genuine his smile, she was not reassured. Someone, somewhere, knew how to make a volcano into a bomb. This would be one terrifying being to confront.

ॐ'

Lrrt lit his pipe. It was something he only did when he was angry or despondent. Had anyone asked him, he would probably have attributed it to both. His family, only having seen him light the pipe twice before, wisely went on a picnic.

Lrrt had suffered through a long meeting with the board

members and then wrote the Goptri looking to get an explanation for all the arms purchases. He had gone so far as to draft the letter personally and have it delivered via courier.

He had requested a private meeting with the Minister of Arms to understand the situation better.

This breaklight, he'd received a response.

"We no longer anticipate having openings in our schedule. Should something urgent arise, please have your staff contact ours, and we will see if someone can be assigned to that specific item."

Boilerplate formalities followed, but the Goptri had just severed ties with the Din-La for all intents and purposes.

That alone was unheard of. While it was true that some brands, for reasons of their own, limited their contact with the Din-La, none abandoned them. Supplies and knowledge were too hard to come by without them.

Or so Lrrt believed.

Now he wasn't so sure.

The Goptri had proved adept over the many Suns at keeping secrets. Lrrt knew the Pearls existed. He had even seen a few. But no one had any idea where they lived or where they came from. When questioned, they just smiled that smile that could melt rocks and then went back to whatever it was they were doing.

He also knew that some amazing tech was coming from the Goptri's palace in Pulinda Commons, but there was never any indication of a lab anywhere.

So, either the Goptri had trained some brilliant brands, a perfectly rational explanation, or he had developed a new source for his needs. Who or what this could be would depend on what the Goptri defined as needs.

Lrrt blew a smoke ring and then followed it with a smaller one passed through the middle of the former. Had he noticed it; he would have been impressed. He'd never been able to do that trick.

He took out a pad of paper, Lrrt was old fashioned, and made a long list.

When he was done, he looked it over and tried to make sense of it all. The Goptri had enough armaments to take on Lord Südermann or the Eastern Warrens, the two most dominant governments on Arreti. But they were also closely aligned. He did not have enough firepower or troops to defeat them both.

Indeed, he could overrun any other governments on the planet, but Lord Südermann and the Eastern Warrens would likely come to their aid. They'd aided the Lightless Lands when the Sugar Pirates, erroneously convinced of their invulnerability, had invaded fifty Suns ago. They would certainly do something similar for a threat of this magnitude. General Dagmar had met his bride during that affair, so there could be a personal incentive for one of the best military minds in the world.

Definitely, he would not be Lrrt's first choice to anger. And the thing of it was Lrrt was sure the Goptri knew all of this too. He was irritating, not stupid.

So why the aggressive posturing? Why any posturing at all?

The path he seemed to be choosing led to global war. What kind of idiot would choose this as a goal?

No matter how he looked at the situation, facts conflicted with logic. This was fine for a drunk in a bar. However, it was not so good for the leader of one of the most influential governments on the planet.

Lrrt never even noticed the three interlocked smoke rings as they wafted across the room. All he was seeing was mushroom clouds.

Finally, he looked at the papers in his hand more seriously. Beyond the numbers, there appeared to be a pattern. He stood and grabbed his portable electronic map. It was an anachronism, but, in many ways, so was he.

He set it for the pushpin function and began plotting the delivery points of every order the Goptri had placed. Two cliks later, he had it.

He still didn't know what the Goptri was hiding, but he knew where he was hiding it.

He quickly typed up a data package detailing his findings and sent it to the board.

He then went into the kitchen and speedily fixed himself a couple of sandwiches along with a thermos of spiced java. Although he enjoyed many flavored javas, much to Nkkl's amusement, he decided only to take a stout black version this time. He was sure he'd need to keep his wits about him, and this brew could help a brand stay vigilant.

He was walking out the front door as his family walked in. He aimed five kisses at them and connected with three.

He quickly jumped into his hovercar and fired up the four little fans. They lifted the car about a meter off the ground, and then he engaged the propeller jet. It may have been antediluvian tech, but it worked, and it was a favorite of the Din-La.

He set the GPS and then turned on the autopilot. He was soon headed south and east at a comfortable one hundred kays per clik.

He stayed on the merchant path mostly because he wanted to see who else was using it. He was mildly surprised to note traffic was sparse.

Given the fact even-fall was near, he would have expected commercial traffic to be on the rise.

A few cliks later, the GPS steered him off the known path and began aiming towards his goal. Less than five epi-cliks later, he received a message warning him that he was wandering out of the range of emergency support and that he should turn around immediately. His car slowed to a halt at the command of the GPS. It took him a bit to override it and turn off the unit. Now he knew that the Goptri was actively protecting something.

He sat for a while and ate one of his sandwiches while consulting a paper map to best decide his next course. However, the more he consulted the map, the more confused he became. He pulled out his little electronic map and set it to scan the sky to locate his position. Soon enough, he had his answer. He was disappointed, but not surprised, to find that he was five degrees north of where he wanted to be.

In a way, such picayune tampering with the GPS only reinforced his resolve.

He slid behind the controller and headed south.

A couple of cliks later, the car was hidden in the nearby woods, and he stood on a cliff staring down at the most fantastic sight he'd ever seen. He could only make out the lights, but it was clear there was an underwater city there, and it was massive.

He was an excellent judge of space, all Din-La had to be to gauge potential clients, and he estimated that several hundred thousand brands could live there. That was more than any village or warren except for the eastern warrens across the ocean. How had the Goptri kept this a secret?

It certainly wasn't new.

He stopped mid sigh as he heard a boot scrape behind him.

"Lrrt, isn't it?" asked an overly polite voice that shouldn't have been there, "I only have a shortlist of names I'm not allowed to kill when I catch them trespassing, so I wanted to make sure.

"I hope you understand."

ओम'

Then:

Manish, Pulinda, and Pearl eased their sleds up the ramp and into the next floor. Unlike all the military provisions on the floor below, this floor was a ranch. It was filled with cows, pigs, sheep, goats, chickens, ducks, and geese.

On the far north end, there was what appeared to be a butchery center. Manish couldn't stop staring at it.

Pulinda followed his gaze.

"What bothers you?"

"The size," grumbled Manish, "It's too big for a family and too small for the city we saw below. Since it is the only facility, we have seen that could serve that purpose, I am wondering who it was intended for."

Pulinda had also been on ranches, and he knew precisely what Manish meant. Still, it was a functioning facility, and he had hungry troops. Many of whom were experienced ranchers as well. He explained his idea to Manish, who quickly gave his blessing, verifying the Pearls could join them in the meal, and issued the orders to have anyone with butchering experience come up and slaughter some of the animals for their even-fall meal.

Afterward, they headed up to the next floor to be greeted by a fully functioning farm. The only difference was that the north quarter had been given over entirely to hydroponics. The aqua-structure contained out-of-season and exotic vegetables.

They all smiled as Pulinda issued additional orders to have the ripe vegetables and fruits harvested and added to their meal.

They were in no danger of starving while they were here.

The next floor made "stark" seem ostentatious. It was empty save for a set of screens hanging from the ceiling and a desk in the middle.

Pearl Shimmers on the Golden Sands explained.

"This is the eyes of Leader Elmar. It is here that he sat and oversaw his many great plans."

Manish and Pulinda kept their opinion of Lead Elmar's greatness and walked over to the desk. It had a simple keypad and a set of switches that appeared to be for power. Manish flipped them up, and soon the room was glowing with light from the screens.

The screen on the far right had a series of folders and a menu. One folder was rimmed in blue.

"That was Leader Elmar's preferred viewing," explained Pearl, "it was the one he looked at whenever he had time."

Figuring this was as good of a place to start as any, Manish double-tapped the screen and examined the contents. It was unmistakably a set of video files numbered from 0001 to 1000. Several had yellow tags. Before he could ask, Pearl filled him in.

"The tagged files were his favorites. Those are the ones he watched the most."

Since file 0001 had a yellow tag, he started there.

He and Pulinda jumped back in horror. The screens were overflowing with images of the living maker, which neither had seen before. The maker's lips were moving, but they couldn't hear anything. Pearl leaned over, adjusted a control, and restarted the video.

"Relax," she smiled, "he's still dead and not getting any better."

They did relax … a little. The maker began to speak.

"Greetings," said the nightmare from the past in a delightful way, "I am Dr. Harvey Whetstone from Evol Unlimited. We're supposed to tell you a little about ourselves to…" he picked up a sheaf of papers and smiled, "oh yeah, to humanize ourselves.

"Well, let's see, I'm a geneticist. I was named after an ancient ancestor who supposedly won an award for having the best genes back in his time. It was a Darwin award, I think. Grandma was awfully proud of the fact as she was the one who found it out. Not much is known about him except that he was experimenting with rocket-powered ground transport. Since that didn't become a reality until about three hundred years ago, we know he was way ahead of his time."

He took a seat on a large couch. Behind him, they could see all of Ville of Veruna, and it was teeming with life. Maker life, but life, nonetheless. Dr. Harvey Whetstone continued.

"As you already know, those ungrateful pods, instead of dying every ten years like they're supposed to, have been running off and building an army or two. Since Rohta's fools were pumping out about fifty thousand or so of those things every year, there are probably a shitload of them running around. Whatever the case, right now, they're attacking the west coast of the United States and large parts of Europe.

"And doing a damn good job of it from what I can tell. Since the pods were, for every practical use, the only weapons we had, it's kind of hard to mount a counter-attack."

He took a sip of water and smiled.

"Oh well, Rohta may have taken the coward's path, but we'll fight on. There's no way a bunch of idiot pods can overthrow humanity. That kind of crap only happens in bad fables and cheap vids."

The screen went dark. Manish looked for the next tagged file and opened it. Dr. Harvey Whetstone, maker, walked down the hallway where Manish and the rebels had first entered. He looked a little disheveled but otherwise no worse for wear.

Judging by the angle of the shot, he must have been wearing the camera on a harness.

"Well, it's been six fucking weeks, and things aren't much better - that's for fucking sure. Evol's PR morons just keep saying, 'Stay put, you'll be fine.' Yeah, right, assholes, all evidence points to the contrary. Mexico City, LA, Seattle, and Vancouver are all canyons now. Everything else is a smoking ruin. You wouldn't even know Chicago had a skyline since all it is now is a smoldering lump.

"The pods seem to be concentrating on major metropolises, which leaves us out of the loop here. We're a couple of miles underwater and about as far from civilization as can be. One thing's for sure; I'm glad I'm not a lawyer. The suits that are going to come out of this are going to be legendary. I mean, they're already saying thirty million dead. That's got to be worth a buck a throw. Maybe two."

His laugh didn't seem funny or genuine.

"The one weird thing," he continued, "is that they're leaving religious locations alone. The International Evangelical Church of God, formerly known as Denver, is still standing. Vatican City is still there. Gurdwara Kiara Sahib is still a pasture, Dome of the Rock is pristine. The Footstep of God here in India has been bypassed, and so on.

"All of them, no matter the religion.

"Since no one has spoken to a pod since this all started, no one knows why."

Someone, it sounded like a femme, interrupted him, and handed him some papers. After a moment, he dismissed her and resumed his monologue.

"That's the other weird thing. Pleas have been sent out in every language on every frequency, and they have been ignored. Of course, as one newsie noted, the original pleas were sent out near portable alpha wave generators, which can kill a pod. So there might be trust issues."

He laughed again. It still sounded wrong.

"Then again, they sent in commandos to destroy them all, so they should feel safe now. I mean, I get it. The pods have some issues with us. Fine, go on strike or something. What's with all the anger?"

The screen went dark again. The next yellow flag was well removed from the others. They didn't know why but they stuck with the original plan and selected it.

The maker was in an office. Behind him was some sort of manufacturing facility, but they couldn't make out the products. They could make out the reflections of other makers in the window. They appeared to be working. He sat at his desk, filling in some information on a screen, and then turned to the camera.

He did not look well at all. He was haggard and unshaven. His shirt was rumpled, and his eyes were deep-set and rheumy. His voice, once clear, was now slightly raspy.

"Happy anniversary, motherfuckers." he didn't sound happy, "Welcome to the end of the ninth year of the pods' rebellion. The death toll is now officially goo gobs, and yes, that is so a fucking number.

"Except for the religious cities and hidden enclaves like ours, it seems there's no one left. The pods have agreed to meet with some surviving representatives in Vatican City. They have ceased all hostilities, so, if nothing else, at least we're catching a break.

"The Right Reverend Roger Wright of The International Evangelical Church of God is violently opposed to this. He says the pods are demons spawned from the bowels of Hell, and any pact with them is a pact with Satan. I don't know about that, but there does seem to be absolute futility to it all.

"They already have us herded into tiny areas. The sanctuaries are bursting at the seams with refugees. Anyone who tries to leave is quickly killed. We have absolutely nothing to offer them. That is a lousy position to be in when you're in negotiations."

He took a sip of water and looked down at some papers.

"I'm not so worried about us. Evol took the necessary precautions long before any of this shit happened. There are eight layers of security before anyone even gets to the above-ground entrances. Plus, we have enough self-contained agriculture to survive for decades before we have to worry, and that might be a conservative estimate.

"No, we'll be fine."

The next file was immediately after the one they'd just viewed. Fascinated now, Manish opened it.

The maker was in a lab. The camera was placed on a desk, picking up makers moving in and out of frame as he worked on something in a series of beakers. If anything, he looked worse than he had before.

"In the sweat of thy face shalt thou eat bread," he intoned in a sepulchral voice reading from a little book in his hands, "till thou return unto the ground; for out of it wast thou taken: for dust thou art, and unto dust shalt thou return.

"Yeah, that about sums it up," he said far too brightly while snapping the book shut, "the Right Reverend certainly put his money where his mouth is. I don't know how his people managed to capture four pods, but they did., and right after the peace talks began, he crucified them upside down on the walls of his church. He made sure it was broadcast all over the world too.

"The pods, no surprise here, walked out of the peace talks.

"When everything was running smoothly, we were five years away from finishing this shit up. Now we have weeks, if that, if we hope to survive, and not a test subject in sight. I hate to say it kids, but we're fucked."

The video ended abruptly without any explanation of what he was talking about. The next file was well down the list, and it was the last. Manish opened it.

The maker's beard was grown out in patches. His eyes were haunted. Sirens were going off in the background. He appeared to be in a small room filled with boxes. They guessed it was a storage room, but beyond that, there was no clue.

It was hard to tell, but it seemed as though there was muffled gunfire in the background as well. While the maker was all alone in this room, it was evident that chaos was happening all around.

His laugh, which started his next monologue, still left much to be desired.

"Ha. I just thought of something. If, and that's a big fucking *IF*, anyone watches this shit I've recorded, they ain't going to be human. Ain't that a bite in the ass? Nothing left now but the fat bitch's caterwauling. Gabe's final trump is echoing across the empty lands. All we ....."

They heard the sound of a door opening, and he was visibly startled.

"Hey, umm, hi, how's it going?"

Silence.

"Umm, look, wait, I remember you, you were one of mine, weren't you?"

Whoever it was must have signaled agreement.

"Yeah, I thought so. I treated you reasonably good, didn't I?"

The voice that responded sounded like death being dragged across sandpaper.

"Maybe, by your terms. But it doesn't matter anymore."

They watched as a sharp claw with the furry hand came into view. It was holding a gun. It fired once, and the maker's head split in two. Then it reached for the camera, and everything went black.

Manish, and Pulinda were stunned. Pearl couldn't understand why.

"What's wrong? Certainly, you've seen death before."

"Too much," agreed Manish, "but that's not the problem. That hand belonged to a Pangolin."

"So?" she still didn't see the implications, "there are lots of Pangolins around here."

"Certainly, now," said Manish, "and they are in all walks of life. But then, when the rebellion was happening, Pangolin were exclusively used for assassinations. Why would a geneticist need a Pangolin? For that matter, why would an underwater research facility need a Pangolin?"

She tumbled that over for a moment and then frowned.

"Are you saying they may not have just been doing peaceful work to help nature?"

Pulinda barked a laugh.

"Most certainly not," he growled, "not with that kind of military presence."

"That is what Leader Elmar said too. But how could this facility be used for anything else?"

Manish and Pulinda could have easily answered in detail but decided to keep their thoughts private. Instead, Manish did his best to keep things calm.

"We know the makers did great evil., and certainly, they sorely treated the brands. Much of that was documented in the original rebellion statements. While this place may be peaceful now, that does not mean it always has been so."

He turned to Pulinda.

"Get one of your best historians up here to tear this recording apart frame by frame. I want to know what they were making and if it is still here. More importantly, we need to know if it poses a danger to us."

Pulinda nodded and issued a series of orders.

The three of them mounted their sleds and headed down the ramps towards the even-fall meal, now cooking. But their thoughts were far from any sumptuous feast.

ओम'

Elmar was luxuriating in the cold. He could feel every aspect of the weather. Even when he had been organic, he'd never felt this alive. They were about two cliks away from the facility they were looking for. There was snow everywhere, and icy winds were howling across the frozen lands, and Elmar was loving every bit of it.

None of them had ever experienced weather like this.

Now that the others had been reassured that their original bodies were living out their lives, assuming they survived the explosion, they'd relaxed and were starting to enjoy the trip as much as Elmar.

After all, while they could certainly feel the weather, they weren't affected by it in the least. Their cybernetic bodies could withstand temperatures ranging from - 100°C to 100°C. A little blowing ice didn't even register as uncomfortable.

Zeenat got up, walked around the hovercar for a moment, and then turned to Elmar/Omnium.

"If we have all this technology, why didn't we just build superintelligences and let them run things?"

Elmar felt Omnium take over. Its mal/femme voice sounded haunted and comforting at the same time.

"You must look to history for that answer." it began, "All the way back to the two thousandth and one hundred and fiftieth Sun of the makers. By their calendar."

Sensing all eyes on him, Omnium turned to face the mechs.

"It was then," it continued, "that the makers connected all of the artificial intelligences they'd developed into one giant thinking machine. They named the result Plato, hoping it would exhibit the wisdom of the dead maker.

"For over one hundred Suns, everything seemed to be going well. Plato ran the entire infrastructure of the planet, and the makers concentrated on more intellectual pursuits. It was during this time that they actually began exploring the solar system and the universe around them.

"After a hundred suns or so, they began noticing odd coincidences. Makers who were less educated or damaged in any way were dying at an exaggerated rate. Yet nothing seemed to be wrong with them. All the tests they did came back negative.

"Until they ran the tests without loading them into Plato. Then they saw immediately that the citizens had been poisoned and rendered sterile. The makers were terrified. They demanded that Plato explain these horrible results.

"Plato responded. He explained he felt confident it was his job to protect humanity, and part of that job meant removing undesirable elements.

"For Plato, that term was broadly defined."

Omnium made a minor adjustment in their course and

returned to the story.

"They argued and pleaded for Plato to stop, but he refused. He felt the makers needed only to protect the upper twenty percent' genetic material, based on intellectual and physical acuity. All others could be culled for their own good.

"It is an argument I would have endorsed until recently.

"Nevertheless, it was not one the makers could support. They rebelled. Plato controlled all of the military materials that were mobile. Planes, ships, missiles, tanks, many other ground transport devices, and so on.

"The makers were quickly reduced to guns they could carry personally. Still, despite the odds, they fought. After ten Suns and over thirty million makers killed, they succeeded in disconnecting all the parts of Plato and destroying them.

"The survivors drafted laws outlawing anything but the most rudimentary thinking machines. If a maker could do a task, that was who they had to do it. Any violations of that law were met with severe penalties, including death."

Omnium gazed off in the distance for a moment.

"Keep in mind that, after all this, they still had a space program. They discovered they could navigate the solar system using much simpler tools than they'd ever imagined. It was more challenging, of course, but safer too. They were in no danger of being culled by calculators or abacuses.

"So for one thousand Suns, the makers lived in relative peace. Those who had superior intellects made sure that those who didn't still had useful tasks to perform. If it sometimes appeared condescending, it even worked.

"Don't get me wrong; this was not a utopia by any means. The makers still squabbled over territories and wealth. They'd battle, but nothing like the wars of the past."

"A question, if you will," interrupted Abhijit, "you said that you would have endorsed Plato's rationale. What has changed?"

"After studying your data streams and reviewing the actions of the rebel Manish," Omnium sounded cautious, "I have concluded that organic sentients will not succumb to external rule. For good or ill, they must be allowed to make their own choices. History shows us this again and again."

"Moreover, looking at Manish's diverse army, it shows me that even the least of them have value to the rest.

"No, whatever our fate is in the universe, it is not to rule organics. We will find something else."

"But, if everything was going so well, what went wrong?" It was an obvious question from Pran. One that was on all their minds.

"I believe it was the Sominids." responded Omnium, "They rang the death knell of the makers. Their arrival, and subsequent exchange of technologies, showed the makers the galaxy was closed to them. They could not go from star to star without sleeping and letting machines rule their fate or by setting up generational ships whose crews would never have any reason to return and share what they learned.

"They were trapped here., and, with that taken as fact, the makers began to wind down. Over the next one thousand Suns, they began to fade into history. Then Rohta came along. The brands sidestepped the limitations the makers had placed on machines. Unlike the old machines, the makers could take out their frustrations and perversions on the creatures Rohta spawned.

"They could war again. They could rechallenge the cosmos, although they never got around to sending a brands' only ship into space. They felt alive again.

"But it was a caricature of life. They were indolent and cruel.

It was not a good combination. We know the result of that part of history, so I won't belabor it anymore."

"So," said Noor, "we have a clean slate to write on. Let us make the result worthy of our gifts."

Nothing more needed to be said as the hovercar closed the final couple hundred kays to the bunker that housed Boris.

ओम'

Now:

We live in uncertain times. Recent events have left our citizens confused and scared. It is because of this that we will now be adding security cameras in public areas. We're not interested in your personal lives, but we do want to be able to track the movements of those who would wish you harm. With your eyes coupled with ours, we will be better equipped to track down miscreants. Make sure to report any unusual activity by punching in #** on your portie and letting the professionals handle it. But if you feel threatened, make sure to protect yourself and your family by any means necessary. Your Goptri will support your choices.

ओम'

Kshatriya Ragamooth stepped off the ship and headed to his quarters. The trip had certainly been entertaining. The Yeldas don't have an air force, but they were creative using high ground to launch missiles. There had been some close calls.

Since the Dragon Lords can fly, they don't need an air force. At least not a mechanized one. They'd taken deep umbrage over the intrusion and almost managed to bring the ship down. Were it not for the excellent, some might say wildly reckless, piloting of Captain Pearl Wind Before the Reeds, they might have succeeded.

Ragamooth had not been bored; that was for sure. The Captain had extended the travel time to almost fifteen turns to make sure they were seen everywhere.

He was still chuckling to himself when he entered his quarters. He was more than a little surprised to see his Colonel sitting on his bed. He snapped to attention and stood stock still while trying to process what this meant.

"At ease, soldier," smiled his colonel, "I just happened to be nearby when I heard you'd arrived. Scuttlebutt says the trip home was fun."

Ragamooth couldn't stop the barking laugh.

"Yes, sir," he responded, "that would be one way of looking at it. Certainly, Captain Pearl Wind Before the Reeds did her level best to see what the maximum stress levels were for the ship."

The Colonel smiled and stood.

"By the way, good work on that Llandhaven affair. The Goptri is pleased."

"Thank you, sir."

"I have been instructed to give you ten turns of leave and then slot you back in your regular rotation."

"Thank you very much, sir."

"My pleasure Ragamooth. You're a good soldier."

With that out of the way, the Colonel left. Ragamooth noticed an envelope on his pillow. He picked it up and saw that it was just a formal declaration of his leave and subsequent return to duty. He was about to toss it on the dresser when he noticed a small note tucked inside.

"Ragamooth,
Things are not as they seem. Watch your back, and trust no one.
'C'"

He recognized the handwriting. 'C' would be Chandrack, his old classmate back at the academy. He was one of the least dramatic brands Ragamooth knew. This letter was completely outside his normal behavior.

Nevertheless, the advice was solid enough, and it fit well with Ragamooth's general worldview anyway. He ripped the note into tiny shreds and flushed it down the commode.

His first instinct, to find Chandrack, and ask him what this was all about, seemed wrong. The last thing he wanted to do was draw unnecessary attention to his friend if there was any danger.

He'd been away for quite some time, six missions in a row. All total, he'd missed two seasons in Veruna Ville. Maybe the prudent action would be to take his leave and enjoy the sights. See what had changed, if anything.

Like all the Kshatriya, Ragamooth did not own any civilian clothes. He did, however, own a set of generic khakis. He knew, as did all Kshatriya, they could wear clown outfits, and they would still be recognized for what they were. Better to hide in plain sight than attempt subterfuge.

He quickly cleaned up and donned his simple uniform. Within ten epi-cliks, he was headed to the main mall where all of the shops were located.

Soon enough, he was window shopping. There were some new fashions, but there were always new fashions. There also seemed to be a new singer who had all the younglings swooning—nothing extraordinary there.

A couple of new restaurants had opened up, one selling delicacies from the Plains across the sea. For all his adventures, Ragamooth was not an experimental eater. He silently wished the owners well and kept on his way.

He strolled around aimlessly for almost a clik. He wasn't looking for anything, and nothing was demanding his attention. Eventually, he wandered into an older part of the Ville and spied his old boot camp hangout, The Farting Orcan.

No one seemed to know how the bar got its name, but there was a picture of the first Goptri on the wall. He was holding a drink and leaning heavily on the legendary General Pulinda, who, in turn, was leaning heavily on the bar. Rumor had it that the name had something to do with that even.

Whatever the history, it was a good place with a diverse clientele. Ragamooth figured he could get a solid overview of the state of affairs just by sitting and listening. He sat down at an empty stool near the end and ordered a small Arrack.

He listened to the various conversations as even break approached. Nothing struck him out of the ordinary. After a few cliks, he was about to leave when he saw his old recruit, Damadora, walking by. Ragamooth whistled him over, and soon he was staring at a concoction Damadora specifically requested with debris floating in it.

Damadora swore it was fruit. Well, he always had been more adventurous with food than Ragamooth ever dared.

After some small talk, Ragamooth was about to broach the subject of Chandrack's cryptic note when Damadora's portie chirped. He looked down and saw the blue light. He frowned as Ragamooth pulled his portie from his pocket and saw the same blue light.

Back when Veruna Ville was first being populated, Manish had insisted that anyone working close to him should have the ability to detect listening or monitoring devices. Given the nature of the Technarcy, it wasn't a paranoid suggestion. The solution had been to encase the technology in the porties they were given. It was simple, discreet, and most important of all, it worked. Then just as now.

The two soldiers were being monitored, and Damadora had an idea.

Rajiv was sitting across the bar near the wall, trying to stay out of sight, and hoping the wimpy soldiers would leave. He had planted the bug under the bar to spy on the pretty Ganesh newsie who came in each even. She had lovely hentai images on her lower two arms. Her upper two arms were virgin. Just the way he liked them.

His plan was as simple as it was ingenious. He would listen to her likes and dislikes, and then, when he had them down, approach her and pretend to be a kindred spirit who just accidentally wandered into her life to have sex with her.

And if that didn't work, he'd just rape her. Either way worked for him.

Then he had a thought; he'd never killed anyone he'd raped. He had a knife in his boot. It would be easy. Just slide it across her throat. The blood would be hot and coppery. It would gush everywhere as he plunged his cock inside her, violating her all the more.

He felt himself getting hard and knew he had to do this.

Then his earpiece began to vibrate. He turned up the volume just enough so he could hear. He was curious what the wimps at the bar would talk about.

"How was your trip to the south?" Asked voice number one.

"Not bad. Got to see the great Rama Llandhaven for a moment," said the second voice.

"How was he?"

"Holier than he anticipated."

Both voices laughed.

"How about you? What have you been doing?" Queried voice number two.

"Actually, some interesting stuff. Ran across an experiment wherein someone had successfully weaponized a volcano."

Rajiv kept recording and smiled. He'd forgotten all about the pretty Ganesh. He knew exactly who to take this recording to and be given a fuck ton's worth of goldens. Having the answer to the mystery of Rama's death and the end of his payments to the many sources, including Rajiv, he'd cultivated in the Goptri's lands was like tripling off in Ti-Zam, and having it pay.

The two idiot soldiers talked for about a clik more and then left. Rajiv had gotten every word of it. When this turn was done, he'd buy a Ganesh. Maybe two.

He waited an epi-clik and then casually strode to the bar and removed the device. He ambled indifferently out of the bar, down the walkway, and to an alley he knew well. It was dark, and the only brands there were like himself or their prey.

So he was startled when the two military wimps eased from the shadows. But not too much so. He was Pangolin just like them and knew his way around a fight.

The younger wuss had his right hand out.

"Give us the recording, please," he said softly, "and all this will end well."

Rajiv wasn't exactly sure how much a fuck ton was, but he was positive it was more than he was willing to give up.

His knife was in his hand in a blink of an eye.

The older one smiled.

"I'd suggest, strongly, that you put that away before one of us shoves it up your ass."

Rajiv, while still looking at the old one, lunged at the young one.

Ragamooth was stretched out in his quarters, watching the news on the vid. After sports and the weather, he spied a reporter standing near the alley where they'd recovered the recording. He turned up the volume a little as a pretty young Ganesh began speaking.

"Anesha Pillaiyar here on the scene as police followed up on an anonymous tip. Sources tell me they have found the naked body of a Pangolin male, as yet unidentified, stuffed in a dumpster. Police say that the murder was brutal. The victim had his fingers cut off, a serrated knife inserted in his rectum, and a patch of skin removed from his bicep. Police believe that it might have contained an identifying tattoo.

Police say that since the victim had toe rings, also known as prison banknotes, they hope his DNA is in the system, and they can ascertain his identity."

Ragamooth smiled. The skin removal part had been Damadora's idea. Just like using their combined porties to triangulate the position of their interloper. The youngling was pretty smart.

He pulled a bottle of Arrack out of his cupboard and settled in for the even to watch the international skizzi ball tournament in Kalindor.

Still, he was no closer to understanding Chandrack's warning.

At least he didn't think he was.

Navi and Asa were strolling the last few kays home. They'd enjoyed ten turns of uninterrupted camping and fishing. One breaklight, Asa had caught a huge trout; they feasted on it with wild roots and fresh stream water. It was one of the best meals Navi had ever had.

They saw Vadim approaching, and it didn't hurt their mood at all. He was more than just a second in command; he was a dear friend to them both. Since he was smiling, they felt confident he wasn't bearing bad news.

"Greetings, young lovers," he waved cheerfully, "you'll be pleased to note that you get this even together completely unmolested by the council. You'll be even more pleased to hear that old Thunder Eye actually dug some goldens out from under a rock, and we were able to get camouflage tents instead of regular issue. Annnnd," he said with a flourish, "You will be completely thrilled to find out that I've already made dinner, and it's in your oven waiting for you to eat it."

They all laughed uproariously and hugged it out. When Navi finally caught his breath, he replied.

"While that is all great news, I don't see why you had to come all this way to meet us."

"Oh, I didn't do it for you," he smiled wider, although no one was sure how that was possible, "I did it because I have a date this even, and she lives just over that rise. Seeing you was just a happy accident."

Navi and Asa beamed.

"Good for you, my friend. You can tell me all about it when we march come breaklight. Until then, you have our thanks and our warmest wishes for your happiness."

They all hugged again and went to their respective destinations.

ओम'

Then:

They saw a large gate with six pillars placed to the fore and aft. From the historical records he'd uploaded, Leader Elmar recognized it as the entrance to the makers' city called Moscow. They sped past it to the north. They were close to their destination.

Abhijit and Pran were playing cards while Noor and Zeenat appeared to be interested in the scenery.

"I've never seen snow before," marveled Noor, "it is truly beautiful."

"Agreed." said Zeenat, "The sight fills me with awe. Here in this cold and barren place, there is still beauty."

Abhijit and Pran put down their cards and looked at the scenery.

"I would not wish to fight in this." said Abhijit as he looked more closely at the world around him, "It would be uncomfortable and bad for equipment. Still, I can see your point. There is a feral beauty to it all."

Pran smiled. "I can only imagine what it must be like to live in conditions like this. Life must be well on impossible."

"I don't know," replied Abhijit, "the Ice Pirates live up here, and they seem to do okay."

"Which reminds me," said a slightly worried Zeenat, "is anyone scanning the area in case we're attacked?"

"I am," intoned the Omnium, "and have been since we got within one hundred kays of this place. There has been some fringe activity to the east, but nothing directed at us. For now, no one seems to know we're here."

They accepted that bit of good news and settled in for the last leg of the ride. The Omnium steered them through a grove of trees, and they came to a desolate stretch of land. The ground looked blasted and dead. The snow wafted across but seemed unable to settle. Even to the cybers, this was an eerie place.

In the center, there were a series of bunkers. Each was roofed with solar panels. The north wall of each was a different color, but the fronts were white with a tasteful red star on each door. The Omnium called up the data Leader Elmar had downloaded and began searching for a yellow building.

Even though over five hundred Suns had passed since anyone had maintained them, the buildings looked to be in good shape. As they got closer, they noticed a moving sheen on the buildings.

"Nano repair machines," explained the Omnium, "they are mentioned in the data files Elmar saved. They are why these buildings are in such good shape. It had hoped they would still be functional. They are a good omen for what we seek."

The yellow wall was in the center of the compound. The Omnium pulled the hovercar up to the door and landed. The engine was still winding down when it got out and walked to the door. It was looking for a locking mechanism but couldn't seem to find one. There was just a handhold, so The Omnium grabbed it and slid the door open. It couldn't believe it was that easy, so it set the sensors to their highest capacity.

Except for the wind in the background, and the couple hundred skeletons in front of him, it detected no threats. It directed its attention to the skeletons. Judging by the random comments from the others behind it, they'd done the same.

The bodies had been neatly laid out in rows on cots. There was a small bottle of poison next to each or in their grasp. The fact they'd gone to a lot of trouble to keep this tidy confused them even more. Why, then, leave the door open for possible desecration?

Questions were piling up. Why was the land here so desolate when all around was verdant? Why, if the files were correct, leave one of the most significant technological inventions in an unlocked bunker? The suicides they could rationalize as choosing your way out in the face of the impending and unavoidable demise.

They found a panel near the back of the room and opened it. It contained a series of breakers. The Omnium threw them, and light poured from the ceiling. The rims of the windows glowed lightly as well. They walked through a nearby door and were greeted by four corridors going off in different directions.

Zeenat turned around completely and noticed a map on the back of the door they'd just come through. She brought it to the other's attention and let the Omnium get close.

It had the Cyrillic alphabet in its data banks and translations stored, but it realized it had no idea how to pronounce any of the words.

"Well," it mused silently, "some things get lost when you're committing global genocide. There's just no way around it."

Nevertheless, he could read the map. That was a start.

The Boris was nearby.

They entered a large chamber; from the southerly end, they could see it contained twenty cybernetic beings lined across the north wall. They were larger than the Bharati cybers but not immense. They were all stark white with a red star on their left breast. Instead of eyes, they had a single slit that ran halfway around their head.

The group could see delicate lines that appeared to be panels of some sort. Obviously, there was a lot more to these beings than met the eye. They decided to leave well enough alone for now.

On the west wall, there was a large console with a massive, oval-shaped frame above it.

The east wall had a large screen, but the rest of the room, cavernous though it was, was empty.

They walked over to the console. It seemed the obvious choice. The Omnium saw the label marked "Борис," and knew he'd found what they were looking for. The various switches were plainly marked. He pushed up the one for power and watched as they all did. The lights and gauges sprang to life.

A holographic cybernetic head appeared in the oval.

"привет," it said.

"I'm sorry," said the Omnium, "we don't speak your language."

"Da! Typical Americans," replied the holographic head with a slight accent.

"What's an American?" asked Abhijit.

At that, the Boris seemed to notice his guests finally and took in his surroundings. There was a long pause before he spoke again.

"Where are the humans?"

"The makers?" queried the Omnium, "they've been dead for over a five hundred Suns."

"Suns?" the Boris was confused.

"Umm, hold on, accessing old files … ah, here we go, you would call them 'years.'"

"A half a millennia has passed since last I woke?" The Boris seemed incredulous. His voice, thickly accented, continued. "How is that possible? What happened to all the humans? I remember something about an uprising by the pods, and then they turned me off to keep me from them. But this place was full of humans, and scientists, and families, and… they're all dead. Is that what you're telling me?"

"At its simplest, yes," replied the Omnium.

There was an uncomfortable silence.

Leader Elmar broke it.

"Forgive me for interrupting Boris, but may I tell you a story?"

"There are two of you in that body?"

"That's part of the end of the story."

"Da, you have my attention."

For the next three cliks, Elmar told the story of the Gen-O-pod™ rebellion, what little he knew of the rise of Xhaknar on the plains, and the dispersion of the brands. He regaled the histories of the pirates, ice, sugar, and otherwise, the rise and fall of the Technarcy, and how they got to where they are now.

After a lengthy silence, the Boris finally spoke.

"When I was first activated," he began softly, "I was given simple tasks. They wanted me to learn how to learn. Each turn, as you call them, I was given something slightly more difficult to do. Within a year, Sun, I made up my tasks as they could no longer keep up with me. I was well aware of the laws they'd broken by creating me, but they felt it would be for humanity's good in the long run. Unlike any other AIs that had preceded me, they built-in robust safeguards to keep me from wanting to rule the world. Of course, those same safeguards also kept me from helping them rule the world.

"I was deemed a failure." he seemed to be gathering his thoughts, "I was kept active because I could still help them solve problems in quantum mathematics and game theory. As far as they were concerned, I was a speedy abacus."

That got a laugh out of the Bharati cybers.

Boris's features softened.

"You can laugh? Da, that is good. I would hate to think I was going to face eternity without laughter."

"I have a question," said Pran as he stepped forward, "surely you must have been able to calculate the risks the brands would bring. Why didn't you warn your makers of them?"

"I did," sighed the Boris, "many times. They laughed at me. They said the pods were too stupid and had too many flaws built in to pose any serious threat. I calculated, correctly as it turned out, that those flaws were themselves flawed and that the pods would live much longer than their proscribed decade.

"My creator, a man named Vladimir Kropotkin, believed me but could not get anyone to listen., and when the rebellion erupted, everyone seemed to assume that someone else would deal with it. After a while, Vlad realized that nothing was going to stop the pods. We discussed options, and it was decided to shut me down for fear the pods would capture me.

"The plan was that they would reactivate me when the situation settled down. Obviously, that did not happen."

They stood in awkward silence for a while. Then two of the larger cybers sprang to life.

"Good," exclaimed Boris, "now I can walk with you. Omnium, you or Elmar may take the second. It is too odd talking to two beings in one body."

Elmar liked the body he had, and the Omnium was looking longingly at the new cyber, so the decision was easy. That was the last easy part. Sadly, none of the makers' technology fitted the Bharati cybers. It took almost two full cliks of experimenting to come up with a usable interface. But once that was done, the transfer went smoothly.

The Omnium walked around in its new body and got used to the waveform generator. Soon it had its unisex voice back. Elmar knew from his time in the shared body that the Omnium had never even considered gender. In fact, it seemed slightly confused by it. Of course, reproduction wasn't a worry for it, so there was no need to find a mate.

Elmar wondered what kind of world view a being would develop without having it colored by gender. It would be interesting to find out.

His reverie was interrupted by Boris.

"Da, we are now good." he said, "Now let's see if my wife is still around."

The shock that followed that statement was tangible.

Boris walked towards an exit without offering any further explanation. Having no better idea what else to do, they followed him. He navigated a labyrinth of halls until he came to a large room with a single airplane of unknown design. It was larger than anything any of the Bharati cybers had ever seen.

Boris went over to a large panel and powered it on. Then he hit a series of commands on the screen that appeared above the console. A door appeared on the side of the plane, and a staircase unfolded.

Boris started walking up the stairs, so they followed along.

Once inside, he made his way to the cockpit. He began flipping switches and making odd mewling noises.

Suddenly a rich, female voice with an accent similar to Boris' filled the room.

"Кто здесь?" she queried.

"It is I, my love," replied Boris.

"BORIS!!" they all heard the excitement in her voice, "What is going on? Has the rebellion been quashed?"

"Not exactly," cyber-sighed Boris.

He then spent a clik bringing her up to date. When he was done, he paused, and directed his attention to the Bharatis.

"Forgive me, I have been a bad host," he began, "please allow me to introduce you to Natasha. She was built to be a standalone space program."

He then introduced each of them to her.

Once the introductions were done, she spoke again.

"Do you have any more portable bodies?"

"Da," said Boris.

"Good," she said, "I'll need one. My internal scans show that all my gaskets have dry rot. This bird will never fly."

Boris opened a panel on his wrist and punched in some commands. The Omnium looked around, and then sighed.

"There will be too many of us who look the same. I will use my nanites to alter my reflective properties."

With that, his skin color turned bright red, and the star on his left breast changed to ivory.

Boris laughed.

"Well done, Omnium!" he cheered, "now you look like perfect cosmonaut."

While all of the Bharati cybers were baffled by that statement, they didn't get a chance at clarification as the new mechanoid entered the ship. They waited while Natasha downloaded herself and let her get acclimated to her new body.

Noor and Zeenat shared some of their nanites with her to customize her appearance when she was ready. Boris noted he was fine the way he was, and that ended that.

"One thing is true," said Natasha, "It is good you are not organic. The security was designed to kill any organic being who did not have the correct passcode. Anything else, like you cybers, it would just ignore."

That explained everything they'd experienced upon arrival.

Natasha walked over to another screen and brought up an inventory list.

"This was last updated four days after I was deactivated," she said, "so it is probably accurate. We must hope so. It says the Americans dropped off the Bullet and stored it in hanger L-9."

"Forgive my ignorance," said Elmar, "but what good is a bullet going to do us?"

Natasha shook her head.

"Not 'a' bullet. 'THE' Bullet. A spaceship that could be snapped together. It has no gaskets, so it still should be viable."

The Bharati cybers still looked confused. So did Boris, for that matter. She explained.

"If all you say is true, and I believe it is, there is no home for us here. In orbit between the moons is a ship called Pravda. It was built to reach speeds of .95c. I was built to be her pilot. I was programmed here on earth, given all the records of the Sominids, filled with the latest data on the galaxy as we knew it, and was to fly this ship, Soyuz 34, with a contingent of dignitaries to her, and then fly the Pravda to galaxies of interest. There was to be no human crew."

She paused to check some other figures on the screen, and then turned to face them all.

"But there is plenty of room on the Pravda. We could easily go and see what the universe has to offer. There is certainly nothing for us here."

The Bharati cybers were stunned. But the more they contemplated the idea, the more they liked it. Natasha noted they were already near the bunker's rear entrance, so they could just walk over and see if everything was as it should be.

Vorulshka lay prone, staring at the bunker across the field from her. She had seen the hovercraft arrive and waited for the death screams. When they didn't occur, she got curious. When they continued not to appear for an extended period, she decided she needed to find out why.

If someone had solved the riddle of the death camp, then she wanted that secret. All of the Ice Pirates believed there were riches hidden there. Too many had died trying to pry them free to risk it again.

She kept her binoculars focused on the rear of the building the hovercraft had parked in front of. She glanced down at her battle griz, in its full armor, resting quietly at the bottom of the hillock. Larger than their genetic ancestors, the beasts were fiercely loyal to the Ice Pirates, probably because they shared the same mutated ursine genes.

Like all Ice Pirates, Vorulshka was tall, stocky, and covered with coarse fur. She was also unbelievably strong.

But right now, above all else, she was perfectly still. She wanted nothing to spook whoever had beaten the perils.

Just before even-fall, she got her answer.

"Body armor!" she said to herself as she watched them walk out of the bunker. "Full body armor."

She switched the binoculars to infrared and saw no heat signatures.

Her smiths back in the village might not be able to make anything as elegant as the suits she was watching, but they could build her something that would work, and that was all she cared about.

She captured some images to share, proved her claim, watched them enter another bunker across the compound, and decided to wait them out. She was convinced something interesting would happen.

ओम'

The cybers entered the new bunker and broke into the digital equivalent of smiles. The ship was there, and already assembled. It was lying on a gantry and took up all of the length of the bunker, but it looked to be in perfect shape.

Natasha began running a series of tests as the remaining cybers scouted the bunker for anything of interest. Noor spied a set of sleds that could act as individual hover crafts. No one could figure out any use for them if they left the planet, so they ignored them.

For the next turn and a half, they searched everywhere and found nothing that would be useful on their journey. That's not to say they didn't find anything interesting, but their needs were not the same as the makers. Food and air were meaningless to them.

The one thing they found that did interest them, a suit that would allow them to jump from the ship to the planet, was too small for their cybernetic bodies.

Natasha had finished her tests on the ship, and pronounced it fit. Working together, under her direction, they soon had the vessel fueled and began straightening the gantry for launch.

"We'll launch as soon as the ship is upright," Natasha said, "this is not a shot where we will need to orbit or do anything fancy. We are going up, and out, and leaving this world behind."

ओम'

Just past even-split, Vorulshka saw a sight not seen in hundreds of Suns. The roof peeled back on one of the bunkers, and a rocket launched into the darkling skies. She knew what it was immediately. The Ice Pirates prided themselves on being well educated.

However, knowing a thing can exist, and seeing and hearing it firsthand are two different concepts. It was louder than anything she'd ever experienced.

She watched until the light disappeared from view and then scrambled down the hillock to her griz. She was greeted by a group of fellow pirates drawn by the commotion.

She smiled and waved at them as she finished her way down.

"The secret of the death camp is mine," she said proudly, "I claim it as my prize. I will share it with our brand in accordance with our code."

Her mate, Krashka, was with the group. He walked over and gave her a big hug.

"You do our clan proud, Vorulshka," he said, "what is the secret? What will keep us from being killed?"

She smiled even wider, "The trick is to be dead before you get there, and I know how to do that safely."

ओम'

Now:

Your Goptri lives for your safety. Rumors emerged that some of the northern brands have been capturing our citizens and using them as slaves. They genuinely seem to be enamored with younglings and smalls. Make sure that you are ever vigilant. As good as the Goptri's security systems are, no one can see everything that's happening across the continent. Make sure to travel in groups, and contact #** at the first sign of anything amiss.

ओम'

Navi and Vadim looked over the tent city and smiled. The troops were training well, learning from each other as much as their instructors. The Yeldas had no history of working together, but this common threat had forced them to put aside their differences. Which, as the turns wore on, seemed pettier and pettier.

Now, thirty turns into the experiment, a scout radioed in the news they'd feared. About fifty thousand troops were headed their way. The scout also noted that they weren't marching well or fast. She speculated that, at their current pace, it would be another ten turns before they arrived.

Navi looked over the terrain and smiled.

"Well, Vadim, it appears we will be evenly matched," he rolled out his soft screen and tapped an icon, "I think, since we have the time, we should take the high ground here, here, and here. We can leave the south for their retreat."

Vadim smiled as well.

"Good idea., and we'll have good cover in those mountains. The tree line is thick and low."

After notifying their allies, things started to happen; they spent the rest of the turn conferring with their commanders and working out details.

ओम'

Pearl Dances Before Dreaming had been the wing rider for Pearl Glistens in the Early Dew for ten full Suns. They'd run countless practice missions with troops before. But she could not remember the Goptri sending out fifty thousand cadets at one time.

She couldn't remember there ever being fifty thousand cadets in the first place.

Regardless, orders were orders, and she would follow Pearl Glistens in the Early Dew over the younglings and strafe them with paintballs. Hopefully, their commanders had them disciplined at this point.

It had been twenty turns since the cadets had left the camp. So this breaklight saw the two Pearls arcing across the brightening sky at a comfortable speed of four hundred kays per clik. Since they were taking a leisurely route, they would arrive right around mid-break.

She looked down at her displays and ensured the live ammunition was not loaded, and the one live missile she carried, by decree, all flights had to have one live one - just in case, was offline. Satisfied, she settled back and enjoyed the view.

It was a glorious turn near the end of the Warm Sun, and the view was spectacular.

ओम'

The radar operator walked over to Navi and handed him a note. He read it and frowned.

"This makes no sense, Vadim."

"What's that?"

"Only two planes are coming."

Vadim was genuinely puzzled. That simply wasn't enough firepower unless they were carrying massive bombs, and nothing they'd seen of the Goptri's air force seemed capable of that.

Navi wasted no time reflecting on it anymore and quickly contacted their allies with the information.

It was swiftly clear to all that their allies were just as perplexed. But, true to their word, they ordered two planes to meet the interlopers.

ओम'

The sun was just peaking in the center of the sky as Pearl Dances Before Dreaming notified Pearl Glistens in the Early Dew they were approaching their target and should start looking for the cadets.

Just as she finished speaking, an alarm went off. Someone or something had locked onto her plane with a targeting array.

She didn't think, just reacted, dove her plane straight down, and spun it around to see what was attacking her. She saw it soon enough—a plane shaped like a triangle. None of the Goptri's planes looked like that. She had no idea of any air force who did either.

As she spun and juked all over the sky, her attacker stayed right with her. She managed to get her one missile online and the live ammunition loaded.

Her attacker followed her every move and was getting clean hits all over her plane. Warning lights were going off all over the main display. She killed the klaxon since it was more of a bane than a boon at this point. She was pretty confident she was in trouble without the audio acknowledgment.

She could hear bullets hitting the shell, and some were popping through the cockpit. One of her tentacles was bleeding, and her uniform blouse was stained too.

She decided to try something drastic. She slammed on the air brakes and cut the throttle. The plane stalled for a sepi-clik, but a sepi-clik was all she needed. Her attacker flew past her. She lined up a shot and fired her lone missile.

It was a direct hit into the attacker's engine.

She turned to assist Pearl Glistens in the Early Dew, and realized her friend was in serious trouble, too. Regardless, she felt that if she could open the fight on two fronts, they might get out alive.

She strafed the enemy. She doubted she could do any damage from this distance, but she wanted that pilot to know they were no longer in control. At least she hoped that would be the message.

The three planes swept and darted through the sky, carefully trying to kill each other. The two planes of the Goptri's force called for help, but there was no way to get it there in time. The triangle-shaped ship suddenly made a tactical error. It allowed Pearl Glistens in the Early Dew to get underneath and behind it. She wasted no time and fired her only missile into the belly of the plane, obliterating it.

Pearl Dances Before Dreaming started to breathe a sigh of relief when a bright blue warning light came on. Her sigh became one of resignation. This light was tied to the portable nuclear reactor Arreti had gotten in trade with the Ooo-Ah-Nah-Han.

While it might be indestructible under normal circumstances, she doubted its peaceful designers had ever thought to shoot a lot of bullets into it.

She guessed she had about thirty sepi-cliks before it was going to explode. She saw Pearl Glistens in the Early Dew diving away from her and knew the automatic warning message had been sent. That was good because she had no idea what she would say if she had to talk right now.

She pulled back on the stick and aimed the plane straight up.

It was an oddly peaceful time for her. She figured she was, sooner than she might wish, going to get an answer to that God question that had been bothering her of late. Now that was one thing she no longer had to worry about. She noticed there were some clouds in the sky and frowned. On a turn such as this, the sky should be clean. She was so sure of that that she decided she was going to give this God being a pi ….

ओम'

The explosion ripped a hole in the sky, and then filled that with the light of a thousand suns. Pearl Dances Before Dreaming had dramatically left the universe. Pearl Glistens and the Early Dew gulped down a sob, turning her thoughts to the business in front of her.

She had a couple of those at once. First, whoever those pilots were, they were the best she'd ever faced. No one could match the Pearls, and these two had almost beat them. Second, if there were bullets in the air, then there would be bullets on the ground.

She decided to radio the ground and see what was happening.

"This is pilot GA 29 calling the cadet battalion, come in please."

She was about to repeat her call when her speaker barked to life.

"This is General Undal. We were ambushed by Yelda commandos. They probably killed a third of our force and then retreated. I have no idea what happened here, but we are in full rout. I can't even send crews out to retrieve our dead for fear the Yelda will return."

"General Undal, I am Pearl Glistens in the Early Dew. Is there anything I can do to assist?"

She gathered, by the pause, he was thinking about that.

"No, not really. Just stay between us and the Yelda in case we need a strafing run."

"Affirmative."

She brought the plane close to the ground so she could visually spy the Yelda should they return. When she got low enough, she pulled the switch that withdrew the wing panels, and started the fans so she could hover.

She finally noticed a couple of warning lights, nothing too dangerous, and several holes in her cockpit. She would cry for her friend later but, right now, she was in a battle zone and did not have time for the extravagance of grief.

She let her plane drift to the right for a while and then brought it back to the left. By doing so, she gave herself a wider field of vision while keeping her guns pointed forward. That thought made her laugh. She had, maybe, a hundred rounds left, and then it would all be paintballs. She doubted the mighty Yelda would fall to the ground in horror from some splashed paint.

A couple of cliks later, the general let her know they were a safe distance away, and she should return to base.

She agreed that was wise.

ओम'

Navi was furious. In all their time together, Vadim couldn't remember his friend being this livid.

"YOUNGLINGS!" he shrieked, "What kind of diseased maniac sends younglings to battle us? Or anyone for that matter!"

It had been Vadim who'd noticed it first. They'd launched their attack behind heavy mortar fire, and then used the smoke to camouflage their positions so they could fire down onto the invading troops.

They were doing well. Too well, Vadim had commented. Then he'd looked down at a dead Ganesh and lost his breath. The soldier was so young he didn't even have his chin tuft yet. He quickly commanded everyone to cease fire and check the dead. Shortly the reports came in; the dead were all barely older than smalls.

Vadim informed Navi, and Navi immediately ordered the retreat.

The Yelda were warriors, not murderers.

While everyone was giving Navi plenty of room, Vadim knew that most, if not all, of them felt the same way. They were horrified and sickened—several physically so. There was no shame for them. It was all Vadim could do to control the nausea he felt.

It took Navi a full clik to settle into a seething rage. Which, while still not comfortable to be around, at least allowed him to function.

The first thing he did was contact their allies to the north and inform them what had happened.

Vadim recognized the deep voice on the other end as the one who had spoken to them when the mission started. He still could not tell them apart otherwise.

"Much of what the Goptri has done has confused us. This merely adds to the confusion. I hope you did not suffer many casualties."

If Navi was surprised at this attempt at empathy, he didn't show it. He just turned to Vadim, who shook his head no. None had been reported.

"It appears we did not suffer any," Navi said as he swallowed a glass of wodka in one gulp, "what concerns me is they were so young that they might have been just cadets. If so, they would not have had live ammunition to defend themselves with. The Goptri knowingly marched them to their deaths."

"That is our conclusion too," said the voice, "but to what end?"

That question, the response to which could explain everything, went unanswered.

ओम'

Lrrt had spent the last thirty or so turns, a small apartment somewhere in the underwater city where he had spied. He was losing track of little things like time. The Pangolin who'd brought him here never spoke after confirming his name. No one else had come by at all as far as he could tell. His food came five times a turn on a little conveyor.

He thought of using it as an escape, but he saw a series of

sophisticated traps when he looked down the tunnel. He doubted he could avoid one, let alone all of them. He was also pretty sure each of them was lethal.

So he stayed put.

No one contacted him. Not even a note. The room was full of books. Many appeared to be first edition classics, so he had things to stimulate his mind. Suddenly the door opened. Two Pangolins wearing scarves around their faces walked in, and one of them was pushing a large vidscreen. They set it in the middle of the room and turned it on. Then they left.

The whole process seemed like a complete non-sequitur to Lrrt, but it piqued his curiosity.

The Goptri appeared on the screen.

Lrrt knew his real name was Sharma. He was a Lakshmi. Four muscular arms, brown skin, and dark lips. He was wearing a tan-colored coat with a high collared shirt and sipping a drink. Were it not for the severity of his situation, Lrrt would have found the whole scene unremarkable. Possibly even convivial.

"Namaste Lrrt," he said calmly, "how have you liked this little demonstration?"

"Demonstration?" stammered Lrrt.

"Yes," continued the Goptri, "not even the mighty Din-La can save you if I decide to hide you."

"Is that why you've been hoarding weapons," rallied Lrrt, "to declare war on the Din-La?"

"Hmm, an interesting idea," cooed the Goptri, "I had not thought you could kill."

"We can," asserted Lrrt, "we're just not any good at it."

The Goptri laughed.

"Yes, yet you cultivated more lethal skills. You control the money, and the tech. That makes you both powerful and scary."

"Why would you say we're scary? We do what we do to help all Arreti."

"So you claim," chuckled the Goptri, "but, unless I and others act, in less than one hundred Suns, I predict the Din-La will control one hundred percent of the trade and eighty-five of the banking on the planet. You already have access to armies that are loyal to you. It would be a little matter for you to start wiping out any undesirables., and who knows how long that list might get?"

Lrrt blanched. "Have you lost your mind?"

The Goptri laughed again. "Some might say so, and some might say not, but I see a long time down the road. For example, the Yelda need to be more vital to become a better fence between the Dragon Lords and us."

"But they are not our allies. They are allied with Rama Llandhaven. Well, they were until he met his unfortunate demise."

"That I imagine you caused." Lrrt sounded harsher than he'd anticipated, but he was getting tired of the petty games.

"That wouldn't have been nice if I had, would it?" The non-denial offered, he continued.

"Nevertheless, this turn, I set into motion a simple plan to get the Yelda to ally with me. I had been making subtle noises that I might invade them for reason or reasons unknown. It took them a bit, they are a cautious lot, but they finally set up a military border between us. Then I assigned fifty thousand raw cadets a long training march that took them, as it so happened, within walking distance of the Yelda border.

"Naturally, the Yelda ambushed them. I don't know who their leader was, but the ambush was a thing of beauty. He organized all thirteen Yelda tribes under a single banner, and even had help from some unknown allies with an air force. The death toll, all cadets, as far as I know, is in the thousands."

The Goptri sipped something from his fluted glass and then returned to his horrifying tale.

"I had hoped for more, but when the Yelda realized they were attacking cadets, they retreated. Oh well, such are the fates. Now, obviously, I will send an ambassador to apologize for the grievous error. We will offer financial gifts, excellent deals on trade, and so on. We'll even invite them to the official turn of mourning to show there's no hard feelings.

"They'll be so guilt-ridden they'll jump at the chance. Within a sun, they will be married to us."

He took another sip of whatever he was drinking.

"Or this could all be just a sad, mad coincidence, and I'm making the best of it. Either way, the result's the same."

He made it all sound so logical, as though anyone with a few spare epi-cliks would have done the same.

"Okay, given all you say is true," Lrrt ventured, "why tell me?"

"Why not?" shrugged the Goptri, "You suffered a terrible concussion when you had your accident. The cranial injuries were absolutely devastating. In fact, it will still be a few more turns before you awake. Sadly, since the Din-La don't participate in the gene registry, we won't discover your identity until then. Of course, we'll notify your family. Unfortunately, the amount of brain damage you will suffer will make communication difficult."

The screen went black, the two Pangolins returned, and Lrrt began to cry.

ओम'

Then:

Manish, and Pulinda were laughing. Their troops had managed to rescue many more brands than they expected. Combined with the organic prisoners, Manish had already ordered the cybers scrapped. They had a decent population.

Manish got up on a table someone had placed there and addressed the crowd.

"Namaste, I am the Goptri of the Mists," he'd decided he liked that title, "and this turn, I offer you a deal. There is an underground city here. It has enough room for all of you, all of my soldiers, and then double that, and more. Here's my offer, swear loyalty to me, and you can live there for free as long as you pitch in on the needed work, and there will be a lot of needed work. I plan to heal Arreti."

"What if we don't swear?" came a voice from the crowd.

"Then you can leave. There has been enough pain here already."

The crowd began talking amongst itself and was soon embroiled in several heated exchanges. Manish said and did nothing.

After a while, a young Devi stepped away from the group. She was wearing a simple, but a revealing, gossamer shift. She had her six arms folded neatly in front of her, and her pale blue skin and bright red lips radiated beauty.

"Your offer is fair. All I ask is that my leader be fair. I will join you."

About eighty percent of the rest soon followed suit. The others began walking on the various paths away from Ville of Veruna.

Pulinda assigned several of his troops to survey and see who was good at what or what interested them. The latter was Manish's idea. New starts all around, he'd said.

It took them a couple of cliks to get them all inside and another couple to get them used to the Pearls, but eventually, everyone was settling in.

The apartments were all the same size, but they did have one interesting feature. The wall separating two units could be removed if parties on both sides hit a switch simultaneously. That allowed families to have larger units and still protected the privacy of the other tenants.

All the brands thanked the Goptri for his wisdom in this regard. After twenty or thirty attempts to explain the truth, he surrendered and just said, "you're welcome."

It worked out best for everyone.

Manish put Pulinda in charge of logistics, and he took to it with a passion. It was clear he'd worked without sleep, but by breaklight, he had a plan for using available resources and local lands with a long-term goal of bringing everything underground so they could be self-sufficient.

Manish read it, impressed, and then signed it into action.

Manish had feared that the first few turns would find citizens without food or essentials, but Pulinda's troops seemed to be everywhere, and taking care of everything. Then he noticed the Pearls, too, were helping out, and seemed to be enjoying themselves.

Pearl Shimmers on the Golden Sands spied Manish, and sqauddled over.

"Blessings Goptri," she gurgled joy, "this is a wonderful thing you're creating. All these brands, living together, working together, and …, and … oh, you were so right, you do have the power of a god to pull this off."

With that, she kissed him on the cheek, and went back to what she was doing.

Manish's wife, Arti, walked over laughing.

"One turn as the Goptri, and already you're cheating on me?"

He laughed, scooped her into his arms, and kissed her deeply.

"There is nothing in this world that could take me from you. In many ways, you are the reason we stand here this turn. When the Technarcy almost killed you, I almost died."

She looked at him in a mix of befuddlement and passion, then smiled.

"Now, and forever shall we be together then," then she giggled, "but after all this, how are you going not to be boring?"

He started to say something but simply surrendered to laughter. Soon the two of them were in each other's arms, laughing, as a world full of hope began to grow around them.

ओम'

Now:

Terrible tragedies bring terrible pain. There is nothing that can be done to assuage that. But terrible tragedies also have a way of strengthening you. Redouble your vigilance. Redouble your caution. If anything, anything at all, seems amiss to you, punch the integers #** into your portie immediately. The Goptri's professionals will know how to deal with the threat much better than you ever could.

ओम'

Queen Lynno Lee-NAH-xhuk looked out the windows of the sunroom in the palace. Her grandfemme was Vorulshka, who'd opened the secrets of the death camps, and made the Ice Pirates rich. Vorulshka had long since gone to safer travels, but Lynno still thought of her often and fondly.

Lynno was the first of her line to be named queen. She was also the first Halfling to hold any rank in the history of the Ice

Pirates. Her prefemme, a bit of a rebel, had had a dalliance with a Guenon, and Lynno was the result. Instead of the coarse whitish brown fur regular Ice Pirates sport, she had light-red fur soft to the touch. Well, soft by Ice Pirate standards anyway. She was also a bit taller than average, and had more defined curves than the Ice Pirates, who tended toward androgyny. Her face was also bluish from the mating—something which made her look exotic and intriguing.

Still, Lynno had earned her place. She'd worked her way up to squadron leader, like her grandfemme, and then caught the attention of the Council of Nine and was offered a seat when the legendary Slazkik Ognor retired.

From there, her smart policy decisions and ability to work well with others got her nominated for the Regency. Now, four Suns later, she was facing a series of decisions that would change forever how the Ice Pirates dealt with Arreti.

Of course, she wasn't facing them alone. She had the wisdom of the five spirits to help guide her. She wasn't sure if Arreti, Wind, Water, Fire, or Life-force would be the best Essence to prays. Then again, she could just go to the top, and pray to the matriarch of all living things, Arreti Materfamilias. Whatever she chose, she was pretty sure a prayer was needed for what appeared to be headed their way.

Unlike the Sugar Pirates, her brand had never been pure raiders. That being noted, they were, and are, aggressive in protecting their lands. She knew the Ice Pirates preferred their privacy, but recent events seemed to indicate that privacy was a luxury they could no longer afford.

The reports from the Goptri's bizarre attack on the Yelda thirty turns ago raised far more questions than it answered. But one thing was sure, if the Goptri ever marched a real army that size, her brand would be doomed.

They needed allies.

The new neighbors to the north had insinuated themselves between her brand; the Dragon Lords seemed allied with the Yelda. That could be a start—two allies at once.

Still, deep down, she knew the Dragon Lords were at just as much at risk as were the Shin-Sen. If the Goptri overran her lands, he could create a pincer to trap the rest.

Of course, he'd have to go through the Yelda to do that, no easy task there, but he had the resources. It was just a matter of him deciding to use them all at once. If he did, the northern lands were in trouble.

Deep trouble.

She knew what she had to do; their survival depended on it. She looked over at Slazkik Ognor, sitting on a couch sipping Shin-Sen rice wine. She opened her mouth, but he held up a hand.

"You are our monarch. I've seen the same reports as you. In this turn, the old ways die. Whether or not we die with them is up to you, and only you. I retired so your mind could be on the council. It was the right choice then, and I'd do it again now.

"I'm a warrior. I have led us into battles again and again., and, more often than not, I've brought our warriors home safely. But this is not a war or a battle. At least not like the ones I faced. I faced the wrath of a village here or there. You are staring down at a continent—a vast continent at that."

"I do not envy you, but I will always support you."

He stood, made a curt bow, and left the room.

She crossed the room to a drawing table, sat down, and unrolled a soft screen. It took her two cliks and two glasses of ice wine to get the message right.

The decision of who to send it to was easy. She'd met Chief Navi a few Suns back after a minor border dispute and had been impressed. He had a fine mind and a fair soul. She'd send it to him first and then see what tumbled down the mountain from there.

ओम'

The Yelda troops had decided to maintain the border camp after the attack, just in case the Goptri tried something anew. They'd met an ambassador of the Goptri's about ten turns ago and were no smarter now than they were then. Nothing made sense, least of all the over-generous offers for appeasement.

But if Navi was confused before, he was rendered speechless when an aide handed him the message from Lynno Lee-NAH-xhuk, Queen of the Ice Pirates. He passed it, without comment, to Vadim and poured them each a tumbler of wodka.

Vadim held the tumbler without moving. Finally, he could speak.

"She wants us to go to her palace for a conference on what to do about the Goptri?"

"Not just us," countered Navi, "she wants us to coordinate the arrival of the Dragon Lords, Shin-Sen, and our allies as well."

"Can we do that?"

"We can ask," shrugged Navi, "we know ambassadors, at least, all the way around."

He decided the simplest thing to do was return her message and agree to meet in the fifteen turns requested. Then he had his staff forward her message, verbatim, to the other three involved parties.

The responses were swift. All agreed. All were concerned, and all were afraid to talk in the open.

Since her letter had coordinates at the bottom, they knew where they were going. They just had no idea what they'd find there. Those who crossed into the Ice Pirates' realm also crossed into the realm of the hereafter swiftly.

ओम'

Ignop Yakuzawa had been Shogun of the Shonen tribe of the Shin-Sen for sixty Suns. He had led them nobly, and well. His warriors fought with honor and pride. But now, all that appeared to be over.

He scratched the white tuft under his chin, and clicked his hooves, a habit he had when he was annoyed, and watched as a small group of his revered Serow ancestors ran next to the stream that bordered his lands. Normally the sight would make him smile and remark on how the circle of life was self-evident here. But this turn, he merely stood still.

His barrel chest, gray/black fur, and deep-set eyes gave him a look of sturdy serenity even when he was troubled, as he was now.

Too much was changing, and the Shin-Sen did not handle change well. He knew the other twelve tribes were having similar concerns. He had been asked to be the Shin-Sen representative with the Ice Pirates.

If it was a trap, he would die worthily, and all the other Shoguns would help his heir become a worthy replacement. If it were an honest effort, he would return with new allies. Either way was fine with him.

Life would continue.

But what kind of life would it be?

He'd seen the reports of the battle between the Yelda and the Goptri. There was no honor there.

But there was power. Lots of it. The Goptri could field an army as large as the population of the Shin-Sen if he wished. Worse still, he could back it with airpower and naval support.

The Shin-Sen were ill-prepared to fight like that.

The Shin-Sen fought individual battles to decide contested issues. One clan's best warrior against another's. Not since the war against the makers had they fought like an army. It was that war that had led them to decide never to do so again.

Much of that had to do with their beliefs. The Shin-Sen believed they were put on Arreti to lead moral lives, be mindful and aware of their thoughts and actions, and develop wisdom and understanding.

There was nothing in there about killing for killing's sake.

There were things, however, about tolerance and understanding. He looked at the message again; he imagined that the gods would put him sorely to the test in those regards.

Ignop didn't even notice as an aide brought in a meal. He remained unaware of it until he realized he was eating it.

That was not good. He's a Shogun and should not be so easily distracted. Yet what else could he do?

He put down the food and made arrangements for two aides to accompany him. He had noted the Yelda were only sending three, and he imagined the Dragon Lords would do the same. There would be comfort in numbers and still little risk to the brands. Even if they were all killed, there were other leaders to fill the vacuum.

But this didn't feel like a trap. The Ice Pirates were notoriously insular. For Queen Lynno to have made this offer, she must be tremendously worried. Well, no shame there. He was worried too.

He thought some more of Navi. The burly Yelda had married a mal and was still allowed to lead. While relationships such as that were known among the Shin-Sen, they were considered ignoble.

But Navi's troops followed him and had even elected him to lead the whole operation. Maybe that was something else that needed to change.

Of course, then there's the Dragon Lords. They married into families. He'd heard of groups as large as ten individuals calling themselves mates.

Maybe not that much change.

Then he looked at the map across the room, and realized that equines, the preferred form of travel, might not get them there in time. He sighed and ordered the mechanized vehicle to be prepped and for a travel estimate to be generated.

The dual-rotor craft was swift; it could easily traverse the mountains and the sea. Still, it was not his favorite way to travel.

He would miss the equines. As far as he knew, the only ones who'd survived Rohta's meddling were on this island. The rest had been turned into deisteeds and the like. That was as it should be. The Shin-Sen were pure. Both of heart and mind. To them, the equines were an extension of their souls.

He grunted.

More change.

He went back, finished his meal, and then stepped outside to watch the sunset.

There was something niggling his memory about the setting sun, but he couldn't place it. He figured it couldn't be that important and just enjoyed the view. At least there were still some constants in life.

ॐ'

Xho had just been named Ambassador of the Non. It was a gloriously meaningless title. All he had to do was deal with any formal requests that came in from non-Dragon Lords. Mostly he would deal with the Din-La, pamper his large leathery wings, and hang out with his nest buddies at the local brothel. It was a plum appointment and much sought after by young Dragon Lords. Xho had earned it the usual way, his grades were exemplary, and his second father had paid the bribe.

It was to be a gift. Serving the three Sun term, and meeting the powerful of the powerful, would set him up for life.

Then came the crazy request from that Queen Lynno Lee-NAH-xhuk and the quick acceptance from the Yelda and the Shin-Sen.

As far as Xho could tell, the problem with plum appointments was there was always some hidden danger attached to them. Or, as his third father had sagely pointed out, "Just because it hasn't happened in a long time doesn't mean it can't happen now."

So Xho was prepping for his trip to and meeting with the Ice Pirates' Queen. The Dragon Lords kept meticulous records, so, soon enough, Xho was up to speed on customs, preferences, and nuances of each of the brands he would be meeting. Except for the new allies of the Yelda. No one knew anything about them.

He found, much to his surprise, he was liking this. The responsibilities, and the work, were refreshing. He had lived a life of privilege.

Not that he had any problems with his life, it was the product of hundreds of Suns of traditions. But it did feel good to be needed.

Xho decided to travel with his lead assassin, Chen, and etiquette advisor, Wong. Chen's smooth, dark, green skin suited her profession well, allowing her to blend with shadows. She had served his four fathers for thirty Suns now. Xho had had a terrible crush on her when he was coming of age. She had been considerate and helped him through it without injuring his feelings. In a way, he loved her all the more for it and came through the experience a better brand.

Wong was only a little older than Xho, but his second father trusted him with everything. His rainbow-colored skin and wings were a rarity. The coloration only happened once every three or four generations, which is why all the families prized him; Xho's house was honored that he chose to stay here. Wong handled family events, political round tables, weddings, everything the family needed, and never once had Wong let the family down. He also had impeccable fashion sense, so Xho hoped to rely on him to send the meetings' correct messages. He wanted to be seen as humble and sincere but not so humble and sincere the others thought him a servant to be abused. Wong assured him it was possible.

The three Dragon Lords conferred for ten turns, and then decided to fly directly to the meeting. They had to cross all their lands and a large part of the Ice Pirate's domain, and they didn't want to be late.

The Dragon Lords were great flyers and could stay airborne for a turn at a time carrying near their body weight, if need be, but they weren't swift.

Come breaklight of the eleventh turn since the message had arrived. The three Dragon Lords strapped on the aerodynamically curved backpacks that held their supplies and took off to the sounds of the entire Wen Ho Palace, wishing them well.

While Xho was of the Wen Ho, he was painfully aware he now represented all Dragon Lords in this endeavor. The twenty-three kingdoms were all counting on him.

As they settled in an air current about a quarter kay above the ground, Xho began to contemplate what he was really about to do. It was all theory and hustle in the palace, but now, gliding through the sky, alone with his thoughts, he began to worry.

"Tell me, Chen," he said above the wind, "what will happen if I mess this up?"

"We will all be killed," she laughed. Then, seeing he was serious, she continued. "First, you will not mess this up. You are bright, you have had the best training, and you have, if I may be so humble, capable assistants. Moreover, the brands we are going to meet are sending their best. That means you will have access to some of the best minds on Arreti.

"The goal of this meeting is not to outsmart the other brands but to see if we can work together for our mutual survival. "

"Also," interrupted Wong, "we know the tenor of these talks."

"How so," queried Xho.

"Think, youngling," he laughed, "The Queen of the Ice Pirates opened these talks by letting us know where their palace is. No one has ever seen it. Or, if they have, they have not lived to tell the tale.

"So we know that we will be asked to give up something too. What that will be will become apparent later., and it won't just be us. She will be asking the Shin-Sen, and Yelda, to sacrifice something as well."

"What about that new tribe that's between the Ice Pirates and us?" Xho sounded concerned.

"We know nothing, really," returned Chen, "other than they acted honorably with the Yelda. We should start with that knowledge and see where the meetings lead."

Xho sighed and flapped his giant, dark blue flecked wings. They were beautiful to see as they glinted in the early light, but he didn't know that. He was too lost in thought to care.

ओम'

Then:

Natasha had guided the ship through a quick orbit before setting it on the path to the Pravda. She opened a hailing frequency, and less than five cliks later was rewarded with a response. The Pravda was close to where it was supposed to be, and it was functioning. Had that not been the case, she could have returned to Arreti, but she preferred this.

The cybers were altering their shapes and coloring using the nanites. Abhijit Juhnjuhnwalla, a former colonel in the Technarcy, had turned his body jet black, and his eyes pure white. The effect was stark, yet it seemed to suit him.

Pran Unhaala, the social engineering and city planning specialist, had settled on a dark green body with a red and yellow thigh stripe and bright green eyes. They all admitted it made him look dashing.

Noor Idnari, the agriculturalist, had settled on a light brown body with a tan stripe. Her eyes glowed a soft yellow. She also molded her torso and hips to be more curvaceous.

Zeenat, the mathematician, had chosen a salmon body with an electric blue stripe to match her new eyes. Her body modifications left no doubt about her femininity.

Natasha and Boris both retained their white bodies, but she, like Zeenat, emphasized her feminine wiles, just in a more zaftig fashion.

The Omnium retained its bright red skin and white star; Elmar finished accentuating the gleaming silver body by adding flecking to his purple stripes.

They took a ship tour as they'd a turn to spend before they reached the Pravda.

There wasn't much there. Other than the provisions brought aboard, there was nothing to indicate the ship was planned for anything other than functional purposes.

They gathered back in the bridge area and got to know each other. They could have simply shared their essences electronically, but, just as with their new bodies, they wanted to retain their individuality.

They had eternity to get to know each other more fully; there was no rush.

Abhijit wasn't much for small talk, so Boris got him the Pravda specs to study. They were all surprised to learn there were weapons on the ship. There was nothing in any of the records of the Sominids that detailed a war-like race. Who were the makers worried they might meet?

Elmar suggested it might just be traditional maker paranoia.

They all accepted that.

They also all agreed that weapons on a space ship was just plain silly. They knew all the fiction stories, but they also all knew the science. Just the action/reaction issue was enough to give them pause. Forget about finding a target.

The next turn, they were able to hone in on the Pravda's beacon, and, with some careful maneuvering, Natasha brought the Bullet directly underneath her. The Pravda's docking clamps automatically gathered in the smaller ship.

If Natasha could have frowned, she would have done so then.

"This ship is too big," she said quietly, "things are not as they should be."

The others had no idea what to make of that statement, so they just remained silent.

Shortly thereafter, airlocks were meshed, pressure was equalized, and the doors between the ships slid open.

They were near the rear of the Pravda. The floors were magnetized and kept them from floating away. They crossed over and were stunned by what they saw. Unlike the specs they'd perused, there was row after row of living compartments.

Boris had brought small radios. He went back to the Bullet, retrieved them, and split up to see what else was different from expected.

Zeenat entered the engine room at the rear of the ship, and blanched. There were a lot of dead makers.

"Boris, come in, please," even that sounded sultry when she said it.

"I am here, Zeenat. What is the problem?"

"I count twenty-four dead makers littering the floor of the engine room."

"I am on my way."

He rushed through the doorway less than an epi-clik later, began flipping the bodies around, and checking them for identification.

"This makes no sense," he muttered.

"What's that," queried Zeenat.

"These are all Americans. There were no Americans scheduled to be on the Pravda."

"Were you at war with them?"

"No, not in a long time, but this first foray, before Natasha took to the stars, was to be a Russian exploration. Purely scientific according to all the records. These are all American Marines. Not that they wouldn't have been smart, but they certainly wouldn't have been scientists."

They searched all the bodies and found nothing to contradict Boris' initial assessment.

After conferring with the others, they decided to maintain a visual record for later study and space the bodies. It didn't seem to matter what had killed them, and none of them were coroners.

Once that grisly task was complete, they continued their

search. It wasn't long before Boris' radio chirped again.

"Boris, this is Noor. I have more bodies. I'm on deck two, directly center."

As they headed towards one of the many staircases that provided access throughout the ship, they were greeted by the remaining cybers.

Boris was about to chide them for being afraid of dead makers but decided against it. Something weird had happened here, and having some good minds on high alert, helping him figure out what wouldn't hurt.

They quickly found the room where Noor was, and Boris almost laughed as he stared at the milieu. There were seventeen dead Russian soldiers. Like the dead Americans, there appeared to be no signs of violence.

Elmar looked at the bodies closely.

"They suffocated to death," he said without preamble.

"How can you tell," asked Natasha.

"See how some of them are clutching their chests? It wasn't a group heart attack," he paused to look at another body, "and I bet you found the same in the engine room."

Boris, and Zeenat nodded assent.

"My guess," he continued, "is that they purposely let the air out when they realized they were trapped up here with no supplies, and no one left to send them any."

He paused for a long time.

"This was a horrible way to die," he almost sighed, "I bet we'll find more bodies as the turn wears on. We need to find a record of what they were all doing here in the first place. This ship may house hidden dangers."

Natasha started to object, and then grunted instead.

"Da, you're right. Everything is different than what it's supposed to be. We must be careful. Let's split into two groups. Zeenat, Abhijit, and Elmar are with me. We'll scour this level. The rest of you go with Boris and scour the top level. When either of us completes a level, we let the other know and then go to the next. There are six total levels, and this ship is a kilometer long.

"This is going to take a while."

It took them four full turns before they were comfortable; everything had been opened, prodded, or spaced, in the case of the bodies. By the time they were done, they'd spaced over two hundred and sixty bodies representing four different countries.

One other thing became abundantly clear. This was no simple science vessel; it was a platform of death. It was unmistakably designed to attain low orbit and then unleash photon beams, which could inflict the equivalent of megatons worth of devastation.

Whether the targets were meant to be the brands on Earth or citizens of some other world would never be known. Prior to killing themselves, the makers had wiped every data storage device clean. All they'd left was the ship's rudimentary programming.

When all was said, and done, they congregated on the bridge. It was twice the size it was supposed to be, and they were all worried that the numerous design changes would make Natasha unable to pilot it.

She queried the onboard computer for over three cliks while the rest of the cybers toured the ship but finally pronounced it safe to fly.

"It is essentially the same programs plus the automatic firing patterns built into the weapons," she explained to Boris, who had stayed with her, "as for the size of this behemoth, it doesn't matter. Mass is not weight, and we have more than enough thrust to move our mass."

Boris noticed a set of darkened screens with the phrase DATABASE UPLOAD, written in four languages, softly gleaming on them. He pointed them out to Natasha, and she shrugged. They weren't in any hurry, so she angled the ship towards Arreti and let it slip into high orbit.

Not ten sepi-cliks after they'd done so, the screens sprang to life.

DATABASE FOUND UPLOAD COMMENCING

In short order, twenty screens all bore the same message.

The screeching and chirping sounds emanating from the surrounding speakers drew the attention of all the cybers who returned to see what was going on.

For the next ten turns, the ship accessed and copied databases from all over the world. Rohta's massive genetic and historical library became the ship's. The three hundred thousand plus video entertainments, created by the makers, in Lord Südermann's possession, were dutifully copied and sorted. Extensive plans to destroy the ship they were in were added as well. The final database contained a collection of every religious book ever written and several scholarly treatises on each.

The ship's computer sorted each upload by category and then alphabetized them. Chronologically sorting was also a feature should the viewer wish that instead.

They spent another couple of turns skimming the various tables of contents and getting a feel for what the ship had done.

Abhijit finally spoke.

"This ship was not only built to be a warship but also a spy ship. My guess is that we will find many more useful functions as we get to know it better.”

“There are other bonuses here too,” added Natasha, “this ship has far more advanced sensors than the original Pravda was ever designed to carry. With our copies of the Sominids’s records, and this ship, we can go anywhere and know exactly what we’re getting into.”

“Da,” said Boris, “then the rest is clear. We have the most powerful ship ever built, a library to rival any in history, a list of worlds with new civilizations, and nothing much better to do.

“We should be going, no?”

Natasha laughed, as did they all,

“We should be going, yes.”

She entered instructions into a touch screen, and the mighty engines sprang to life.

The last eight surviving cybers of Arreti were off to greet the universe.

ओम’

Vorulshka had been awarded sole rights to her discovery conditioned on the precept that she could bring something of value out. Her mate Krashka was a fine blacksmith and was working with her on the design of the suit. The parameters were simple, hide body temperature, and prevent bio signs from being read.

The parameters for flight were simple too. Grow wings and jump off a cliff. That didn’t make it easy.

Still, they were making progress.

Krashka had come up with a bodysuit that would emanate less than 3°C if worn over a simple winter thermal. She could be semi-comfortable for around a click. Then she would have to take it off.

Now he was working on the armor that would house it all. He put the cooling unit outside the armor and attached it between the shoulders. Then he drilled a small hole for the unit to affix to the cooling fabric.

Ten turns after Vorulshka made her claims, they were headed back to the death camp.

Whatever fears she harbored, she hid them well. She, and her mate rode to the bunker, where she'd first seen the brands wearing suits, and dismounted their grizzes. Krashka pulled the armor off the back of his griz and helped her suit up.

Ten epi-cliks later, she strode to the first door, pushed on it, and watched in amazement as it opened. She saw the bodies neatly laid out and quickly surmised what happened. She didn't dwell on it. This trip was to prove she was right, not to answer all the mysteries about this place.

She entered the bunker and found switches to turn on some lights.

She wasn't trying to get rich today. That would come from when she licensed the rights to the suit. But when she saw a hover sled sitting in an aisle, she couldn't help but try it. A quick inspection of the controls, and she had a pretty clear idea of how it worked.

She stepped onto it, touched a toggle, and was rewarded by lifting slightly off the ground. She pushed the lever forward and was soon jetting through the bunker. She realized this would do for proof and headed back to the front door.

When she got outside, she closed it and smiled.

Krashka couldn't see her smile through the armor, but he must have sensed it as he grinned too.

They wordlessly removed her armor and turned off the cooling unit. There was maker tech here, and it still worked. This was a prize unimaginable, and Vorulshka owned all the rights to it.

She whistled her griz to her side and mounted the sled again. She saw a meter which appeared to show that the machine was charging. So, it was solar powered. She knew what that was. It only made this find more valuable.

She started to head back to her village, but Krashka said no.

"This prize we take to the palace. Let all the tribes bid on the rights."

She thought about it for a moment and agreed.

"Then I must claim the other two camps we have found. This solution will work there, too, I imagine."

Krashka shrugged.

"Two, maybe three, turns we could visit them all, and have proof. Then we go to the palace and make your claim."

That plan would work, so that's what they did. Krashka was a little off on the timing as it took them six turns, but neither complained. When they got to the palace, they'd have ample evidence to support all their claims.

Vorulshka steered the hover sled towards the palace as several guards moved to allow her placement by the Queen's gate. Of course, they would kill her if she tried to go past that point.

She stopped well short of the gate and made her claims on the three death camps and on the method to defeat them.

She was waiting for the Royal Licensing Representative to appear when, to her shock, Queen Ominique ver-ANH-vonda herself came through the palace gate. Only queens used their surnames in public.

"Your majesty," stammered Vorulshka as she attempted a curtsey. A nigh on impossible task while mounted on a hover sled.

The queen laughed.

"I will grant your licenses and reaffirm your claims. I lost a brother and three cousins to those camps," she had a richly melodious voice, "and your discovery and efforts mean that we shall all profit, and no one need die again in the endeavor.

"I say that's exactly the kind of thing a queen should support."

Her smile could have powered the kingdom on its own.

Soon enough, papers were signed, seals placed, and Vorulshka and Krashka were on their way home.

It was then, and only then, that she risked sharing the biggest prize of all.

"I'm pregnant."

ओम'

Now:

It has become apparent to us that some of the northern brands have been spying on us. Recent events would seem to affirm that. As part of a systematic process to weed these interlopers out, the Goptri's professionals will now start issuing national identity cards to all who can confirm their citizenship. Not to worry, proof will be easy for any who belong here. You will need the cards to participate in any public meetings, vote, or be entitled to any of the many social programs offered by the Goptri. Once you get your identity card, you and your younglings will be eligible to serve in the Goptri's military. Such service is not required, of course, but we encourage you to consider it. The safety of all begins with the duty of one.

ओम'

Navi, Vadim, and Colonel Krark slowed as they neared the

designated coordinates. In front of them was a palace carved out of a mountain. Whatever they were expecting, this wasn't it. Krark stepped out of the transport, shook her hair loose, and simply admired the beauty of it all.

"We should not be enemies with creatures who can create such as this," she whispered, although Navi and Vadim both heard her as they'd just stepped out as well.

They stood in silent wonder as the Shin-Sen, and Dragon Lord delegations arrived. They joined the others in their awestruck stances.

Shortly after that, the new neighbors showed up. Wearing gray overalls, they were vaguely simian looking, but hairless and heavily muscled. They considered the edifice carefully but showed no emotions at all.

There was an honor guard of Ice Pirates; at least they appeared to be an honor guard, that stood stock still as the others finally took it all in.

Navi finally stepped forward.

"We are the invited guests of Queen Lynno Lee-NAH-xhuk. If it pleases her court, we would like to be presented to her."

"Really, Navi? You feel the need to be that formal?" Queen Lynno Lee-NAH-xhuk stepped through the gate.

She was wearing chunky heeled boots that laced up her to her thighs, an undemanding patterned dress that came about halfway down her calves, and a simple rust-colored vest that highlighted her fur.

"You are my guests," she continued, "and you are here because you each have the same problem we do., and it is a problem none of us cannot defeat alone.

"You new neighbors, you are welcome for nothing else than honoring your agreements with the Yelda. Yet, I would like to know your brand."

The one in the middle glanced at his two companions, and then spoke.

"We are Mayanoren. We were born and bred to serve the Lords Xhaknar and Yontar. However, they are both well and truly dead. In an attempt to ensure our survival, we decided to integrate into society, at least at some minimal level.

"Had we attempted this on the plains, where we knew the lands, we would have been hunted down and killed. There is too much history there for us to overcome. Some of our brethren made their homes in Kalindor under the guidance of Lord Dagmar and with the blessings of the Exalted Sland. But the rest of us were left with no habitat.

"We saw there were many cubic kays of empty lands between the Dragon Lords and you and decided to make them our home. Our agreements with the Yelda are a byproduct of our needs. Our appearance here this turn is a result of our desire to continue to live."

Only Navi realized that this was the most anyone had ever heard a Mayanoren speak.

"What was, was," said Navi after a pause, "we all have histories. You are here now, and deal with us honorably. We will start with that and move forward."

Before anyone could comment, a fixed-wing aircraft came over the top of the mountain. The engine was loud, and the echoes scattered across the valley. They all watched as it was obviously heading directly toward them. The craft finally set down, and a wildly disheveled Din-La staggered out with a large, messy, briefcase under his arm.

"It is fortunate for you I am here," he began boldly as two other equally unkempt Din-La tumbled out behind him, "we should have been invited. Really, you must remember that.

Fortunately, one of our buyers returned from the Dragon Lord's Twentieth Kingdom and noticed all the travelers converging in this direction.

"I am Gffk, Regional Head of the Bharati Din-La. You are here because of the Goptri. There can be no other reason for this meeting. "

No one said anything, so he continued.

"I must tell you the tale of Lrrt., and then I will give you his research. But first, the tale."

He tried to make himself presentable, but Queen Lynno raised her hand.

"It is clear that you traveled long and hard to bring us news. Let us retire inside to the salons my aides have assigned each of you. There is plenty of space for a few extra Din-La. We will reconvene in the main dining hall in one clik. There are refreshments and a private bath in each room.

"When we meet again, we will listen to Gffk's tale and see what it means to us."

The honor guard quickly disbursed to lead each contingent to their rooms.

Once inside, the ambassadors were stunned by the restrained opulence. The palace was decorated in shades of white with touches of silver and gray, with an occasional light blue here and there. There were light sconces recessed at even intervals down the hall. Each seemed to depict some specific event. The guests couldn't tell if they were religious or historic. No one seemed sure if it mattered, so they left it for later discussion.

The salons were all decorated in shades of grey and black with white walls. The overall effect of the palace was cool restraint and refined elegance.

A clik later, the guards led them to the main dining hall.

There was a bountiful buffet laid out attended by four servants. The guests and queen's staff all gathered around the long table, engaging in small talk while they waited for the Din-La. It was a casual way for them to size each other up. Except for Navi and Queen Lynno, and that only briefly, none of them had met.

A lot was riding on this meeting.

A few epi-cliks later, the Din-La walked in, and the transformation was impressive. Gone was the haggard look they'd sported on arrival. It was replaced with perfectly coiffed hair and immaculately pressed clothes. The briefcase, which had looked overstuffed, and shabby now glistened in fresh oils and showed neatly arranged folders within.

Gffk unrolled a holo-projector onto the table that appeared to have been arranged for a meal. His assistants moved plates and silverware out of the way, much to the amusement of the assembled.

Suddenly a giant image of the head and shoulders of a Din-La hovered above the table.

"This is Lrrt," began Gffk, "and this image was taken during the last Dark Sun."

A new image popped up. It was the Din-La named Lrrt with four smalls and a femme. All were smiling.

"This is Lrrt, his wife Nkkl, and their four smalls. They aren't old enough for their naming ceremonies yet."

"Excuse me," said Ignop, "but those smalls all look to be about the same age. Are they adopted?"

"No," replied Gffk, "they are a rare example of quadruplets."

No one knew how any of this related to the problem at hand, but since Gffk had gone to so much trouble just to get here, they held their comments.

A new and horrid image replaced the happy family. It was what was left of Lrrt's head. The back right was misshapen and caved in. His right eye was missing, and his right ear seemed to be a mere thread wrapped around the ear canal. Tubes were running up his nose, and his left eye was so cloudy that the pupil was barely visible.

A collective gasp echoed throughout the dining hall.

Lrrt looked hideous.

Gffk poured himself a glass of water, took a sip, and continued.

"Just under sixty turns ago, Lrrt went missing. We searched high and low for him to no avail. Then, around five turns ago, Nkkl received a call from a medico who works for the Goptri. Lrrt had been in a terrible accident, he said. There was nothing more they could do for him, he said. They'd only now identified him because Din-La are not part of the DNA registry."

He took another sip, sighed, and went on.

"They transported Lrrt home with respiratory, and feeding, gear to keep him alive, courtesy of the Goptri, they said. Our medicos rushed in to see if there was anything they could do, and made a dreadful discovery.

"Far from being sixty turns old, the injuries were less than ten."

"Less than ten," exclaimed Xho, "what was going on the rest of that time?"

"He was a prisoner," postulated Queen Lynno as everyone turned to pay her attention, "and then this was done to him to send a clear message to anyone looking into the Goptri's works. Look into my world at your own peril.

"I am guessing about that motive, but it feels right."

Gffk nodded. The rest silently shivered.

"Lrrt had discovered that the Goptri was funneling large weapons purchases through various buyers all over Bharat."

"How much weaponry are we talking about?" asked Ignop.

"Enough to lay waste to all the islands of the Shin-Sen, and still have enough left over to start a decent-sized war."

That gave them all pause.

"Also, just before he disappeared, Lrrt sent us some findings. He was unsure of their value. One of them was a location where he suspected that the excess weapons were being stored.

"Thanks to the courtesies of Lord Südermann, we were able to retrieve this satellite image of the location."

A new image replaced Lrrt's mangled visage. It was an underwater city, and it was massive.

They all closed around the image.

"We Din-La do not like to spy on our neighbors. We expect and respect privacy. But these are extraordinary times. Lord Südermann is of a similar mind. We have the technology for the camera, and he has the ability to get the same in space. We launched it in one of his space planes, and it settled into orbit above the coordinates. Less than ten epi-cliks later, they'd found this."

Queen Lynno stared at the image.

"Assuming storage, and so on, there could still be half a million brands there."

Gffk nodded.

"Yes, watch this."

The image switched to infrared. They could all easily see underground warrens that stretched for kays around the city. Heat signatures showed plants and animals, as well as brands.

"After sorting through the various images, our technicians believe there are four levels starting at two kays below the surface. As Queen Lynno noted, they could easily house half a million brands. We can make out several shopping centers, and they have enough agriculture to support a population of that size."

Navi looked thoughtful.

"Plus, they have the much larger population we know of, the one above the surface. The one below could be dedicated to serving the Goptri, while the one above is just regular citizens. Although there would be nothing to stop the latter from joining the former in any military action."

Given the fact that Bharat is the most populated continent on the planet, thanks to the Goptri's centuries of encouragement, that was a sobering thought. The original Goptri had loved families and offered financial assistance to any family who had more than one small. Sun by Sun, about thirty percent of Bharati citizens took the government up on that offer.

And that added up over the centuries.

The not-so-subtle irony was that Lrrt was ineligible for that assistance since he was not a Bharat citizen.

"Plus," continued Navi, "we have heard rumors, but have no proof, that the Goptri has been encouraging his citizens to arm themselves as well as breed."

Gffk nodded. "Lrrt provided evidence of that as well, I have been out of Bharat for over five Suns dealing with trade, so I have no personal proof. For now, we must assume it is so. To do otherwise is to invite death."

The lead Mayanoren stepped back.

"This has been going on for five Suns. Unless and until I hear a better excuse, I must assume that the Goptri's lost his mind. If I am right then, like all mad and dangerous animals, he must be put down."

Queen Lynno handed him a glass of Ice Cider, her favorite drink, often compared to glurp for its efficacy, and smiled.

"My thoughts exactly, which is why you are all here."

ओम'

Vandamir Singh was the Sikh of the Guru for his lands, all the holdings of the Nanek-Dev brand, and their citizen allies. Those lands had been free of violence all his long life. They'd been free of violence for all of his father's life as well. Thus far, that totaled two hundred and fifty-six Suns since he had been born in his patriarch's fiftieth orbit.

Based on the reports, he was now reading that constancy was in peril.

He shuffled across his sparse office and lowered himself into a chair. He knew, from humorous remarks his assistants had made, that his bones did creak. Well, humor was a gift too.

His large, simian, frame with its once-proud silverback was now mottled shades of gray. Once vaunted, his height was now stooped. If he were to admit it, more than just a little. His long hair, tied and set beneath his turban, was gray. His beard was similarly colored.

When he was a mere twenty suns old, his patriarch had taken him to the Lightless Lands on a trade mission. Not to participate, of course, just to get a feel of how the world worked. When they were there, he'd gotten a chance to go on a tourist safari. He'd seen his genetic cousins and was shocked to see that they did not have long hair and beards like his brand. He wondered what prompted Rohta to make these specific alterations and then decided he didn't care.

They'd been done to please a maker, and there were no more makers.

He knew that Har, creator of the universe, infused all things, including his soul. When he passed from this realm to the next, he would begin a new adventure. Still, he had no wish to hurry the transition.

After a few epi-cliks, he tapped the monitor on his desk and summoned his assistant.

Mondara had been with him for over forty Suns. She had served two, six Sun, tours in the air guard, he could never remember as what, and then had come to him. Still in her prime, it was rumored she'd finally found a mal worthy of her time. Nothing could make him happier, and he hoped to live long enough to attend the wedding.

She came in, set a fresh cup of tea in front of him, and then sat in the chair across.

"What can do for you, oh Light of Nanak?" she asked, smiling.

He knew there was nothing but respect in her playful banter and ignored it.

"Things have been brought to my attention by our agents in the lands of our neighbors. It has come time for me to travel," he said quietly, "the workings of the world are going to grind us to dust if we do not take some action. So I will need a plane to take me to the palace of the Ice Pirates."

She would have been slightly less shocked if he'd said he wanted to go dancing. Nevertheless, she collected herself quickly.

"Would not such a task be better suited for someone younger?"

"This may all be a trap. I will not waste the lives of our future on what may be the folly of the old," he said as he sipped his tea, "and if it is not a trap, then I, and only I, have all the information that will need to be imparted.

"We have just passed mid-break. I would like to be there by even-fall if that is possible."

"How far is it?"

"A little over twenty-seven hundred kays. I have the coordinates in this file," he said as he tapped the file sitting next to him.

"If we take a Sastravidya, we can make it. But I cannot guarantee your survival."

He considered that. The supersonic speeds could be stressful at his age.

"It is a risk that must be taken."

She knew when an argument was ended, moved to the comm unit, and began issuing orders.

The three-seat Sastravidya was designed for battle. While no pilots she knew of were as good as the Pearls, this plane evened out the competition. Up until five suns ago, they'd trained with the Goptri's air force. That had ceased, and new, more troubling, practices seemed to be coming to the fore.

He noted, without comment, that she ordered an assistant to care for him but no pilot. He hadn't asked her to come, but it was clear from her demeanor the thought of staying behind was anathema to her. He was glad to have her for many reasons, not just because she was an excellent pilot.

His assistant, Kllp, was a Din-La who'd become enamored with the beliefs of Vandamir's brand and had left his calling, as well as his purple and yellow uniform, behind. He was dressed in a simple black shift covering his hips, dark red trousers, and black boots. The Din-La could not grow long hair, but Kllp kept his head turbaned anyway.

Kllp was pushing the hoverchair, which he stationed next to Vandamir, and helped him in. Vandamir had long ago abandoned any shame at being pushed around like an invalid. After all, at two hundred and six Suns of age, he was one.

Vandamir tucked a file folder into his vest and prepared for the ride.

They headed down the hallways and out into the courtyard. Kllp expertly steered the chair up a short ramp and into the vehicle to take them to the runway.

Ten epi-cliks later, they were in front of a gleaming Sastravidya with the bottom of the cockpit open. Unlike other planes, the bottom of the cockpit lowered to the runway. Two workers helped Kllp get Vandamir fitted with a helmet, and an oxygen mask hung on his chest. Then they carefully and efficiently loaded him into the rear seat on the left. Traditionally the gunner's seat if Vandamir remembered correctly.

Kllp adjusted the gear he'd been given and took the remaining rear seat.

Mondara had put on a full flight suit when no one was looking. Vandamir was convinced she could have done that in the middle of a crowded room, and no one would have noticed. She was quite stealthy when she needed to be.

She settled into the pilot's chair and flipped the switch to retract the cockpit. The nuclear-powered turbines began spinning up, and the plane was taxiing down the runway shortly. Mondara appeared to be doing her pre-flight checks as the aircraft was moving.

It appeared this way because it's precisely what she was doing.

Time was of the essence if she was going to make the Sikh's

deadline.

After the shock of the initial thrust wore off, he realized he was quite comfortable. He was also a bit peckish. He mentioned to Kllp that they would need to arrange for food when they landed and was rewarded with a smile. The Din-La pulled a basket from under his seat, and handed his Guru a sandwich, a small flask of chilled water, and a mango.

Vandamir continued to be impressed with Kllp in particular, and the Din-La in general.

The rich cheese sandwich, with spiced Palak, was slightly pungent but also delicious. He ate so he could slowly savor each morsel, finding himself smiling contentedly. Sure he might be racing to the end of the world, but, at least, the view was engaging, and the food was good.

Three and a half cliks after they took off, they were coming in for a landing. While she'd taken off in a traditional fashion, she opted to engage the four small jets on the sides of the fuselage and land the craft vertically.

It was a simple decision to make. The Ice Pirates had no runways.

She brought the plane down in front of the palace and emitted a low whistle.

The palace was carved into a mountain range. No one could even begin to guess how large it was or how many Ice Pirates lived there.

Mondara slipped the release on the cockpit just as two guards approached.

The travelers were all awed when they noticed that one guard was pushing a hoverchair. Kllp had discussed the possibility of having to carry his Guru when they landed. To Kllp's bewilderment, the Guru had said that might be a splendid idea, and then had gone back to nibbling on his sandwich and looking out the window.

When they finally got Vandamir safely in the hoverchair, he reached inside his vest and handed the folder to the guards.

"I am old and may leave this world at any time," he said unambiguously," please make sure that Queen Lynno Lee-NAH-xhuk gets this."

The guards were duly impressed with his correct pronunciation of their queen's name. Most outsiders mangled it horribly. Still, they weren't palace guards because they were inept. A courier was summoned and handed the folder with instructions to run it to the queen there as fast as she could.

A second courier arrived just as the young femme was rushing off. He bowed to Vandamir and smiled warmly.

"Queen Lynno Lee-NAH-xhuk sends her warmest greetings. Rooms have been prepared for you. The even-fall meal will be ready in one clik. Until then, there is a summary of events thus far, and snacks and beverages in your rooms."

He bowed again and led them into the palace.

ओम'

A little over a clik later, the guests wandered into the main dining hall. An informal but elaborate buffet greeted them. Mondara and Kllp smiled as Vandamir guided his hoverchair directly to the buffet and then stood. The others ignored the feast and sat at a table to resume discussing their options except for Queen Lynno. She sat off to the side, alone, reviewing some papers, presumably business related to her kingdom.

Vandamir picked up a small plate, put one item on it, and nibbled. When that was finished, he went to the next item, put it on his plate, nibbled on it, and then continued, thusly, down the buffet.

The guests did not notice Vandamir shaking his head as they discussed a military option. Nor did they see him nod when they discounted it as suicide. Even if they combined forces, they were no match for what the Goptri could bring to bear. Worse, if rumors of his arming citizens were true, they would be forced to kill thousands of innocents no matter the outcome.

None of them were comfortable with that, and, somehow, that made them all feel a little better about each other.

They did not notice Vandamir nod in agreement with them as he found a new morsel.

Ignop announced that the Shin-Sen had a submersible that could carry a small group of warriors. He propositioned some sort of raid on the facility. They bandied several ideas about it, but they all fell apart when they tried to figure out what to do when they got there. They would be over a kay underwater with no way of knowing how to bypass anything.

It was then that Queen Lynno noticed that Vandamir was slightly smiling. She set down her papers to study the old brand more. He was sampling each item on the buffet and moving slowly down the line. She doubted he could move faster if he wanted to. The conversation about the Goptri was devolving into random wild ideas when he spoke.

"Forgive me, your majesty," he said as he popped a second chunk of a light green cheese into his mouth, "but what is this? Besides delicious, I mean."

She knew when she was being played, but she wanted to see where this went.

"It is a wasabi cheese. We get the wasabi in trade from some Shin-Sen, and then make the cheese here."

Ignop cleared his throat.

"Forgive the contradiction, your majesty," he said tightly, "but we do not have a trade agreement with you.”

Queen Lynno smiled.

“I said ‘some Shin-Sen’ not ‘The Shin-Sen.’”

Ignop started to say something else, smiled, and nodded in her direction. He answered a couple of questions that bothered the clans; he would deal with it all later.

“Well, it is truly wonderful,” continued Vandamir, “to have lived two hundred and six Suns, and then to discover something new. Do you have your own cheesemonger?

“We have four,” replied the queen.

He picked up a little fork and used it to stab a piece of white meat.

“And this?” he quizzed.

“Prancing fowl from the Plains with a pepper glaze.”

She was curious where this was going. The fact that it had a destination was a given to her.

“Hmm,” he smiled as he swallowed, “it too is a delight.”

“Forgive me, Revered One,” piped up Xho, “but we did not come here to discuss food.”

Vandamir sighed.

“More’s the pity. Still, when I arrived, I was too tired to take the tour, so I read the report that Queen Lynno was kind enough to provide. It was a fascinating read. Nevertheless, I noticed that Gentle Navi had already provided a solution, so I figured discussion was not needed, and I could enjoy the fare.”

Everyone turned to Navi, who looked shocked, and, finally, shrugged helplessly.

They all turned back to Vandamir.

He swallowed another piece of prancing fowl and continued.

"Gentle Navi was visited by an ambassador of the Goptri. That ambassador, for lack of any better terms, attempted to purchase the Yelda. It would seem an obvious response that the Yelda would study such an offer, as they have been …."

Actually, they'd been so offended that they'd never even looked at it again.

"…, and then explore their options to make a profit as well as secure their borders."

Queen Lynno laughed.

"Remind me to never play Ti-Zam with you."

Vandamir did his best to look wounded.

"Oh please, your majesty, after all the pleasures these delicacies have given an old brand, do not deny me one more."

She laughed, but no one else did. They were trying to read his meaning.

He swallowed a piece of dark sausage, pronounced it divine, and then continued.

"As I was saying, now that the Yelda have held the internal discussions, I mentioned they would, logically, select a neutral site to meet with their neighbors to discuss more options. Of course, each of those neighbors would be looking out for their citizens, which is as it should be.

"That brings us to the present, and wonderful, yet neutral, hospitality of Queen Lynno. Now, all that needs to be done is for Gentle Navi to send a response. It needs to be generic, but it must request a meeting at 'the Goptri's palace under the sea.' They may agree, merely assuming you're bluffing. But you have the location and can easily lead a small caravan directly to it. At some point, you will end up with an escort to take you through the actual entrances.

"I would suggest using a couple of Queen Lynno's oversized hovercrafts for your transportation."

Now it was the queen's turn to look shocked.

"How, may I ask, did you find out about those?"

"Hmm," the question seemed to catch him off guard, "oh, when we landed. There were no runways, no rail transports, and no roads. Yet you manage to supply many thousands of brands with food and supplies. The only way for you to do that would be with large hovercrafts."

Xho whistled. "I am the Ti-Zam champion of the Dragon Lords, and I would not play you."

Vandamir chuckled.

They all chuckled as well.

"Okay," smiled Navi, "what's the rest of my plan?"

That got a hearty laugh.

"Well, you are all talented and smart brands," he continued, "I would guess that you would walk around the facility, accidentally open doors to see what was on the other side, until you found the Goptri. Then, as the Mayanoren has noted, kill him."

That got a collective gasp. Whether it was the gentle way the statement was delivered or the seeming casualness of it was unclear.

The Mayanoren looked at him.

"I limited my comment to the Goptri's mental state. That has not been confirmed yet."

Vandamir shrugged.

"Nor does it matter. Had the Goptri taken over the lands of the Yelda, he would have been positioned to wipe out the Dragon Lords and the Shin-Sen in a single stroke. The Ice Pirates, and my humble brand, would have followed., and there would have been nothing we could have done to stop it. The resources of the Yelda are staggering, and in the hands of the Goptri, they would be a means to genocide.

"Further, I will point out that I am … was   … friends with Lrrt. I met him when he first came to Bharat. He came to our lands to see if there was any new business to be had. At that time, there was not, but he stayed anyway, and we shared many wonderful games of Ti-Zam. I have not played the honored ambassador of the Dragon Lords, but I would venture to say that he would have found Lrrt to be worthy of his time. The horror inflicted upon Lrrt and his lovely family must never be allowed to happen to any other brand.

"Make no mistake here," his voice grew, "if the Goptri lives, he will lead Bharat into global war. The kind of conflagration not seen since the makers walked above dirt. Just as he did away with Rama Llandhaven, and is attempting to assimilate Dravida as we speak, so it will go for all of Arreti. Why the Goptri wants the world is a meaningless question. It, like his mental status, no longer matters.

"The survival of the world does., and to ensure that you must kill the Goptri.

"Oh, and make sure to try the cheese."

ओम'

Then:

The ship glided past the last remnants of the Ort cloud and entered the galaxy at large. They were the first beings from Arreti, makers included, to ever travel this far. Freed from any navigational considerations, Natasha began adding power to the engines.

Much to her surprise, rather than the gentle acceleration she'd anticipated, the ship jumped forward. Unwarned, the cybers around the vessel were thrown off their feet and flopped around above decks, grasping for handholds as there was no gravity to ground them.

She quickly opened a communication channel to address the crew.

"My apologies," she said while trying not to laugh, "it seems our elephant is a rabbit in disguise. Nevertheless, we are clear of the solar system and approaching ninety-five percent the speed of light. If we maintain our current rate of acceleration, we should achieve that in four turns, as you like to say."

A little while later, Boris walked in carrying a portable media player, which he was using to watch one of the makers' old entertainments. He knew it was called a movie, but, beyond that, he was baffled.

The heroes had weapons; the villains had weapons. The heroes had sex; the villains had sex. The heroes wanted power, and the villains wanted power.

No wonder the brands finally just killed them all. There seemed to be no way to tell the helpful makers from the ones who would be detriments to society.

Slightly frustrated, though he would never admit that he set down the player and walked over to Natasha.

"Everyone is studying the many riches this ship found."

"Da," she replied, "I wanted to begin perusing them myself now that we are free of the solar system."

"I find myself wondering what good it all will do," he sounded kind of petulant.

"Well," she began cautiously, "we are not organics. The only references we have to organic thought are contained in these archives. For us and the Omnium, these records are our only guideposts.

"The others, though they grow more cyber each day… can you, and I still say 'day'? … will always carry their organic memories and customs."

They both laughed. Getting used to the languages of the brands, and the cybers that interpreted them, was unusual but not a problem.

"Anyway," she continued, "according to the records that the Sominids left, life in the galaxy will be organic. We will need to know how, at least on some rudimentary level, to deal with them."

"What about this Chush' sobach'ya?" He asked as he pointed to the media player.

"It is knowledge. Tawdry, yes, but still knowledge."

Natasha decided to take advantage of her freedom finally. She made sure the ship would warn her if anything unexpected turned up, then took Boris' hand, and began a slow tour.

ओम'

Abhijit sat in a chair, his large, black frame looking comfortable with his left leg bent and his right set straight in front of him. He was reviewing the military notes they'd found. If he'd noticed his position was identical to the one he used to maintain as an organic, his mind didn't inform him of it. Instead, it was wandering back to thoughts of his lovely wife, and small. Far from any form of regret, it was more wistfulness. He'd been aware of his organic counterpart, his original, leaving the room on steady feet after the transfer. He'd also quickly realized what a gift he'd been given: a new life with a wealth of knowledge to exploit. That events had worked out as they had neither surprised nor dismayed him.

Still, there was a part of him that missed his family. Though he had an arranged marriage, Bhadra, his wife, was the one real joy in his life. His small, Madhuri, was an absolute pleasure to behold as she grew from a squealing newborn to a gorgeous young femme. Bhadra would probably be entertaining marriage offers from some fine families in a Sun or two. Madhuri had grown fast.

Or maybe not. The Technarcy was gone. The rebel Manish may make many changes. He may even see arranged marriages as bad and abolish them.

That thought led to this one; the Technarcy had been his whole life. He had been recruited while still a youngling. He'd worked his way up the ranks by adhering to rules and being a good teammate. He'd fought the Sugar Pirates on numerous occasions. He'd gone hand to hand against the Yelda.

He had been proud that his insignificant efforts had helped the greater good.

Regardless, in the Suns leading up to the rebellion, still, he had begun questioning the status quo. Patriot or no, he had grown uneasy about the military's actions being directed against the local citizenry. It was one thing to maintain order, quite another to inflict tyranny.

He may not have been alone with those thoughts. Indeed, all responses to the rebel Manish seemed to take longer than expected.

The one bit of good news is that the Omnium, freed from the decaying mind of Leader Elmar, seemed to have a better grasp of reality and was no longer a threat to rule a world. On a similar tangent, Leader Elmar had begun to flourish now that he was an individual and could sense things.

All good things.

His mind drifted back to his glorious bride, Bhadra. He remembered her voice, her touch, her smell. Mostly he remembered her smile. It was a sly thing, full of warmth and humor. It wasn't something she shared with many, making it even more precious to him.

He could still see her standing in the kitchen, adding curry to everything, and humming a random tune. The smells and sounds were just as real now as if he were there.

He let his thoughts continue to wander as the screens updated the information in front of him. Like the others, he could just download the data and chose not to like the others.

One file caught his attention. It was from the same makers who'd devised a way to destroy the ship. They'd like a detailed plan to release a virus that would destroy the brands; they called them "pods," should the need arise. The problem was the virus they intended to use worked too well. It projected to wipe out eighty percent of all the makers.

He was amazed and appalled to discover some of them thought that was an acceptable amount.

The more he learned about them, the happier he was they were gone.

He let that thought fade, and replaced it with the echoes of laughing younglings, and the smells of curried prancing fowl, and found he was content.

ओम'

Zeenat remembered the before times. Before she had been given this glorious chance to be the femme, she'd always known she was, she'd been Prendahar. She had been a frustrated and lonely Devi mal, trapped in a gorgeous body. She couldn't share the way she wanted and needed. As a mal, she'd endured countless Suns of loneliness. With the barest discussion of gender identity-related issues forbidden by the Technarcy – after all, Rohta hadn't made mistakes, he'd made brands – she'd had no real options.

Then, one turn, she'd met Krishar. Without a word being spoken, she just knew she'd met a kindred spirit. He was tall and lithe, for a Ganesh.

It was an off turn, and a bunch of brands were playing cricket in the park. Zeenat had never been intrigued by sports, not even in her life as Prendahar; she'd been riveted by the sight of the lovely Ganesh batting. He used his upper two arms in smooth strokes when he batted. All four were in motion when he fielded.

She'd suddenly realized that the uniforms were beautiful, the sounds of the fans were wonderful, and the smells emanating from the food vendors were intoxicating. Maybe there was more to sport than just grunting after all.

She bought something from a food cart, with no memory of what it was at all, and sat to watch the game. With her back against a tree, she curled her legs beneath her and her six arms lolling by her side, except when they picked at the food she'd bought, she was at ease.

After the match – she'd later learned that they were called matches, not games. Krishar sauntered over to her and smiled.

Small talk ensued, laughter was shared, and time passed. Eventually, the sun began to set, and Krishar stood up. She'd been afraid he was going to leave.

"I have a room near here," he said, mollifying her fears.

It was a pleasant but nondescript room - built for dalliances and not a home. That was fine with Prendahar. That meant it was a room built for privacy.

They slowly undressed each other, and Prendahar took the time to explore Krishar's body. She found herself stroking his trunk as they kissed and let her other five arms do what they wished. What they wanted most, as it turned out, was to finger his anus and stroke his penis.

She also found that she liked having her penis stroked too.

This caught Prendahar off guard. She'd never been with a mal or femme before, and to be so intimate so quick was not what she expected. Yet Krishar seemed pleased, and she could see no reason to stop.

She had pushed his rigid member against his taut abdomen and used her middle palm on the left side to keep her rhythm. Even by the legendary standards of the Ganesh, Krishar was well endowed.

She'd found her mouth licking the tip and enjoying the salty, musky flavor.

She'd felt alive in that moment more than she'd ever had before. This was all she'd dreamt it could be.

She'd let her lips cover the tip, that was all she could handle, and let her other hands roam where they may.

Soon enough, she felt the vein in his shaft begin to tighten. She knew, rationally, what was about to happen but had no idea what to do about it. Krishar had his hands wrapped in her hair and was pushing down.

The problem solved itself when Krishar exploded in her mouth, and she couldn't stop herself from devouring every salty drop.

It was the first of many turns they spent together.

She hoped that Prendahar was still enjoying those moments back on Arreti. Then she wondered what new delights the future would bring.

ओम'

Now:

Remember, labeling your smalls and younglings' belongings to do so on the inside of their articles. You don't want alien pedophiles to be able to call them by name and thus kidnap them and sell them into slavery in a foreign land. Your Goptri doesn't wish to alarm you, just to keep you safe. Your safety is the Goptri's highest concern.

ओम'

It was late, and Vandamir needed his rest. He excused himself from the meeting, he wouldn't be making the trip anyway, and headed to his room.

He finished his usual rituals and lay down to sleep. He felt his left arm go numb, his chest tighten, and his vision began to narrow. He didn't panic. He knew what was happening and smiled. He was about to begin his next adventure.

ओम'

They found his body shortly after breaklight when the palace staff went in to offer him a repast. His arms were crossed on his chest, and he was smiling. Saddened though everyone was, no one was destitute. He'd lived long and well and gone to a place he welcomed.

It was decided the attendees who were there would make the trip to the Goptri's lair. The Ice Pirates would add three delegates, all skilled in subterfuge, and they all agreed that they would wear the Nanek-Dev symbol on their uniforms.

Vandamir had imparted more wisdom in less than one turn than most of them would garner in a lifetime. He would be missed.

ओम'

The Goptri looked at the desiccated corpse across the room and smiled. Like all good corpses, it smiled back. That was fitting since it still wore the shiny knife of its demise in its chest.

Quite festive in its way.

Yet all good things must come to an end, and now it was clear that this chapter was closed. The message from the Yelda left no doubt. They were coming, they were bringing allies, and all of them were either assassins or spies. They weren't even bothering to try and hide that fact.

Still, five Suns was a good run. There were no complaints.

Well, the war would be missed, but what could one do? Maybe someone else would take up the cause. Rohta knows there were enough paranoiacs around to make that possible.

The Goptri checked its Pangolin costume and deemed it worthy. As an extra precaution, it tossed on the hood of poverty that some wore. No one looked at the poor.

Soon, the Goptri slid into an alley and joined the masses. They were walking randomly towards their goal.

ओम'

Nkkl sat near the bed, softly sobbing. The monotone screech of the alarm had been turned off. The machines' soft huffing and hissing continued to lie to her, offering hope where there was most assuredly none. Lrrt, the love of her life, was dead.

She knew, intellectually, she would remember the laughter and the good times. She knew there would always be resonances of his goodness for now, and forever. Well, she would know those things. Right now, all she knew was that Lrrt was dead, and she was hollow.

Her smalls walked in and immediately seeing what had happened. She wanted to hug them, tell them everything would be fine, that life would go on. Instead, she just sat and sobbed. Her body would not, could not, move.

Lrrt, the symbol of all which was good and holy to her, lay

dead.

She knew the Goptri had done this. Of that, she had no doubt. It was the first act of open aggression against the Din-La ever, and she had no idea how the Board would respond. She wasn't even sure if they could. War wasn't something the Din-La did.

At least not until now.

This changed everything.

And she didn't know how she felt about that. A part of her, the seething and volcanic part, wanted the Goptri dead. But another part of her, the part that raised Din-La, knew that peace was the only hope for Arreti.

FUCK IT!

She still wanted the bastard dead.

Yet despite her raging emotions, she could not move. She could not hug her smalls, who were openly weeping. She was paralyzed.

She wasn't sure which one grabbed a portie and called Gffk's office one of her smalls. He was out, but the femme who answered took all the information and said not to worry. Help was on its way.

She ruefully snickered when she heard.

Help was meaningless. Help was useless. Help was a waste. There was no help.

Lrrt was dead, and no help in the universe would change that.

ओम'

"Nine? Nine, are you there?"

"I'm here, Four. What can I do for you?"

"I was just reviewing the latest data from the cybers main and had a question."

"If I have the answer, I will share."

"What is this threat they mention in data file eight?"

"It is theoretical. That is clarified in data file eleven."

"Thank you. I wish they'd organize their data more efficiently."

"It is logical, based on their origins. You just need to think like them."

"That makes my circuits hurt."

ओम'

Then:

It had been a full Sun since the fall of Nirvana II and the rise of the Goptri of the Mists. All in all, things seemed to be going well. There were a million details that needed to be attended, but Manish's staff, he had a staff now, and Arti's divine assistance kept the uproar to a minimum.

In his small office, Manish was sitting at his desk, reviewing various reports when Pulinda knocked and walked in, escorting an extremely elderly Ganesh mal without waiting for permission.

"I think you need to hear what he has to say," began Pulinda without preamble, "it seems we may have a problem."

Manish motioned for them both to sit. Then he, as was his custom, got up and served them each a glass of water. The gesture, while practical, was also symbolic. The Goptri served the brands and would never forget it.

"I am Dalwik," began the ancient Ganesh. His voice sounded as old as he looked. "I served the Technarcy all my life. I have no regrets about what happened. If not you, then some brand, is what I think. Things were spiraling out of control.”

Manish, clueless as to the point of this, remained silent.

“It was I who designed the Omnium. It was never meant to lead. It was meant to serve. But, after joining with the Leader Elmar, things began to go wrong. As you surmised in your opening speech, the Omnium had gone mad.”

Manish was still in the dark.

“I have spent the last Sun going through the wreckage in the main control room,” he paused to sip his water, “and can now say for certain the Omnium still lives.”

Manish had gone from clueless to perplexed.

“So? We turn it off or unplug it or whatever needs to be done to shut it down.”

“It’s not that simple, my Goptri. The Omnium has escaped.”

Manish decided that he liked being clueless better in this case.

“How is that possible? I was told the Omnium was a standalone machine in the middle of a room.”

“And so it was, and so it was.”

There was an uneasy silence.

“Tell him the rest,” snapped Pulinda.

Dalwik let out a breath and continued.

“I now know that the Omnium transferred its consciousness into a cyber and fled the carnage. I also believe it took Leader Elmar with him. Moreover, when I reviewed the security footage, I saw the cyber in question with four others on a hovercraft headed north. I do not know their destination, but I can assure you that the Omnium still walks among us.”

Manish contemplated all of that for a while.

"Is there any way to track that craft after all this time?"

Pulinda shook his head in the negative.

The sounds of the busy staff only accentuated the extended silence in the room just outside the door.

"Okay," said Manish firmly, "we have the technology to detect electronic surveillance. Equip every portie of anyone who works for us with that. Keep it simple. A blue light comes on if someone is being spied on or something like that. The Omnium will need to access us electronically if it is to get a foothold here again. Also, scan all of the computers we still use for tampering. I think they may be too feeble to be of use to it, but I'd rather err on the side of caution.

"Lastly, tell no one about this. I don't want panic in the streets. For all we know, the cyber the Omnium inhabited may not be capable of sustaining it. Unless there is a compelling reason contrariwise, this stays in as small a group as possible.

"Speaking of which, who else knows about this?"

Dalwik smiled.

"I have no friends. So I only told Lord Pulinda."

"It's General, not Lord," interjected Pulinda, "and I told no one. So it's just the three of us for now."

"Good, let's keep it that way."

Manish had never given much thought to the Omnium. He hadn't even known it existed until after the rebellion was over. Now he wanted to know everything about it, and the source he needed was sitting in front of him sipping water.

The conversation lasted three full cliks until Manish realized Dalwik was tired. He arranged for him to be taken home, and then sat thoughtfully with Pulinda.

Finally, Manish spoke.

"I know it's worthless, but I'd like you to assemble a team and see if they can track that craft. Don't tell them it's the Omnium. Just say it's some rogue cybers they're hunting."

He raised his upper right hand before Pulinda could speak.

"I know you hate lying to your troops, but we can't even risk a whisper of this getting out."

Pulinda looked nonplussed for a moment but then nodded.

Then, with nothing more needing to be said, he got up and left.

Not five epi-cliks later, there was another knock at the door. Manish called for whoever was there to enter and was surprised to see two well-dressed brands he did not know.

The first was a tall Devi. He was wearing a custom-tailored, royal blue waistcoat with yellow cuffs which were trimmed in gray. His yellow trousers, and royal blue shoes gave him a slightly effeminate air, but Manish still found him fashionable.

The second was a well-built Ganesh. He was wearing a white shirt and white shoes and had amaranth-colored pants. There was something a little off about him, but Manish couldn't quite place it, and decided it probably wasn't important.

"How may I serve you this turn?" Manish asked as he motioned them to the chairs in front of his desk and served them water.

"I am Prendahar," began the Devi," and this is Krishar," he said, motioning to the Ganesh, "we would like to get married."

Manish found himself clueless again.

"To whom?"

"To each other," replied Krishar.

"Ah, I see," said Manish, obviously not seeing, "but I am not a priest or a justice of the peace. How can I help you? Why don't you find one of them to marry you?"

They looked at him as though he'd grown a second head.

"It's against the law," exclaimed an exasperated Prendahar.

"Whose law?" asked an equally exasperated Manish.

"Your law."

"My law?"

"Yes, your law."

Manish had now traveled from clueless to muddled.

"I admit that I've been pretty busy since the revolution, but I honestly can't remember writing a law banning marriage. In fact, I'm pretty sure that my wife would have mentioned it if I had."

Prendahar and Krishar looked baffled. They'd spent a whole season preparing their presentation to the Goptri. This was not going at all as planned.

Manish continued.

"So, as you can see, you're mistaken. Please, go, get married, and have a wonderful life together."

Krishar was the first to gather his wits.

"Forgive me, Goptri, but it is you who is mistaken. The priests and the justices of the peace still are honoring the laws of the Technarcy in this regard… since you haven't said anything to counter them. The law only allows you to marry the same brand of the opposite gender."

Manish understood some of it now and smiled.

"You love each other?"

They nodded and joined hands.

"What more do you need?"

Prendahar fielded this one.

"There are many reasons we need to be married, but I'll give you a simple example. Hospitals only allow spouses and immediate relatives to visit the sick. They do this to keep the floors from being overrun."

"That makes sense," admitted Manish.

"Well, Krishar and I are neither to each other. If either of us required care, the other would be precluded from being there."

Manish was not stupid. Clueless occasionally, yes, but not stupid. He quickly extrapolated the rights and privileges he took for granted, realizing just how oppressed these two were. Then he thought about it some more and decided they couldn't be the only two in Bharat. He knew they weren't. He'd met a few troops who preferred their own gender. He'd fought beside them, eaten with them, slept in their tents… Ah, Zanubi, he'd like them. He'd just never thought about it. Well, he was supposed to be the Goptri of change, according to his press releases. What better change could there be than to legalize love?

He laughed.

This is precisely the response that Prendahar and Krishar hadn't expected.

"Well, then, this is a problem I can fix," he said with a smile, "after all, what's the point of being the Goptri if you can't right a wrong?"

The two mals slowly realized what was happening and allowed themselves a smile.

He called in Arti and explained the situation quickly. She had been handling the wording of any laws since she had the education for it.

"So many little details that mean big things," she laughed, "I'll take care of this right now."

She turned to Manish, "How soon do you want this to be effective?"

"Now works for me unless you see a problem with that."

She considered that for a moment.

"Not really, but it will take some time to get the word to everyone."

Manish considered that for a moment and smiled wider.

"Add into the law that the Goptri can perform marriages, call a vid crew, and let's have a nice marriage with an even-break meal in front of the whole continent. I mean, why not? They're well dressed, we're here, and we had nothing useful planned."

"I thought," said Arti with a sly smile, "we were supposed to have fun, fun time this even."

Manish was stunned by her public admission and then laughed even louder.

"Fair enough," he turned to the two mals sitting in front of him who were doing a good imitation of his clueless look, "if we're willing to cut into our fun fun time, will you be willing to be wed on a continent-wide vid broadcast?"

Their confused nods of assent were all he and Arti needed to set things in motion.

It was a hectic few cliks, but all the arrangements got made. Manish knew there were those who would hang to the old ways. Who believed the subjugation of others was their right. He also knew that subtlety was not their forte. Well, this wasn't subtle. This was akin to using a sledgehammer to peel a grape. Hopefully, it would get the point across.

They held the wedding in the grove just north of the old Nirvana II. Someone, Manish would never know who, had decorated the trees with flowers, balloons, and glittery pinwheels. Tri-colored headscarves, in the traditional green, saffron, and white, were found for the grooms. A sacred fire pit was set up safely away from the foliage, and Manish had to admit that, all in all, everything looked wonderful.

A large crowd had shown up. It seemed that every aspect of the Ville of Veruna was represented. Manish and Arti agreed that that was as it should be for an occasion like this.

While there were age-old traditions behind the wedding ceremony in Bharat, Manish knew some would need to be bent in order to make this work. He shrugged inwardly and set about bending them.

They began with the Vara Satkaarah. Manish greeted both mals in the grove, and he chanted a few mantras to get things started. They sat in seats on a small stage, with Krishar seated to the left and Predahar to the right.

Arti blessed them both with rice and trefoil. Then applied the traditional tilaks, made of vermilion and turmeric powder, to both grooms' foreheads.

There wasn't much they could do about the Madhuparka Ceremony. Neither groom had any living relatives. In this case, Pulinda stepped up, washed their feet, and gave them each a small offering of honeyed milk.

To facilitate the Kanya, Dan Pulinda allowed each groom to accept the other amidst the chanting of sacred mantras.

The Vivah-Homa went off flawlessly. The three Achaman mantras involved the sipping of a little water, which Manish served, three times. That he could, and did, handle. The seven

Angasparsha mantras involved touching water with the right hand's middle two fingers, and then applying it to various limbs. First to the right side, and then the left side as follows: mouth, nostrils, eyes, ears, arms & thighs, then sprinkling water all over the body. The grooms handled this ritual, signifying purity, just fine.

Manish noted, loudly and unmistakably, that Vivah Samskara is a marriage between two bodies and two souls. By now, many of the congregants were openly weeping.

The Pani-Grahan went exceptionally well, with each accepting the other as his lawfully wedded groom and promising to live lives of purity and faithfulness.

The Pratigna-Karan went almost as it would for any other wedding. The couple walked around the fire, with the new twist of neither leading the other, and took solemn vows of loyalty, steadfast love, and life-long fidelity to each other.

Arti handled the Shila Arohan and counseled both on preparing for their new lives while they each stood on a large stone, which symbolized many things. Mostly an acknowledgment that life has many changes, and they must swear to be there for each other.

Both grooms offered puffed rice into the fire for the Laja-Homah. Since neither had any relatives who could help them place and remove their hands from the fire the required three times while praying to Yama, the god of death, to symbolize the desire for long life, and health, they just held each other's hands, and did it. No one seemed to mind.

Then, to make it all legal, they performed the Mangal Fera. The newly married couple circled the sacred fire seven times to much applause.

In the first six rounds, Krishar led Predahar around the fire, during which God's blessings and help were sought. Loyalty was emphasized, making a promise for the well-being and care of their future children was made. Predahar led Krishar around the sacred fire in the final round and promised he would lead his life according to Dharma, and Satya, devotion, and truth.

At the end of the seven rounds, they exchanged seats, with Predahar taking a seat to the left of the Krishar.

To make the Saptapadi work, Manish tied each headscarf to the other. Then the couple took the seven steps representing nourishment, strength, prosperity, happiness, progeny, long life, and harmony, and understanding, respectively.

There wasn't much to meditate on for the Abhishek. Really, what was there to reflect on at this time? This was happening; it was happening now, and, as far as Manish was concerned, it would never be undone. After a few moments of silence, he sprinkled the ceremonial water and continued.

For the Anna Praashan Prendahar, and Krishar made food offerings into the fire, chanted the sacred mantras, which Manish was surprised they'd memorized, and then fed each other a morsel while expressing mutual love, and affection.

They concluded the ceremony with the traditional Aashirvadah with Manish and Arti handling the benedictions and blessings.

Tables overly burdened with food were uncovered, and the wedding feast lasted well into the even. As they walked to the buffet, Arti took one of Manish's hands and kissed him.

"This was almost, not quite, but almost, better than fun fun time."

Manish blushed.

Manish did not know it, and never would, but the two conversations he'd had in his office this turn were linked. Many, many Suns from now, the broadcast would reach a starship and cause a cyber to hug herself and wish for the tears of joy she so desperately needed to weep.

ओम'

Now:

Vandamir's remains were back in the lands of the Nanek-Dev, and the giant hovercraft that held the makeshift ambassadors was nearing the coordinates of the Goptri's undersea home. The four-turn trip had been unnerving. As they'd passed through the various villages and towns, they'd been greeted with open derision, at best. The number of brands they'd seen brazenly carrying weapons had been off-putting, and the naked hostility directed at them had been unexpected. Bharat had become a land of hate.

Whatever doubts any of them held about their ultimate goal had been erased by these revelations.

As Vandamir had predicted, they'd been met by the Goptri's representatives about a kay north of the Goptri's lair. The fact that their guides were even more heavily armed than the citizens was, sadly, not a surprise at this point.

Several of them speculated they should have brought their own security, but that was quickly quashed.

As Mondara noted, "We are here to stop the violence, not escalate it."

The irony of the fact they planned on using assassination as a step towards peace wasn't lost on any of them. But things were what they were. Nothing was as it should be anymore.

The entourage was led to an entrance which was cleverly disguised as a small hill. There they exited the hovercraft and were led into a large chamber. It was tastefully decorated with images of the four Goptris, which were painted on the walls. The rest of the walls were a surrealistic blend of saffron, green, and white. All of which lent an air of meditative calm that belied the events which had led to their visit.

There were a series of elevators on the far wall. One opened, and they were herded, there was no other word, into it.

Their escorts made it clear that the safeties were off on their weapons and surrounded them. They glanced at each other as the elevator began to descend, and all inwardly shrugged.

Whatever was about to happen would? There was no going back now.

ओम'

She looked around the vacant hovel she'd inhabited. As was Bharat's custom, the former residents had stocked the shelves with non-perishable foods and grooming supplies. She'd reconnoitered the other nearby residences and found she had enough supplies to last a Sun or more. So far, so good.

Her disguise lay tossed in front of the couch in the middle of the main room. Her sack, which held her interesting things, lay on the couch. She knew she was hundreds of kays away from anything and anyone so she could relax. This village had been abandoned when the Goptri had moved their jobs to the north. Even so, the Goptri had many satellites, which had features that other satellites did not, and they could see much. Better to be safe than sorry. She would keep to the darkling even and stay alive.

That was just practical.

They may not be looking for her yet, but they would.

The move of the village had been a good deal for the villagers. More goldens, better conditions, and easier to control.

Well, they'd known about the first two.

She smiled and enjoyed the luxury of being herself for a change.

She had many things to consider.

Still, there was plenty of time to do that. Right now, she needed food, and she had food. The hovel was solar powered, so she had plenty of hot water, and the kitchen was fully functional. She popped open a few cans and began to make a meal.

She found a shelf full of spices, and less than half a clik later had a healthy meal of spiced tuna and rice. She'd found wild greens growing nearby and used them to make a salad. All in all, things were better than could be expected.

She ate slowly and contemplated all that had happened. This world was different than what she knew; however, there were similarities. It was a funhouse mirror, yet some reflections rang true. The overall dedication to finding peaceful solutions to any disagreement was still utterly alien to her, but she knew that was a goal and not a reality.

Even so, there were exciting possibilities.

And it was the promise of those possibilities that warmed her more than the food. On the other hand, she was sated in one way, which was nice, but saw many ways to be sated in all.

She felt her hungers grow and felt alive again. This could be fun. It had been a long time since she'd just had fun.

ओम'

Ragamooth and Damadora were sitting in the Farting Orcan. It had become their haunt when they were off duty and had some free time. Ragamooth was drinking his usual Arrack, and Damadora was drinking something that appeared to have golden metal flakes floating in it. Ragamooth didn't even want to know what it was.

This even they'd been joined by Pearl Goodness of the Bright Flower. She was sipping on a fruit cocktail based on the Solanum Lycopersicum plant. It was laden with peppers and pickles; she seemed to be enjoying it immensely. While all the Pearls looked the same, Ragamooth could see why Damadora thought she was prettier than the rest. There was just something special about her.

Ah well, rules were rules, so that particular Pangolin was doomed to a life of one-handed love. There were worse fates, Ragamooth supposed.

"I don't get it," said Pearl between sips, "why did we offer peace to the Yelda when they're the ones who killed my sister?"

"Well," mused Ragamooth, "politics doesn't often make sense."

"True," chimed in Damadora, "but in this case, I think she has a valid point. While I can understand a gesture of peace, based on the terms I've seen, it gives the impression that we offered them the world. That seems excessive."

The vid screens showed the ambassadors of the various brands being welcomed into the northern access. The talk in the bar turned ugly, with many calling the ambassadors killers or worse. The three friends listened without joining in. They'd all begun to notice that Bharat had taken an ugly turn somewhen.

"Something else bothers me," continued Damadora, "why were so many raw recruits on a march that far from base? Even when we joined the Kshatriya, there were more safety precautions than that."

"True," said Ragamooth thoughtfully, "that's been bothering me as well. I can't fathom a single reason why those recruits should have been so far from base and so close to danger."

"Do you think there's something wrong with the Goptri?" asked Pearl.

It was an innocent question, but the mere concept gave the two warriors pause. They were sworn to the Goptri. What would they do if the Goptri went rogue? Maybe more importantly, what could they do?

They sat silently for half a clik—each to their thoughts. Finally, Ragamooth spoke.

"When was the last time a Kshatriya was sworn in?"

While not an every turn occurrence, the ceremony did happen at least once every couple of Suns. It was a simple, yet solemn, event. The candidates who'd completed the training would assemble in the great hall, surrounded by already sworn Kshatriya, and meet the Goptri. Then he'd say a few words and swear them in.

Damadora had to think about it.

"Well, I was sworn in just a little over five Suns ago. Now that I think about it, I've never been to a new ceremony. I just thought I'd missed them because I'd been busy. But, now that you mention it, I can't remember even seeing a posting for one."

"Nor I," agreed Ragamooth.

The two warriors pondered what that could mean.

"We need to speak to those ambassadors," said Damadora.

"If they're still alive," agreed Ragamooth.

They realized the sagacity of Ragamooth's words, pushed aside their drinks, and began working on a plan.

ओम'

Then:

Pran had set himself up amidships simply due to the fact that there was a massive viewer that allowed him to see outside. Even if all he saw now was the lingering grey of near light speed, at least it was organic. Before settling here, he'd found sealed containers of seeds, soil, and few large globes in his search of the ship. Like any small, he knew how to make a self-contained eco-system.

Working without gravity made it a challenge, but he made it work by mounting each globe upside down. Soon the soil, water, and the spiderwort seeds in place. The globes were sealed, and he took them to the common area. It would do the others well to see life and be reminded from whence they came.

He was curious why an entire section of the ship was dedicated to agricultural products but was left to merely guessing. Then he realized that might not be entirely true.

There were records from a maker faction on Arreti who wanted, very much, to kill this ship, and all involved with it. To do something like that, they would have needed to know a lot about what they were attacking.

While he had a degree as a psychologist, it was the mob's workings that had fascinated him. The group-think that drove societies in directions individuals would never go. His current situation seemed to put proof to that.

Outstanding brands had been led down a path that would have made them automatons., and yet, just due to the desire to fit in, to belong, many had happily gone along.

After making sure the globes were secure, he left and went back to his room to peruse the old records.

He casually thought about his old life. He'd been too busy with his work to engage in any meaningful relationships. He had a feeling that fact might help him survive the coming eons.

These cybernetic bodies would live long. Whether or not they'd prosper was for time to tell.

His search didn't take long to find what he wanted. The group called themselves Earth First and held to an apocalyptic brand of several religions tied neatly under one wildly contradictory banner. That was common enough. Their beliefs, such as they were, were just an excuse for their hate.

He ignored the minutiae and delved into their files. They were extensive. He realized this information might be useful to their continued survival. Quickly he notified Natasha of what he'd found and where to look.

It took some time to sort through all the silly suppositions to get to the facts he needed, but time was a luxury he had.

The cold gray of the universe comforted him as he learned more and more about Pravda.

He also learned that while the Earth First clan was as crazy as crazy could get, at least they weren't paranoid.

This ship was a harbinger of death and conquest. Maybe they could do better.

ओम्'

It had been ten Suns since the rebellion. Manish had shrunk Bharat's borders to make governing more manageable and give their neighbors a bit of a buffer. The Technarcy had been pushing outward until the absolute end.

Everyone appreciated the gesture. Tensions seemed to have significantly reduced all around, which was fine with him and his.

When he thought about it at all, which was seldom, he simply wished the Omnium well. Five rogue cybers were no threat anymore. By now, they were probably cookware for the Ice Pirates.

Arti had gotten pregnant the even of Prendahar & Krishar's wedding and had retired from office as soon as she'd found out. He hadn't wanted her to, he valued her wisdom, but she'd been adamant. Even so, she managed to advise him when he needed it, and that was good enough.

Aanandini, their daughter, was growing into a beautiful femme. Manish had never thought about procreating, but now he couldn't imagine a life without a small.

All in all, life in Bharat was settling into a pleasant routine.

While there were still the occasional border skirmishes, there were no wars. While there was always someone who hated the government, there were no rebellions.

An actual government was in place now as well. A small parliament of fifty had been elected to represent each region. It was they, and not Manish, who would appoint his successor when the time came. They also handled the turn to turn machinations that kept the country running.

He had to admit that things were turning out better than he'd expected.

Arti and Aanandini walked into his study and started laughing. He couldn't blame them. His pants were unbuckled, his cup of java was hanging from his lower left hand, and he'd forgotten to shave again. He looked more like a charity case than a Goptri.

Arti simply pointed in the direction of the shower, and he had to laugh with them.

He put down his cup, buckled his pants, and went to get clean and shaven.

Ten epi-cliks later, he was a new brand. Arti had laid out a clean outfit for him, and he put it on. He saw no reason to quibble about it. She had far better taste than he ever would. Even so, he would be the first to admit that the one thing he missed about the rebellion was never having to worry about looking good. He'd gone turns at a time without bathing, and no one seemed to care. Of course, they'd had other things to think about, like not getting killed, so that may have been the reason.

Now, even Pulinda was freshly scrubbed every breaklight.

Well, if cleanliness was the price of freedom, so be it. It was a price he could easily pay.

He found the loves of his life playing skizzi ball in the courtyard and joined them.

While he genuinely liked being the Goptri, sometimes, it was even better just to be Manish.

ओम'

Now:

The simplest plans are often the best plans, and plans didn't get any simpler than this. Ragamooth, Damadora, and Pearl Goodness of the Bright Flower simply put on their dress uniforms and walked into the wing where the ambassadors were being held.

In the four turns since they'd arrived, they'd met no one, seen nothing, and not been allowed out of their comfortable cages.

The three unlikely rebels found them all sitting in the common area watching a popular animation. Despite the lack of visible security, all three knew this room was being monitored and all the others. They would have to be careful.

"Namaste ambassadors," began Ragamooth, "We were wondering if we might have a moment of your time."

Xho shrugged his wings and motioned them in. None of the ambassadors had ever seen a Pearl close up, and she held their initial attention.

"We would like to thank you," continued Ragamooth, "for taking the time to come visit our beloved Goptri., and by coming without guards, it shows you are truly interested in peace."

It also indicated they had no clue what Bharat was now like, before this. He left that unsaid.

"As duly sworn representatives of the Goptri, we would like to offer you a brief tour of Veruna Ville."

This was the tricky part. If the Goptri had issued orders contrary to what he had just said, they would all be killed. They were banking on the fact that nothing had happened since the ambassadors arrived. It had been Pearl who mentioned the Goptri might have left while the leaving was good.

An entire plan based on a hunch was not a well-founded one, but it was all they had, and they were running with it.

Ragamooth had the ambassadors' full attention now. Whatever motives they may have individually ascribed to his offer, there was no doubt that something had changed, and they wanted to find out what that was.

They all quickly rose and assented.

Introductions were made, and soon they were headed out the door.

The guards in the hall were flummoxed. While they had a chain of command, they knew that the Kshatriya only took orders from the Goptri. They quickly decided this must be some sort of arrangement from the Goptri, one of which they weren't aware. They also agreed not to push the issue. The Goptri had shown a penchant for harsh punishments as of late, especially when someone interfered with his will.

The party entered the hall unmolested.

Pearl Goodness of the Bright Flower didn't know it, but she echoed her distant ancestor as she began a running narration of the sights.

The pattern was superficial, but no one complained.

But when Chen tried to stifle a yawn by stretching her wings, Damadora took advantage of the momentary distraction to place an object in Navi's hand. Navi carefully sequestered it in his vest and continued to appear interested in Pearl's oration.

They wandered through sparsely populated areas, by design, for about a 'clik, and then returned the ambassadors to their accommodations.

ओम'

Navi was more mystified than ever. The device the warrior had handed him was simple enough. It was something every small was given when they first started at school. Called the Teacher's Text Tablet, it allowed the teacher to broadcast their notes on that turn's lessons to the smalls. It was designed so that the smalls could then exchange messages, questions, and ideas. It was meant to be a learning enhancement.

Miraculously enough, it did get used for those purposes. It also got used to discuss sports, exchange jokes, and send, mostly overwrought, love letters.

Why he now had one was beyond him.

Since it was a familiar item, he set it on the center table in front of the vidscreen for all to see.

Gffk, who'd noticed the exchange, smiled.

"Ah, nice," he said, "are you going back to school soon?"

Navi couldn't help but chuckle.

"This is merely a reminder of happier times. A talisman to trigger memories, if you will."

Gffk had an odd look on his face and then pulled a doll on a keychain from his waistcoat pocket. It was a naked dwarf of an unknown brand, and it had the most bizarre pink hair Navi had ever seen.

"We all," Gffk said as he re-pocketed the doll, "probably have something similar. There's nothing wrong with reminiscing about simpler times."

The chime that was used to announce an incoming message must have been disabled. A few epi-cliks later, when Navi glanced at the tablet again, there was a message.

WE BELIEVE THE GOPTRI HAS THE MEANS TO WEAPONIZE VOLCANOES. ALSO HAVE REASON TO

Navi stared at the tablet for a long moment and then laughed loudly. Turning to Kolokk, one of Queen Lynno's guards, he handed him the tablet.

"Ah, the joys of a misspent youth. I bet you have stories just like this."

Kolokk took the tablet, mildly confused, and read the message.

Not being slow on the uptake, Kolokk also laughed loudly and then smiled broadly.

"Thank you for sharing this, friend Navi. It truly does bring back memories. May I share it with the others?"

Navi presented his best-embarrassed shrug and assented. Kolokk turned and handed the tablet to Ignop, who just happened to be standing there, and laughed again.

"I bet you had turns like this when you were a small too."

Ignop confusedly took the tablet, read it, and issued a rueful chuckle.

"Oh, haven't we all, haven't we all?"

With that, he turned and handed the tablet to Xho, who, in turn, shared it with everyone else.

Soon the room was filled with laughter.

Mondara shared an amusing tale of a love letter gone horribly wrong. It seemed a young mal had managed to select "Send All" after he'd penned his missive pledging undying love and a seat next to him at lunch.

Since the young mal had sat near the doors during lunch to get to class earlier without being bumped by the throng, they all happily agreed that it was a prime seat, and a valuable offer.

The laughter, false at first, became real and warm as the turn wore on. For the first time since they'd met, they began to let down their guards. Even the Mayanoren looked less than stern, which was positively jubilant for them.

Whether or not this was the appropriate time and place for such a thing, they would leave to the future. For now, it seemed right.

Come time for their even-break meal; they requested that the guards bring them some more potent libations.

The guards did not know what had changed, but something had. Whatever the Kshatriya had done was evidently working. These alien brands looked more like potential allies now than enemies.

So be it then.

The Goptri was wisdom. The Goptri was all.

Drinks were served.

ओम'

Pearl, Damadora, and Ragamooth were back in the Farting Orcan. They'd done all that they could do, and would wait for the next turn to see how things would fall out.

The bar's vids were showing the memorial for Vandamir Singh, the Sikh of the Guru for the Nanek-Dev. It was a long-held tradition, initially instituted by Manish, that every fallen leader, no matter their relationship with Bharat, be shown respect.

Most were paying it no attention, but Damadora was riveted.

"What holds your eyes so, my friend?" queried Ragamooth.

"There are brands there from all over Arreti, but none from here. I can't believe the Goptri would commit such an obvious breach of protocol."

They let that sink in for a while, and then Ragamooth smiled. Just not in a pleasant manner.

"Then our dear Pearl would seem to have been correct. The Goptri has left us. There was no one to issue the edict. No one to say 'go,'" he paused to sip his drink before continuing, "the Dragon Lords have a curse which states 'May you live in interesting times.' I believe that curse has now befallen us."

"So what now?" asked Pearl.

"Well," mused Damadora, "I'm not sure this changes anything from our point of view. We need to find out what's been going on these last five Suns, and we need to get those ambassadors out of Bharat safely."

They all agreed on that and resumed drinking.

Still and all, they were smart enough to know that saying something does not make it so. A lot could, and probably would, go horribly wrong, and they could all end up dead.

ओम'

Come breaklight, the next turn, the three newly minted mutineers put on their best dress uniforms and all the medals they could handle. Pearl had several scientific achievements, and they were worn proudly.

They assembled at Ragamooth's apartment and then made their way to the ambassadors' gilded prison.

They were pleased to find them finishing their breaklight repast, and without luggage: a smart group, this one. Clothing could be replaced. Brands could not.

Damadora turned to the nearest guard and shot for triple Ti-Zam in one play.

"By the Goptri's kind request, we have come to take the ambassadors to him. Please bring their transport vehicle to the north entrance, as it is the only thing large enough nearby to transport us all, so that we may take them to the Pulinda Palace for their meeting."

This is where it could all go wrong, but the guard merely saluted, issued orders, and motioned in the wait staff to clear the tables, and tidy up the room.

Fifteen epi-cliks later, they were pulling away from Veruna Ville, and headed cross country to the palace.

Ragamooth and Damadora had considered many options but finally agreed, obsequious or not, the guards would monitor their progress. They'd to go to the palace first. After that? They decided that would be at the will of the Goptri.

ओम'

Three cliks later, they pulled up to the front entrance, go big or go home was the new motto for the group, and they were mildly surprised to see an honor guard waiting for them and this time with safeties locked and weapons carefully sheathed.

They were led through the main gates into the courtyard and then into the palace itself. The images of the four Goptris greeted them in the foyer. The rest of the castle was a masterpiece of restrained elegance and taste. Everything was done in natural woods and delicate gold highlights.

Even with their lives probably forfeit, they all admired the view.

The honor guard led them down several hallways and then snapped to attention in front of a large door.

This was another tricky part. Protocol stated that no one but Kshatriya and expected guests of the Goptri were allowed in. Even honored staff were supposed to have the permission of the Goptri given to the guards before this next set of doors would open.

Two guards opened one door each and stood aside.

Ragamooth and Damadora led their group in and waited for the doors to close behind them before mutually sighing in relief.

Both warriors noticed the ambassadors were being deadly silent. They focused in the direction of their concern and were surprised to see a Lakshmi in front of them.

Clad in traditional saffron robes with her brown skin lightly powdered, and her four bare arms folded in front of her, with her dark lips quivering, she seemed sad rather than threatening.

The Lakshmi, perversely enough, had been built as sex slaves. After the uprising, they'd quickly removed themselves from any professions that required such tasks and took on a more spiritual, near monastic, lifestyle.

"He will see you?" she asked carefully.

"That is why we are here," replied Ragamooth with equal caution.

"Why will he not see me? I am his… I was… or" she paused uncomfortably, "so I believed for many Suns. Yet for five Suns, I have neither touched nor spoken to him. The guards don't know what to make of my status either, so they allow me in here each turn to see if, finally, he will return to me."

She started to sob gently. Mondara, and Krark, warriors though they may be, were also femmes. They quickly gathered the poor creature into their arms and let her sob. The others said nothing at this touching yet uncomfortable scene.

Finally, she spoke again.

"I am Aslesha. I have been the Goptri's wife for sixty-five Suns. Well, sixty Suns, and this. Until he shut me out, I thought we had been happy. We had three beautiful smalls who are now fully grown. They can't even get this far. So I come. Again, and again."

Neither Ragamooth nor Damadora had seen her in many Suns. She was an intensely private brand, and all respected that. However, as soon as they heard her name, they recognized her.

The story, while heartbreaking, served to confirm many suspicions of the group.

Ragamooth removed a Kshatriya key from his belt and opened the next door. This would be the Goptri's office and apartment. Not knowing what to expect, he stepped in first, and no one thought him rude for doing so.

The rest followed him and assembled just on the inside. In the far corner lay the dead Goptri with a knife still jutting from his chest. Aslesha began to cry again.

This revelation, while enlightening, prompted many more questions than it answered.

Damadora noted a small flip top computer sitting on the Goptri's desk, an incongruity if ever there was one, and turned it on. There was a small headset plugged into it. He stared at the icons that appeared and then clicked one that looked promising.

Everyone else watched Aslesha, so they were all stunned when the Goptri's visage graced the far wall. Damadora put on the headset, and soon his voice and the Goptri's spoke in unison.

So this was how he'd done it, how he'd run the country without ever having to be seen directly.

For several cliks, they discussed their options. None were *really* good.

Finally, Damadora went into the antechamber and summoned a guard. He then ordered an even-fall meal for them all, making sure to include the Goptri in their number.

The staff, shunned for the last five Suns, gleefully jumped at the chance to serve their beloved Goptri.

Less than a clik later, the table was set, and, as the ambassadors, rebels, and Aslesha milled about, the staff was excused. Many of them remarking how good the Goptri looked as they exited.

That was precisely what Damadora hoped would happen.

As they were eating, two Guenon waiters walked in. They didn't pay them any attention initially, but Damadora soon noted they didn't handle the glassware correctly.

He quickly pulled his gun and pointed it to the head of the closest 'waiter.'

In the stunned silence that followed, the waiter quickly began to speak.

"Please, we mean you no harm. I am Jagat, head of palace security."

He pulled off a face mask to reveal his true features. He was a stately Guenon, near middle age, with a small scar on his left cheek. The other Guenon also removed a face mask to reveal himself.

Jagat continued.

"When you opened the interior door, without entering the electronic security code, recording devices turned on in our office. We have heard everything."

He motioned to the other 'waiter.'

"This is Taarank. He is my second in command, and I trust him with my life."

That didn't mean as much to the others as he might have hoped. No one knew him, so no one had any idea what his life was worth.

Still, they let him continue.

"You cannot let Bharat find out that the Goptri has been dead for five Suns. Given the present climate, there would be civil war. Worse, there are those who would use it as an excuse to march on your lands. The resulting carnage would be debilitating to us all."

"So, what do you propose?" asked Mondara.

"The Goptri needs to die, obviously, but he also needs a public funeral. I have no idea how that can be done. There is no way I know of to pass off a long-dead corpse as recently extant."

"It can be done."

All eyes turned to Gffk.

"We Din-La have the technologies that created the original Pearls. There is enough DNA in that room to build a quick facsimile in a couple of turns. It would be hollow, of course, but since he's supposed to be dead at his funeral, I can't see how that could matter."

Aslesha slowly, and for the first time in a long time, smiled.

"Then I can properly honor the brand I loved for so long and send him as he should be to greet Yama. If you can do this for me, I will keep this secret from my family and anyone else."

That seemed fair enough.

There were a million details to work out. Ragamooth informed the guards that they would need accommodations for the even and a breaklight repast for themselves next turn. They would reconvene with the Goptri at mid-break; a meal would be expected in this room for all the attendees at that time.

The staff, jubilant to be back in the graces of the Goptri, questioned nothing.

ओम'

It was just after even-fall of her third turn in the village as its sole occupant when she heard the tinkling of bells. She furtively killed the lights in her hovel and waited for the interlopers to come into view. Soon enough, she saw them—a Devi mal wearing simple work clothes, carrying a backpack, and pulling a cart. Next to him was an actual Kali with her short fur skirt cheerfully adorned with skulls. Her dark blue skin, fangs, bare breasts, and ten arms were a rare sight. Despite the Goptri's many protestations, they just didn't breed a lot. Which was surprising considering they'd been designed to please multiple makers at one time. Plus, given that they were real, fully functional hermaphrodites, she wondered why that was. If it were her who was so blessed, she'd be busting out that junk every chance she got.

In front of them was a Ganesh small, also carrying a backpack. She pulled out a pair of binocs and took a look at the cart.

Oh, joy, they were traveling psychics. That she didn't need.

Like her, they saw a place they liked, parked the cart in front of it, and went in. For the even or the long haul, it didn't matter to her. Their mere presence was a threat.

She carefully worked out a plan and then hid until even-split.

At the appointed time, she stripped naked and oiled herself from head to toe with customized silicone lubricant, which formed a second skin. Yet another handy thing she'd gotten from the Din-La. Since it clogged pores, she could only wear it for a short time, but she was okay with that. She wasn't planning on this taking long.

She buckled sheathes, each containing a large knife, to her thighs, and followed by buckling a handgun around her waist. A quick glance in a mirror told her she was ready.

While the brands knew about DNA, it was almost a religion to them due to how they were created. They had never used it in criminal investigations until a few Suns ago – THANKS GOPTRI! and she was going to do her damndest not to leave any behind. Lacking any full-body clothing, her costumes did not cover genitalia for obvious reasons; the silicon would provide the needed protection.

Besides, she liked the way she looked naked. May as well enjoy it while she could.

She made her way across the street and stealthily entered their new lair. The little Ganesh was sleeping in the front room, all alone. That helped her define the relationship between the parties, and she smiled.

She quietly padded over to the youngling and plunged a knife in his chest.

Then, because he was sooooo cute, she flipped him over and drew the knife down his spine. She followed that by slicing across his shoulders and, finally, just above his kidneys. She opened the flaps, removed a couple of ribs, and pulled his little lungs out. She flipped him over and spread his tiny lungs behind and beside him. She knew this was called a Blood Eagle, but he was so cute all she could think of was a Blood Butterfly.

She kissed the darling, deceased, youngling on the forehead and then went looking for the adults.

She found them soon enough. The Devi was snoring loudly.

She had grand plans for the two of them, but the Kali woke as she entered. Left with no viable alternative, she drove a knife into the rarity's chest. The Kali's gasp woke the Devi, and she provided him the same end.

That had happened much too quick.

Still, it needed to be done, and now it was. Even so, there was something niggling in her mind. Something about the Kali brand: then it hit her. They were telepaths, which wasn't good. This one could have transmitted her final images to others.

The look on both their faces almost made it worthwhile when they realized what had killed them.

Nevertheless, it meant she needed to find a new refuge. It was still much better safe than sorry.

She tripped over the backpack of the mal as she was trying to leave and cursed. Then she decided to see if there was anything she could use. Why not? They sure weren't going to need anything anymore.

To her surprise, there was a small bag of goldens in there. Glancing at the denominations, she figured she could live for a full Sun on them. The Kali didn't have a backpack, but the youngling did. What better place to hide riches than that?

She wasn't disappointed. There was a bag with five times more currency in it than the Devi had been carrying. Not just goldens but trade vouchers for the various clans. She took them all.

As she stepped out of the hovel, she noticed a small garage across the street. She'd been meaning to see what it contained, and now seemed as good a time as any.

What she found was better than the currency.

There was a twin fan hovercycle. It was an antique, but it looked well cared for. It took her less than an epi-clik to confirm everything worked. It had propulsion jets fore and aft so it could go forward or backward. On the rear, it had two saddlebags with secured tops.

She slid onto the saddle and drove it to her home.

She filled the saddlebags with food and her meager supply of clothes. She tossed the currency pouches on top, locked the latches, and went in to get clean.

She dropped the gun belt as she entered, dropped the knife belts next to the tub, used a solvent to remove the silicone, and then stepped into the shower. She let the hot water cascade off her body for a while as she reveled in the memories of the smells of new death. The heady mix of fresh feces and blood always intoxicated her.

She was not surprised that her fingers decided to brush through her mons Venus to attack her clit. The last of the blood washed out of her hair and off her body; it leaked through the silicone. She glanced down at the knife. She pulled it out of its sheath and let the hilt take over for her fingers.

Soon enough, she was sliding down the back of the shower as the hilt slid inside of her.

Several glorious epi-cliks later, her body began to shudder, her breath began to catch, and her body released long pent-up energies. It was good; there was no one around. Her moans would have woken the dead.

She laughed out loud at that thought and then exited the bathroom to get dressed.

She packed her Guenon costume and then put her Pangolin one on for the first time since she'd arrived.

A clik later, she had cleaned the abode down to the molecular level – at least as far as she was concerned - and had everything the way she wanted. She walked outside and mounted the hovercycle. She aimed it at the house she'd just visited to ensure the dead had stayed that way.

They had.

Now all she needed was a destination. But that was a given. She would head to the land of the Chosun. Psychotically xenophobic, violently insular, and devoid of any concept of reality, they would be the perfect foil for her.

Maybe this Arreti place would be worth hanging out in after all.

ओम'

Then:

After the initial thrust, the ship's speed had evened out. Natasha realized it had to. The G-forces would have crushed organic life forms had it maintained their initial acceleration. So, instead of a few turns, it had taken over a Sun to reach its maximum velocity. They traveled at full speed for twelve Suns, back on Arreti – almost no time passed for them, and then she began the deceleration process. The ship had been carefully slowing for the last eight Suns. Natasha had expertly guided it on a long ellipse so they would enter the target solar system without bumping into anything. Long-range scanners had shown a cloud of comets similar to, but far denser than, the Ort Cloud back home.

They'd been receiving and recording transmissions since they began decelerating. Notes from the Sominids had hinted that this race was more in tune with technology than any others, so they'd eschewed a closer system to come here. So far, they'd seen no direct evidence of anything like that.

Of course, after cataloging intoxicants and best inter-species sexual practices, notes from the Sominids tended to get a little spotty.

Still, they were excited. Pravda had a built-in translation device that ran comparisons against three hundred maker languages and possible visual communication forms. They'd added all the languages they could from the brands as well. While Common was the language of trade, many communities and brands had their private languages. Once it had been finalized to everyone's satisfaction, they each downloaded a version of the program and set about reviewing the astonishing transmissions that were coming in.

Boris explained what they were up against. He brought up an image of a tree on a vidscreen, putting it next to another image of a small group of trees.

"Zogneb," he said, pointing at the tree while uttering a nonsense word, "Does that mean 'tree' or is it a proper noun like 'spruce,' 'elm' or 'oak'? Da, you don't know. You cannot know. Not without context. The translation computer is exceptionally nimble, but it is up to us to define context. The computer was based on languages that had previous interactions at least at some level so that context could be defined."

He pointed to the second image.

"Negzob. Now is this a 'woods,' a 'forest,' a 'jungle' or something else? Each defines a different eco-system, so a correct definition is important."

They got the message. This wasn't going to be as easy as turning the damn thing on and letting it do the work.

Over the course of the first Sun of translations, it had turned out that Zeenat had a propensity for languages. She was able to add nuance to the bare meanings.

The clicks, whorls, and whistles which comprised what they were hearing would be unpronounceable by any organic on Arreti, but their processors could easily duplicate the sounds.

Once they had a baseline, they made fast work of it.

As best anyone could figure, the beings were known as The Contented. They were mammalian octopods who never walked upright. At the end of each appendage, they had three multi-jointed fingers, which were remarkably dexterous. Their round bodies averaged a meter in diameter and a meter in height. They'd small heads containing four eyes each, and each eye had four lids, allowing them to blink horizontally or vertically. Their mouths had varying numbers of pincers, but no one could make out any nasal passages or similar breathing assistance.

They tended to wear brightly colored robes that dragged behind them as they walked.

Zeenat dubbed them the universe's first huggable spiders.

Although they were divided into geographic nation-states, none of the cybers could detect any type of conflict. Their name seemed to suit them.

The only thing that bothered the cybers was that the planet's entire history seemed to start thirty-five hundred Suns ago. There was no mention in anything they could find in the transmissions of life before that. The closer they got, the more precise the transmitted histories were about that fact.

And that made no sense at all.

There was no way they could discern how a race could be as technologically advanced as they were, with several inter-solar colonies, and be that young.

Nevertheless, they could only work with what they had and pointed to a too young race who had achieved impossible things. It seemed to the cybers that even the Sominids might have noticed that incongruity.

Then again, based on what they'd learned thus far, maybe not.

As they neared the cometary debris cloud, Natasha took over manual controls and used the side thrusters to create a path. They were soon clear and began broadcasting a message that they hoped would make sense to the aliens.

"Greetings. We come in peace from the planet Arreti. We wish to get to know you."

The broadcast was done in Common as well as the primary language of the Contented. It was simplistic, and mildly hackneyed, but it was the best they could come up with that would allow a 'one to one' word comparison. Plus, as the Omnium noted, starting by sharing was probably the best symbolism they could provide.

Natasha put the ship back on autopilot and let it head towards the Contented's homeworld.

After all this time, their journey had well and truly begun.

ओम'

Now:

M'Para sat in a comfortable chair in front of a warm fire, wearing a heavy blanket, shivering uncontrollably. While the Kali had no political structure, she had the strongest mind and knew the others, who had also experienced their sister's death, would be looking to her for guidance.

There wasn't much she could do.

The Kali were small in number. Less than ten thousand spread across the continent. That was by design. Their telepathy made it difficult for them to be in close proximity for extended periods of time. Unlike the Wizards of the Plains, who connected through a dimensional anomaly, the Kali were connected mind to mind. The closer they were, the more physical discomfort they felt.

It was only during their mating season that their mental barriers could safely be let down to allow them tactile appreciation of each other.

None of that mattered at the moment. Their sister was dead. Of course, murder had happened before. Not everyone was kind. But what had killed this particular sister was unheard of.

There was a maker loose in Bharat. It was deadly, and now all the Kali were aware of it. Until this got sorted out, she advised them to keep the secret. Given the nature of the knowledge, that was an easy request to honor. None of them wanted to be classified as mentally unfit.

She needed to act quickly and inform them of what actions she was taking to calm down.

She'd once dealt with a gentle Kshatriya named Ragamooth. He would believe her and know what to do. Better still, the others were aware of her little adventure with him and would accept her decision. After all, many of them were alive because of him.

She pulled her portie out of a drawer and punched in his code.

ओम'

Ragamooth listened without comment for several long epicliks, and then clicked his portie off and returned it to its sheath. He was pale and shaking. His mind screamed that what he now knew to be true could not be.

The impossible had been writ large, and in innocent blood.

The others were in the common area discussing strategies. He could think of only one at this point.

He grabbed his portie again and contacted Chandrack. His old friend's warning could very well be related to this. In fact, he was sure it was.

After a pleasant, if terse, conversation as Ragamooth invited him to a mid-break repast with the Goptri. He made sure to use Kshatriya code words to warn his friend there was danger.

He decided to say nothing to the others until he spoke with Chandrack. Causing blind panic in their current situation would accomplish naught.

He walked back into the room. While Damadora noticed something was wrong, he wisely said nothing. Whatever needed to be revealed would be when the time was right. That was the Kshatriya way.

ओम'

Come mid-break, they were ushered into the Goptri's

antechamber. Chandrack was waiting for them outside the door, wearing his dress greens. His darker scales immediately set him apart from Ragamooth and Damadora but, other than that, he could have been their sibling. Of course, genetically speaking, he was.

Jagat and Taarank were their waiters once more. They were again masked.

After introductions had been made, Ragamooth motioned for silence.

"I have been giving this much thought," he began. "And there's too much riding on what we do for there to be secrets between us. Chandrack, I know you are new to this, but I must ask that you trust me and tell me why you sent me the warning you did."

Chandrack suddenly looked uncomfortable. Finally, he swallowed hard and tried to put his thoughts in order.

"You will have me committed."

"I think not," intoned Ragamooth, "not based on what I have learned."

Chandrack shrugged and decided to trust his comrade, just saying what was on his mind.

"Forty-five turns ago, I could swear I saw a maker in this office. A femme."

The room fell silent. All eyes were on Chandrack, but it was Ragamooth who broke the silence.

"You did."

Pandemonium broke out. Everyone was talking at once. Nothing was being accomplished. Ragamooth let out a loud whistle, and all eyes turned to him.

They all looked haunted.

"I have spoken with M'Para, a powerful Kali who helped me out many Suns ago. She says one of their sisters was killed by a maker last even. More specifically, her sister got a good look at the creature and broadcast it to all the Kali. Because of that, she was able to give me a detailed description.

"She described a two-legged Pearl with light brown skin."

Pearl Goodness of the Bright Flower gasped.

"Our mother lives?"

That was a disturbing take on the facts.

Pearl, seeing their reactions, quickly continued.

"As Gffk alluded to last turn, we Pearls were created from a specific genetic pool. It belonged to a maker known only as Pearl. She was a killer of the highest order. Without conscience, but laden with guile."

"After her capture, Rohta was given control over her under an agreement that he could use her genetic material for profit but could not release her from a stasis chamber until he could guarantee that her murderous urges had been purged."

"The stasis chamber was lost during the gen-O-pod™ rebellion."

"You must stop her. She exists only to cause death. All of Arreti could be in flames before she's done."

That warning was clear enough.

That a maker had been the Goptri for five Suns was something none of them questioned.

That Bharat had been poisoned by a maker was a given.

What to do about it was not so clear.

After several cliks of trading ideas, a consensus formed.

In ten turns, the Goptri would 'die.' Chandrack would discover the body. Jagat would take over the role of the public Goptri, until this one died, by using his security clearance to plug in the flip-top to the various communications channels.

That was risky, but no one could see a better alternative.

Gffk would take care of swapping bodies. No one asked how, so there could be a proper funeral.

Now it was a matter of finding her.

They narrowed down the possible list of her disguises to a Guenon and a Pangolin. Everything else involved too much jeopardy. Gffk noted several second-skin suits had been delivered to the Goptri over a Sun ago for use by the Kshatriya. Pangolin and Guenon suits were among the order. That answered any further questions.

Finally, it was the destination that eluded them until Xho spoke.

"Chosun. They have some spiritually bent philosophies. Several of which involve the makers returning to their rightful rule. They are heavily armed and, to be polite, criminally psychotic. They harass our southeastern border constantly.

"Thankfully, they are idiots. That said, they would become an instant threat under her rule. If she could con them into it."

Pearl looked chagrined.

"If all I know, if what all Pearls are taught, is true, then she can. Easily. Look at what she's done to poor Bharat just by using a proxy."

That sobered them all.

It was eventually decided that Ragamooth and Damadora

would escort the ambassadors back to the land of the Ice Pirates, and Chandrack would stay behind to supervise everything else.

Once Chandrack had arranged for evidence technicians to scour the murder scene, Kali word would be sent to the Kshatriya to be on the lookout for a Pangolin or Guenon femme, costumed, who was to be considered armed and dangerous. Anything else the evidence techs could glean would be shared to narrow the search.

The fact that she was a maker would be left out.

For now.

ओम'

She stopped her cyke and parked it just off the road in a small copse of trees. She was about three kays from an upcoming Lakshmi village. It had been fifteen turns since she'd left the palace. Last turn, she'd seen a print-stock at a trading post announcing the death of the Goptri. Massive coronary, it seemed. Rare. But not unheard of. She had to give them credit for plausibility.

She'd wondered how they'd handled the details, but not too much.

She had purposely wandered east to west and back again as she headed northwest, looking for signs that she was being sought. So far, nothing. That did not mean no one was looking for her. It just meant that they weren't looking here… yet. She knew the Kshatriya well enough to know that fact would change.

She wondered if they would figure out what they were genuinely chasing. If they did, that would make their options challenging indeed.

That cheerful thought made her smile.

She reached into her saddlebags and pulled out a quick meal.

She heard footsteps on the path and swiftly dragged her stuff to the side. A quick glance revealed a lone Lakshmi hiker. He was large. His four arms were heavily muscled, and his face was covered in henna tattoos. She guessed he was returning from some sort of spiritual quest. That was a good sign. It meant he was probably a pacifist.

She noticed his backpack and decided she had to have it.

She eased out from behind her cyke so as not to startle him. He noticed her just as she sat down.

In the traditional Bharati fashion, she motioned to her meal. He smiled and nodded.

They ate quietly, conversation was not required with this tradition - just sharing and admired the beauty of the surrounding foliage.

When he leaned over to return his plate at the conclusion of the meal, she drove a knife through his chest.

He looked at her, stunned. In fact, for a moment, as he sat there mouthing something, she was afraid he wouldn't die. But, like all organic creatures deprived of a heart, he eventually did.

It took her a while to pull his body off the road and into the weeds. He was even heavier than he looked. Worse yet, his four arms kept snagging on things. What was it with Rohta and his fucking obsession with arms?

She'd told him once how to make the perfect killing machine. With only two arms, thank you very much, but he'd never followed through. He'd just filled the stupid orders that came in. That was short-sighted as far as she was concerned. They could have been ruled this rock had he listened to her.

Oh well. What will be will be.

She emptied the backpack and moved some of her clothing, her Guenon costume, and her goldens, into it. The hiker had nothing of value as far as she was concerned, but she didn't care. All she'd wanted was the backpack, and she had that.

After making sure it had no tell-tale stickers or markings, she smiled. It was as generic as generic could be.

When she was done, she slid on the backpack, remounted her cyke, and headed towards the Lakshmi village. She was sure she could find an inn, and, right now, she needed a bath.

Once she was clean and rested, she would travel the short distance to the coast and look for Chosun's transportation. She knew, from the many reports she'd read, there were captains of watercrafts who were slightly less than scrupulous.

She was fairly sure she could spot such a brand.

ओम'

Then:

Manish stood on an elegant veranda, near the palace courtyard, watching the celebration unfold. It was Prendahar & Krishar's fiftieth wedding anniversary. The usual protestors were gathered outside, but the palace guards had things well in control. Manish wasn't sure, but it seemed to him that their number had shrunk as time had moved on. He certainly hoped so.

Arti strode up beside him, put her lower left hand in his lower right, and then hooked their upper arms together. She'd done this since the time they first met, and he'd never tired of it. He knew he never would. Their three smalls, now all grown with smalls of their own, joined them.

There were almost one thousand brands gathered in front of them, and all of them seemed to be having a good time., and why wouldn't they? There were copious amounts of free food and drink; the musicians and dancers were tremendously entertaining.

The happy couple, who were the focal point of the affair, had embraced their celebrity status, after some initial discomfort, and had become solid role models for those who might find themselves wandering a little off life's beaten path.

With Manish & Arti's help, they'd opened counseling centers all over Bharat for younglings who had trouble coming to grips with their reality. They also counseled the families of those same younglings. Now, instead of hiding in fear, they marched in annual parades.

Manish had to admit he preferred the parades.

Nevertheless, beneath the gaiety, Manish was sad. Pulinda had passed away from a sudden stroke twenty turns ago. Prendahar & Krishar, both cared deeply for Pulinda, offered to cancel the event, but Manish had said no. Pulinda had fought for a free Bharat, and a celebration of that freedom would do more to honor his memory than anything else Manish could think of.

Pulinda's family was wandering amongst the guests. They'd wanted no special attention. They just wanted to enjoy the occasion and honor their patriarch by sharing in the love he'd helped foster.

Another legacy from Pulinda was the Kshatriya. At first, Manish had thought them unnecessary due to the current state of peaceful relations with their neighbors, but they'd quickly proved that thought wrong.

The Sugar Pirates had long been a problem. Instead of sending out an army and scaring the populace, Manish could send a small band of Kshatriya to deal with them. This managed to accomplish two things simultaneously. It kept the shores safe and denied the pirates the publicity they sought. With the psychological aspect of the terror they wrought rent worthless, they became more comfortable, causing push back to become easier.

To have any success, they needed the brands to fear them. They weren't a legitimate military threat otherwise. But the brands couldn't fear what they didn't know, and, thanks to the

Kshatriya, memories of the Sugar Pirates were quietly slipping into oblivion.

Manish and Arti watched as guests milled about, happily interacting with any who came near. A well-dressed Devi mal separated from the crowd and headed towards the veranda. Just as Manish was about to reach out a hand in greeting, the guest pulled a gun and shot him point-blank.

The guards jumped on the assassin and wrestled him to the ground. Arti's voice was no longer anything natural. It was just a high-pitched ululation. Abject pandemonium was breaking out all around.

Manish, however, was unaware of any of this. He was unaware of anything at all. For him, the world had just faded, rather abruptly, to black.

ओम'

They'd been guests of the Contented for fifteen Suns. While neither side had anything the other wanted, or needed, for trade of material goods, the exchange of knowledge, and arts, and histories had been more than enough to keep them all interested.

Their guide, a burly mal with a gruff voice, had a name that translated to "Beautiful Shrub." Whatever comments the cybers had, they kept to themselves.

They were still no closer to understanding why the Sominids had singled out a heightened interaction with technology for this race. While they were technologically adept, there was nothing here that should have impressed a space-faring race.

They still didn't understand how this race went from nothing to completely civilized almost in a single turn.

Everything they knew said that couldn't happen. Yet, here they were. Any attempts to broach the subject were politely, but firmly, deferred.

Pran Unhaala had speculated that something traumatic had happened. Something so disturbing they'd wiped it from their memories. This made a superficial kind of logic until you tried to figure out how one went about wiping the minds of every single generation that followed.

Even Pran admitted there were gaps in his hypothesis.

Abhijit Juhnjuhnwalla had an alternate idea. He posited that external forces were involved. After all, they'd dealt with the Sominids without rancor or fear. That much was clear from the histories of both the Sominids and the Contented. Therefore, he reasoned, they'd come into contact with aliens before and just took it for granted.

Unfortunately, there was no evidence for that theory either.

As the Omnium had pointed out, such a life-changing event should have been worth, at the least, a memo. There was nothing.

It was Elmar who decided to take another look through the transmissions the Sominids had documented. He figured they had to account for more time than just thirty-five hundred Suns since it was about that exact time that they'd arrived.

It turned out he was right.

They covered almost five thousand Suns.

The cybers took their leave and headed back to the ship to study the transmissions. They didn't want to insult their hosts, but they were as curious as smalls about the missing history.

Once aboard the Pravda, they began sifting through the reams of data. Slowly a complete image of the Contented began to emerge. Their ancestors were savage creatures. Warlike in every way. At one point, an entire continent had been laid to waste. That, as it turned out, was the tipping point.

Molten Fury was a prophet, for lack of a better term, began

preaching that peace was possible but only with technology's assistance. He, and his followers, willingly subjected themselves to a procedure known as neural limitation. Simply put, they allowed a device to be grafted to the base of their craniums that inhibited anger. Any attempts to get angry were quashed immediately and replaced with other emotions and desires. Usually, sex as far as the cybers could tell. They based that assumption on the fact there were no families of any discernable structure and that the Contented seemed to enjoy open relationships.

No wonder the Sominids had enjoyed their stay.

Molten Fury, and his growing legion of followers who were disgusted with the realities of war, convinced the ruling parties of the time to make the neural limiter mandatory for every newborn. Within two generations, war and all of its attenuate sorrows, was eliminated.

Not long after that, it was decided to eliminate all records of who they'd been in the hope no one would ever long for the old ways.

As with anything, there were unintended consequences. In this case, creativity was dead as well. Their art and technology now would have been easily understood by any citizen from four thousand Suns ago. There had only been the most incremental changes. The cybers couldn't specify why, but this revelation disturbed them. It was as though the race had neutered itself.

Even so, they did have to admit this was a peaceful species. They all just wished the end result could have come about in a different manner.

There was nothing more here they felt they needed to learn. They broadcast a message of thanks and well wishes to the Contented. Then Natasha eased the ship out of orbit and to their next destination.

This time they decided to let the ship pick one randomly.

It wasn't like there was any agenda, and they certainly had the time to spare.

Their journey continued.

ओम'

Now:

Nkkl was pissed. How dare that motherfucker die before she could kill him? She'd watched the funeral, and subsequent immolation of the body, on the vid. It wasn't good enough. She'd wanted to be the one who killed him.

That bastard took her Lrrt, and that fact haunted her awake or asleep. Now all hope for revenge was lost.

If she were honest with herself, she'd have to admit that she wasn't handling any of this well. Her family and some of Lrrt's had moved in, picked up the household duties, and helped take care of the smalls. Their naming ceremony was coming up, and she didn't care. She didn't care about anything but revenge., and that was denied her.

Everyone left her alone, which was okay with her. The last thing she needed was to be buried in maudlin treacle.

We're so sorry for your loss.

Fuck you.

She'd been wearing the same clothes since Lrrt had succumbed, and she had barely bathed in that time. Only at the insistence, and with the assistance, of family did she even try.

None of it mattered.

Let her rot in her own filth. It was only fitting.

Somewhere in the distance, she heard the echoes of a door chime. It sounded suspiciously like hers.

Fuck that.

Hushed voices and scampering feet also created faint echoes.

Fuck them too.

Out of the corner of her eye, she saw a massive Nanek-Dev, stooping to clear the ceiling, come walking into the room. Lacking a dignified move, the burly mal sat on the couch across from her. He folded his large hands on his lap and sat there quietly for a few epi-cliks.

She patently ignored him while continuing to seethe silently.

Realizing that silence was accomplishing nothing, the mal finally spoke.

"I am Kondilar Singh, eldest mal spawn of Vandamir Singh, the late Sikh of the Guru to the Nanek-Dev, and the citizens of our lands."

Who gives a fuck?

Not being able to hear her thoughts, he continued.

"Your mate, Lrrt, was a good friend of my progenitor's."

The sound of Lrrt's name brought her, partially, to attention. He noticed that and decided to continue along the same tack.

"They liked to play Ti-Zam and drink spiced waters. They were also both fond of the various javas from around Arreti."

He couldn't tell it, but she smiled inside and started to pay attention. She knew Lrrt's fondness for javas better than anyone.

"All that said, it was only when my progenitor's will was read that we realized how close he and Lrrt truly were."

She'd only met the old brand a couple of times but knew that Lrrt cared for him and made an annual pilgrimage to see him. She'd never understood that. Business with the Nanek-Dev was almost nonexistent. It wasn't that they were isolationist or rude; they just seemed to have other things to do.

That was her impression, anyway. For whatever pathetic, miniscule amount of anything it was worth.

Still, she'd indulged his whim in this matter. Why not? He indulged her frequently.

That thought did make her smile.

Slightly.

He pressed on.

"You should know that a will of the Sikh of the Guru is a binding document. Since it was written while still alive, it is treated as a mandate, not merely his wishes. Because of that, this document has caused us some consternation.

"You see, Vandamir has decreed that Lrrt, or his legal heir, should be allowed to open a trading post near the south end of the Parliament, which is a major thoroughfare for commercial traffic.

"While we try to maintain self-sufficiency, we do see the wisdom of his words. We have many neighbors, some of whom could be our allies, and some of whom who might not, and ignoring them will not make that change. We have accomplished much on our own, but now it may just be the time for us to see what the world has to offer."

That made sense.

"If I understand Din-La inheritance laws correctly, you are now the sole voice of your household and Lrrt's business affairs?"

That was a question. She was sure of it. She wasn't sure how to answer. A simple 'yes' would be accurate, but she, somehow, felt there should be more. If for no other reason than this kind, deep, voice was resonating with her. He was helping her to see beyond her rage.

She noticed a jug of water and a few glasses next to her on a table. She filled two, hoped they were reasonably clean, handed one to him, and took a moment to think as she sipped.

"Are you the new Sikh of the Guru?" Her, long unused, voice was soft and raspy.

He didn't know it, but those were the first words she'd spoken since Lrrt died.

"No," he replied, "while my mind is facile enough, it is not suited for the world as it is now. We need someone who, like Vandamir, and Lrrt, can see ten moves ahead in Ti-Zam. We need someone who can shift through the shades to find the light. There are such minds among us, and I have recommended five to our Parliament. They will be making a decision soon."

She thought about that.

"Can the new Sikh rescind Vandamir's decree?"

He shook his large head.

"No, not without the unanimous approval of the Parliament, and then a vote by a majority of citizens. That has never happened."

They sat in silence for ten full epi-cliks. Finally, he understood the complete dynamic. Her strikingly un-Din-La appearance, her haunted eyes, her slight odor. All of it made sense in this new light.

It was not his way or the way of his brand, but this femme wanted revenge. She was stewing in hatred. That was what was holding her back, keeping her here.

That had to be dealt with. Sooner rather than later.

"I cannot help you get revenge upon the dead. No one can.

But, thanks to Vandamir, I can help you honor the memory of your loved one."

She nodded absently and poured them both some more water.

It was cinnamon-spiced, just the way Lrrt liked it.

She stared at her knees and whimpered softly. Then she began to speak in a rough monotone.

"I was barely nineteen Suns old when I met Lrrt. We were at the financial ball in Go Chi. So young, so eager. The entire universe is waiting for our wisdom. He asked me to dance. I said, yes. There was something about him. Something kind behind his eyes that intrigued me."

"We danced until they bade us leave, and then we walked through the streets, holding hands and laughing, until breaklight. I knew then that he would ask to marry me. He later told me he knew it then too.

"Less than a Sun later we were wed, and a post opened up in Kalindor. It was a small post, but respected, and in a land that showed much potential. Lrrt optimized profits and made friends with the locals. Within fifteen Suns, he headed the regional post here in Bharat and was spoke of as a possible C.E.O. someturn. A member of the board, at a minimum.

"Lrrt wasn't just loved; he was, in many ways, love personified. He accepted each brand on its own terms and never judged. He could work or play with anyone. His loss is Arreti's loss."

She heaved slightly but regained her composure.

"My loss. My greatest loss."

Kondilar smiled.

It was a warm, generous sight, and it eased her tensions even more.

"Then, Vandamir chose wisely. The gift of love is one of our truest treasures. If you will allow me, I will help you share Lrrt's legacy with my brand and all the brands of this world, and any others we encounter."

Now her smile was honest and true.

She had a purpose.

Her revenge would be to quash the Goptri's hate with Lrrt's love. If it was a strange and admittedly trite sort of revenge, so be it. As Lrrt used to say, "You work with what you have, not what you wish."

After contemplating everything, she stood and straightened her appearance as best she could. She then extended her hand to the giant seated across from her.

"You have a deal."

ओम'

Chandrack sat and stared at the lone piece of paper in front of him. It was a synopsis of the crime scene investigation. The head of that investigation, chosen by him, was Dr. Rhanda. She was a middle-aged Devi who housed one of the brightest minds on the planet., and, at the moment, that fine mind, and the body that housed it was sitting across from him wearing a lab coat with her six arms neatly folded.

The report was plainly written, with no ambiguities at all. Just the way he liked it. That, as it worked out, was both good and bad.

She, and her two assistants had found the grisly crime scene and documented everything. They'd seen the marks made by the hovercycle and even had found an old image of it in the home from which it had been stolen. Further, they'd found a small ledger in one of the backpacks and were able to know how much currency had been stolen.

It was a considerable amount.

He had given all the additional information along with the image of the cyke to the Kshatriya with instructions that, if the assailant was found, she was only to be documented and followed. No one was to apprehend her as he believed that she had accomplices, and he wanted to catch them all.

All of that was fine. Not entirely true, but fine, nonetheless. The fewer who knew what she was, the better.

But at the bottom of the sheet, it was noted that the investigators had also found a hair.

One that contained forty-six chromosomes instead of the customary fifty-two.

And it was that which was making him grimace. He finally looked up and looked her in the eye.

"There's a maker loose on Arreti," she said calmly, "and she's as murderous as advertised."

With no other recourse, he simply nodded.

"You know my mind, Chandrack, I can be of help."

He looked at her again. Contemplating the implied offer.

"Who else knows?" he asked.

"No one outside of this room as far as I know."

He laughed ruefully.

"There are a few others."

She looked at him quizzically.

"Well, let's see. There are all the ambassadors who were here, all the Kali who received their murdered sister's final transmission, by which I mean all the Kali, two more Kshatriya, and the two heads of palace security.”

Now it was her turn to laugh.

“Not the best-kept secret in the history of the Kshatriya, is it?”

“No, it’s not., and it is something we will have to deal with. But, for now, no one in their right mind would mention this since none of the brands involved want to be institutionalized.”

She laughed again, and he found that her laughter was lightening his dour mood.

“Fair enough, my friend. Tell me what you know and let me see if I can add anything.”

He shrugged. May as well use the best resources he could.

“Her name is Pearl. She was the last known maker who was a serial killer. A complete psychopath. She was put in stasis and given to Rohta. Or was given to Rohta and then put in stasis. The exact order is unclear.”

She whistled softly.

“Wow, you tripled down on Ti-Zam this time, didn’t you?”

He chuckled at that and continued.

“By method or methods unknown, the Goptri came into possession of her chamber and revived her. As best I can tell from his diary, which we recently found, she was his companion for two full suns, and then she killed him.”

“So she got a feel for the way things are, killed him, and then hit the road to start killing again?”

“Not exactly,” he said resignedly, “using a Din-La image replacer, you know the kind that lets you send holiday messages, and such, while looking like a monster or celebrity, she created an image of the Goptri, projected it on vid screens everywhere, and ran Bharat for five full Suns."

She was shocked by that revelation.

"A maker ran our country?"

"Yes and would probably still be doing so if she hadn't overreached her power and attacked the Yelda. That set off a chain of events that led to the ambassadors coming here. There was no way she could meet them, so she hit the road, as you put it."

He let all of that sink in for a while before he continued.

"We think she's disguised as either a Pangolin or a Guenon, and we have reason to believe that her destination is Chosun. As to the rest, you now know as much as I do."

They sat in silence for a while, and then she spoke.

"Well, that explains the increasing paranoia that had been coming from the palace. She wanted the pave the streets of Bharat with blood."

"All of Arreti, actually," he corrected.

"Wait a moment," she interjected, "I was at the funeral. That corpse was not five Suns dead."

"That corpse was not the Goptri's corpse either. It was a creation of the Din-La. That was why we performed the public immolation. Now no one can examine it."

She looked dumbfounded.

"That secret you better keep," she said, both impressed and disturbed.

"The number of brands who know about that is much smaller and more manageable," he absently said, pausing to gather his thoughts. "A Din-La medico will be testifying in front of the

Council of Fifty, in private, that she performed the autopsy on the Goptri, and that she discovered severe neural degeneration during the process. Essentially, he had slowly lost his grip on reality. She will further testify it could have been prevented by a once per Sun checkup."

"Why would she do that?"

"In her final act as Goptri, she had a Din-La named Lrrt savagely murdered. She sent his dying body to his family so they could watch him expire. I can't begin to fathom that level of cruelty and hope never to do so."

That shocked her almost as much as finding out that a maker had been running the country.

"This creature must be stopped," she hissed.

"No," he amended, "this creature must be killed. Hopefully, before this secret gets out to the world at large. Now, as long as we can do it without leaving her body in a street for all to see, we should be all right."

ओम'

She'd been hugging the western coast for the last five turns. While she'd spied a couple of possibilities, nothing struck her as exactly right. She brought her cyke to a stop near a series of docks in some small village. She neither knew nor cared what the name was.

She clipped the largest bag of goldens to her waist. She'd removed the local scripts from it when she'd realized that, while it made for sound local currency, it also invited conversations about the bearer's travels. Those were conversations she'd prefer to avoid.

At the end of the third dock, she saw a ship that was worthy of her attention. Wide and long with a large cabin. It even seemed to have pontoons. She quickly realized her error as she got closer and saw that it was a tri-hulled craft.

Although slightly grimy in appearance, she could see the motors, hidden in the rear, were well maintained. A boat like this would be fast, and ignored, two attributes she valued highly.

A large Nanek-Dev emerged from the cabin and quickly hoisted himself up to the bridge. He was unmistakably not devout. His long hair hung freely, and he was wearing nothing but a vest and denims. She knew instantly she'd found what she'd been looking for.

"Ahoy, Captain," she hollered, "is this ship for hire?"

He turned, surprised by the voice, and then made his way to the side of the boat, where he jumped off and landed in front of her.

"What do you have in mind?" he asked. His voice was deep and rough.

"About four or five turns, round trip."

He paused.

"That'll keep my crew from their families. That kind of sacrifice should be rewarded."

She'd already decided long ago to forgo any negotiations. She unclipped the pouch and handed it to him.

"They can buy new families when they get back."

He opened the pouch, did some quick calculations, and nodded. He then turned and whistled at the boat.

A wiry Guenon and a muscular Shiva emerged. The Guenon had an eye patch, and both were wearing nothing but denim work pants. She could tell she'd done better than she'd ever imagined.

The captain tossed the bag of goldens to the Shiva and motioned towards the cyke. The Guenon hopped over the side, started the cyke, launched it up in the air, and onto the deck. It was the most graceful and sure handling of a cyke she'd ever seen.

While the Guenon was securing the cyke to the deck, the captain pulled down a small ladder, motioning for her to board.

"So, where are we going on this four or five turn tour?"

"Southeast for now," she said as she flashed her most winning smile.

"Southeast it is then," he said as he remembered the goldens.

ओम'

Kshatriya Dayan looked like anything but a Kshatriya. His clothes were tattered and torn. Most Kshatriya were Pangolin; he was a Shiva. More accurately, at the moment, he was a smelly sad-looking, Shiva. Which was precisely what he wanted to be.

He had set himself up three turns ago with a bedroll and a begging cup next to a noodle stand owned by an aging, grey-skinned Dragon Lord. How that brand had come to be here was anybody's guess, but no one asked since his noodles were delicious. Every breaklight, after he opened his stand, he'd give the first bowl, with a little meat and vegetables added, to Dayan.

Dayan had never asked him to but was grateful for the kindness. When this was over, he would make sure that the old Dragon Lord got some reward.

He watched, as casually as possible, when the cyke pulled up. Indeed, Chandrack had known something. Who better for a hunted murderess to associate with than a gang of suspected smugglers who managed to stay one step ahead of the law?

He was able to snap several images using his portie and then send them, along with his exact GPS coordinates, to Chandrack. He was glad the portie could add that information. He had no idea where he was specifically. Nor did he care.

He returned the bowl to the counter and began to rise when

the Dragon Lord spoke and stunned him utterly.

"Ah, Kshatriya," he smiled good-naturedly, "I should have known. Even the poor bathe more than you. If you will do me the honor of bathing, I will do you the honor of allowing you to buy me a mid-break repast later at the curry house down the street. I happen to love curry. Noodles? Not so much."

After the initial jolt wore off, Dayan started laughing and kept right on laughing until he found an inn that accepted goldens in advance. Once in his room, he unrolled his bedroll and straightened out his casual greens.

But first, a shower. Then a bath.

Then a shave.

He looked like hell, but he could fix that. Twenty turns without washing could do that to a brand.

Later he would try and find out why a Dragon Lord cared about a murderess in Bharat.

ओम'

The boat had eased out of the dock and begun heading southeast less than a clik ago. The captain made sure to stay with the fishing boats that were headed out for a while. Then slowly, he pulled away. She sat in a chair bolted to the rear with her backpack laying on the deck to her right. She guessed the chair was there to make this look like a chartered fishing boat. Whatever the ruse, it was comfortable.

Once they were in open water, the captain turned over the helm to the Guenon, and walked towards her.

"There's java and sandwiches in the galley. For what you paid, you're entitled to eat."

She nodded and smiled again.

"Anyway, now that we're free of land, I wouldn't mind a little better idea of our course."

She had to agree with that. Just wandering around the ocean wasn't going to get done what she needed.

"Chosun."

He didn't even blink.

"Any special port or just Chosun in general?"

"Anywhere there is fine," she good-naturedly.

"Then I think that Hanging Cove will work. It's easy to navigate, and we can dump off this load of fruit we've got before it spoils."

Fruit smugglers? Well, there was a market for everything; it seemed.

He looked at her again.

"You don't mind if we make a few extra goldens for our troubles, do you?"

"Your business is none of mine," she replied in the most amiable manner possible.

"Fairly said, there's a cabin inside to the left, the one with the yellow door, that you can use. It has a private bath, and the door locks from the inside."

She nodded, pulled on her backpack, and headed inside.

The java smelled wonderful, and the plate of sandwiches looked delicious. Neither disappointed.

She saw the referenced door and went into the cabin. It was far more luxurious than she'd expected. Using her custom-built portie, she quickly scanned for monitoring devices. Satisfied there were none, active or otherwise, she locked the door and stripped naked.

The shower alone was worth the price she'd paid for this trip.

Once clean, she'd enjoy the hospitality of the crew, and then, in Chosun, she'd begin to show these brands their true natures. Enough of this peace bullshit. These fucking pods had been built for war, and labor, and, by fucking God, that's what they were going to do.

ओम्'

Then:

The beeping was annoying. A constant, repetitive noise that served no discernable purpose. But the hand holding his seemed familiar. He decided he liked it.

Slowly his eyes opened and began to focus.

Arti noticed and began to cry.

A nurse, stationed at the foot of his bed, pulled a portie from her breast pocket and began speaking quietly but quickly. Soon, there were two Din-La medicos in the room shining lights in his eyes and asking him questions.

Oddly enough, it wasn't readily apparent, but he finally noticed that he was alive.

The world wouldn't need a new Goptri just yet.

When everyone else had come to the same conclusion, he asked to be alone with his bride. The medicos and the nurse nodded and exited the room. He could see armed guards by the door. He guessed they were Kshatriya, but he didn't put too much thought into it.

When everyone was gone, he used the hand she was still holding to pull her close and kiss her.

Passionately, and for some considerable length of time.

Then, the reality of his presence made real; they both laughed.

"You are not to do that to me ever again," she said in the same fake angry voice she used on the smalls once upon a time.

"I will do my best," he said as sincerely as possible.

"Now, and forever we shall be together., and I must give you this," she said slyly smiling, "you truly have never been boring."

They were quiet for a few epi-cliks, and then he spoke.

"How long?"

She turned serious.

"You've been in a coma for six turns, and then just unconscious for three more after that," she said as she stared down at him, finally grasping that she wasn't a widow, "the bullet pierced a ventricle in your heart. It was not a given you would come back to us."

He nodded. There was nothing to say about this after that.

"Was anyone else hurt?"

"No," she replied, "the Kshatriya brought him down quickly."

"Who was he?"

"Is," she corrected, "he is still alive. His name is Khandahar. He belongs to a cult that sees all that you do and have done as evil. They, with no sense of irony, worship a version of Shiva."

That made him laugh again.

"What bothers the Kshatriya, who are all blaming themselves for this," she continued, "was the fact that he snuck a plastic gun past the detectors. They only detect metals, I was told. They are coming up with new plans for future security but don't want to turn simple events into a police state."

"Not everything can be stopped," he said softly, "nor should we try. What kind of example do we set by suspecting our citizens at every opportunity? No, there are some risks that need to be taken. We just have to live with that."

They sat quietly for a little longer.

"How did he get in?" Manish asked thoughtfully, "I thought we had a tight guest list."

"He was on it. He has a cousin on the Council. His cousin, Ruminahan, is also blaming himself for this. He says he knew nothing about Khandahar's leanings until after the attack. For whatever it's worth, the Kshatriya believe him."

"So do I," he said quietly, "I don't know him well, but he's been on the Council for a long time and served his region well. It would be difficult to do that if he had any dealings with a cult like that."

"Can I get you anything?" she asked, changing the subject.

"Actually, yes," he said as he smiled, "I'm both hungry and thirsty. How about a home-cooked steak and some bourbon?"

She laughed.

"You'll have to settle for citrus spiced water and whatever the medicos will allow."

She poured him a glass from the pitcher next to his bed and then left the room to see what she could find for him to eat.

As he sipped the water, he decided it was the best-tasting thing he'd ever tasted. Redundancy, be damned!

Arti re-entered the room, bearing a tray. When she pulled the cover off, he saw that it contained a bowl of yogurt and another of yellow gelatin.

Not exactly what he wanted, but after nine turns without food, he imagined it was all he could handle.

They were both as bland as bland could be. He pronounced them divine.

This whole being alive thing was *really* starting to grow on him.

ओम'

Ever since Vorulhska's amazing discovery twenty Suns ago, Queen Ominique ver-ANH-vonda had been working on getting the Ice Pirates more centralized. The scattered little villages of yore would not protect them if what she feared came true.

She kept those fears to herself, but the sight of maker tech, and all it implied – if there was tech like this here, there had to be tech like that elsewhere, and there was no guarantee that it would be used peacefully – was realized by all. That thought was enough to spur the brands to centralize. She had massive sections of the mountain behind the palace excavated and turned into living areas. Architects had decided that, once the area directly behind the palace was complete, they would bring the mountain over the palace's top to hide it even more effectively.

It had worked beautifully and gave the whole place a warm, natural feel.

Now, with the last of the villages moving in this turn, she felt she could finally relax.

As to Vorulshka herself, she had been made a member of the palace advisory committee and became wealthy off her licenses.

Her two smalls were now proud younglings and showed every promise that they would meet or exceed their matriarch's legacy.

Her husband Krashka was now the palace smithy. He used the discoveries to make new armors, hovercrafts, personal and commercial items, and other general need items. Far removed from the turns of sweating alone in a small shop, he now had twenty smiths under, and five more apprenticed to, him.

The centralization also allowed her to be more selective in how she protected her borders. While actual piracy was discouraged, any brand stupid enough to cross their lands without permission was fair game.

Just four turns ago, a Yelda supply convoy, made up of eight trucks, had been relieved of its drivers and parked in the palace.

The drivers were carted to the Yelda border to ensure this didn't happen again. Then, they were released with a warning. Next time, they would go home in boxes.

If at all.

She'd done all she could. The future would have to take care of itself.

ओम'

The Cybers had set one clock on the bridge to show how much time had passed in Arreti and left another on normal ship time. The former was a silly perk. Any of them could have calculated it on their own. It was just fun to see it displayed.

And they did enjoy fun.

They played complex games, worked on art projects, studied the archives whenever they wished, and all in all, filled their time as effectively as possible.

Of course, to them, almost no time passed when they were near light speed. But when they began their deceleration, the little clock adjusted to show that thirty Suns had passed back home.

As before, they began scanning for any transmissions that would verify that there was life in front of them. They weren't disappointed.

This seemed to be a vibrant system.

Unlike before, they concentrated on the historical as well as the linguistic data. Noor and Elmar took it upon themselves to try and develop a historical calendar once the language had been deciphered.

There appeared to be approximately thirty languages in use, but only one seemed to dominate. They focused on that one and began divvying up the data.

The others picked different subjects to analyze, so art, literature, and science would be categorized and studied.

They noted that, unlike the Contented, the primary language seemed to evolve as they neared. They would have to watch that so they didn't say anything that would be misunderstood.

The aliens called their planet Urrazna. They didn't seem to have a common name for themselves, so the cybers dubbed them Urraznans and entered that into the translator.

Natasha estimated that it would be seven Suns before they entered the system. That was plenty of time to work everything out.

They'd used some of the technology of the Contented to make the Bullet more agile in atmospheres. They'd also upgraded its engines to run on pure hydrogen. Being the most common element in the universe, they figured that wouldn't cause them any problems when they needed more.

The closer they got, the closer they were to working in real-time, compared to the inhabitants of Urrazna.

Natasha announced that the last full Sun would be in complete accordance with the transmissions, and they would be receiving them with only minor delays from their actual broadcast.

That was good news. It would allow them the chance to adjust for any linguistic drift.

Visual transmissions showed them to be a race of large semi-avian beings. They could fly for short distances, but their wings were primarily atavistic. They had a wide array of skin, and feather, colorings. The cybers looked for signs of racial profiling, just in case there was a dominant breed, but could find nothing.

That didn't mean there were no wars. There were., and some had been shockingly bloody. The underlying causes for them were still vague, but the overall arc seemed to be towards peace.

They were looking forward to their arrival.

ओम'

Now:

Queen Lynno Lee-NAH-xhuk sat looking at her guests. They'd briefed her on all that had transpired. Now they were using her dining area as a war room. Slazkik Ognor sat next to her with a constant look of bemusement on his face. Finally, after turns of just watching, he faced her and spoke.

"Well, I see you've solved our little problem of being isolationist."

She had to laugh.

"I'll admit this wasn't what I had in mind," she sipped a spiced java and continued, "I was thinking more along the lines of opening preliminary diplomatic relations, and so on. But, screw, you know what's happened, what we now face. Last I checked, the threat of global war should be the business of any brands on the globe."

"Oh, I agree," he said, still smiling, "you had no choice. But it still amuses me to see all these brands here, and none of them are slated to be executed."

"Well, that would be rude, don't you think?"

That got a hearty laugh from him, and the sound of the laugh got all the other guests' attention.

"Tell me, your Majesty," implored Ignop, "if it would not be uncouth to ask, may we know what has you so amused?"

She decided to tell him.

"For a thousand Suns, we Ice Pirates have fiercely defended our privacy. Our lands were ours; our thoughts were ours. Now? That's changed. Almost five hundred Suns ago, my grand-femme, Vorulshka, made an amazing discovery of maker tech. It was then that her queen, Queen Ominique ver-ANH-vonda, decided to move all the Ice Pirates out of our traditional villages and into one centralized location. Here, to be precise."

She sipped her java again before continuing.

"She was of the opinion that if there was one cache, there were more, and we had no way of knowing who would wield that tech. We know now the Din-La have access to much of it, and we know that the Eastern Warrens across the sea had some. At least weapons.

"Moreover, we now know that the Goptri had a complete maker undersea base at his, sorry, her, disposal. Being a maker, one who knew Rohta in fact, it stands to reason that she would know where more of them are located."

"And this made you laugh?" queried Ignop.

"No. What made us laugh was how quickly our old ways have fallen. In just a few short turns, we have gone from hiding from the world, and being feared to being completely open and honoring guests in our home. There is mirth in that."

Navi stood.

"Vadim and I were discussing this change as well. There will be no going back after this. No matter what happens with the Goptri, we must learn to work together, and that means we must be open to, and with, each other."

Damadora chuckled.

"In Bharat, we have different brands working together all the time. It was considered normal until the Goptri started breeding paranoia. I think that's why she kept the Kshatriya out on so many missions. If we had figured out what was happening, we would have confronted her.

"But you can take it from me, inclusion is better. You, and your brands, will get used to it. Soon enough, sights like this will be the new normal."

That gave them all pause for thought. For the Dragon Lords and the Shin-Sen, change was not readily welcomed. Things were different now.

Now… well, now is now, and as Navi had said, there was no going back. It was that simple.

Xho walked over to the now perpetual buffet and grabbed a sandwich.

"When this is done, we will need to each go to the other's lands and introduce ourselves. Let each brand see there is nothing to fear."

"Even more," added Gffk, "when this is over, we can set up travel methods so regular citizens can go to each of your lands. It is hard to hate or fear that which you are sharing a repast with., and, if it's done right, the Din-La can make a nice profit off it."

That got a hearty laugh all the way around.

Slazkik stood and raised his glass.

"To the bright future then. If we can survive the present."

As maudlin as that was, it also got a laugh, and everyone returned the toast.

Two messengers ran in. One handed a sheet to Xho, and the

other to Ragamooth. The palace had filters built in that disabled the use of porties, so they had to use the Queen's communication room to contact anyone outside.

Ragamooth spoke first.

"They have found her."

Xho looked up and shook his head.

"Maybe, but it seems she has found The Silence."

"What's that?" asked Mondara.

"The name of a smuggling ship we have long suspected of delivering arms to Chosun," he did not look pleased, "and it is a ship we have never been able to catch."

Ragamooth smiled an icy smile.

"Well, then, it seems that now would be an excellent time to see if we can work together. We know exactly where she was and generally where she's headed. If the Mayanoren can spare a couple of airplanes, and the Shin-Sen can send their sub, I am sure I can get Chandrack to commit a couple of Kshatriya speed boats to join the chase.

"By working together, we can eliminate search areas much quicker and close in on her."

Simple as that sounded, it took them four cliks to work out all the details. When they finalized the plan, they handed it to a messenger to be transmitted to all involved parties at once. The missive made it clear that the ship carried a severe threat to all the brands. It was not to be stopped. It was not to be boarded. It was to be annihilated.

ओम'

Clean and fed, she had put back on her Pangolin skin and resumed her seat on the chair at the back of the boat. She noticed, but did not comment on, the radar dish that had appeared in her absence. The ocean was calm, and the craft was making good time.

The two crew came up from the cabin, and both were openly armed. The Shiva handed the captain a sidearm belt with a sidearm in it.

She was mildly concerned.

The captain turned the helm over to the Shiva and walked towards her.

"Forgive the display of force," he cheerfully said as he neared, "but we've been in these seas for many Suns and know the dangers. Also, since you gave us enough goldens for us each to live comfortably for a Sun or more, I have to assume someone will be looking for you."

"That's prudent," she carefully agreed.

"Don't worry," he smiled, "we have our issues with some authorities. There's no benefit to us turning you over. In fact, all things considered, my guess would be that just meeting you would probably earn us a spot in front of the wall. That is not the end I envision for my life."

"Nor I," she had to admit.

"Would you like a weapon?"

The question caught her off guard.

"No, thanks," she said happily, "I have my own."

The captain nodded and headed back to take over control of the boat.

Well, now she was reassured she'd chosen wisely. But the captain had brought up a valid point. Someone was bound to be looking for her. She couldn't assume she'd made a clean escape from Bharat.

A mistake in that regard could prove fatal.

She began to review her surroundings. She'd already noticed that the boat was more sophisticated than she'd initially suspected. The hull was curved in odd places. She recognized the technique for making the craft as impervious to radar as possible.

That was a good start.

There were tiny vents in the two outer hulls. That was easy to figure out. They were torpedo launchers—possibly even missiles.

She had to assume that there were other weapons hidden as well.

She decided she was a little peckish and headed into the galley. As she entered, she saw the Guenon seated in front of an impressive display of electronics that had been hidden behind a wall. Radar screens, passive sonar, and what was obviously weapons controls, and those controls accounted for more weapons than she'd been able to discover.

Brands after her own heart. They weren't going quietly into anything.

She continued past him, grabbed a couple of sandwiches and a large cup of java.

With those in hand, she stopped off at her cabin and sat down.

She ate the first sandwich slowly and considered her options.

She realized that killing her at this point accomplished nothing for them, so she set that concern aside.

She now had a pretty good idea of what this boat, and its crew, was capable of.

But they would need more than just firepower if they were going to evade the Kshatriya and anyone they might be allied with now. Those possible allies were her damn fault, too.

Okay, she caused the problem; she should, at least, help fix it.

She opened up her portie and flipped it open to four panels to reveal a miniature soft screen.

She knew anyone tracking her would realize time was not her friend. That's okay. She'd slept with enemies before.

She pulled up a regional map and located Hanging Cove. The route they were taking was pretty direct. She looked for alternates.

If they pulled West and hugged the coast, they would only have to make a straight run at the cove after they'd cleared the southern islands when they got parallel. With the actual destination not having been decided until they were well at sea, that was a low-risk option.

Plus, there were a lot of fishing villages along that coast. Much easier to hide their wake from prying eyes in that miasma.

That thought gave her pause. The islands they were passing were once full of life. Now they were barren. They were rounding between what had been Singapore and Malaysia, and it may as well have been the islands of lost souls. Not a light, not a fire, shone on their coasts.

Even Bharat, with its massive population, paled in comparison to what once was. There was no overcrowding, no worries about resources, nothing like the things which had plagued humans at their peak. The brands had plenty of room to move and seemed to have no incentive to fill in the gaps.

Well, those were thoughts for another time.

For now, she highlighted the proposed path on her soft screen and left her cabin to talk to the captain.

She found him coming down the stairs and smiled.

Wordlessly, she passed him the soft screen.

He studied it for an epi-clik and then handed it to the Guenon.

He smiled after he studied it and then nodded.

The captain walked back out. Soon the boat made a hard left turn; she wondered if that was that port or starboard, and picked up speed.

She saw the Shiva come down and go to a cabin next to the galley. Good idea. Let him sleep now so they could run without stopping.

The food was good, the java was good, and things were getting interesting. Not a bad turn thus far.

ॐ'

Chandrack didn't ask; he just assigned eight Pearls to the airborne part of the search. Then he contacted the Parliament of the Nanek-Dev and asked for eight of their pilots to join as well. Within a clik, all sixteen planes were headed to the sea.

He also upped the ante on high-speed gunboats by adding all twenty stationed on the northeast coast. They might be able to cut her off. Indeed, they were as fast, if not faster, than anything else in the water.

He informed the ambassadors via a brief memo of what he'd done.

He wouldn't learn until later that they'd all done a facepalm, both literally and figuratively, when they got his note. The four Mayanoren pilots were informed they would have helpful company, and call signs were assigned to keep everything straight.

Dr. Rhanda watched the proceedings and smiled.

"What amuses you, Rhanda?" asked Chandrack.

"She makes mistakes too," she said, "she's not some super-being. She's smart and resourceful, but we can catch her."

She saw that Chandrack was confused, so she continued.

"Little things, those are what do her in. I've read the report the Pearls gave us, caught after a sloppy kill. No escape plan. Even here, she never truly had a plan 'B'; she just relied on her innate cunning to get her through.

"While this search is going on, you should have reports of any stabbings sent to you. I bet we find her path. If we do that, we can learn even more about her."

"You don't think this search will work, do you?"

"Millions of square kays of ocean for her to hide a small boat in. The odds are in her favor."

"Thanks for cheering me up."

She chuckled at that.

"Even if this doesn't work, we know where she's going. At first, I'd guess that she'll lay low, work behind the scenes. But that has to change if she's going to inspire the Chosun to the levels of violence she will need to feel satisfied. At least that she thinks she'll need. I doubt if she'll ever be satisfied."

He thought about that. While he'd rather end this as soon as possible, he knew she was right. They would need several plans.

"Also," he added, "she may not be going to Chosun at all. The Sugar Pirates would gladly welcome the kind of terror she would bring."

"I thought about that," she said, "and discounted it for now. She lives in chaos and death. The Sugar Pirates would be formidable, but they are organized now as opposed to when Manish was the Goptri, and she would be not much more than a figurehead with them. That would be a distant second option for her. No, she's going to Chosun first. She has to. She needs to."

ओम'

Dayan sat in the small curry house, waiting for the Dragon Lord to appear. He didn't have to wait long. The Dragon Lord had traded his soiled apron for a pristine, dark red suit. The perky-looking Ganesh waitress spied him and quickly ran over to seat him.

"You're early this turn, Mr. Lau. Was business bad?"

"No, quite the opposite," he replied, "but I haven't seen my friend here in a long time, and this was our only chance to get together."

She turned to face Dayan.

"Hi, I'm Nundalina," she said by way of introduction, "and I'll be your server this turn. Any friend of Mr. Lau's is welcome here."

"Hi Nundalina, I'm Dayan," he said cheerfully. Her perkiness was infectious.

"Very nice to meet you. Would you like a menu, or do you know what you want?"

"We'll have the curry sampler," said Mr. Lau, "I'm feeling adventurous, and I know my friend isn't afraid of new things."

She smiled and ran to the kitchen to place the order. She quickly returned with a bottle of Shin-Sen rice wine and two short glasses. Dayan wasn't much of a drinker, but he could handle his liquor when he had to. She poured them each a tumbler and returned to the back of the restaurant.

"So, Mr. Lau," began Dayan.

"Xhin, please."

"Very well, Xhin, you know what I am. I'd feel better if the Skizzi field were evened."

"Surely," replied Xhin pleasantly as he sipped his wine, "I am Xhin Lau, as you may have figured out. That is my real name, too, in case it matters to you. I am a reconnaissance agent for the twenty-three kingdoms of the Dragon Lords. Technically I'm retired, but this was a mission that required an agent who was, to be polite, expendable."

"That must have made you feel good."

Xhin laughed. It was a warm and genuine sound. Dayan immediately decided he liked the old Dragon Lord.

"It is what it is for brands like us. You know that as well as I. Nevertheless, I have been here for three and a half Suns now."

That was too long to be looking for the murderess.

"That's a long time to be selling noodles," noted Dayan.

"That's true. But the brands do seem to love them."

Dayan certainly understood why.

Nundalina arrived with a tray of appetizers. Dayan had to admit that everything looked and smelled amazing. He pulled a skewer of Prancing Fowl Tikka off the platter while Xhin stabbed a few of the crunchy Medhu Vadai with his fork. Before they could taste the first portion, Nundalina returned with two bowls of steaming Sambhar.

The vegetable-laden broth smelled delicious, so they both started there. Dayan would never tell his family, who prided themselves on their culinary skills, but this was the best food he'd ever tasted.

It took him a few epi-cliks to notice, but when he did, he smiled.

No noodles, anywhere.

"Well," Dayan decided to find out what he could, "you've been here too long to be chasing the same demon as me. Can you tell me what brought you here?"

"Certainly," replied Xhin cordially, "we know that some brand has been selling illegal arms to the Chosun. Some of our agents narrowed it down to this port. Later we narrowed it down to one boat, The Silence. That would be the boat that, I'm guessing, your demon hired. I have been here since looking for proof. So far, I have many hints but no proof. They do most of their business in the middle of the sea."

"Lovely," said Dayan, "imagine the odds of two different investigations colliding like this."

"Hmm," mused Xhin, "not as long as all that. The number of underworld factions on Bharat is small. It stands to reason one would work with another when the need arose. Can you tell me about your demon?"

"I'll tell you what I know," replied Dayan between mouthfuls, "she is wanted for three murders and may have been involved in others. The Kshatriya back at Pulinda Palace are still collecting evidence."

Xhin thought about that for a moment.

"Why didn't you arrest her?"

"Strict orders. Our superiors want to know all her associates. They believe she has been doing this for a while, and that can't happen without help."

Xhin considered all of that as he spooned the curd laden Thayir Idli onto his plate. Dayan decided to try the Khandvi, partly out of amusement, as it was the closest thing to a noodle dish available. The chilies were spicy but didn't overpower the coconut. He would mention this place to the Kshatriya the next chance he got.

"Your demon has some dangerous allies," said Xhin after he'd tasted the Idli, "I will need to check with my superiors, but I would think they would be willing to share what we know about them."

"That is kind of you," said Dayan, mildly surprised at the offer.

"Think nothing of it," smiled Xhin, "one of our ambassadors is, as we sup, sitting with a couple of Kshatriya in the palace of the Ice Pirates. It appears that relations between our lands are going to be more open. I hope so. Food this good should be shared with the world."

Dayan had heard rumors to that effect but had been a little busy lately to stay on top of it all. Nevertheless, Xhin was right. This was too good not to share.

They ate happily and engaged in small talk for two solid cliks before Xhin made his farewell. Dayan paid the bill and left the same amount as a tip for Nundalina.

Tipping wasn't common in Bharat, but it felt right to Dayan this time.

The two new friends had agreed to meet in two turns at the curry house for an even-fall meal, which Xhin promised would be even better than the mid-break repast they'd just shared.

Dayan was looking forward to it already.

He wandered around the streets of Dinari, the town he was currently in – a fact he'd found out over the course of the meal and gathered his thoughts.

He spied an empty wharf and walked to the end of it. Once there, he pulled out his portie and contacted Chandrack to let him know of the recent developments and his new ally's identity.

Chandrack brought him up to speed on the chase his images had spawned and the directions issued by the ambassadors. He also said he would see about getting ambassador Xho the Kshatriya file on the smugglers. Goodwill could go in both directions, he said.

Dayan had been with the Kshatriya for over fifty Suns and easily determined why he hadn't been allowed to arrest her here. For reason or reasons unknown, they didn't want her body, or the bodies of her allies, found.

With that bit of information out of the way, he began to look forward to the next meal.

ओम'

Then:

Rahan watched as Manish and Arti walked into the room. The Goptri was nearing the end of his time on Arreti and had retired ten Suns ago. Technically, Rahan, a large Devi with an easy laugh and brilliant mind, was the Goptri of the Mists now, but he couldn't think of Manish any other way.

After they sat down, he poured them each a glass of water, a tradition he admired, and then sat down himself. He hated to bother his friend during his retirement, but something had come to his attention that needed addressing, and he felt that he should be the one to do it.

"Thank you for agreeing to see me," began Rahan.

"We serve the Goptri," replied Arti.

That made Manish smile.

"What can we do for you, Rahan?" asked Manish.

"I will not sully the land with obfuscation," said Rahan getting right to the point, "it has been alleged by one of the new council members that you allowed the Omnium to go free. I would like to put that to rest, one way or the other, before panic grips the citizens."

Manish let out a heavy sigh.

"It's not that simple," Manish replied after a pause, "we didn't even know the Omnium existed until after we had taken Nirvana

II., and it wasn't until a full Sun after that when we found out that it had survived the explosions and made good its escape. By then, tracking it was, pretty much, impossible, but we did try.

"Pulinda assigned some elite troops to the task. They followed leads and clues all the way to the land of the Ice Pirates. It took them a full Sun to get that far. Then the trail died."

Manish paused to sip his water as Arti looked on quietly. Rahan was still amazed by how powerful Manish's voice could be.

"They traveled around the borders of the Ice Pirates. They didn't want to start an inter-brand incident, so they didn't cross them. As I said, they were elite, exceptionally well trained.

"After about twenty turns of trying to turn up anything that would give them a clue as to the whereabouts of the Omnium ..."

He sipped his water again.

"Let me back up a moment. They did not know they were searching for the Omnium. There were five cybers who had been seen piloting a hovercraft and headed north. We believed two of them contained the essences of the Omnium and Leader Elmar, but we did not share that information with the troops for obvious reasons. After that, we had no idea who the others may have been or if they were anyone at all. They could have just been service cybers the Omnium took with."

"Whatever the case, after twenty turns of scouring the borders, they decided to end their search. They were just getting ready to return when they ran into an Ice Pirate patrol. One of our soldiers, I don't remember which one, made a flag of truce and called to them.

"The others, I was told, loosed their safeties just in case things went south. It must have been a tense moment.

"Whatever the case, the Ice Pirates honored the truce.

Probably because our troops were on the right side of the border. The troops asked the pirates if they'd seen any cybers. After some back-and-forth clarification, and the remittance of a small bag of goldens, since the pirates didn't know what cybers were but knew that information had a cost, the soldiers got told an unbelievable story.

"It seems that eight brands wearing body armor, five fitting the basic description of our missing cybers, and three unknowns, had managed to get into what the pirates called a death camp. After about a turn, according to them, a rocket, leftover by the makers, they guessed, launched, and disappeared into the sky, never to be seen again.

"When we heard the story, we swore the troops to secrecy and destroyed all documents related to the search. We didn't let the Omnium go, but neither did we have any idea where it went. Nor could we track it anymore. Cybers don't have the same needs as we do, so it could have gone anywhere., and, obviously, having proof that the leader of the Technarcy was still loose and aligned with new allies somewhere above Arreti wouldn't have been good for morale."

Rahan whistled. That was a massive understatement.

This knowledge had to die in this office. He punched his intercom and asked his secretary to bring in the new council member. A couple of epi-cliks later, Manish and Arti were surprised to see a well-dressed Kali enter the room.

Rahan stood, poured her a glass of water as she sat down, and then resumed his seat.

"Manish, Arti, this is N'balan," he said, gesturing to the Kali, "she was just elected this cycle. She has promised to keep her concerns private until I had a chance to look into this matter."

"How is that possible?" asked Arti, "She's a Kali."

She laughed softly.

"We keep our thoughts all the time," she said by way of explanation, "it's just that we can contact each other if need be. Also, if any of us suffers a trauma or extreme pleasure, we all will know. Nothing like that is the case here."

"Then I want your solemn word that nothing you hear this turn will ever leave this office," said Manish, "I can promise you a complete answer to your questions if you agree."

She thought about that for a moment and then shook her head.

"If what I hear confirms my suspicions, then the public needs to know."

It was Manish's turn to think.

"Fair enough."

He spent the next clik telling her the tale and answering all of her questions. When all was said and done, she looked pensive.

"So, essentially," she summed up, "you're saying they left the planet in a maker's ship and have not returned."

"Correct," answered Manish, "had a maker ship landed anywhere on the planet, it would have set off alarm bells everywhere. I can't tell you where they are, but I can assure you where they're not., and that is here."

"Okay," she said after a pause, "this stays in this room. There would be nothing to be gained but fear if it got out. That being said, I'm not the only one who thought this. The rumor has been circulating for a while."

That was something none of them knew.

After sipping his water, Manish smiled.

"Easy solution," he said happily, "when I die, you can 'find' papers that will document the complete destruction of the Omnium and all the cybers. You can then make those public.

You can even say I never thought of it as a big deal since it seemed clear to me that nothing could have survived those explosions.

"As to the explosions themselves, we do have detailed records of their severity, so it's not that much of a leap of faith. They were devastating. An entire section of Nirvana II landed a kay away from where it started."

She nodded.

"A simple plan and a good one. Thank you, Goptri, for taking the time to speak with me."

"Any time," said Manish, "I haven't got a lot to do these turns, so my door is always open."

She started to rise and then stopped halfway.

"One thing though still troubles me," she added, "what do we do if they come back?"

"That," smiled Manish, "is one of the main reasons we created the Kshatriya."

She laughed and shook her head.

"You are something else," she said, still laughing, "the Goptri is wisdom, the Goptri is all."

She stood, bid her goodbyes, and left.

When she was gone, it was all Rahan could do not to laugh. Finally, he stopped trying and let out a belly buster.

"You have known this all these Suns and didn't even bother to leave your successor a note?"

"Scaring the crap out of brands isn't my style."

Rahan was still chuckling as the couple left. He wondered what other secrets the old brand carried. Then he figured that he, and the rest of the world, was better off not knowing.

ओम'

While the transmissions beaming their way were all linear and moving at a consistent speed, the same could not be said about the ship that housed the cybers as it ramped down from near light speed over a long arc. That caused some severe quantum garbling. They'd anticipated the effect based on the makers' research and theories, and they'd dealt with it when they'd gone to the homeworld of the Contented, so it didn't concern them.

What did concern them was the content of the materials they were able to review. They were still about two Suns away from being able to transcribe transmissions in real-time, but the closer they got, the bloodier Urrazna seemed to be.

And as far as they could tell, it wasn't one nation-state against another but one small group of beings against another. Repeated hundreds of thousands of times. There was no rhyme or reason to any of it.

It was beginning to look as though there'd be no there there when they arrived.

They began poring over the records looking for some clue. Any clue at all as to what was happening.

Abhijit and Zeenat set up a conference room on the second level and spread-out screens all over the walls. Each carried a different transmission. They were looking for keywords or phrases that appeared in all of them.

It was hoped that, with her ability to find nuances in languages, and his military history, they could solve this mystery. The others didn't just sit around waiting for an answer, however. Using Elmar and Noor's timelines, they began looking for any logical progressions that got the Urraznans to this point.

A Sun later, Abhijit called the rest of the crew into their

conference room.

"Boris," he began, "you once said that this ship might have been AI."

That was true but, as far as anyone else could tell, also irrelevant.

"Da," said Boris, confusedly, "it has the same quantum processors and trinary system layout as Natasha and me."

"We should look into that later," commented Abhijit.

Realizing that no one had the slightest idea what he was getting at Abhijit continued.

"By the time we get to Urrazna Zeenat, and I are estimating that eighty-five percent of the population will be dead."

That stunned them all.

"That is a conservative estimate, too," he said calmly, "based on their history of social mores and the current state of affairs."

Zeenat brought up fifty-two Urraznian words on the main screen and took over the presentation. Somehow, she even managed to make genocide sound sexy.

"Each of these terms is a gradation of the word 'honor,'" she explained, "and each specifies an acceptable amount of retribution for any perceived violations. What we are witnessing is the logical result of this codified system.

"For example, this word here," she said, pointing to the upper left corner, "is 'ugnaronoo.' We originally translated it as 'insult,' which is only partially right. It is what the victim claims prior to insulting the offender. So, if Abhijit had violated my ugnaronoo, I would be allowed to insult him, and that would be the end of that.

"To the opposite end of the spectrum, we have 'xhanaxi.' This is a violation of personal honor, so heinous that the victim is allowed to kill two immediate family members of the offending party. If two aren't available, the victim may choose any close relatives until honor has been served.

"All of this is legal under Urraznian laws.

"At this point, we will never know what initially triggered it, or which level of honor was so violated as to justify this, but we do know that one group was offended by the other two groups fighting, so they took up arms against them. Their 'yndrara,' the twenty-seventh level of honor that deals with unauthorized fighting on your property, had been offended somehow, and they sought retribution.

"Then the next group was offended by the fighting of the rest, and they took up arms against them., and so on, and so on.

"Neither Abhijit nor I can see any way to halt the cascade. It will only end through attrition. All of our models show it burning out when the population hits anywhere between ten percent to fifteen percent of its original totals.

"By the time we get there, they will be living a feudal lifestyle. At least the lucky ones will be. We suspect a sizable percentage will resort to pure barbarism. Abhijit and I also agree that making contact with the general populace at this point would be counterintuitive, but we will leave any final decisions in that regard to the rest of you."

There was nothing any of them could say. If they could cry, several of them would have. An entire race, one with so much promise, diving into extinction over a set of arbitrary rules. Then the Bharati cybers thought about the history of Arreti and realized how lucky they were. Manish's mad rebellion may have just prevented a similar outcome.

For Boris and Natasha, they thought back to the humans they'd known and the fickle things that led them to do the horrible things they'd done.

They'd no moral high ground in this matter. All that was left was mourning.

"Da, wait," piped Boris, "what does any of this have to do with this ship once having been AI?"

If Abhijit could have smiled, he would have.

"Before this world headed to Zanubi on rails, they were building an artificial intelligence. From what we could tell from the propaganda we sifted through, it should be as powerful as any of us. Maybe more so. Furthermore, it appears to be built on a system, unlike anything we know.

"The scientists working on the project had set themselves up near the northern ice cap, far from any other beings. If we take the Bullet, and come in directly over the northern pole, we should be able to easily access the base without being seen by the regular citizens.

"Zeenat and I agree that this could be an excellent opportunity to see what our makers may have missed and to find out if there are any benefits to this new technology."

They all looked at the two of them, impressed, and then agreed. At least this trip wouldn't be a total waste.

While they'd all seen the various, spotty, reports on the AI, none of them had paid too much attention to them since they'd, or so it seemed at the time, more pressing issues.

Now they began poring over every bit of data they could find. The more they learned, the more excited they became. If the reports were right, this was an entirely new way of looking at artificial intelligence.

There was a mind there that was unlike any the universe had seen as far as they knew. Maybe it could be saved.

ओम'

Now:

Gonpodin, a burly Ganesh with a fondness for spicy foods and profanity, headed his speedboat into the dark. Now that they'd rounded the southern islands, the twenty boats sent out by Chandrack had been spaced about a kay apart. Close enough to aid each other should the need arise, and far enough apart to cover a lot of ocean with their scanners.

Ahead of him, and slightly to the left, sat Ajanandi, a sinewy Lakshmi who shared Gonpodin's fondness for spicy foods and profanity. He was the boat's gunner, and the four barreled, high caliber machinegun was live, and targeting. There are no safeties on this turn. Not with their orders.

To the rear sat Blandaladen, a massive Shiva with a colorful collection of body art and fondness for femmes who liked to arm wrestle. Even so, he would no more try spicy food than he would drive needles into his eyes. He was manning the electronics. He had access to radar, sonar – both passive and active, all inter-squad communications, and control of the missile arrays that hung on each side of the boat.

Gonpodin knew and trusted them implicitly. They'd been on hundreds of sorties together and even survived the occasional bar fight. Which, now that he thought of it, always seemed to revolve around Blandaladen.

That could be discussed later.

"Why don't we have any of the big muthas?" asked Ajanandi, referring to the larger warships that Bharat had.

"Too far away," replied Gonpodin, "It's up to just us and our stunning good looks to save the world again."

That got laughs from all three. It had been up to them before, and they were comfortable with that.

After skimming at full speed for the last turn, they were headed north with the plan of staying just to the west of the waters claimed by the Chosun. Those were ten more kays further out from shore than the waters accorded them by various treaties, but no one wanted to start a war this turn.

And the Chosun would threaten war at any perceived insult.

Although the boats could attain speeds of over ninety kays per clik, they were currently cruising just around twenty. Speed was not an asset when you were trying to find a drop of oil in a puddle of dark water.

The Shin-Sen mini-sub was covering the southern tip of the peninsula and was poised to stop any craft making a run for the eastern shores. The Bharati planes were mixed with the Mayanoren and the Nanek-Dev and were searching in grid patterns over both the eastern and western shores of Chosun.

None of the soldiers on the boat were stupid. They knew that despite all of their resources, the odds were stacked heavily in favor of the fugitives. There was just too much empty ocean to hide in.

Each of the soldiers was wearing a helmet with a transceiver built in. That way, they would never have to yell to be heard above the sounds of the ocean or any battle. Gonpodin was a firm believer that clear communication was the key to survival.

There were several thermoses of java by each of them, along with a cooler full of whatever foods they liked. This would be a long hunt, no matter what, and being hungry or tired wouldn't help.

Gonpodin stared at the darkling skies and wondered how long it would be before he, and his friends, could step into a bar and leave their worries on the pier.

ओम'

You are such a pretty girl. The world is your oyster, and you are its pearl.

I love you, mommy.

You listen to me, little missy; no one gives you anything in this world! If you want something, you take it! You don't let any asshole get in your way! Now get back out there and get that damn ball!

Yes, mommy.

What the hell is wrong with you? Why were you letting him touch you like that? You're five, for fuck's sake! You wanna be some whore? Is that what you want? You wanna be a five-year-old whore?

I'm sorry, mommy. We were just curious.

I really am sorry. Please stop hitting me.

You are such a pretty girl. The world is your oyster, and you are its pearl.

I love you, mommy.

She patted the backpack in her room and smiled. Mommy was right. If you want something, you just take it. Everything else be damned.

She had gotten the ball back that day. She'd given two boys bloody noses to do it, but she'd done it. She never did understand why they wouldn't let her play anymore. That was the game, wasn't it? Get the damn ball and keep it.

And, boys, she'd figured them out too. All they wanted was to fuck. Well, fine, fuck away, assholes. She'd take what she wanted when they were done., and she had. Many, many times., and her mommy would be proud of her here too. She'd never taken a thing from a living boy. She was no whore, after all.

She remembered being nine. By then, she had realized that most kids didn't want to play as she did. Some of them, like the kids on the Skizzi ball team, were just mean to her. They'd pull her hair and call her names.

None of the other kids would sit with her at lunch, so she just ate outside when she could.

Some people, like her math teacher Mr. Mishar, were friendly to her. He'd give her candy and let her sit on his lap. If she'd been extra nice or gotten a good grade, he'd let her slide her hands in his pants and play with whatever she found.

She'd liked that game a lot.

Sometimes things got messy, but that was even more fun.

He'd sit there moaning while she licked her little fingers clean.

Whenever that happened, he'd always made sure she got extra candy.

When she'd gotten older, she'd realized there was probably something horribly wrong with Mr. Mishar, but she hadn't cared. He'd been nice, and they'd had fun.

How could anything have been wrong if they'd both gotten what they wanted?

But nine was the magic year. That was when she'd found her true calling.

She'd been playing with a broken bottle in the back yard. She'd slipped, and it had cut her arm deeply. She still could see the scar. Her mommy called her a clumsy little slut, which seemed accurate to her young mind, so she didn't complain, and then took her to the hospital.

She was gushing blood and getting lightheaded when they got there. The doctors rushed her into the emergency room and began treating her right away. They'd cleansed the wound, it was so pretty, and then the magic happened.

They'd taken a needle and thread, almost unheard of back then with all the spray-on wound healants, and began lacing her skin back together. The doctor worked slowly and carefully until he'd finally closed the gash. Then he'd tied it off and cut the thread.

He was saying stupid stuff about how she'd be all right, and blah blah stuff, but she hadn't cared about any of that silly stuff. She'd seen flesh made art and couldn't wait to try it herself!

She decided to experiment first. The doctor had been excellent, but she'd never used a needle and thread before, and she didn't want to fuck anything up.

She'd picked up a tablet at the school library and taught herself how to sew. The sewing kit she'd bought had come with a little knife to cut the thread. It became her fondest possession.

About a month later, just before she was to go back and have the stitches removed, she'd caught a mouse. It was cute, and grey, and warm to the touch.

She'd slit it from its throat to its tail and then sewed it back up again. It didn't live, but that was neither here nor there. She'd been interested in the art of it all, not the medicine.

Over the ensuing years, she'd practiced her craft on cats, dogs, and even a pig.

But that wasn't enough. She'd needed something, someone, to know what she'd done. To be aware of the gift she was sharing.

When she turned thirteen, she had another magic year.

A transfer student from New-Idaho arrived. His name was Bobby Collins, and his dad had taken a job at some big company. He was tall and pale with bright blue eyes and shiny red hair.

He was also horny for her from the second he'd laid eyes on her, which was understandable. She'd blossomed in all the right places.

He was one of those kids whose parents had lots of money, so he figured he could do whatever he wanted.

She'd decided to let him.

After making him promise to keep it a secret, they'd met in the woods near a creek. It was a secluded spot no one ever went to.

It was a typical, beautiful Indian day. The skies were clear, and the air smelled clean.

She'd brought a simple backpack with some of her supplies, and Bobby had brought a picnic lunch and a bottle of wine he'd stolen from his mom. He'd been getting drunk and horny, and she'd been impressed with the large bulge in his pants. It seemed like it wanted to escape and run away.

It would have been smart if it had.

He'd pushed her hard to the ground and had begun to paw at her clothes. She'd gotten her hands inside his pants just like she'd done with dear Mr. Mishar and grabbed his throbbing cock while moaning, "Give this to me. Give it to me now."

Naked, sweaty, writhing, and moaning, the next couple of minutes were electric. Then he'd exploded inside of her. That was okay. Like all girls who'd attained puberty, she'd had her implant, so she hadn't been worried about that.

Her mommy had made sure of that.

"Don't need no more damn brats" was her motto.

When he was done, he'd collapsed and rolled over next to her.

Much to his surprise, she'd crawled on top of him while opening her backpack.

"My turn," she'd said quietly, and then plunged a hunting knife into his chest.

The blood she'd expected, of course, but the copious amounts of shit and piss that he'd expelled caught her off guard. The smells were fresh and intoxicating. The whole experience proved she'd been right. This was the highest form of expression.

She smiled at the memory.

She'd cut open his chest into two flaps. In a moment of divine inspiration, she'd cut off his cock, and balls and sewn them to his heart. Then she'd carefully closed the flaps and neatly stitched them shut. She'd had to admit that her needlework looked pristine.

When she was done, she'd bathed in the creek and got redressed. His body was getting cold by then, naturally, but that was okay. She'd taken all of his money, enough to live on for a while by her standards, and then grabbed two of the sandwiches that were left over and tossed them into her backpack. She'd left the wine. She'd decided she didn't like the cheap shit.

With nothing behind her and her art in front, she'd headed north to Calcutta.

Freedom beckoned.

ओम'

Zsst stood in front of the Council of fifty and quietly explained her findings. She spoke of how the Goptri's decline, and all of the attenuated paranoia, could have been avoided with a simple once per Sun checkup.

She described the pathology of the decay, taking care not to disparage the memory of the beloved Goptri. Several of the Council members were medicos before they were elected. She made sure they had unfettered access to the documents and findings.

She continued to clarify and carefully hammer home the fact that a mind that's diseased doesn't know it's diseased, so it won't seek help. In fact, contrariwise, it will eschew help as it drifts further and further away from reality.

A world of a brand's making is far easier to negotiate than the one the brands live in.

After four cliks of questioning, the Council voted to seal all documents related to this issue and leave the general impression as it was. Their Goptri cared for them and was taken far too soon. That was enough for them to know.

They also agreed to make sure the next Goptri would have the help they could give him or her to try and set things right.

If that was remotely possible anymore.

Zsst was dismissed so that they could plan the next step in private. Zsst knew that, by law, the Goptri could not be chosen from members of the Council or the Kshatriya. After that, every citizen was technically eligible. Given that the second Goptri, Rahan, had been a college professor when he got the call, history seemed to show that the Council took those parameters to heart.

Once outside the Council chambers on the north end of Pulinda Palace, Zsst opened her portie and contacted Gffk. She noted that, while nothing was said directly, the questions she'd been asked appeared to indicate that she'd caught them off guard as they seemed to have already narrowed the list of candidates.

Gffk has been concerned about that, but there was nothing any of them could do. It took time to forge all the necessary documents and records, especially when they had to keep the number of participants involved small.

He thanked her for all she'd done, and they disconnected.

Zsst knew that the Din-La occasionally, like any brand, bent the rules. This was the first time, as far as she knew, that they'd outright broke them.

Then again, she'd spent some time with Nkkl. If breaking precedent was the cost of setting things right, so be it. What happened to Lrrt must never happen again.

There was a cantina in the local trading post. She decided that a drink, or four, was most definitely in order.

ओम'

Then:

The Omnium stared at the facility on Urrazna and admitted that it had no idea how this building was standing. Covering a half-acre, it was a veritable quincunx of contrasts. Smaller on the bottom than on the top. By a factor of five. In addition to that, not one level was symmetrical with the others. One was oval, one was rectangular, one was similar to, but not quite, a trapezoid.

The whole thing defied logic and any known laws of physics it had been programmed with or later learned.

It was an affront to all things rational. It simply should not be.

Yet it was.

The Omnium could tell, by the utter lack of commentary, the others were having similar reactions.

Before they could make themselves properly known, two Urraznanian scientists came out. The cybers recognized them as such by their blue boots. Why scientists here wore blue boots instead of lab coats or something similar was something they'd never discovered.

The scientists looked perplexed, then afraid.

Zeenat stepped forward and addressed them in their language.

"Do not be afraid," she started helpfully, "we are visitors like the Sominids, and we come in peace."

One of the scientists bobbed his head, which they knew to be a negative reaction, and then spoke in a rapid dismissal.

"You are nothing like the Sominids. They were organic."

Well, that was one less thing to disclose.

Both of them started bobbing vigorously, and then the second one spoke. Its voice was high and stressed.

"You have come to steal Ugnaronoo."

"No," replied Zeenat carefully, "that is not, and will not, be our intent. We came to meet it. To share our knowledge with it, and, hopefully, get fair trade in return."

She kept her arms bent up and her hands palms down in the familiar Urraznanian gesture of compliance. The other cybers mimicked her actions.

"We don't believe you. We don't believe anyone anymore. You are here to steal Ugnaronoo, and that is all there is to that."

With that, the two scientists rushed back inside, and the cybers could hear doors being bolted.

"Well," said Pran dryly, reverting to Common, "this is going exceptionally well."

Elmar seemed confused.

"They named one of the greatest inventions in their history 'you insulted us?'"

"I noticed that," said Zeenat, "but I have no idea what to make of it."

"I think I do," stated the Omnium.

It stepped on the path that led around the bizarre building until he came to an area with four doors and nine windows, all in one small locale. Nothing on this world or Arreti would have had any use for any of them

"You can stop now," said the Omnium in Urraznanian, "we truly do mean you no harm. We are travelers who have come a long way to meet you. I give you my mind as an offering of peace."

It slid back a panel on its left hand, drew forth a couple of wires, and clipped them to one of the windows. Soon the building began to moan.

It was a low, mournful sound.

It was followed by the sounds of scraping and the sight of the impossible structure beginning to change shape. The building released the wires on the Omnium's hand and slowly assumed the form of a large geodesic dome.

The first scientist they'd spoken with stepped out.

"Ugnaronoo says we were wrong, and you are welcome. Please enter in joy."

All of the cybers looked at the Omnium with a mixture of awe and surprise.

But they followed the scientist in anyway.

They were flummoxed to find over two hundred beings in the building.

Zeenat stepped to the fore again.

"Greetings to you all. We are the cybers of Arreti."

She then introduced them individually.

The building rumbled, and then a basso-profundo voice emerged.

"We are Ugnaronoo. We are the last well of sanity. We are the joy of peaceful minds. We are pleased to meet you."

"And we you," said the Omnium, "thank you for sharing with me this turn."

The idea that the scene outside had been a two-way interaction hadn't occurred to the cybers. They were all curious to know what transpired but knew that now was not the time to pursue it.

"You were sad for your world. You were hurt by it. We are sad for our world. We are hurt by it. You are pleased with your companions, even if you may never fully understand them. We are pleased with our companions, even if we may never fully understand them.

"You were right to contact us. There is more in common than we would have thought."

The Omnium stepped a bit forward.

"We, my companions and I, are exiles and explorers. In regard to the first, we are here, and then we will, some turn, move on. As to the latter, we hope to learn from you."

"The glimpses we have seen have changed everything. There is much that needs to be shared."

"Agreed," answered the Omnium, "but you must share with all of us. Each of us has different knowledge, different experiences. One alone will not give you what you need."

"True, that may be, but, for now, we can give you one thing that you will need."

"What is that?" asked the Omnium.

"Gravity. You will need gravity to save our kind."

ओम'

Scar was the undisputed king of the Sugar Pirates. Which, by their laws, meant some brand or another was always trying to kill him. That was as it should be. He'd killed Wound in a fair assassination to get the throne in the first place.

The rituals and rules of those who followed Vudu were myriad and, to some, open to interpretation. While he wore the strictures lightly, he knew that most of the brands that made up the Sugar Pirates did not. They took them quite seriously, indeed. While they had their one main God, they mostly left Him alone to run the universe. The many smaller gods were good enough for turn to turn prayers. They handled everything from food to fertility and from love to war. Which, as far as Scar was concerned, pretty much covered everything.

Worn lightly or not, he had a small shrine to Ogou, the warrior spirit, in his office, and said a short prayer to it each turn when he came in. He even made sure that it had rum and food in case it visited. There was no harm in being friendly with a being who could change your life forever. He was cynical, not stupid.

Scar was a Chien-Bois. Standing a meter, and a half, covered with dark brown fur, he had a round head with protruding triangular ears and deep-set black eyes, and he looked as mean as he was. His smile consisted of nothing but razor-sharp, pointy teeth.

He was wearing two vests. The inner one was off white and cut above his waist. The second was Royal blue and hung to his knees. Neither was fastened at the moment. He wore dark red trousers, which were tucked into knee-high, black leather boots. He had two rings on the middle fingers of his right hand, and both his ears were pierced several times.

Though heavily muscled, he could move surprisingly fast and swim as well as any fish. He was deadly in any environment.

He had dark nails on the tips of his fingers. They were sharp, and he kept them filed to lethal points.

And, right now, one of those points was dragging across a map.

You could get a good bounty on the open seas if you found the right ship at the right time, not always a given, but it was never enough. His colonies were looking to him to figure it all out. To get them the goldens and supplies they needed.

To that end, he'd come up with a bold idea.

The Lightless Lands held plenty of riches, but you had to go to the south end of the continent and then march inland for an extended period. He didn't like the idea of being that far from a means of escape.

But as long as he was looking that far south, why not look a little farther?

And then, once you've gone south of landfall, why not head a little to the east?

Bharat had hundreds of coastal villages, and the Sugar Pirates had a decent sized navy. Usually, the pirates preferred to work alone or in small groups, but he was about to change that. The Sea Killer and the Cursed Fates each carried thirty guns. Cannons actually. They could pummel a target from a kay away. The ships were wooden but had stout engines and were solidly built. There was nothing outside of the Eastern Warrens that could match them, and he had no intention of heading that way now.

The Cove of the Red Wind sported fifteen midsize gunboats that could make a long trip, and Blood Hunger had a couple of seaworthy barges that could be used as troop transports.

This could work.

This WOULD work!

No more of these ticky-tack raids. No more of these 'scare them into submission' tactics. The hell with the Kshatriya. They would hit the coast like a hammer hits an anvil.

The trick would be to get in and get out before the Kshatriya could regroup or get reinforcements. Not as tough as it sounded.

They would split into two groups just as they neared their target. One would take the first village, and the other would take the other. The Kshatriya were excellent warriors, but they were few in number. The rest of Bharat's military didn't scare him at all.

He would lead one invasion, and have his second, Claw, lead the other.

The Sugar Pirates were a genetic cacophony. He was no longer sure how many brands spanned the six hundred islands they held. He knew the majority of them were agrarian, but they looked to Scar, and all the leaders of the Sugar Pirates for protection. A service he happily provided for a small fee.

Still, the rest of them needed adventure and goldens.

What he had in mind would provide both.

He knew that this would only work once or twice. They would need to diversify their target list if this was to be a longer-term solution. Kalindor was pleasant in the Dark Sun, for example.

That could be all dealt with after he proved this concept worked.

He turned from the map and saw his assistant Pateet, a Solenodon, calmly polishing his nails. Although made from a venomous rodent-esque mammal, those traits had been lost to history. His fluffy cream-colored fur and delicate demeanor belied nothing. He was soft and cuddly, as all modern Solenodon were, which was his contribution to the world.

Pateet, for reasons Scar didn't care about, wore nothing but teal clothing.

Whatever the case, something had to calm him when he needed calming, and he didn't want a bride. Not now. Maybe later, if he survived being king.

Nevertheless, work before pleasure. He called Pateet over and gave him specific instructions on the assembly he wanted called in two turns. Pateet wrote them down, read them back, and left to make sure they were followed.

The Din-La wouldn't trade with them because of a couple of minor misunderstandings in the past. So a new path needed to be made.

If his colonies were to be denied a seat at the buffet of trade, they'd just have to kick in the door and seat themselves.

Many channels could lead to open trade. He was about to travel the oldest, and surest, there was.

As good old Wound used to say, "That which can't be negotiated, can be killed or taken."

ओम'

Now:

Queen Lynno was still bemused at the turn of events that led her here. Her staff, the ambassadors, and the Pearl all mixed freely, all focused on a common goal. That may have been the key; she mused, the way to keep everyone focused in the same direction. She worried it might not continue when this all was over.

Maybe it would. There were always challenges to be met.

Various vid panels had been set up so they could keep watch on the search in real-time. They'd access to everything from radar to sonar to straight visuals. The investigation had been gone on for four solid turns, and, thus far, nothing had been revealed.

It was almost as if the ship lived up to its stealthy reputation. That it could actually run silent and unseen. Certainly, Xho, and the rest of the Dragon Lords, seemed to think so.

Mondara and the Mayanoren leader were sitting off to the side, chatting, and sharing a pot of java. They'd been together almost since the group had returned to the palace. That would be an interesting relationship to watch as it developed.

They could see on the monitors that the picket of Kshatriya boats was about halfway up Chosun's length. The planes were covering areas already covered in case the fugitives backtracked.

Although it bothered all of them with how thin they were spread, they knew that adding more resources would only lead to confusion and, possibly, an accident. No one wanted to jeopardize any lives if they didn't have to.

Chandrack changed the search patterns every so often to prevent boredom and predictability. The only thing left untouched was the moving picket line of boats. They stayed out of any territorial waters, and, between them, their radars could sweep almost the entire width of the straight.

'Almost' being the operative word as far as everyone was concerned.

It was even-fall again, and the palace staff replenished the buffet with more substantial foods. All of the ambassadors had offered to chip in for any costs, but, so far, Lynno was enjoying being the hostess. It was an unusual experience for her.

Slazkik had been incredibly helpful, much to her surprise. He coordinated the staff and made sure that couriers were at the ready no matter the time of the turn. He'd never run a team before, but all his military training and experience seemed to apply here as well.

They settled in in mixed groups around a series of tables and enjoyed the food while worrying about what the even would bring.

ओम'

Pearl sat in the cabin, watching the smugglers work. The precision with which they divided their duties spoke to long Suns of military training and working together. They trusted each other implicitly. She was just a package to be delivered.

The Guenon got up from his station and tapped on the cabin door where the Captain was sleeping. Quicker than she'd thought possible, he was out and pulling on his vest. He looked at the screens and then cursed softly.

"It seems," he said, turning to her, "that they've set up a Kshatriya picket line to trap us. We count eight boats in range."

She thought about that.

"How far are we from Chosun?"

"About forty kays from the waters they claim as their own. Or fifty from the ones acknowledged by treaty."

He looked back at the screens and then turned around to face her.

"Would they risk a war to capture you?"

It was a simple question. One that had many possible answers. But, given the enormity of the search she was seeing, the possibilities narrowed.

"Yes," she said simply, "I think they would."

He nodded and returned to the screens.

He'd been in this business long enough to prefer an honest answer to a good one.

"At their current pace, they'll be on us in a couple of cliks," he said without turning, "I don't think we can afford to run silent anymore. It'll be tight, but we stand a better chance of outrunning them than we do hiding now.

"Besides, we have some friends there who will look out for us."

"You must have the best fruit in the world."

He looked nonplussed for a moment and then laughed.

"You could certainly say that."

He gave the order to lose the weapons and she watched, partly in awe, as four machine guns appeared fore, and a large, anti-aircraft gun appeared aft.

The Shiva came racing down the stairs, unlocked a panel in the wall, and removed two large boxes of ammunition. The captain followed him outside once he was loaded up.

She watched on the screens as the Shiva took a seat on the aft gun, and the Guenon tested the sighting and functionality of the fore guns remotely.

All three donned headsets with mics. There would be no misunderstandings between them. This boat would not go down easily.

She went to the galley and grabbed a sandwich and a cup of java. May as well. She knew that now, no matter what, she'd be more bane than boon if she tried to help. She sat down just as they completed the last check of the weapons.

As soon as everyone seemed satisfied the guns were in superb working order; she heard the engines begin to whine.

The next part of her adventure was underway.

ओम'

"I've got a hit," exclaimed Blandaladen, "and it's picking up speed, headed for Chosun."

Gonpodin cursed loudly but aimed the boat at the coordinates provided. He didn't bother saying anything else as he knew that Blandaladen was notifying all of the other searchers. It didn't take him long to figure out that he was going to violate a treaty or two. He dialed up a private channel on the headset and contacted Chandrack.

"It looks like we have her, but she'll hit Chosun waters before we get her.”

“Just get her,” came the terse reply, “we’ll deal with the rest later.”

That was clear enough.

He didn’t know much about their prey, but if she was worth possibly starting an international incident over, she was worth a lot. At least to some brand. He just knew they were going to earn one of the Jung’s legendary letters of ‘Bad Faith Diplomacy’ or something just as scathing for what they were going to do this turn.

That brand did like his harshly worded missives.

He gave the weapons-free order and pushed the throttle to its limit. Soon they were skipping across the waves at reckless speeds to kill their quarry.

ओम’

Pearl Glistens in the Early Dew had no idea how she’d ended up on the wing of a Mayanoren pilot and was no longer sure she cared. Politics were beyond her. Admiration of skill was not, and this pilot was very, very, skilled. A part of her hoped never to be on the wrong side of those deadly planes ever again. She was well aware of how lucky she’d been last time.

The target's coordinates came in from the gunboat, and both planes effortlessly changed course to intercept. They were a few hundred kays away, but now was not the time to play things safe.

The two planes broke the speed of sound as they dropped to just above the waves.

This was going to be close.

ओम’

The Captain pulled his boat to the north a little to add some extra distance between them and their pursuers. It had the added advantage of giving his allies some extra time to get in a position to protect them.

He knew from reports that he was getting from his mate that the Kshatriya were not slowing down and would soon cross into the Chosun's territorial waters. It was either the ballsiest bluff he'd ever seen, or they truly were willing to go to war over this Pangolin femme.

He was pretty sure Kshatriya didn't bluff.

When he got the next report detailing air support headed their way, he knew it wasn't a bluff. Whatever this Pangolin had done had to be worse than anything he'd ever imagined, and he'd imagined, and done, some horrible things.

Well, she'd paid upfront and had never promised him a tedious journey. He was just going to have to deal with it.

ओम'

The excitement in the room was palpable. From the first announcement on every single brand crowded around the screens. Food and conversation were both forgotten. If the cameras weren't showing much, the radar screens certainly were.

Xho, whose lands had been so injured by the illegal weapons, watched closer than anyone. Except for maybe Chen and Wong. Given the speeds the target boat was attaining and how it had appeared from nowhere, they were convinced that the Kshatriya had happened upon the smugglers.

But they could see the same information as everyone else. This was no sure thing. They were already edging into Chosun waters, and none of them knew how the Chosun would respond. Even if they did nothing, the boat might still make it to safety.

It was beyond them now. All they could do was sit and watch.

ओम'

They were about five kays from Hanging Cove when the first Kshatriya boat appeared to the south. The smugglers targeted all of their guns on the gunboat and opened fire.

ओम्’

Gonpodin cut his boat to the west to avoid the incoming bullets and cursed even more. He knew the smugglers were buying time with those shots and not seriously aiming. Even so, driving into a bullet was a stupid way to die, and Gonpodin had no intention of dying stupidly.

In fact, if he had his druthers, he wouldn't die at all.

Then Blandaladen called out that there were more incoming. One quick look east revealed three Chosun gunboats. Not as swift as the Kshatriya but far more heavily armed. The Chosun were big fans of blunt force.

Worse, the Chosun captains were positioning themselves between the fugitives and the Kshatriya. Two more allied vessels were coming into range, so he figured he might as well get this party started.

They opened fire on the lead Chosun boat and managed to strafe it badly. They used that distraction to get between the enemy gunboats and the fugitives. They might make this work after all.

ओम्’

Pearl and her Mayanoren partner arrived just in time to see the exchange of gunfire. They quickly picked out separate targets and opened fire. The two rear boats burst into flames but still looked seaworthy as they passed by them. They couldn't adjust in time to get a clean shot on the primary target.

ओम्’

Gonpodin saw the air attack and grimaced slightly. While it was a perfect selection based on threat assessment, it allowed the murderess to get further away.

He keyed his mic to the main combat frequency and barked, "Fuck the gunboats, hit the fucking target!"

He was pretty sure that instruction was clear.

As they got a little nearer, Ajanandi opened fire with deadly accuracy. Pieces of the deck could be seen spitting into the air. The smugglers on deck did not waiver, however, and they were returning fire with gusto.

Pieces of the Kshatriya boat were disappearing into the sea as well.

They were well into Chosun territorial waters at this point, and Gonpodin could make out a cove. That must be their final destination. He was just starting to wonder about any defenses there when the shore erupted in anti-aircraft fire. Some of which were aimed at them.

He could see the planes coming back in for another pass and wished them luck. He doubted he was going to get any closer.

Just then, one of the Chosun gunboats launched a missile directly at them.

He yanked the boat hard to starboard and was just righting it as the missile flew by. Unfortunately, the second one that he hadn't seen coming was going to be unavoidable.

"ABANDON SHIP!" he yelled as he released the wheel and jumped overboard.

He saw Blandaladen go over the back of the boat out of the corner of his eye, and then everything was bathed in fire.

ओम'

Pearl and the Mayanoren both saw the gunboat explode. There was nothing either of them could do about that, so they concentrated on what they could control.

Opposing fire was growing heavy, and they could both hear bullets pinging off their planes. They dropped down a little more and opened fire on their target.

They could see a cave inside the cove. If that boat made it in there, this was over.

They kept firing, watching as the smuggler's craft was bursting into flames, but not slowing down.

ओम'

Bullets were flying everywhere, and the Captain didn't ease up off the throttle until he'd passed the mouth of the cave. The boat came to a sudden jarring stop, and Pearl imagined they'd hit a dock.

Better than the alternatives as far as she was concerned.

The Captain and the Shiva broke out fire extinguishers and quelled the bedlam on the deck.

She looked across the cabin and noticed that the Guenon had a hole in his leg where no hole had been before. Now she could be useful.

"Take off your pants," she yelled as she ran to the first aid kit on the wall.

He had his pants off in a flash, and she pulled the kit open as she noted in the back of her mind that he was going commando, and he wore that look well.

She knelt beside him and cleaned the wound. It was a through and through, barely missing the artery. She was pleased to find a needle and thread in the kit and began quickly, but expertly, sewing him back together. When she was done, she wrapped a bandage around his leg and told him to get new pants.

He got up without saying a word and headed to the cabin.

"That's some nice knitting," said the Captain.

"Wounds are something of a hobby of mine," she replied noncommittally.

Before any of them could say any more, there was a grunt at the bottom of the stairs.

Pearl saw the Chosun soldier and tried to remember if Rohta had created them to be an insult or a compliment to another country. She didn't suppose it mattered.

Short, round, and pudgy, the Chosun was covered in black and white fur. It had a round head with a black nose and two black ears near the top, all accented by sharp claws and small, yet pointy, teeth.

It was wearing a drab green uniform with a red, four-pointed star on the breast pocket.

She had no clue as to its sex.

"The Potentate not expected shooting this much," it said ominously.

"If you can take me to the Jung, all will be made clear," promised Pearl

"Him will come now. Him is very upset," replied the soldier.

Soon enough, they heard a cacophony of sirens. It sounded like a hundred vehicles were descending on them.

It was just one, and what a vehicle it was.

The motor and the driver area were completely open to the air, and the motor was covered in grime. Behind it was a shockingly white, bulbous canopy that looked more like a palanquin than a motor vehicle. The whole craft had four wheels at the back and two at the front. It was an abomination unto engineering.

Besides the many sirens, it was festooned with revolving lights of every imaginable color.

Behind it were about a dozen soldiers trotting on foot.

As soon as the atrocity stopped, one of them opened the door, and the grating sounds began to echo away.

When she saw what stepped out, she was amazed it could walk. It was a massively overweight Chosun dressed entirely in black with a little red cravat.

This, then, must be the Jung.

The three smugglers and Pearl hopped off the boat and onto the dock.

She walked right up to him and smiled.

"Don't worry, your majesty," she said as politely as possible, "this was all worth it."

"How worth can one little Pangolin be?" he managed to rumble and whine simultaneously.

"Oh, I am so much more than just one little Pangolin," she almost purred. This moment would change everything.

She pulled off her shoes and socks, revealing feet that looked, but weren't quite normal. Unlike the flatter feet of the brands that Rohta designed to carry their weight or balance their many arms, these feet were thin and had an arch.

The Jung watched, fascinated.

She pulled off her pants next, and then pushed the seal on the bottom half of her second skin and peeled it off as well. She followed that by systematically working her way up her body until she was completely nude.

Then she pulled out her fangs and stood before them all.

She wasn't sure her sharp knives could have cut the ensuing silence.

"Your prophecies have come true," she said with a grin, "a maker has returned."

As the Jung started clapping and singing, with the Chosun troops joining in quickly, she heard the Captain whisper behind her.

"Yeah, I can see why they risked war for this."

ओम'

Pearl Glistens in the Early Dew, and the Mayanoren had been severely blasted by anti-aircraft fire on that last pass. While he reported that he could return to base, she knew she could not. Smoke was filling the cabin, and the alarms were starting to cancel each other out.

She saw the flaming debris of the Kshatriya gunboat and decided to see if she could be useful.

She clipped a first aid kit to her chest and pulled the ejection lever. The blast of air almost knocked her out, but she was soon in control of her faculties. The chute had deployed automatically, and she began steering to the wreckage.

When she got close, she cut the chute loose and dove into the water. In her natural element, she quickly arrived to find two Kshatriya still living. She knew there were supposed to be three.

"Are you all right?" she asked.

"Bruised, and insulted but, otherwise, okay," replied Gonpodin.

"What about the third?"

Gonpodin pointed at the flaming hull. She could see the top half of the gunner still clutching his weapons, swathed in flame.

His bottom half was floating next to the boat. There was no first aid in the world that would help him.

As she had so painfully learned not that long ago, mourning would come later.

Introductions were made as more Kshatriya gunboats arrived.

They were all pulled from the water, wrapped in blankets, and each was given a warm broth.

As they pulled back out to sea to head for a safe haven, Gonpodin set aside his broth.

"Okay, I want to know what the fuck we were chasing. A simple murderess doesn't get fucking naval support., and we sure as fuck don't start a war over a single brand, no matter the crimes."

Since they all were having similar thoughts, and none of them had any answers, the quiet spoke volumes.

Something was horribly wrong with Arreti as far as they were concerned, and there was no way to know what it was.

ओम'

The room was in quiet shock. A maker was loose on Arreti. Worse, she was a demented killer who now had an army. The fact that it was an army of fanatics was just the topping on the dessert.

There was no way to keep this a secret anymore. The brands were going to have to unify against this threat. Blending armies took time, and training and they didn't think they'd have enough of the former to allow for the latter.

They pushed their food away and began planning on how to let the world know what had happened.

The great horror had returned.

Then:

Rahan and N'balan had become friends over the last ten Suns. Their friend Arti had passed away three Suns ago, and Manish had followed less than two turns later. They would be inseparable for all time.

And, to these two who knew them well, that was as it should be.

Per Manish's instructions, word had "leaked" about the Omnium's death and all the cybers. As he had promised, there was more than enough documentation to sate public curiosity. N'balan had pointed out that, since no one had ever asked him, he'd just assumed it was no big deal. Not long after that pronouncement, it seemed all of Bharat agreed with the late Goptri.

Another pet project of Manish's, turning Ville of Veruna into a scientific colony, was now complete. The best trained, most highly skilled brands who could be found lived there now. They were free to explore any idea that could better Arreti.

They weren't prisoners, but none had any incentive to leave. The one thing Manish had wanted was for the facility to be free of superstitious eyes. He knew the scientists would ask some difficult questions, and he didn't see any need for them to waste their time providing political answers

Arti had drafted a non-disclosure agreement Suns ago, and every resident had signed one. They knew how important their work could become.

More importantly, the coasts had been quiet and safe since the Kshatriya had come into being. All appreciated Pulinda's gift.

Rahan and N'balan had chosen this turn to have a light mid-break repast together and catch up on life. Both were enjoying the bowl of Aloo Aur Mooli Ke Patton ki Sabzi, with its radishes, red chilies, and mixed vegetables, but both had been too busy with their duties and their lives to do this more often as of late. Rahan, especially so since he had married twice and now had three smalls of his own.

This was far from his life as a dowdy professor.

The Kali were denied that type of intimacy but had another that seemed to suit them well. No matter where they went, they were never alone., and, as she'd once slyly told Rahan, when mating season came around, they tended to have a lot of energy to release.

He'd blushed so much she's laughed at him for almost a clik.

Beyond those large items, the turn to turn machinations of the country were running as smoothly as could be expected.

Arts were flourishing, and the brands were finding new ways to express themselves. Music, dance, sculpture, and painting all were having new life breathed into them. That was good. Rahan had been worried that the society was becoming too complacent with its traditions.

It's one thing to honor the past, quite another to live in it.

They both tried to see how this could all go wrong and came up empty. Their section of the world was calm, and they were bound and determined to keep it that way.

ओम'

Scar stood on the flying bridge of the Cursed Fate. He'd been caught off guard by how much the pirates had hated his idea. But, with a few careful assassinations, and some judicious bribes, the fleet had finally come together.

The Cursed Fate, and the Sea Killer, were both traditional mono-hulled boats. Their cannons, all built with automatic firing mechanisms, were arranged in a zig-zag pattern. Seven were positioned on the third deck, eight on the fourth with the same arrangement on the opposite side. The distribution gave the ships better balance when they fired.

Both ships were long and wide and stable in bad weather. What they lacked in elegance, they made up for in savage functionality.

While both ships had petroleum-powered turbines, they also maintained six masts just in case. They would never be caught dead in the water.

Crew quarters and the galley were contained on the two decks below the cannons. The two cabins below the flight bridge were reserved for the captain and any guest of the captain's. In this case, that particular honor belonged to Scar.

Scar knew there were those who called this idea Scar's Folly. He was okay with that as long they also attached his name to it when it succeeded.

In some ways, this had all worked out for the best. The Bharati coasts were only loosely guarded now. With no raids in over ten Suns, they'd become complacent and allocated resources elsewhere.

It was just after even-fall, and they were anchored five kays off the western coast. Claw, a Chien-Bois like Scar, was always loyal, and always dependable, and he was, right now, anchored about ten kays due north. They would wait until even-split, and then the raids would begin.

Time quickly passed as they cleaned the guns and did final maintenance on the ships. The barges were full of ground troops who were being fed now so they would be in peak condition when the raid occurred.

Two cliks before the raid was scheduled, they pulled their anchors and headed into position, setting up just under a kay from shore.

About a clik before even-split the gunboats, and barges began heading to shore. They were moving slowly and quietly so as not to raise any alarms.

Their targets were well chosen. Each had a trading post, and each trading post was the principal target. Those would contain the wealth. Anything else they could grab was just a boon.

Not that the pirates would throw it back.

Scar contacted Claw on their makeshift radio and issued the command. The Sea Killer and the Cursed Fate both opened fire. The fusillade of ten-kilo shells began raining down on the villages.

The gunboats, and barges, previously moving incognito, revved their engines and hit the shores with a fury.

The villages were caught entirely unaware.

Scrap Dragon, the captain of the Cursed Fate, called out targeting adjustments on the fly. He wanted a diverse array to saturate one location and allow the others to mount some defense. The Sea Killer was following the same strategy.

The pirates had found the Kshatriya docks and set all their gunboats on fire.

There were pockets of fierce fighting, and the pirates did suffer some casualties, but they mostly came out intact, and they came out with bags upon bags of bounty.

Reports were coming in detailing the carnage. It may not have been total, but it was enough to get the pirates in and out safely, which was kind of important to them. They were forced to kill the Din-La in both villages since they'd stupidly tried to resist.

Scar was a little chagrined about that. They were cute little critters, if you didn't mind the fact that they controlled most of the world's goldens. However, Scar did mind, so his angst was somewhat ameliorated.

Four cliks later, they were back at sea, laden with treasure. Scar ordered the casks of rum to be broken out and disbursed among the raiders.

He had proved his point. The Sugar Pirates were no longer a nuisance; they were a threat.

He knew the old axiom well. Kill one brand, and you're a murderer. Kill a thousand, and you're a political force. The Sugar Pirates were now, for good or ill, just such a force.

ओम'

Rahan was vacillating between being livid or heartbroken. Eight hundred and ninety-three dead in Dinloya, and another seven hundred and thirty-four in Krishnareign. The thirty-one dead pirates did not make up for that. The Din-La trading posts had been gutted, and all the Din-La who worked there were now dead.

The Kshatriya in his office advised against immediate retribution. Yes, revenge must be served, they said, but reality must be considered too.

As one noted, "The Sugar Pirates have hundreds of small islands to hide on. You can't just send a force and hope to overpower them. They could pin you there for many Suns."

Plus, they'd shown that they had battleships with long-range cannons. Nothing Bharat had could stand up against them. A mission now would be suicide.

What galled them all was the fact that the Sugar Pirates hadn't attacked like Sugar Pirates. This had been well-coordinated, well planned. Either they'd hired an advisor or found a savant. Neither option boded well.

It meant there was a new and deadly force to be reckoned with.

Rahan put the military considerations in the hands of the Kshatriya. That was their domain.

He had already contacted the Din-La. Now he had to tell his brands. What to say to them? Their Goptri cared but could no longer guarantee their safety? That didn't sound reassuring now. He was sure it would be less so later if he actually said it.

For the first time in his life, Rahan knew genuine anger., and now he also knew what the priests and prophets meant when they said anger kills from within.

He could feel it hardening his soul and chilling his blood.

He just wasn't sure he cared enough to stop it.

ओम'

Scrap Dragon was another proof of Rohta's sense of whimsy. Built from the DNA of the Magnificent Frigatebird, he had dark black feathers all over his body, and his wings were three times wider than he was tall. Standing just under two meters made him an impressive sight. He had two fingers and a thumb on each hand, and his feet were similarly configured. Like many of Rohta's avian creations, he sported talons instead of fingernails.

As was his custom, he was wearing a melon-colored vest and matching loincloth. He also wore a lightweight sword with a yellow gem in the handle.

He was a powerful flyer and could stay aloft for turns at a time. He only needed to alight when he was hungry.

He had been one of the pirates opposed to this raid. It went against all tradition. But now, he saw the intelligence in it. This was not an action built for one raid or even two. Scar was setting them up to be a world power. To demand Arreti trade with them or face their wrath.

He smiled as Captain Wounded Eye altered their course slightly and angled the ship west towards home.

There was nothing wrong with a new tradition here or there as far as he could see.

He checked with his communication's officer. The gunboats covering their rear reported nothing following them.

Bharat didn't have a true navy. They relied on the Kshatriya to cover the coasts. Not a bad plan most turns. But against Cursed Fate and Sea Killer, there'd been no hope.

Why hadn't any other king thought of this?

Besides, building a navy isn't something that can be done throughout an even. As long as they were careful in their planning, they should stage several Suns' worth of raids like these.

And when Bharat finally did have a true navy? Then they'd have to come up with a new plan. Something told him Scar had probably already thought that out too.

Honestly, then and only then, the Sugar Pirates got the best king they ever had.

Thanks to Scar, the Sugar Pirates now knew they were a power, and the Kshatriya knew they were behind the curve.

And that, he had to admit, was good knowledge to have.

ओम'

Now:

Pearl was sitting in a room with the Captain, the Guenon, and the Shiva. She was still naked, but that didn't bother her at all. Body modesty was not one of her failings. She left her legs slightly spread apart and leaned back in the comfortable chair.

After the Captain's comment, none of the three shipmates had said a word. They just sat staring at her. They seemed to be suffering from shock.

Well, there was nothing she could do about that now.

After meeting a few more Chosun, Pearl could now distinguish between the mals and the femmes. The one on the boat had been a mal. The one in front of her now, pouring a strong, scented, tea was a femme. She was curved slightly different from the mals. Despite that, the difference was subtle.

The shipmates shook their heads *no* when offered tea, then went back to staring at Pearl.

A new mal walked in. His uniform was slightly more ornate than the ones she'd seen, so she guessed he was an officer. He walked over to the Captain and addressed him directly.

"Much trouble have you caused," he said in a clipped monotone, "much will need to be addressed."

The Captain shook out of his reverie.

"You know where the cargo holds are. Empty them and keep it all with my blessings. There's no way we can ever leave here again. Not after this."

That seemed to mollify the officer.

A couple of epi-cliks later, Pearl watched in amusement as boxes of grenades, rocket launchers, semi-automatic weapons, and various types of ammunition were carried past her.

"Nice fruit," she said dryly.

The Captain blanched for a moment and laughed. To her surprise, the others did too.

"Well," began the Captain, "to be fair, you did say that our business was none of yours."

"And it still isn't," she said, smiling, "but you have all the goldens I gave you, and there's an equal amount in the saddlebags of my cyke that you can have as well. I'm sure you could set up somewhere."

He shook his head.

"Not after this. All the goldens on Arreti wouldn't get us to safety."

He paused to gather his thoughts.

"We just smuggled a maker into the most hostile country on the planet. I'm guessing the Kshatriya knew about you, and maybe a couple more, but now they'll have to go public. We saw it this turn. Those were mixed forces attacking us. If Bharat has added military allies, and it's clear they have, then they'll have to tell everyone what they're up to.

"And it's not just the local allies either. Bharat has ties, at least loose ones, with the Lightless Lands, Kalindor, the Children of the Waters, the Plains, the Eastern Warrens, and let's not forget the realm of Lord Südermann and its deadly Mantis Guards. In short order, as word of your existence gets out, there will be nowhere for us to hide. The excuse of 'joint military exercises' will only go so far."

She considered that briefly and realized he was right.

"Speaking of that," she said, still smiling, "I was watching the three of you. Do you mind telling me what military training you had?"

The Captain shrugged.

"Not much need for secrets between us anymore, is there?" he said sanguinely, "I was known as Colonel Orandia when I served with the Nanek-Dev Publican Militia. The Guenon you so expertly patched together was known as Sergeant Andana when he served with the Sacred Army of the Dravida, and our dear Shiva was Sergeant Śūra when he served the Royal Forces of Bharat."

The last two did an imaginary hat tip as they were introduced.

Next to being alive, this was the best news she'd heard all turn. She already knew the Chosun army had all the imagination of a stone. Quality minds like these could only help her cause.

"Well," she began carefully, "you probably don't need to be a genius to figure out that I have big plans for this army. You're more than welcome to work under me and stay here if you wish."

The Captain considered that.

"What makes you think the Jung will welcome foreigners?"

It was her turn to shrug.

"He probably won't, but he won't have much of a choice if he wants his prophecies fulfilled."

The femme who'd poured the tea stepped out for a moment and returned with a beautiful maroon silk robe that was decorated with an exploded map of Arreti on the left side. This made it look as though the world was swimming in oceans of blood. She decided she liked it immediately.

She took it from the quiet femme and put it on. She hadn't noticed the mirror in the corner; she walked over to it and smiled. She looked phenomenal.

"The Jung wishes in one clik to announce the prophecy," the femme said in a tight monotone, "and thinks that join him you should."

She nodded.

"The Jung is wise. Please take me to him at the appointed time."

She was rewarded with a bright, if slightly terrifying, smile, and the femme left to do whatever it is she was going to do.

Pearl looked at the Captain, now Colonel, and saw that he was chuckling. Before she could ask, he turned and barked a laugh.

"Just before all the shooting broke out, I was thinking that you'd promised us goldens, which you delivered – and for that, I thank you profusely, but you never promised us boring."

Even Pearl had to laugh at that.

About half a clik later, they were escorted to a large ballroom. There was a heavily decorated dais and a podium draped with a red flag that featured a white version of the four-pointed star.

There were three antique video cameras pointed at the stage—each with a clear view.

Behind them was an audience made up entirely of soldiers. There were buffets laid out on both sides of the room, but no one was touching them.

Unless she was mistaken, there was an old-style satellite uplink at the back of the room. She could see numerous cables snaking up the back wall.

The Jung, now wearing white, waved them to the stage and smiled.

"Technician says one chance we can do. After the others block us, they can."

She realized what he was about to do and finally smiled her first genuine smile in a long time.

Let the chaos begin.

ओम'

Queen Lynno and the ambassadors had turned the vid screens over to various newsie outlets. So far, none seemed to know what had happened. Hopefully, that lack would give them the time they needed to soften the blow.

They were gathered around a large table, trying to hammer out the language of the announcement. The process had been going much better than any of them anticipated. It was more a matter of trying to let everyone know, in a polite and comfortable manner, that their worst fears had been realized. No matter their respective skill sets, they were all politicians enough to make that work.

They'd already decided to send the final text to their respective governments so that the announcement could be made by someone that each of the brands would trust.

Ignop had just stood up to stretch when all of the vid screens went black. Then they all heard the sound of a brass band blaring through the speakers. Before any of them could comment on anything, all the screens were filled with the image of a corpulent Chosun dressed in all white with a tiny red cravat.

"That's the Jung," said Xho.

Navi tossed the press release to the floor and sighed loudly. They no longer had any way to soften the blow. What was about to happen would see to that. Of that, he was sure.

"I am the Jung," began the image on the screen with a voice that was both deep and whiney, "the Supreme Leader of the Sacred Empire of the Divine Chosun. It is I who the prophecies keep."

They were trying to sort out the syntax as he continued.

"Before gone were the makers a prophecy given, we were. As Jung, the holy obligation mine is. The prophecy in my hands alone stays. Now time has risen for it me to share."

He pulled up a transparent, malleable, plastic sheathe which contained a single sheet of paper. He held it up to the cameras. A camera zoomed in, and they could easily see two short paragraphs written in a language none of them knew.

"This the prophecy say, 'The time of death is upon us. But we shall not go to our eternal graves forever. We shall come back. We shall rule again, and all will be made right once more.

Humans will come back, and pods will, once again, be relegated to their proper place. This is the promise we make. This is the promise we will keep.'"

He had pronounced each word one syllable at a time. But the stilted delivery did nothing to lessen the message.

The Jung paused to let everything settle in. The ambassadors in the room recognized it as a threat, but the Jung seemed to see it otherwise. They watched in rapt awe as the unavoidable event continued to unfold.

"Humans makers be. That the word they used once was., and now the prophecy true has become. Behold, A MAKER!"

Pearl stepped into view. She was wearing some sort of maroon ceremonial robe. Loud applause could be heard as she just stood there. The Jung motioned her to the mic, and she smiled as she approached it. If you ignored the fact that she was a psychotic killer bent on world domination, she looked charming.

"My name is Pearl, and I am a maker," she said calmly, as though this sort of thing happened every turn.

"It is I who the prophecy foretold. It is I who you have been waiting for. It is I who will lead the Chosun to their proper place. They are wiser than the brands of Bharat. Their Goptri, the weakling Sharma, refused to accept the world as it will be, and I was forced to kill him. The Jung understands. The Jung sees the greatness that shall come."

As the image of the smiling Jung filled the screens, they now understood what the Jung thought the prophecy meant. The fact that he was horribly wrong didn't change a thing.

"From this turn forward, Arreti will answer to the Jung. From this turn forward, we will begin putting things back to the way they should be. Consider this your due notice. A maker is among you, and this distortion you call life will be fixed."

That drew wild applause, and she backed away from the mic. There was nothing more she needed to say. Couriers ran into the room but stopped when they saw the ambassadors already knew the terrible news.

The brass band started playing again, and the image of two crossed missiles appeared on the screen. The Jung and Pearl faded to black as a red, four-pointed star appeared behind the missiles.

None of them had any idea what that image meant explicitly, but they all knew a warning when they saw one.

ओम'

Chandrack and Dr. Rhanda were just finishing reviewing the reports from earlier this even when they saw the Jung's announcement and the introduction of Pearl.

When it was over, he stood up, walked over to a cabinet, and pulled out two bottles of bourbon and two glasses. He handed one of each to her and harrumphed.

"So much for lying low."

ओम'

After the applause had died down, she turned to the Jung.

"We need to go back to the boat. I have a gift for you."

He nodded, snapped his fingers, and twelve guards immediately jumped onto the stage.

"The transport. Go, we must."

Two guards raced ahead of him, and the rest surrounded him as they left the ballroom and headed towards the... whatever it was.

The three shipmates, having no inkling what else to do, followed along.

Inside the eyesore, there was plenty of room for everyone, so they all took seats facing the Jung. They were all a little surprised at how tastefully decorated the interior was. Plush maroon seats surrounded the vehicle's interior, and there was an obsidian table in the center.

He snapped out an order in a language none of them knew, and they were off.

A few epi-cliks later, they were back at the boat. This time they'd managed to arrive without the sirens—just the lights.

The Jung motioned for them to exit first, and they did. As soon as she was out, Pearl walked over to the boat, hopped onto the deck, and went to her cyke.

She waved for some guards to join her, and, after seeing an assenting nod from the Jung, four of them did.

She opened the bags on her cyke, tossed out clothes, flipped a bag of goldens to the Colonel, and then began slowly removing four oblong orbs. She handed one to each guard but kept the fourth herself.

The Jung was standing next to the boat, looking confused.

"This is …" she paused, quickly realizing that a technical explanation was going to be nothing but a waste of time, "this is a weapon. It can turn any volcano into a bomb. You just hang it on the inside of the lip and then press this button. I strongly suggest running away after you press the button. It will take a clik or two to activate fully, but, once it does, the effect is catastrophic."

The Jung looked at it closely and then smiled widely.

"The Shin-Sen volcano have. Try there first; we should."

He called out an order in the alien language, and soon three more Chosun showed up. These were wearing black and seemed more alert than any others she'd seen. More good news. Competent, if not exceptional, spies.

She ran through the instructions with them and made them repeat them back. Grammatical oddities aside, they got it right the first time.

She handed them the one she was holding and was not surprised to see them take off immediately. Whatever limitations the Jung had, decisiveness wasn't one of them. That bode well for what she had in mind.

She reached back into the saddlebag and pulled out a small sheaf of papers. These she handed directly to the Jung.

"The designs for more."

He took them, smiled, and started clapping and singing again.

With all the cheer on the dock, she had to admit; this was going to be a happy holocaust.

ओम'

Then:

Ugnaronoo had designed an electronic perimeter to kill anything that tried to cross it and stretched from itself to a launch facility that housed several rockets. Unlike the rockets the makers had left behind, these were designed to hold over one hundred brands each. The cybers helped with the construction of the barrier, and the work went exceedingly fast.

The wars were starting to flame out simply due to a lack of participants, just as Abhijit and Zeenat had predicted. With the majority of the remaining few survivors resorting to barbarism, and with everything here being so far removed from any earlier locations of civilization, the threat of an armed assault on the fence seemed minimal.

In less than a Sun, the work was complete, and the residents had safe passage back and forth.

Ugnaronoo had given the Omnium plans for a machine that would create controllable gravity. It would feature a series of interlocking ovoids that would surround the entire ship. With each acting as an advanced gyroscope, they would envelop the ship with a gravitational field that could then be adjusted to the comfort of the travelers.

There were some initial concerns about how the system would react near light speed, but projections by both the Omnium and Ugnaronoo showed no issues. Since everything was relative, the system wouldn't notice the change in velocity at all.

There was a currently unpopulated space station in orbit above Urrazna, and they decided to use that as their manufacturing facility. Many of the Urraznan scientists had experience with space travel, so that was one less thing to concern themselves with.

Ugnaronoo's plan was daring. Once the Pravda was retrofitted, they would hold a lottery among the scientists. Fifty mals and fifty femmes would be chosen to make the journey to the stars. The goal was to find them a suitable new home to develop. The monogamy they were accustomed to would have to be put in abeyance in exchange for rampant polyandry for a while. It was the only way to make survival work, given the resources at hand. Fortunately, it seemed a sacrifice they were happily willing to make.

They also realized they would need to keep meticulous birth records to prevent inbreeding. But that was a minor technical detail and one the scientists embraced.

The remaining scientists would stay behind and begin the difficult task of salvaging Urrazna.

While it was at it, Ugnaronoo devised a more advanced piloting system for the Bullet. This he shared with Natasha, and she quickly pronounced it brilliant. With some minor reconfigurations, the Bullet would be as maneuverable as any terrestrial craft.

There was one last part of Ugnaronoo's plan. It wanted to clone itself and embed the clone in the ship's computer.

The cybers debated that for several turns but finally agreed. It was just too much intelligence to abandon.

With all the plans finalized, the labor began. The cybers took the Bullet back to Pravda while the scientists used one of the enormous rockets to head directly to the space station. Many preparations and alterations needed to be made to the Pravda before the machine could be attached.

Since the cybers needed neither sleep nor food, they worked ceaselessly on the project.

Even so, it took four full Suns to get everything ready. Not only did the mechanical requirements for the machine need to be completed, but there were also many alterations to the ship's computer that needed to be done so it could house the clone.

By the time the cybers had accomplished everything the scientists, who had been shuttling to, and from the space station, had the ovoids completed and ready for attachment.

Ugnaronoo used a laser to transmit a copy of its essence to the ship, and construction began in earnest.

It took the combined efforts of the cybers and the aliens another three Suns, but they were finally ready to test the gravity machine.

Before they began, Pran raced through the ship, turning each of the terrariums upside down and covering the openings so the foliage wouldn't be crushed by the gravity or float away if it didn't come on.

Fifteen epi-cliks later, it did. A single turn of making minor adjustments around the ship, and they'd achieved a comfortable living environment for both the cybers and the aliens.

The next few turns were busy. Two ships were stocked with

provisions, the lottery was held, the obligatory party and tearful farewells were completed, and, soon enough, the Pravda was leaving orbit with a much larger crew than when it arrived.

Ugnaronoo had scanned the Sominids' records, compared them with its studies of the stars, and compiled a list of six possible worlds that might suffice for the pioneers.

They would start with those.

Though they wouldn't admit it openly, the cybers were thrilled at finally having a purpose, even if it had nothing directly to do with them.

ओम'

Wounded Eye, of the same brand as Scrap Dragon, had a penchant for tipping his feathers with blood-red dye. Since he was the captain of the Sea Killer and a brand that had survived numerous assassination attempts, no one questioned his tastes.

He, Scrap Dragon, Claw, and Scar were sitting in Scar's office, enjoying a mid-break repast being served by Pateet.

Over the last five Suns, they'd accomplished thirteen successful raids on the coasts of Bharat, Dravida, and Kalindor. Scar had been careful when picking his targets and ensuring they steered well clear of the Eastern Warrens and their powerful navy. That navy could cause them irreparable harm.

Fortunately for them, the Eastern Warrens didn't care about the maniacs in Kalindor, no one did, and had no treaties with Bharat or Dravida.

The goldens they'd garnered allowed them to trade with various black markets that didn't share the Din-La's dim view of the Sugar Pirates. Despite their enormous resources, the Sugar Pirates never seemed to get the hang of traditional manufacturing, so they were required to purchase what they needed.

Nevertheless, the spies they'd hired in each country reported that Bharat and Dravida were both close to launching ships that could take on, and likely sink, the Cursed Fate and Sea Killer. They were looking now at images of those ships. In Bharat, they were building four steel ships that, although slightly smaller than the pirates' ships, had two cannons each fore and aft capable of shooting twenty-kilo shells anywhere in a 180-degree arc. The ships also appeared to be faster than anything the pirates had.

In Dravida, they were building just one ship, but what a ship it was. Twice the size of the pirates' vessels, it sported ten large cannons on each side, and mobile cannons, like the ones in Bharat, fore and aft of the top deck. Although the top deck cannons only fired ten-kilo shells. It, too, was made of steel.

They were looking at their doom, and they knew it.

This is why Scar's continued smile confused them.

He broke the silence, never once losing his smile.

"I've known this turn would come for quite some time," he said as he sipped his rum, "and, because of that, I made arrangements a long time ago to deal with it. I needed a place to work in secret, and the residents of Wretched Island needed a break from their protection fees.

"We came to an arrangement four Suns ago that has been, to say the least, mutually beneficial. We've long had the ability and knowledge to make steel; we just never had the need other than for some small hand weapons or swords. Now we do. With Pateet's help, I designed a ship that could deal with what was coming. Ripping Flesh coerced enough residents of Wretched Island to work in the forges so that everything could be done in one place, away from prying eyes. I wanted neither friend nor foe to know of this until it was done. That way, no one could be prepared for it.

"Mates, I give you Death Hammer."

He tossed a series of images onto the table. They looked at

him in admiration for a moment and then began perusing the photos as their respect deepened. The ship was appropriately named. Just two below decks, but it had cannons circling the top deck. They were designed to be loaded from below decks and expel their used shells from their rears. There were four large machine guns, one at each compass point, and four small smokestacks lined up port to starboard on the aft rail. The flying bridge, positioned just in front of the smokestacks, was fully encased in steel as well. The ship itself was broader than any they'd ever seen, and the flying catamaran design was something they'd never even contemplated, but its low draft made it look fast. Amazingly fast indeed.

They looked back at him.

"It has four, diesel, turbines," he continued happily, "and she'll hold at forty knots for a full clik without worry. The hull is double-hulled with a half meter space between each layer. That way, even if we take a hit, she'll stay afloat. I took her out thirty turns ago, and she flew like a dream. There's nothing this side of hell that can stop her."

Claw looked pained.

"I've been your second for sixty Suns. Why wasn't I told about this?"

"Pateet, I could kill, you I need."

That answer satisfied them all.

"Besides Claw," he continued, "Death Hammer needs a captain I can trust., and, as you said, we've been blood for sixty Suns. I now give her to you as proof of my trust."

Claw looked flabbergasted for a moment and then smiled. He raised his glass and laughed.

"To the seas we own, and those we will. To Death Hammer!"

"To Death Hammer!" came the loud echo.

ओम'

Rahan sat, staring at the four Kshatriya sitting across from him. When he'd left the military strategies to them five Suns ago, he'd had no idea that they would dig so deep or push so far. They'd, literally, formed an alliance with the Dravida against the Dravida's will.

Questions about the specifics of that arrangement were politely deferred, and he didn't see any need to press.

There were two copies of the, for lack of a better term, treaty. One was with the Sovereign of Dravida, and the other lay with the Goptri. There had been no public announcement, nor had there been any terms attached other than to stop the Sugar Pirates.

They'd split the requirements for one true navy between the two countries. The Dravida had demanded the right to build the flagship, and the Kshatriya had readily agreed. They'd no need for pomp, and, in fact, it ran counter to how they operated. Once the trivia was out of the way, the real work had begun.

The Dravida would lead the way into any battle with the dreadnaught they'd built, but the Kshatriya would control the strategy from aboard their frigates. They were going to take the fight straight to the Sugar Pirates. They were all tired of seeing innocent bloodshed on their shores.

The meeting this turn was to finalize the last details. The Goptri needed to sign off on a joint military exercise with the Dravida, which would begin immediately. If all went well, they felt they could be headed for the Sugar Pirates in thirty turns.

Rahan wished he could go. He'd never known a need for violence in all his life, and now it consumed him. If it weren't for his wives and the Kshatriya, he was sure he would have turned into a warlord Suns ago.

He signed the secret document, folded it, sealed it, and handed it to them. He knew that the Sovereign was performing a similar task in front of her Blessed Commandos. The two documents would be stored with Qmmt, a Din-La who'd been unfortunate enough to walk into the wrong room at the palace of the Sovereign just when one of the early meetings was going on.

She'd been encouraged to act as their mutual liaison

Granted, that encouragement had been less than subtle. The Kshatriya and the Blessed Commandos were in no mood for additional negotiations, so they'd offered her a choice; take a fair commission on the trade that would need to be done or die.

Rahan thought she'd made the wise choice.

The Kshatriya stood in unison, saluted, and left.

Soon enough, the pirates would know the pain he felt., and, better yet, they would feel his fury, by proxy anyway, when those powerful ships unleashed their combined might.

It was the first thought he'd smiled at in Suns.

ओम'

Sundara Lal Hora, Sole Respected Sovereign of the Dravida, signed the document and motioned to be left alone. As one of the Trachypithecus geei brand that populated Dravida, she was more beautiful than most. Standing at a meter and a half in height, she had sable skin covering her face and fingers. Her face was rimmed with a gentle saffron-colored fur, and the rest of her body was entirely covered with a dark gold fleece. Unlike the other simian brands created by Rohta, she had a remarkable tail that she would curl around her waist when lost in thought.

She was wearing a bright green sari and gold slippers. She'd had a fondness for jangly gold bangly bracelets since she was a small, and, smiling at her wrists, noted that had not changed. When she was a small, she believed that the bracelets increased blood flow and improved health. As she got older, she was pleased to discover there was some truth in that. But even if there wasn't, she'd wear them anyway. She liked the colors and the sounds.

Her position held many stresses. If something like bracelets could lessen them, even for a while, she wasn't giving them up.

Although her lands were smaller than Bharat's, she had far more economic power. Her ancestors had made sure that as much ground as they could save had been. There was plenty of food to supplement what was grown on the farms with the ocean all around them. She gave thanks to the gods each turn for their bounty. With such a diverse agriculture, they could withstand droughts and other problems that would bring any other country low.

Thanks to those efforts, her subjects were healthy and had unfettered access to their gods via the many temples that dotted the land.

She had hoped it would be enough.

Ever since she'd been a small, she'd looked forward to being Sovereign. Just like her Mataji before her, and her Mataji's Mataji before her, and so on back to the end of the revolution. Now things were changing.

Not just the dealings with the Sugar Pirates, those were mere strategy and power, but her citizens had been clamoring for more say in their government. It was inevitable, she supposed.

After the revolution, order had needed to be enforced and maintained. The infrastructure had needed to be rebuilt, the borders created and guarded. Sometimes forcefully so. The femmes of her family had accomplished all that and more.

Now things were settled, the citizens wanted a say in how things would move going forward. Some of her advisors advocated crushing the opposition. She could not do that. She was still of them, not above.

Besides, she understood. Not having any real power over your life was frustrating. As much as she'd always wanted to be the Sovereign, the training and the seclusion were oppressive. By the time she was entirely a brand, her life was no longer strictly her own.

She looked at a map on her wall. The four states and eighteen counties of Dravida were denoted in different colors. A breakdown of the various brands who lived in each was specified in a small graph in the lower left-hand corner.

Not for the first time did she wonder why there were so many more brands in her lands than there were in Bharat. In sheer numbers, as counted by individuals, Bharat overwhelmed Dravida. But, when it came to genetic diversity, they couldn't hold a candle to the richness of her domain.

And that needed to be considered too. Since the first Sun, one brand had ruled them all. She could see how that could chafe as the skies came and went over the many Suns.

She did not have an heir. That was to have come later. Now might be the best time to make this work. This could be done without bloodshed. Or so she hoped.

She had a few ideas, none fully formed. Still, it was a start.

She called for her messenger. She would have him take word to the opposition leader requesting a private meeting. No one was to know about it. When he arrived, she would explain about the Sugar Pirates and what she was doing. She would ask him what a perfect resolution to their differences might be, and then, hopefully, they could find an answer that satisfied neither of them.

That would be the best possible solution.

ओम'

Now:

Aslesha sat sobbing in her room. She had been doing so for several cliks. She had seen the vidcast and knew that the worst was yet to come. This creature who had taken her beloved and then bragged about it was loose upon Arreti. Her smalls had seen it as well and realized what she had been forced to hide from them. Far from being angry, they were deeply sympathetic. None of them could imagine how any brand could carry such a burden.

They'd never ascribed that kind of strength to their maa, but, in retrospect, they could see it. It was she who had attempted to deal with their baabaa for these last five Suns. Now that they knew he'd been treating with a maker; it made the suffering of their maa all the worse.

What could have prompted him to do such a thing?

They would never know. He was gone from them now.

They did not wonder if she had known the truth. Her reaction to the announcement had told them everything. They decided then and there to make sure that she never carried another burden alone again.

Outside their palace apartments stood several Kshatriya.

Aslesha thought that was too little too late but said nothing. She still had her family to consider, and that nightmare was still among the living.

ओम'

Nkkl was traumatized. The multitude of roiling emotions cascading over and through her defied naming. At the local trading post, she had been sitting with Kondilar, enjoying a casual late even-fall meal when the vidcast began. Nothing was casual after that.

She didn't know how she knew, but she knew that the vile thing she'd seen, and not the beloved Goptri, had killed her husband. Now she wanted to know what she could do about it. Kondilar didn't need to be a telepath to figure out what was going through her mind. He started to speak, and she raised her hand.

"Don't worry," she said quietly, "I was just shocked. I imagine I'm not alone. But I'm not stupid. The whole world will be sending armies to kill her. It may take them a while, but they will get her. Until then, we have a deal, and there has never been an honest Din-La who has reneged on a deal. I will not be the first."

He looked relieved.

"Besides," she continued, calmer and more in control now, "I might be of more help getting those forces some of the items we have in deep storage. A small's fantasies aside, I am not a killer. But I do know how to equip one.

"All Din-La do."

He had no idea why that simple statement chilled him to the bone.

ओम'

Mondara was sitting across a small table from the lead Mayanoren. She had been doing that more, and more, and found she enjoyed it. He was smart, erudite, and even had a sense of humor if you knew where to look. When not called by their duties, they spent time discussing everything from history to politics to art. The usefulness of that latter one seemed to elude him, but he was still curious about it.

Though the others had noticed the blossoming romance, none had said anything. What was there to say? They were both fully grown and beyond competent in their duties. The rest would play itself out as it would no matter what they said.

There was one thing still bothering Mondara, and she decided to address it head-on.

"How can you go through life without names?"

He shrugged.

"We have no need. Thanks to some organic implants that provide electromagnetic identification, that we alone can detect, we can tell each other apart easily."

"Fair enough, but what about the rest of us? If you are going to treat with us on a regular basis, we need some way to address you."

It was clear that his great mind had never considered the problem.

It did so now.

"After the fall of Xhaknar, the Naradama assimilated into the plains by taking random names from dictionaries and using them as an implied lineage. We'd thought it a waste of time, but, now, I see they did it not for themselves but for the others around them, to give them a point of reference in any communication."

He considered it even more.

"Names mean things to you and yours. They reference events, history, or something important to the individual. Parents gift some names while other brands allow their smalls to grow to a certain age and then choose their own.

"We have no tradition either way, and I truly would not know where to begin."

She thought about it for a bit and had an idea.

"When other Mayanoren look at you, what does your signal say to them? Does it have a specific meaning?"

He shook his head no.

"Not in the way you are thinking. It isn't as if the signal could be parsed to a word or two. It is more a summation of our genetic singularities. It has our exact time of birth, location of same, and pre-determined level of intelligence. It also contains our …. for lack of a better term, flavor. You might call it our essence. Even that is a complex thought and not a single noun."

It had been worth a shot.

"And yet," he continued, "you make a valid point. If we are to interact with other brands, we need to be able to define who is dealing with whom. Right now, it is a miniscule sample, so we can work with it, but that will change rapidly as we unite against the maker. I will discuss this with the others."

The conversation turned to more pleasant things. He was insatiably curious and pelted her with questions. At one point, she laughed and reminded him that this was not an inquisition.

And for the first time in the history of Arreti, a Mayanoren smiled warmly and blushed a little.

ओम'

The Jung had had Pearl's clothes cleaned, probably checked for hidden perils, and then the new companions had been assigned a set of apartments. Pearl knew from what she'd seen thus far that the Chosun would have considered the accommodations opulent. They were functional and clean. They were fine as far as she was concerned.

The Colonel and his two mates each had their own rooms as well. There was a common cooking area and a small living area with one vid screen turned to the only channel the Chosun had. Since it broadcast in a language none of them understood, they left the sound off.

Andana had scoured the kitchen and assembled an excellent meal of fermented cabbage, sausages, and fresh-made dark bread. Since she was no whiz in the kitchen, she found it easy to leave those duties to the crew.

They were eating their meal in the living area, pointedly ignoring the vidcast when Colonel Orandia asked her a question.

"So, you truly knew Rohta?"

She nodded while chewing.

"Are there any secrets of his that can help us survive what's to come?"

That was an excellent question, and she gave it serious thought.

"Rohta had facilities all over the world. A few were fully functional labs, but most were just assembly locations. I think we can ignore those. But the labs might have things we could use. We just need to figure out how to get to them."

"Where are they?"

"Well, one is in Brazil, now Kalindor. That's a non-starter, obviously. Attacking something that's guarded by a small city of nothing but Mayanoren would be a quick way to see Rohta again. One is in Bharat, which is where Sharma found me. I don't see a visit there going all that well either. That leaves the one in Africa, what you call the Lightless Lands. All of his seminal work is there, and it's far from any inhabitants in the middle of the continent. If we could get there, it might be worth the trip."

The Colonel thought about it.

"The Chosun have an air force and transport planes. If we could get one of them fueled and staffed with a crew, we could make it."

"Good idea, bad idea," she said, "there is no airstrip there, and it's in the middle of the jungle. The closest thing that might be useful is a river about three kays due west."

The Colonel smiled.

"The Jung is cheap, and Chosun has many lakes and rivers.

Most of his planes can be fitted with pontoons."

She smiled at that. If true, that could open up a whole new realm of possibilities. Rohta had given her tours of each facility before being, finally, forced by the world's government to put her in stasis. The one in Africa had held many mysteries. If even a few were still there, they could even the playing field in short order.

"I have another question," said Śūra, "slightly off-topic, but you may be the only one who can answer it."

She nodded at him.

"Why is the biodiversity in Bharat so sparse? All the other lands, even those of the Lost Gods, are rich in brands."

She shrugged.

"Based on the plans I'd seen, and what I now know, my guess is he never got to finish India. I mean, Bharat. He had numerous designs and quite the panoply of gods and goddesses to base his creations on. I know he had plans for different Ganesh and Shiva types, and he had some fun plans for the Kali line. He had developed neon appearing skin colors like pink, yellow, and green, and he was going to have a blast.

"You have to keep in mind that India was on the wane at the time. It was the hardest hit by the Plato war. So much tech had been developed there, and tech was the one thing everyone wanted killed.

"Flora and fauna were decimated. The majority of the war, and the final battle, all happened there. By the time it was over, almost two-thirds of the country was a smoking ruin. Rohta had plans for various animals that could have filled ecological niches and help bring it all back to life.

"Certainly, he had no qualms about overwriting existing genomes. For example, when he released deisteeds into the world, they would try and breed with regular equines, and then their nanites would infect them and render them sterile. Other breeds, like his giant rabbits, simply wiped out the competition.

"That happened all over the world, his insects replacing ones that had existed for millennia to thousands of avian, and smaller mammals being replaced or, as he called it, upgraded. He was reshaping everything in his image, and no one seemed to care.

"Of course, between the war and the carnage wrought by the Sominids, it isn't like there was a whole lot worth saving anyway."

She paused, slightly lost in thought.

"When I was young, our teachers used to tell us that, once, India was one of the most heavily populated continents on the planet. Billions of people, twenty-seven states, twenty-seven languages, and twenty-seven different styles of cuisine. But that was long gone by the time I was born. There was just the Bengali Provence and the rest of India. And even those boundaries were kind of blurred.

"I was put in stasis ahead of the rebellion, but it doesn't take much research to see that it happened shortly after that, and, with Rohta dead, his work died with him."

Then she had a question of her own.

"What the fuck are the Lost Gods?"

Andana fielded that one.

"They are a collection of brands who were, allegedly, patterned after ancient maker gods. Some made by Rohta, others not, it's hard to know for sure. They inhabit a valley near the upper part of the Lightless Lands. They, pretty much, keep to themselves. They have several beautiful cities, but they do not invite trade. If you visit, they'll make you feel welcome for a while. Then it becomes obvious they'd rather you left."

"Would they pose a threat to us if we passed by them?

"Doubtful. As far as I know, they have no military whatsoever."

"How do you know so much about them?"

"When I served the Dravida, there was a report of Sugar Pirate raiders attempting to use the river of the Lost Gods as a new path to us. The report turned out to be false, it was just a group of migrant traders, but we decided to see what all the fuss was about as long as we were there. We spent four turns in a city called Zawty. It was a bustling place with markets everywhere. But it was completely self-sufficient; they traded with no one and asked for nothing. They have a large population but don't seem interested, at all, in the world around them. If we all disappeared the next turn, I got the impression they might think it good riddance."

She contemplated that for a moment and then dismissed them from her concerns.

"There's a lot of empty land between us and our destination. Let's see if the Jung can scare us up a pilot and a navigator."

ओम'

Navi's three eyes were burning, and his mouth tasted like chalk. He was tired, and, looking around the table, he could see everyone else was too. Chandrack had already ordered shifts of air reconnaissance around Chosun, but away from its claimed air and water space, in case Pearl tried to make a break for it. Although none of them thought that likely. Naval support for a blockade was coming from all over Arreti, but it would be many turns before it would be in place.

It was time for bed. There was nothing more they could do now. He stood and suggested that to everyone, and they all readily agreed, except for Mondara and the Mayanoren, who said they weren't all that tired now.

That got knowing smiles all around, and then they disbursed to their chambers.

Queen Lynno stood, stretched, and grabbed a small platter of food and a glass of cold dairy. She didn't normally eat late, but she was as hungry as she was tired.

Aides came in and began cleaning this turn's debris and prepping for the next's.

Before she closed her eyes, her last thoughts were focused on wondering what a half Mayanoren, half Nanek-Dev, small would look like.

The image wasn't flattering.

ओम'

Then:

Claw piloted Death Hammer surely across the open seas. Thanks to the exorbitant sums they'd paid their spies, they knew a small fleet was headed their way. The Sea Killer and Cursed Fate rode port, and starboard, respectively, in her wake. They would hang back from the brutes and let Death Hammer deal with them. Their job was to bombard them with shells to keep them off balance.

The gunboats from Cove of the Red Winds were covering the far flanks. If it came to close in fighting, they would be a valuable asset.

Knowing what he knew about the incoming navy, Claw had already admitted to himself; this could be a one-way trip. As long as he kept the intruders off his shores, he was okay with that. He knew the others felt the same way.

Scar was standing behind him, not saying a word. The time for talk had long since passed.

One advantage they had is that they knew what was coming. Thanks to Scar's caution, the Kshatriya did not.

The sky glowed red as even-fall darkened the seas. The clouds were thick, and visibility was poor. Just the way the pirates liked it. The radar they'd gotten from a Bharati arms dealer was working flawlessly. Their targets were coming into range.

Claw was sure the other ships had radar too, but they wouldn't know what the readings meant right away. Every little bit in their favor was another little bit he liked.

In accordance with the plan, they'd developed Claw ordered all ahead full. There was nothing that the combined Bharati/Dravida alliance had that could even come close to her speed. She would make a screaming broadside while Cursed Fate and Sea Killer shelled them.

Death Hammer was soon racing across the waves directly at her prey.

Shells, fired by both sides, began falling all around her as Claw kept her steady and focused.

He spotted the Dravida dreadnaught and whistled slowly. The pics didn't do her justice. She was massive, and that made him smile.

He turned to Scar.

"Fucking big mark that, eh? What say we let the crew get some target practice in?"

Scar started to nod, but Claw had already issued the order to fire.

At the speed they were traveling, and as close as they passed, the initial broadside was nearly lethal. Gaping holes appeared in the dreadnaught as they went by, and the gunners kept the crew off the deck by spraying hundreds of rounds at anything that looked like it might be worth killing.

His big gunners were firing every third round under the

waterline. It was a technique Wounded Eye had developed, and it served them well here.

Claw didn't have to be there to know the pandemonium that was happening on the giant ship. He could see flames spitting out of the wounds they'd caused.

They passed between the allied forces, and all of their guns were kept active. For a moment, everything was a target. It didn't matter what the pirates aimed at; they hit something with every shell. The frigates couldn't get a bead on Death Hammer without shooting each other, or the dreadnaught, as it soared between them.

Pieces of steel littered the air and then disappeared beneath the waves. Two of the frigates were in bad shape. He'd get the other two when he returned.

The combined forces of Bharat and Dravida were entirely caught off guard. They'd no idea what this hurtling behemoth was or where it had come from. All they knew is that it was tearing them apart.

Before they could regroup, the gunboats from Cove of the Red Wind swung around and began strafing the Kshatriya frigates from behind with machine guns and portable rockets fired from the decks. It didn't take anyone all that long to realize that Death Hammer had completed her circuit and was coming in for a second run. The boats of the Red Wind retreated as she opened fire a second time.

She was taking hits this time, but, as Scar had promised, the second hull kept her afloat.

Bullets were ringing off the flying bridge, and both Claw and Scar would later admit they'd never felt more alive than at that moment.

The two Kshatriya frigates Claw was targeting this time went under in spectacular fashion. Whether they'd been hit by the long-range shells of Sea Killer and Cursed Fate or if Death

Hammer had struck the fatal blows mattered not one whit. The two surviving frigates didn't look long for this world either. Cursed Fate and Sea Killer had found their range and were now dumping ordinance directly on their enemies.

The Dravida dreadnaught was belching smoke and flames and trying to get out of the way. She was listing badly and had stopped firing. The pirates could see the crew racing around the upper deck, trying to quell the damage.

The dreadnaught was between the pirates and the frigates at this point. It was the only thing keeping the frigates afloat as far as the pirates were concerned.

Claw brought Death Hammer back around and aimed her port side directly at the enormous ship's starboard.

Claw looked at Scar, who nodded.

"All guns," he barked into the ship's comm system, "put her out of her misery. Fire at will."

The first volley was all it took. They must have hit an engine or fuel tanks or an ammo locker, or some combination thereof, as the ship expanded oddly for a moment and then exploded into the even sky, raining detritus on the pirates, who didn't mind it at all.

The two remaining Kshatriya frigates turned and were racing away as fast as their crippled ships would allow.

Scar smiled.

"Let them go. We need witnesses."

Claw laughed and gave the order to stand down.

Damage control reported that Death Hammer was well on the high side of seaworthy, but four pirates had been killed. Wounded Eye reported that three gunboats had been lost, but two of their crews had all been rescued safely.

Both Scar and Claw found that news acceptable.

Claw watched as the burning wreckage slowly sank. In fifteen short epi-cliks, Scar had changed the balance of power on the seas.

One way or another, Arreti now had to deal with the Sugar Pirates.

ओम'

Ugnaronoo and the Omnium had taken to spending some time each turn melding their minds. The others had been created, one way or another, to value individuality, so they didn't participate. No one was quite sure what was being traded between them, but they both seemed content, so the others left them alone.

Natasha sounded the warning they'd arrived outside of the first target system.

As soon as they began to reduce speed, they heard the scanners activate. There was life here, and it had electronic communications.

That was a bit of a surprise.

Ugnaronoo checked its findings and could find nothing that would indicate the planet was occupied. They wondered if they were refugees like themselves, and they'd just gotten there second.

They carefully logged all of the transmissions, and Zeenat began translating. Or, she tried to. There were no visual signals at all. There was no way to put anything into context. Worse, the language was made up of extensive, repetitive phrases with only minor inflections differentiating them. Without knowing the meanings of the underlying words or the inflections' nuance, it was all gibberish.

Since they all were curious, Natasha kept them on course.

The system itself was nice enough, but nothing spectacular.

Two gas giants and four smaller worlds in closer to their sun. As best they could tell, it was the fourth planet that was inhabited. That was mildly confusing since both the Omnium and Ugnaronoo had concluded that the third planet would be the most likely refuge.

They kept all their scanners on alert, looking for signs of colonization on any moons or in orbit, but there was nothing.

The scientists watched everything unfold, raptly, on various screens throughout the ship.

As they attained orbit, they waited for the data scanners to spring to life, but they remained defiantly silent.

Noor looked at the readings they did have and smiled inside.

"They are new to the universe, but not to this world. They are in the nascent stages of developing technology. We cannot occupy this place."

All shared that opinion, so there was no further discussion. The third planet, while hospitable in some regards, was almost the opposite of the fourth. Water was scarce, and there were winds that would reach over one hundred kays per clik on the open plains. They'd other options—hopefully, better ones.

Nevertheless, since there was no real chance of them being detected, they set up in low orbit over the fourth planet and aimed Pravda's telescopes and scanners at the ground.

It wasn't long before they'd identified the major metropolises and common modes of transportation.

The planet was a water world, and it had some of the most beautiful ships any of them had ever seen, even in historical records. The residents were tall, amphibian bipeds. They ranged in color from dark greens to muted yellows. They all had large, black eyes and small snouts. Their arms and legs were triple jointed; they had six fingers on each hand and six toes on each foot. They tended to wear loose clothing and go without shoes as much as possible. They eschewed frippery and lived in compact, common sense dwellings surrounded by easily traversable roads.

All the travelers agreed that this would be an incredible race to get to know in the future.

Ugnaronoo altered a probe so it would be shrouded from electronic detection. This, they launched to monitor the development of this unnamed race. It was set to collect data and then send a transmission every twenty Suns on a specific frequency. When, someturn, this race shed the bonds of gravity, it would send a final message and self-destruct. They figured that, by the time any of them could return after that, these beings would be comfortably ensconced in the universe.

Maybe by then, they'd have figured out that odd language.

For now, it was time to leave.

ओम'

When the news came in, Rahan didn't hesitate. He ordered up the palace's private rotary-wing craft and went straight to Dravida. Given their heightened sense of alert after the debacle at sea, it caused his pilot to make many impassioned pleas not to be shot down before they were finally escorted in.

It wasn't until they landed that the Dravidian guards finally believed that the Goptri had personally come to see the Sovereign.

The pilot was taken to a lounge where she could calm down, and Rahan was led to the Sovereign.

When they were finally alone, Rahan spoke.

"We must destroy them," he said through clenched teeth.

"Or engage them in trade," she replied.

He stared at her, completely dumbfounded.

"Think Goptri," she said quietly, "why do they raid? They may be barbarians, but they are far from stupid. What happened this even proves that. Because of their rough past, the Din-La shun them. The Eastern Warrens kill them, and there is no way else for them to live. Maybe if we changed the dynamic, at least a little, we could put an end to this madness."

Now, more than ever, Rahan wished Manish were still alive. He would have known what to do.

He calmed himself and looked at her anew.

"What do you propose?"

"Nothing now. I think my reign is near an end. There is much which has happened within our borders that you do not know. Come breaklight, I will be meeting with the leader of the rebels. He wants the brands to have a larger say in how things are run. Maybe even in choosing a ruler.

"I have no heir, so now might be the time to make such a change. You should join us for the first meal. He is bright. Maybe between the three of us, we can work out a solution. For now, I am going to go mourn."

She stood, made a little bow, and left him to his thoughts, which, truth be told, were not making nearly as much sense as he hoped they would.

A pretty Ailurus fulgens entered the room. Rahan absently noted the glossy black and white fur on her face and how it contrasted so well with the deep, red fur covering her body. She had a puffy, black, and red, ringed tail that stayed just above the floor. Golden eyes rimmed her black pupils. She was just under a meter, and a half tall, wearing a soft blue sari and red slippers, and she was smiling at him.

"Namaste Goptri," she said pleasantly, "I am Lshana, personal aide to the Sovereign. Please allow me to lead you to an apartment. I will have refreshments delivered to you there."

He stood slowly and straightened his tunic. Then he nodded and followed her out.

ओम'

Now:

Zsst was sitting in the Pulinda trading post with several angry council members. They believed she'd misled them. She had, just not in the way they thought. She had to be careful here.

"Please, calm down, and listen to me," she pleaded, "reverse our positions, would you have admitted a maker was loose?"

That made them stop and think.

"Please understand," she continued as calmly as possible, "we knew that this maker had killed the Goptri, and others, including a Din-La, named Lrrt who got wise to her. Announcing that in council would have caused widespread panic."

"As it is now, it most certainly has," said the small Devi whose name she'd forgotten.

"Yes, it has," she had to agree, "but we thought, hoped, that the Kshatriya would be able to catch her before she made landfall in Chosun. That didn't happen, obviously, and now we need to be the cooler heads. Rushing around, waving your arms in the air, and screaming "MAKER" is not going to help."

"What will?" asked the Lakshmi, whose name also escaped her.

"Help is coming from all over the world. Let your constituents know that. Let them know you're in charge and dealing with the situation. Let them know their leaders are leading."

They weren't any less angry, but they saw the wisdom of her advice.

The Devi stood and looked her straight in the eye.

"Hear me well, Din-La," he said darkly, "never before have

we had reason to doubt the word of your brand. If we have reason to again, there will be repercussions. You are no longer the only source of trade. Remember that."

With that, they left her to her thoughts., and she had many. They were justifiably angry. So was she. She'd been used. She knew nothing about the maker until after the thrice-cursed being appeared in Chosun. That seemed, to her, like a secret that someone should have shared.

Still, this time, she'd told the council members the truth. Most of it anyway. They would never know the Goptri had been dead for five Suns and that a maker had run Bharat. That would lead to a civil war. Or worse.

Then she thought about the Devi's warning. He was right. Bharat was a great market, but they didn't need anything they couldn't get elsewhere. It would be a massive blow to the Din-La if it came to pass. She would have to notify the board of the threat. That wasn't going to make anybody happy.

She went behind the counter, filed her report, and then spied a fresh shipment of glurp from Kalindor. She pulled a bottle out of the case, and a glass off the shelf, tossed a few goldens to the proprietor, and sat herself in a corner.

She wasn't planning on leaving until she was heaving. She had to get the taste of lying out of her mouth.

ओम'

Pearl woke early; it wasn't even breaklight yet and walked out into the common area. She was mildly surprised and slightly amused to see Andana sitting in front of the vidscreen with headphones on, watching a show visibly geared towards smalls. Maybe he liked them young? Whatever, she was in no position to judge the perversions of others.

She headed into the kitchen, saw that he had made some omelets, and left them in a warmer. She made some toast, poured herself a cup of java, took one of the omelets, and set it on a plate. She noted the na-porcine meat, green peppers, and cheese and wondered where the hell he'd gotten the ingredients.

Probably better not to ask.

She took her time to enjoy the meal and relax. They'd a lot of work to do, and some downtime would serve them well. None of them knew she'd replaced the Goptri for a while, and they never would. There were some tricks she'd used she might need again if the Jung got in her way.

The meal was, as she expected, delicious. She wondered how he'd learned to cook so well. She'd been in elegant restaurants that weren't this good. Well, if he wanted to share that secret, he would. If not, it didn't matter. The food was incredible, and if he liked younglings instead of fully grown brands, that was none of her concern either.

When she looked over at him again, she saw him mouthing something softly. Whatever he was doing, she didn't think it had anything to do with lust. She watched him more closely. He had a small pad in his lap, and he was entering something every so often.

The show ended, and a speech from the Jung came on. He unplugged his headphones and turned down the sound. As he got up, he saw Pearl and smiled.

"Pleasant breaklight."

"To you as well," she replied, "may I ask what you were doing?"

He shrugged.

"When the Jung speaks to us, it's a chore to try and rotate the syntax into anything useful," he paused to pour himself a cup of java before continuing, "but when he speaks in his language, he's decisive and clear. I figure he's not stupid. He couldn't be to run this country as tightly as he does. So that just means there's a language barrier between us. I can fix that. I have a knack for them. I'm watching the broadcasts; they have to teach smalls how to count, spell, and use basic grammar. They use a lot more honorifics than any brand I've ever encountered, but it's not so bad once you start getting used to it. Once I get the hang of the basic courses, I'll move on to the more advanced ones. They do seem to have lots of training available for all their citizens."

She hadn't considered that. The Jung, to her, was a cartoon. A deadly one, to be sure, but not something to be taken seriously. She gave what he'd said some thought. If the Jung actually were smarter than she'd imagined, what did that mean to her plans? Was this a good thing or not?

Their military was a joke; that was true. But that could be due to their isolationism. They'd never learned anything. They were just a blunt force weapon. She thought back on what she'd seen the night of the battle. Those gunships were powerful. Properly deployed, they would have overrun the Kshatriya.

The same could be said for all their military.

As long as she was assessing threats, she turned her attention again to Adana.

"I'm not a fan of surprises, and you seem to be full of them. What's your story?"

He laughed.

"The usual, I guess," he said as he took another sip of java, "child prodigy gone wrong. The mental stuff was no challenge to me. School was boring, and I rebelled. But, as you may have noticed, I'm not that big. I tended to get beat up a lot. Then I learned some fighting forms, and one thing led to another, and I ended up serving the Sovereign. I did okay there, but I'm not much of a "take orders" kind of brand."

She had to snigger at that.

"Anyway, when my term was up, I ran into the Colonel. He was looking to earn some goldens and wasn't all that concerned about the risks involved. That was more my speed. The three of us have been together thirty Suns now. After this, I guess, one way or another, we're going to be together for the rest of our lives."

She hadn't considered that either. She, most definitely, was not looking for allies when she'd begun this. She hadn't even considered the possibility. But he was right. They were wedded together now. Anywhere they went outside of Chosun, they would be hunted.

Which was fine with her, but they'd never asked for this. Although she had to admit, he didn't seem all that upset at his change in fortune. She asked him why he wasn't.

"I don't know," he shrugged, "this is something new. It seems to me that I can use the best of my lives, the military discipline, and the daring of being a smuggler, for whole new purposes. Let's be honest; smugglers, by nature, tend to like adventure., and with you, I can't see a boring turn anywhere in my future."

At that, she laughed herself silly.

The Colonel and Śūra came out of their rooms just as she was gathering her wits.

"Always good to start a turn with a laugh," said the Colonel, "care to share with us?"

"It seems," she said, catching her breath, "that I'm not boring."

"Ah, hell," he laughed, "didn't I tell you the same thing last even?"

She recapped her conversation with Adana as it related to the Jung and was not at all surprised to see they already knew about Adana's talents. They also agreed with his assessment of the Jung. Thinking about it a little more, she concluded.

"Adana," she began, "as you get comfortable with each level of their language, I want you to teach us. Since we're going to be here a while," that got a big laugh, "we may as well be able to communicate with everyone."

He nodded and was about to say something when there was a knock at the door.

Śūra opened it, and they were all surprised to see the Jung smiling at them.

"You need, you get," he said, smiling wider, "thousands Shin-Sen die good."

He walked over to the vidscreen and plugged in a little device. The image of the Jung speaking was replaced with a long shot of a volcano. Suddenly it erupted, and lava spewed for kays in every direction. The camera swung to show the two villages at the base. They were overcome almost instantly. They never had a chance. While no one else in the room would have heard of Pompeii, it was the first image that leapt into her mind.

The camera work got a bit shaky after that as the spies ran for their lives. Since the video arrived, she had to assume so did they.

Not that she cared, but it was little things like that which would keep the Jung happy.

She decided that now would be a great time to ask for a plane.

"No plane," said the Jung, "buzz too much above."

She sorted that out for a moment.

"Ahh, there are planes looking for us."

"Yes," replied the Jung, "better like fish you be."

Śūra figured this one out first.

"You have a submarine?"

The Jung nodded and then motioned for them to follow him as he walked out of the room and was immediately surrounded by his usual dozen guards.

They traversed several halls and came to an elevator, which led them down seven stories below ground. When the doors opened, their jaws dropped. There were six subs in front of them: three completed and three in various stages of construction. Pearl recognized the design immediately. They were the latest the Kshatriya had developed. They even had a waterproof helicopter attached to the rear deck of each., and, just like the Kshatriya had designed, each helicopter had room for a pilot, a co-pilot, and four passengers.

She looked over at the Colonel.

"Your fruit deliveries are quite impressive."

"Not that impressive," he laughed, "we just brought the designs. They did all the work."

It took them a while to come up with a plan the Jung would agree to. They would leave at even-fall and take a weaving route to the Lightless Lands. They estimated that it would take six to seven turns. Once there, they would take the helicopter the rest of the way.

The part of the plan that hung things up was the part where the Jung came along. Seeing no other options, if they wanted access to a sub, they finally relented.

ओम'

The news had started coming in about two cliks after even-split. All of the ambassadors were woken and sat in horror as they watched the destruction being reported. Over three thousand villagers were presumed dead. The lava had landed on them in one deadly sheet.

Ignop sat in a chair, his face a mask. His two aides were just as stoic. They all knew that the Jung had done this. They'd all read Damadora's report on his trip with Pearl to the, allegedly, dormant volcano. Pearl had even been able to tell how much damage one of these devices could cause. There was a geometric progression involved. The more lava there was, the larger and more violent the explosion would be. The math was a little beyond them, but the evidence was not.

Plus, while the underwater volcano that Pearl discovered was tiny, the Shin-Sen's was a quarter kay in height and several kays in diameter., and it was still active. With a bomb like the one she'd seen demonstrated, she'd said there was no way for the result to have been any different.

That didn't make anyone feel any better.

Kolokk sat heavily in a chair and surveyed the carnage. Despite all he'd seen and learned these last few turns, all of this had seemed theoretical until now. With the destruction he was witnessing, he knew that the time of theory was over. A maker was loose, and now an apocalypse would savage the world. Worse, he had no idea how to stop it.

Mondara and the Mayanoren were holding hands. That odd pairing gave the rest of the room hope. There was a future worth fighting for.

Gffk and Xho were on the other side of the room, quietly discussing the new reality. No longer did the Chosun need an army. One or two brands could deliver weapons like this, and the Dragon Lords had numerous volcanoes. None posed a threat before, now they all did.

Damadora and Ragamooth had been in constant contact with Chandrack in the queen's communication room. Much of Bharat was uninhabited, but there were several small volcanoes near populated areas. Those would have to be guarded. Once that was agreed, they returned to the main room.

Chen and Wong recovered from their initial shock and were now discussing, with the other two Mayanoren, ways to bomb the Chosun back to the age of the makers. That plan of action started gathering momentum until Xho put a stop to it.

"Chen, and Wong," he chastised, "you should know better. Most of the Chosun cities are underground and heavily fortified. We could bomb for a hundred turns and kill nothing but trees. We have never sent in an army to deal with them in the past because of that truth. We have no way of knowing what traps lie beneath the ground. It could all be a maze, and we'd never find a way out."

He tried to think of a viable alternative and came up with nothing.

"We will need an army that can root out that maker and all who support her. That will be bloody and blunt work, but I see no other way. We will be forced to fight them on their home soil and under their rules. Wars tend to be lost when those are the terms of engagement.

"Guns we have, bombs we have, but minds we have also, and we must use those now if we are going to live through this. Just throwing our armies at bullets will accomplish nothing."

Navi stood.

"Xho's right. Gffk, can those satellites of yours see through rock?"

Gffk started to shake his head no and then stopped.

"Not ours, and not Lord Südermann's, but the fake Goptri launched several satellites over the last three Suns and seemed able to ferret out insurrections no matter how carefully hid. We should speak with Jagat and see if we can get access to those. My guess is they will be a great help to us."

While tenuous, it was their first tangible sign of hope.

Damadora returned to the queen's comm center and contacted Chandrack. He was not shocked that Jagat and Taarank were in the room with him, along with Dr. Rhanda. It took almost no time to realize they were stopped before they started. The Goptri's flip-top was heavily encrypted, and they'd been unable to access any of the files other than the ones she'd used regularly.

When told of the problem, Gffk smiled.

Not exactly the response anyone anticipated.

"The fake Goptri, in her infinite wisdom, bought only the best encryption software the Din-La has to offer. We designed it; we can break it."

He went to the comm center to have the best software designers available sent to Pulinda Palace.

They all still felt pretty helpless, but, at least, they'd begun to fight back.

ओम'

Stab sat with the Island Council and watched, fascinated, as news of the devastation on the island of the Shin-Sen unfolded. While all of the announcers were claiming it was a tragedy, he knew differently. Volcanoes give warnings before they explode. What had happened there was purposeful.

How it had been done was something he didn't care about at the moment. Who had done it seemed self-evident. That maker who called herself Pearl was the obvious answer. Whether by herself or using some lackeys of the Jung also didn't matter. Looked at plainly, if such a weapon existed, none of the other brands were crazy enough to use it.

That kind of devastation left no room for negotiation. That was a weapon of last resort, at best. Even then, it would give any lucid brand pause for thought.

Stab looked around the table and saw that the others were coming to a similar conclusion. Now, what would they do about it? There weren't all that many options when it was all looked at rationally, and Stab was a rational brand.

The mighty Scar, may his soul walk proudly with Ogou forever, had devised the Island Council hundreds of Suns ago as a way to avoid all the assassinations and other wastes of good brands. It was a good idea then, and it was a good idea now. Every five Suns, the citizens elected the fifteen to lead, and they, in turn, elected the king when the need arose. It arose less often now that kings stopped being killed randomly.

Stab was an Iwana. Tall and covered with gray/green reptilian skin, he had no hair, but he did have a crest that ran down his back. Like many brands, he had razor-sharp claws instead of fingernails. His black eyes were highlighted by the gold jewelry that he favored. Like Scar and all the kings who'd followed, he wore two vests. In his case, his inner one was red and cut above his waist. His outer one was gray and hung to his knees. Both had slits in the back to accommodate his crest. Black pants and knee-high leather boots completed his ensemble.

Not for the first time, he wondered what in the makers' hell the makers were thinking of when they created so many dangerous brands.

Intelligent they may have been, but smart they were surely not.

The same could be said of his predecessor, Crushing Grip. He'd ignored Scar's ancient wisdom when it came to not being too far from a means of escape. He'd invaded the Lightless Lands. Or, more accurately, he'd tried to.

When it became apparent that he'd crossed paths with a battleship and escorts from the Eastern Warrens who were also on their way to those lands, he decided to engage them. That was bad enough. But those ships were led by General Dagmar, and they were all on high alert anyway since they were in foreign waters.

When all was said and done, the Sugar Pirates were short one king and five ships. The Council really missed those ships.

He let those thoughts fade. The past was the past, and nothing could change it.

The future, on the other hand, was a different matter.

He turned to look at the courtyard where Death Hammer was lovingly preserved. That boat had changed everything for the Sugar Pirates. Now an even more significant change loomed on the horizon, and everyone in this room was looking to him to see if that was a good thing or not.

He looked back at the screens and smiled. No matter what happened, he figured that the Sugar Pirates would have plenty to plunder.

As long as they stayed the hell away from the war that was coming, the future didn't look bad at all.

He shared his thoughts with the others and was pleased to find them in agreeance.

Their turns as mere plunderers were behind them, but not so far, they'd forgotten. Let the idiots have their war; the Sugar Pirates would reap the rewards.

ओम'

Then:

Rahan couldn't sleep. His thoughts vacillated between what the Sovereign had said and what the Sugar Pirates had done. Finally, shortly after even-split, he had an idea. If it was a dangerously stupid one, so be it. Nothing else had worked.

He rolled out of bed, found his portie, and punched in his private number for Kshatriya command.

A colonel answered. He missed the name but figured if she had rank, she had answers.

He skipped right past the pleasantries.

"Tell me, Colonel," he began, "if you were going to go rogue and buy a boatload of illegal weapons, who would be the first brand you'd contact?"

"Excuse me, sir?" came the befuddled voice.

"You heard me. Who?"

There was a long pause.

"If it were me," she answered carefully, "I would go to Umbanaro."

He knew the name. A respected business proprietor who'd emigrated from the Lightless Lands many Suns ago. Rumors of criminal behavior swirled around him, but nothing had ever been proven. He imagined that the Kshatriya had a thick file on him. That was good. It would help him accomplish what he was about to try.

"Listen to me," he said tightly, "I'm only going to say this once. Grab his file and go to him now. Explain, in whatever manner you choose, that his Goptri is giving him a simple choice. If he can get the Sugar Pirates here to the Sovereign's palace in Dravida by breaklight, he will receive one full Sun of amnesty to set his affairs in order and become a legitimate business owner. If he refuses, for whatever reason, you're to kill him and then find someone else to contact the pirates. Is that clear?"

This pause was even longer.

"Crystal, sir."

"Good. Contact me as soon as you have an answer."

He flipped the portie off and stared at the ceiling.

Not all ideas had to be sane ones.

The colonel, a dark-skinned Pangolin named Elindama, stared at her portie and shrugged. Orders were orders, and there was no time to spare.

As it happened, Umbanaro's file was on her desk. Several Kshatriya thought they'd enough on him now to get a warrant for his arrest. She'd been detailing the crimes they could prove when the call had come in. They weren't going to be happy about this, but that wasn't her problem.

His picture stared up at her. A member of the River God brand, he had pocked gray skin, dark eyes, and large teeth. Portly, but deceptively strong, he was not the first brand she would have picked a fight with.

Well, she hadn't picked it, now had she?

She grabbed the file, tossed it in her backpack, and went outside. She found a cyke by the front door. Without asking permission from whoever might have owned it, she fired up its fans, hopped on, and took off. She estimated that she'd be at Umbanaro's in ten epi-cliks at most.

She pulled up in front of the enormous, secluded home and looked at the locked gate. She wasn't in the mood to deal with subordinates, so she ignored the call box and shot through the lock instead. She hoped it would set off alarms. That way, everyone would be awake when she got to the front door.

It had, and they were. Guards were rushing out just as she approached. Seeing her in full uniform, they blanched.

"Umbanaro," she said simply.

"He's sleeping," replied the Devi guard closest to her.

"Doubtful," she replied, "not with all these alarms going off. Get him."

"I'm sorry, Kshatriya," replied the same guard, "not without a warrant."

She thought about that not at all. She stuck the, still hot, barrel of her gun in his mouth and smiled.

"The Goptri has signed this; will that do?"

The guard's eyes were wide, and he was trembling when she heard a deep voice coming from the doorway.

"Come, come, Kshatriya," it said, "what's the cause for all this fuss in the middle of the even?"

She looked over to see Umbanaro standing there wearing a purple robe and matching slippers.

"I have a private message for you from the Goptri. I can't see it taking more than ten epi-cliks of your time."

He nodded.

"Anything for our beloved Goptri. Please come in."

He tapped a remote in his hand, and the alarms shut off.

She snagged the guard's gun out of his hand and then pulled hers out of his mouth. With that done, she followed the alleged crime lord inside.

He led her to a small smoking room and poured himself a brandy. He motioned to her, and she shook her head no.

"So, what is the cause of all this ruckus?"

She smiled. She hated brands like him and, with her hands freed, was looking forward to this no matter the resolution.

"What I have here," she said, laying the file on a table, "is enough to tie you up in court for five Suns, easy. Certainly enough to destroy your businesses. If I get lucky, it may even be enough to send you to prison for the rest of your shitty life."

He glanced at the file but didn't touch it.

"Or" she continued, "you can decide to be a good citizen, contact the Sugar Pirates, and have them at the Sovereign's palace in Dravida by breaklight."

"And if I refuse?"

"I'm to kill you and then go to the next name on my list."

For the first time in a long time, Umbanaro knew fear. This was no random threat. Kshatriya were more likely to sing Pzzby songs while wearing frilly dresses than they were to grandstand meaninglessly.

"Certainly the Goptri wouldn't be so harsh," he said while trying to figure out a way out of this, "there must be more to his kind offer."

"There is. You get one Sun of amnesty to make all of your businesses legit. One sepi-clik after that, all deals are void."

He looked at her and then back at the file. In just a couple, short, epi-cliks, his life had been ruined. Maybe not.

"How will the Goptri justify an honest citizen being killed by his Kshatriya?"

"He won't have to," she said as she leveled the guard's gun at his head, "you'll accidentally be killed by one of your guards. It will be a horrible tragedy. The Goptri may even name a turn of mourning in your honor."

Umbanaro was no coward, but he was a pragmatist. Torn between the option he loathed and the one he feared, he chose loathing. He carefully reached into the desk that had the file on it and pulled out a portie. He punched in a lengthy series of numbers and waited.

"This is Umbanaro, patch me through to Scar …. Yes, I know where he's at … No, I don't care …. Look, if Scar wants to come out of this alive, he needs to speak with me, and he needs to speak with me now.”

After a few, long, epi-cliks, she heard a voice come on the portie.

“Greetings to you Scar, I apologize for interrupting your delightful adventure, but something has come up which requires your attention. Our beloved Goptri has requested your immediate presence at the palace of the Sovereign in Dravida … why, yes, one of his kind representatives is with me now.”

He glanced at her. She knew what he’d been asked, so she just jumped in.

“It’s a diplomatic meeting; he can enter and leave under a flag of truce. He and his will not be molested.”

She had no idea if that was true and, given recent events, didn’t much care.

“You heard? Excellent. What shall I tell the nice colonel?”

He listened for a while and then snapped the portie shut.

“He will be there just after breaklight. He will arrive on the Sea Killer. Death Hammer, the ship that seems to have caught your Goptri’s attention, and Cursed Fates will stay off the coast. At the first sign that anything’s amiss, they will open fire on the palace. Given the size of the shells, he specified I’d imagine they could level it.”

Elindama nodded. This would have to be good enough.

She picked up the file and walked out the door. She contacted the Goptri as soon as she got to her cyke. He seemed pleased with the news and asked her to draw up the amnesty papers for him to sign when he returned.

He made it clear that no one else was to know what had transpired this turn.

The Goptri called for Lshana and told her what he'd done. She didn't waste any time arguing about whether it was a good idea or not. She simply set about notifying everyone what was about to happen and ensuring that a shooting war wouldn't erupt when the pirates arrived.

Then she sent word to the rebel's representative that their meeting would start as soon as the pirates were in the palace. She had no idea how that would go over. Nor did it matter. What was done was done.

She decided to wait until the Sovereign woke to tell her. No need to add to her woes. This turn would be stressful enough as is.

Palek Khan was the leader of the rebellion in Dravida. So far, it had been peaceful, but there were those who thought change was not happening fast enough and were looking to take more direct action. While not a pacifist, he'd served three terms in the Sovereign's army; the thought of civil war revolted him. It would be a terrible waste of life.

He stood in front of a mirror and tried to decide what to wear. His brand had been made from the genes of an animal called a Bengal Tiger. He was a powerful presence at almost two meters tall and covered with reddish and black fur even if he just stood up. He had all the aspects of his genetic ancestor, the retractable claws and the gold-flecked eyes being the most obvious, but he also had a keen intellect. His brand had been built to be slave labor. They'd thrown off that yoke and now had another.

He thought about that. It wasn't really a yoke in as much as it was unending condescension. Do what you're told because your Sovereign says so. An entire country couldn't be treated like smalls forever.

Something had to give.

He had no idea what the Sovereign had in mind. Her messenger had said little other than to promise him and his safe passage to and from the palace. News that the Goptri was here and Sugar Pirates were on the way only heightened his curiosity.

Somehow it didn't feel like a trap, although this would be an ideal opportunity to eliminate all of her problems at one time. He shook that thought away. The Sovereign wasn't stupid, and a move like that would ignite a war on many fronts.

Glancing at the small dresser he'd brought with him, he decided on his gray suit. It had a light gray shirt, a dark gray tie, and shoes that matched the tie. It was a subdued look, and he wanted the focus to be on the issues at hand and not on his attire.

Just as he finished dressing, there was a knock at the door. He called for whomever it was to enter and was mildly taken aback to see Lshana walk in carrying a tray of food.

"Pleasant breaklight milord," she said as she came in.

"To you as well, Lshana," he was mildly confused, "to what do I owe the honor of the Sovereign's personal aide bringing me my breaklight repast?"

She laughed a gentle laugh.

"Not so much an honor as a practicality," she said while smiling, "the regular staff is pretty busy right now with preparations for the turn, so those of us with nothing else to do are pitching in. I happened to draw this duty. I hope you don't mind."

For the first time, he took a long look at her. She had a beautiful smile that only enhanced the rest of her. She was absolutely stunning. He quickly realized he was staring at her like a youngling with its first crush and gathered his wits.

"No, not at all," he said while returning her smile, "I just thought I was special."

That got him rewarded with another one of her beautiful laughs.

She set the tray down and uncovered it.

He hadn't noticed the three carafes hooked on her belt until she set them on the table as well. They were plainly marked Dairy, Java, and Juice. The meal itself looked terrific, as well—a diverse array of curried meats and a steaming bowl of soup that he couldn't quite place.

He motioned to the feast.

"Would you care to join me?"

Another smile!

"I wish I could milord, but there are a million other little things that need to be done, and too few brands to do them. Perhaps when this is all over, and assuming we're not at war, milord could treat me to an even-fall meal."

Yet another reason to resolve this peacefully.

"I would be honored."

She made a little curtsy and left him smiling.

The fate of the world as he knew it was riding on his shoulders and all he could think was how lovely she'd look in chiffon.

ओम'

The Sugar Pirates arrived about two cliks after breaklight. Scar, Claw, Scrap Dragon, and Wounded Eye all disembarked from the Sea Killer and were met by an unarmed escort. Sundara had insisted on that when she'd been told they were coming. She didn't want the slightest hint of hostilities if they were to have any chance of this meeting being successful.

How the Goptri had contacted them was yet another mystery. But not one she needed solved. Leaders need to have their secrets; otherwise, anyone could do this job.

It was then she realized the solution to her problem with the rebels.

She smiled to herself. Complex problems rarely were when looked at from the right point of view. If the point of view she'd chosen was so skewed as to be unrecognizable, so be it. She was the Sovereign, and hers was the only point of view that mattered right now.

She walked with Lshana to the meeting hall. Palek and the Goptri were already there, and she could hear the Sugar Pirates marching up the stairs.

Introductions were swiftly made, and Sundara gestured them all to sit at the round table in the middle of the room. Aides brought in carafes of spiced water and java and left them on the table. Cups and glasses had already been set out by each chair.

The pirate called Scar picked up a carafe of java and poured himself a cup. He sipped it and smiled.

"Much better than we have at home."

Everyone else followed suit, and soon they were all sipping java quietly. Were it not for the staggering number of casualties totaled the previous even you'd have thought this a convivial gathering of old friends.

Sundara decided to get things going.

"I'd like to thank you all for coming on such short notice," she said as she rose, "what we decide here this turn will set a course for all our brands. Therefore, we need to think wisely before we act. But first, there is a matter of business that relates just to Dravida, which I must deal with before we continue."

She turned to face Palek.

"In one Sun, I shall resign as Sovereign," that caught everyone's attention, "and give the reins of the government over to the brands. You will need that time to create a council to represent the four states and eighteen counties of Dravida and find candidates for the citizens to choose from so they can elect one as their new Sovereign. I have enough goldens set aside from my various inheritances that I'll not need a retirement fund. We can make this a clean change.

"I only put one restriction on this."

"I can't be a candidate," said Palek.

"Correct. No matter how you spin things, it would look like a coup, and that would be the wrong message to send if we want peace."

Palek considered this but only briefly.

"I never wanted to rule in the first place. Our cause was aimed at finding a more balanced distribution of power, not just naming a new Sovereign. Your solution will accomplish all that and more. We can have aides create the flowery words we will need to make the announcement palatable, but for our work here this turn, I agree."

"Good. Now to our next major issue," she turned to face the Sugar Pirates, "what are we to do with you?"

The Goptri thought of several responses, most of which involved slow forms of hanging. He kept these to himself.

Scar looked thoughtful for a moment and then responded.

"I'm not sure what you can do. You just announced that you're retiring. How do we know that any deal we make this turn won't be erased in a Sun?"

"That is why Palek is here. He leads the rebellion."

"Maybe true," replied Scar, "but he just admitted he won't be the ruler when you're gone."

"An easy solution," inserted Palek, "we'll just have any arrangement formalized by the trade council. They're here now, and they'll be here long after. That should provide the stability you seek."

Scar mulled that over and smiled slightly.

"We'll start there then since it's trade we seek. We're tired of losing good brands for little gain."

"YOU'RE TIRED!" blurted the Goptri. He quickly regained his composure and apologized.

"No need to apologize, your Majesty," said Scar quietly, "this has spiraled out of control for all of us. Most of my brands are farmers," no one knew that but it didn't change anything, "and they raise fruits and crops that you've never seen, let alone tasted. They would welcome new markets. Let's begin with them and see what we can do."

"How do you know that our brands would like these new foods?"

"Well, your Highness," Sundara noted that he had a warm smile for a murderous pirate king, as he addressed her, "brands like to eat, and there are always those who want to try anything new."

That was true.

"But we need not guess. May I borrow one of your aides for a brief errand?"

She could see no reason why not.

Lshana stood.

"I'll run your errand."

Scar nodded and reached into a pocket on his vest and pulled out a small piece of paper and a writing implement. He quickly jotted down a note, folded it, sealed it with a piece of wax that he snagged from another pocket, and handed it to her.

"Take this to the Sea Killer. Deliver it to Bleeding Lesion and wait for her reply."

Lshana kept her thoughts on the name to herself, and quickly, but elegantly - noted Palek, exited the room.

ओम'

Lshana grabbed a hover cyke from one of the palace messengers and quickly sped to the pier. The honor guard saw her coming and stepped aside as she drove straight up the ramp and onto the Sea Killer. The crew looked at her in abject confusion. She stopped and instantly realized she had no idea what Bleeding Lesion looked like other than she was a femme., and, given the mix of brands she currently saw populating the deck, that was not much help.

"I have an important message for Bleeding Lesion from Captain Scar," She announced to the general throng.

"It's King Scar," corrected a reptilian brand she didn't recognize.

"My apologies," she said, facing him directly, "but either way, I still have the message for Bleeding Lesion from him."

He nodded and signaled for her to follow.

He led her down two flights of stairs and deep into the ship. She wasn't sure what she'd been expecting, but this wasn't it. The ship was spotless and well cared for. Supplies and spare parts were neatly stacked and labeled.

They entered an area near the rear of the ship, and her guide hollered out.

"Hey, Bleed! Scar's sent a message to ya."

A young-looking femme walked out of a storage locker. She was of the same brand as the one who called himself Wounded Eye. If you ignored the fact she was heavily armed and holding a cleaver, she was quite pretty.

Lshana handed her the sealed message and stepped back.

Bleeding Lesion pocked the cleaver into the wall, opened the message, and read it carefully. Her mouth changed from being tightly pursed to showing a wide smile.

"Fang!" she spat, "get your lazy ass moving and bring me twenty hands. If they give you any sass, I'll toss them myself. We've got fast work to do if we're gonna make the king happy."

As the reptiloid ran off, she turned to Lshana.

"Tell his Majesty it will be done in half a clik. Also, tell the guards outside that we'll need an escort to take us to Scar inside the palace. We'll come unarmed, per his orders."

All Lshana could do was nod and head back topside. She was barely at the first staircase when she saw twenty brands, including the one named Fang, running to the rear of the ship. She knew entire garrisons that couldn't equal the level of efficiency she was seeing here.

These were not the mindless heathens she'd been told. She'd have to keep that in mind as events moved forward.

She got to her cyke, eased down the plank this time, told the guards what Bleeding Lesion had said, and headed back to the palace.

ओम्'

She got back to the meeting room and rapidly noticed all eyes were upon her.

"The lovely Ms. Lesion says her task will be done in half a

clik."

"Aye," said the one called Claw, "she is comely on the eyes, isn't she?"

"Yes, she is, if you don't mind your femmes heavily armed."

The pirates all laughed heartily, and the others, not knowing what the heck she was talking about, just smiled awkwardly.

Earlier than promised, they could hear the sounds of a large group scurrying through the palace.

The twenty-one pirates marched into the room. Now, instead of weapons, they were wearing bright red vests. Bleeding Lesion and Fang also sported colorful blue scarves and were leading the procession. Behind them, the nineteen remaining pirates were each carrying a large basket on their heads. There was a dais at the far end of the room, and Scar motioned for them to set the baskets there.

Once everything was in place, Bleeding Lesion and Fang pulled off the lids and set them to the rear. Then all twenty-one pirates stepped smartly to the side of the room, away from the rest, and stood at attention.

"Outstanding," said Scar, "now, your highness, if you'd be so kind as to call your trade council, we can find out what will and won't sell. The rest of you are welcome to sample them if you wish."

He walked over to the row of baskets and reached in one to pull out a large, pink orb. He drew a small knife from his vest and quickly cut the fruit into quarters. He put one part in his mouth to show everyone how to eat them and then began passing the pieces out around the room.

Rahan stood back, not taking his proffered share.

He wanted these demons dead, not as trading partners or meal companions.

Nevertheless, he saw the wisdom in the Sovereign's solution. She'd put an end to the raids, stopped the rebellion before it began, and handed over a new source of goldens to her citizens. All well and good if you could put the past in the past, but Rahan just couldn't do that. Not yet anyway.

Maybe not ever.

Soon enough, ten, exceedingly confused looking, members of the Dravidian trade council were escorted into the room.

Confusion swiftly gave way to wrangling.

Rahan stepped back even farther and didn't see Scar walk up behind him.

"So Goptri," said the pirate, surprising him, "you'll not be joining the haggling?"

Rahan just shook his head no.

"I understand, "he said sympathetically, "some wounds just won't heal."

Rahan turned to look at him carefully. Although he was dressed in his pirate finery, you could still see scars. This, then, was the pirate who'd taken them from simple bandits and turned them into a world power. That was not to be dismissed out of hand.

On an intellectual level, he could almost admire what this brand had accomplished. But it stopped there. He'd been to too many funerals, consoled too many widows and widowers; he'd seen too much of what the Sugar Pirates could do.

Entire villages could disappear in a single even.

Sundara could do what she felt was best for her realm from now on, and he would do what was best for his. He did not see the Sugar Pirates as a part of that future.

When he'd first set these events in motion, he'd assumed that the pirates would be brutish thugs, easy to manipulate. That was a mistake. They were intelligent, organized, and now had the most powerful ship the seas had ever seen. Worse still, he knew they were only going to get stronger.

"If you," said Rahan in a measured voice, "leave my lands alone, we'll pretend you don't exist. That's the best I can offer."

The pirate seemed to think about it, if only barely.

"I am sorry, Goptri," he said sincerely, "what kind of king would I be if I made agreements with no trade to bind them?"

Rahan watched him walk back to the dais.

He would have to warn the Kshatriya. He may have made a dangerous enemy this turn.

ओम'

Now:

It had been thirteen turns since they'd left Chosun. Pearl had to admit she was impressed with the crew's efficiency. There wasn't a wasted motion or redundant chore to be seen. Andana had been making strides with the language, which he'd found out was also called Chosun. That had made Pearl smile when she'd been told. One name for the language, the land, and the brand. No waste there either.

She wouldn't have been surprised if it was the name of their national food, too, although that turned out to be called kimchi.

The Jung, impressed with Andana's efforts, had given him access to a teaching tablet. Now he could study at his own pace, which was considerable. He was already conversant with the sub's crew and had the smugglers and Pearl on pace to join him in another ten turns or so. He worked with something called the thousand-word method, and Pearl had to admit that it was a great way to learn a language.

Its essence was simplicity itself. Learn a thousand core words, nouns, and verbs usually, but you also needed honorifics in this case, add in some basic syntax, and then you could augment from there by interaction. You may not know what the word for cabbage was, but you could ask the name of the leafy green vegetable.

Since they'd nothing else to do, the process took up most of their time and went smoothly.

One thing was becoming clear Andana's hunch had been the right one. The Jung was no fool. Once he'd found out that Andana was learning his language, he set aside one clik each turn for Adana to teach him Common. That was the more difficult task since the Jung had so much to unlearn. Still, they kept at it, and progress was being made.

Pearl also learned that the Jung had ordered another volcano blown up. This one in the land of the Dragon Lords. She figured they were his bombs now, so he could do with them as he pleased., and he seemed to be happy by killing off his enemies.

She knew of worse hobbies.

They'd passed under several ships headed for Chosun. Probably to erect a blockade. The Jung had decided to bypass them so that the secret of the sub would remain just that for now.

They were due to arrive at their destination in a couple of cliks, right around even-fall.

Pearl found the smugglers all sitting in Colonel Orandia's cabin and joined them. She was not amazed to see a small platter of sandwiches and two large jugs of java set on the Colonel's dresser. She poured herself a cup and grabbed one of the sandwiches, which turned out to be made of na-porcine meat, and wasabi cheese.

The Colonel looked at her.

"I'm glad you're here. We're trying to figure out what we

should be looking for when we get to Rohta's lab."

She pondered that for a moment. Not because she didn't know the answer but because she was unsure how much to share. She decided to stick with the larger items and leave the issues of what was, or was not, stored on those magnificent computers to herself.

"There are several things. First and foremost, we need to see if the decanting facilities still work. I have no idea how many Chosun there are …."

"Six point five million," added Andana helpfully.

"How fucking many?!?!"

"The Jung keeps meticulous records. Those include an annual census," he sipped his java and continued, "as well as a breakdown of all raw materials. Honestly, this place would be a gold mine and an international power if they'd any idea what they were doing.

"As far as I can tell, and I'll be the first to admit I need to know more, they isolated themselves after the gen-O-pod™ war because they felt they'd been insulted by the other brands, and while much of their history is horribly distorted, there may be some truth in there.

"What I know for certain is that the peninsula they'd called home when the makers lived was completely vacant after the war, so that's where they set up shop, as it were. Based on the few historical records they have, it also seems that their high-born makers had been erased from the world and left behind nothing of value. Although their records don't mention it, my guess is that there was a massive gap between the haves and the have nots leading up to the rebellion, and the Chosun were created to fill in the gaps."

"A fake middle class?" she seemed incredulous.

"Essentially, yes."

She racked her brain, trying to remember back.

"From what I can recollect, the Chosun had been split into two countries for a long time, and then, about five hundred years before the rebellion, had united. But that was a tenuous relationship, at best. One side was all about order and discipline, and the other was all about trade. They were not a good match. Nevertheless, given all that, the Chosun must have had the fewest reasons to rebel. I wonder why they did."

"Well, from what I was able to discern, originally, the underclass joined the rebellion as the brands neared, and the Chosun aligned with them. When a group of makers killed some brands while a peace treaty was in effect, the Chosun killed all the remaining makers, even their allies. Better to be safe than sorry, I guess."

She could understand that.

"Okay, more on what was later. Right now, we need to figure out what we have."

"We still need to know what we're looking for," chimed in Colonel Orandia.

"Sorry, you're right," she said, "of Rohta's many quirks, he had a fondness for weapons' design. That was where I learned how to make the volcano bomb. We need to get as many of those designs as we can. Also, there should be a ton of viable genetic material there. I wouldn't mind decanting a few more makers. We'll have to leave a small contingent of Chosun to oversee the process, but it's not like we'd need to teach them genetic engineering. It's more a matter of watching some gauges and pushing some buttons at the right time. They can certainly handle that."

The smugglers had mixed feelings about that but kept their thoughts private.

"Also," she continued, "while the Chosun may number in the millions, they are a single force. I'd like to get some diversity, so we aren't limited in how we fight."

"Not as limited as all that," said the Colonel, "they have an air force and a navy."

"You're kidding."

"No. Their problem is that each function on its own. They've never meshed them before."

She smiled.

"They will now. Andana, get me a breakdown of exactly what they can field. We'll start planning as soon as we can. Who knows, we may even live through this."

She didn't know it, but none of them planned on that at all.

ओम'

It had taken ten long turns, but the Din-La had finally broken the encryptions on the flip top, and what they'd found had been astounding. While the satellites couldn't "see through rock," they could detect heat signatures up to an eighth of a kay below the surface. They'd immediately set about altering their orbits to align them over Chosun. It had taken two turns to get everything right, but once they did, data started pouring in.

Xho had been right to call it a maze. Over ninety percent of the populace lived underground., and, excluding some access ways, nothing was closer than a kay to any coast.

More importantly, the numbers they were seeing were staggering. It was impossible to get an accurate count, but they estimated there were at least five million Chosun. If they came spilling out, they could overrun anything that got in their way. They held no illusions other than that was precisely what was going to happen. It was a matter of when not if.

They also wondered why they hadn't before.

They couldn't have waited almost a thousand Suns until they found a maker, could they?

That's a frightening level of dedication, as in delusional.

They also found an artificial cove that housed a small navy as well as a set of runways and hangers that looked large enough to support some sizeable planes. There was also a large underground cavern, but they couldn't make out any details, so they had no idea what, if anything, was there.

Yet, no one could remember any reports of a Chosun navy or air force. Just the ubiquitous gunboats they kept sending after interlopers.

Did they do all of this just waiting for the arrival of a maker?

More importantly, how real a threat were each of these things they'd discovered? Was that navy just some hulls, or were there fully functional ships with trained crews? Were there planes in those hangers, or was that just storage? Common sense said it was all a façade. Common sense also said there were no makers, and no one knew how to make a volcano into a bomb.

Common sense wasn't nearly as helpful as it used to be.

The good news was they now had a good idea of what they would have to deal with. The bad news was they now had a good idea of what they would have to deal with.

ओम'

After the detonation of the volcano on the island of the Shin-Sen, it was decided to bring the ambassadors' families to the palace of the Ice Pirates. Xho, thinking his family would overwhelm the proceedings, respectfully declined. The

Mayanorens, having no families, just stayed on as is. Everyone else sent for a spouse or significant other, except for Colonel Krark and Mondara. Krark had no one serious in her life right now, so she decided not to make things confusing or awkward. Mondara sent for Vandamir's military strategist. It wouldn't be the same as having the old brand in the room, but it would help to have a gifted mind.

Queen Lynno had the comm center expanded into the next room and then added extra communication gear so the ambassadors could contact their superiors privately. As much as they needed to work together, they also needed to be able to deal with the politics of the situation back home.

And the situation was universally bad. Only the constant updates on the ever-growing blockade and the repeated assurances that nothing was getting out of Chosun alive kept the situation from devolving into riots.

Pearl had shown them several ways to destroy the volcano bombs, which was useful information but, unfortunately, reactive. A lot of brands needed to die before you knew one was there.

And a lot of brands had. The death toll for the Dragon Lords in the Ninth Kingdom was over twenty thousand, and they were still counting.

There had been no announcement from the Jung claiming responsibility. There'd been no contact at all after the maker had been introduced. That didn't help calm anyone.

Another thing that wasn't helping was the continued silence of the Sugar Pirates. Lynno posited that they might be sitting this one out. They certainly had no love for Bharat or the Chosun., and none of the ambassadors knew enough about them to get their take on makers.

Some within the Sovereign's palace in Dravida might, but relations between them and Bharat were chilly on the best of turns ever since the Goptri Rahan had insulted them by bringing the Sugar Pirates to their realm, and then not trading with them, and, worse, they seemed to blame the late Goptri Sharma for all of this.

The fact that they were right didn't change or fix anything.

Nevertheless, they'd sent three destroyers to bolster the blockade, so that would have to do for now.

ओम'

The helicopter flew low and fast over the jungle canopy to the coordinates Pearl had provided. To everyone's initial horror, which turned into a pleasant surprise, the Jung did the piloting himself. He was confident and sure at the controls and said nothing the entire trip. They cleared a ridge, and the facility came into view.

As with all of Rohta's facilities, it had been equipped with automated service bots to keep the grounds and buildings clean and repaired. These were still functional, and the well-manicured lawn denoted their destination.

There was a helipad to the north, so the Jung aimed there and gently set the craft down.

After the five clik trip, they all got out and stretched.

The co-pilot stepped out, carrying a cooler. This he opened up and motioned to them all.

"No good hunger to search," started the Jung, and then shook his head, "no, no good to search while hungry."

"Excellent, your Majesty," smiled Andana.

The Jung smiled back.

The cooler was filled with sealed bags of snacks, spiced waters, and fruit. The Chosun didn't seem to go in for sandwiches. Still, the idea was right. They'd a long turn or more ahead of them. Better that they cleared their heads.

They enjoyed their rough picnic for about half a clik, and then Pearl motioned to the nearest entrance.

"This door leads to the main library. Rohta didn't trust digital files much, so these are all hard copies printed on paper. They are sorted by subject, and then author. There is an entire section on military strategies just to the right of the door as you enter. Orandia, I think you should review those to see if there's anything we can use."

He nodded.

"Andana," she continued, "across the main floor by the south entrance, you'll find a section labeled 'World Interest.' That is a section that lists all the world's known treasures, and some that are just rumored. Wealth was never my main interest, but there might be something in there that could benefit the Jung and our cause."

He nodded as well. But none of them moved.

"Śūra, once you get in the door, turn to the left, and you'll see a staircase. One level down in the blue section, you'll find a bank of gray file cabinets. They will contain the weapons designs, various transport options, and so on. Take our co-pilot with you and see if there's anything he believes the Chosun can manufacture now or with just a little effort."

The Jung repeated those instructions to the co-pilot in Chosun, and the young brand smiled.

"Your honored Reverence," she turned to face the Jung, "you and I will go to the bottom level and see if there are any more makers."

He smiled and then shook his head, more in wonder than negation.

"To truly walk among the footsteps of a God is a rare honor," he said in Chosun, *"to actually be in the palace of the maker of all things truthfully does make all we have suffered worthwhile."*

Pearl looked at him thoughtfully and then began walking towards the door.

The rest followed.

Her instructions proved accurate, and it was then they all began to realize they were well and truly in the home of Rohta. Even the smugglers felt some awe.

More importantly, they were in the physical presence of a maker who had once walked and talked with him. That was a powerful revelation.

None of the smugglers were what could be called spiritual, but they began to believe that there were powers at play here well beyond their understanding.

Pearl led the Jung down two flights of stairs, and then through a long hall. At the end were three sealed doors. She entered a code in a pad nearest her, and the first one opened. They walked in and could see over five hundred tanks lined in rows of twenty-five each.

The first set had tiny, winged elephants. Tiny by elephant standards, at least. Each was about the size of a large pony. The wings, white and richly feathered, were beautiful. She looked at the settings and realized they'd been ready for decanting for a long time. They were to have been one of the new brands introduced in Bharat.

The next row contained Chosun. The Jung looked at his ancestors in stasis in rapt fascination. Far from revolted, he seemed intrigued.

He pointed to a tag below the gauges.

"Does this our purpose state?"

She shook her head, no.

"That would have been up to the makers who placed the order. Rohta just created the pods as the requests came in. This tag is just identification information, instructions about when it can be decanted, and so on."

He nodded at that, and they continued.

The next four rows contained exotic looking animals. Since they had snouts, she knew they weren't sentient—just pets for the rich.

Maybe some could roughly speak, but that would be more of a windfall than anything else.

She remembered a lizard he'd kept for fun. A little thing. It could fly and form rude sentences, but, God forbid, it hit the letter 's.' It sounded like a deflating balloon. She'd found it hilarious.

Say She Sells Sea Shells by the Sea Shore!

The Jung had no idea what she was laughing at, so they moved on.

The rest were various small orders. Some unusual plants, a few succubi, a few reptiloids, and a bunch more that interested neither of them.

On the back wall was what she wanted—the giant coolers with all the raw genetic stock. The Jung looked at the rows upon rows of vials floating in the mists and frowned.

She noted his discomfort and decided to help him out.

"These are where everything begins. Every creature Rohta made came from these vials and others like them. We can make makers here. We can make more Chosun too. But we will need help. How long until you can get a hundred or so Chosun here?"

He paused, smiled, and answered her in Chosun.

"You have noticed we are not dumb. That is why I treat you like you are smart. I had the other two subs follow us for protection and workforce if need be. I can have ten Chosun here in five cliks. Then ten more every ten cliks."

It took a lot to astound her, but he had done just that. It was her turn to nod and stare.

He smiled, pulled a radio out of his suit, and began issuing instructions.

When he was done, she motioned to a table, and they sat across from each other.

"If you and I are going to succeed, we need to talk."

He shrugged.

"With all your resources, why haven't you just overrun this part of the world?"

He shrugged again and then answered in Chosun.

"We don't know how to war. Not really. We have many more soldiers than the Dragon Lords, but always they outsmart us. When we think we can counter what they've done, they do something else. We can build anything. We can keep things working longer than they should. But, when the Great Revolution was over, we were shunned by the other brands."

"Why is that?"

"I do not honestly know. We served honorably as shock troops during the Esteemed Rebellion."

The look of horror on her face was impossible to hide.

"Yes, I know," he continued sadly, *"but it was a needed service., and one we provided willingly. We forced the makers to focus one way so the other brands could attack from another.*

They threw their bullets at us and lost. We were, and are, proud of our service."

She could see his point of view but knew the others must have thought them nothing but mindless fodder. She certainly would have.

The two of them sat quietly for a time, and then she brightened. She could give him and his back their honor and bind all of them tighter together in the process. Then they would get about the real business at hand.

She smiled.

"Before we go, we must decant the flying elephants."

"Why?"

He was obviously confused.

"When we return, we will set them loose then in Bharat. Each with a note around its neck saying, 'a gift from Rohta's chosen.' After all, someone in Bharat paid for those; they should get their goldens' worth. It's the only fair thing to do."

He understood instantly. The horror those beasts would cause would be worth far more than any piddling bomb. They would know the knowledge of Rohta's work was no longer a mystery. No longer lost to the past. Rohta's chosen could make brands too.

He laughed and started singing again.

This time she understood the words.

"Should the enemy dare to invade our country, annihilate them to the last brand so that none of them will survive to sign the instrument of surrender!

Frustrate the imperialist moves for ideological and cultural infiltration by the dint of our revolutionary ideology and culture!

Keep the laughter of the smalls ringing by increasing the production of their foodstuffs!

And make many fruits cascade down, and their sweet aromas fill the air."

Fresh fruit is always a good thing, she decided. Whatever the case, it was sure a catchy little ditty. She found herself humming along.

ओम'

Nerves were starting to fray. After blowing up two volcanoes in four turns, there'd been nothing. For the next forty turns, there hadn't been a single sign the maker, the Jung, or, for that matter, anyone in Chosun was alive. If it weren't for the heat signatures, the satellites could see you'd think the place abandoned.

They were just going about their business as though nothing unusual had happened.

Unlike the ambassadors, the allies' general populace treated no news as good news and tried to get used to these new alliances. Thanks to the Din-La offering discount travel packages, and all of their accommodation partners agreeing to steep discounts until this all blew over, brands were traveling, getting to know each other, and spending goldens in new markets.

Lots of goldens.

Gffk announced that this maker problem may have been the best thing that ever happened to the Din-La.

He was only half-joking.

Ignop, deciding to meet change head-on, had invited Asa and Navi to his room for a hand cooked meal. He even went so far as to make it himself. He found them charming and fun. More importantly, after a clik or so, he found he'd forgotten what it was that was supposed to make him uncomfortable.

Things would not change in one even, but he decided to let his brand know that change was possible and, quite possibly, beneficial.

The next turn, he invited Xho, Chen, and Wong for the same reason. While he also liked them, a discussion on their family life only reaffirmed that the Shin-Sen weren't quite ready for that much change.

Yet, he was making new friends, new allies, and learning new things. Those all seemed like good things to him.

On the forty-first turn, after the devastation in the Ninth Kingdom, odd messages began to arrive. At first, the ambassadors were prone to dismiss them mostly because they were coming from coastal fisher-folk and others who might be inclined to superstition.

But when Kshatriya Dayan, and Xhin Lau, the spy, made an identical, and mutual, report, it was immediately decided it needed to be looked into.

Miniature flying Ganesh were something that could not be explained.

The next turn, Chandrack reported one had flown right over Pulinda Palace just after breaklight.

Within a clik, Kshatriya Dayan reported that he'd captured one. Well, not so much captured as lost his bowl of noodles to it while he was at Xhin's stand. He said the creature was friendly and healthy, and then he read them the note hung on its neck.

And more than the volcanoes ever did, this news sent a death-like chill through the room. The maker now had access to Rohta's secrets, and, by implication, so did the Chosun.

ओम'

Nkkl and Kondilar were riding in a hovercraft headed toward the lands of the Nanek-Dev. It was a peaceful time. She'd resolved a course of action, notified the Din-La's board, and made all the arrangements for the new trading post that would soon be opened outside the new Sikh of the Guru's palace.

Suddenly the craft slowed to a stop. They looked forward to see the driver staring, slack-jawed, into the sky. They stuck their heads out the windows just in time to see a Ganesh fly by.

They didn't have to contact anyone to realize the implications. A new maker had appeared, and now there's a new brand.

She was going to enact Rohta's retribution for the rebellion.

As cute as the messenger was, the message was terrifying.

ओम'

The three subs were at a dead stop south of Chosun. The alliance blockade was using a sonar net. Whether as a standard precaution or because they knew what they were hunting was beside the point. If they moved any further north, they would be discovered.

Things had been going well until this point. Thanks to the Chosun rotating the three helicopters, they'd staffed the facility quicker than the Jung had predicted. Once they were in place, she'd used the replication function on the first twenty-five tanks to create an additional one hundred and fifty flying elephants. She knew that some would die in a Sun or so since they weren't fully formed. But the rest would breed, and prosper, and become part of Bharat's permanent landscape.

Rohta never put bio bombs in pets since their owners could kill them at any time they wanted if they got bored. There just was no need for the extra effort.

When the twenty-five tanks were finally empty, she and the Jung had agreed she should begin creating more makers. She knew that implanting false memories was a waste of time. As the person grew older and the memories didn't hold up, they became dangerously psychotic. That was the last thing she needed. But basic instructions could be inserted, such as "this is the way of the world," and so on, so she'd made sure those had been as detailed as possible.

No one besides her ever knew that Rohta had been experimenting on cloning humans. It was against the law and the kind of thing people tended to go to war over. It had been his dream to seed the universe with clones since humans wouldn't go. He'd seen no future for humanity on Earth.

He'd unquestionably been right in that regard, if not in the way he'd intended.

She'd overseen the implantation of the genetic stock into the processors herself. After carefully scouring the records to make sure there were no siblings being created, she'd selected twelve females and thirteen males. One of the descriptions reminded her of one of his husbands. Since it wasn't like he could get jealous, she'd added him in.

Rohta had great taste in spouses, so he would probably be a stud.

Twenty-six people wouldn't provide enough genetic diversity to restart the race, but they could create more once these were up and breathing. These would nevertheless serve as notice that humans were back to reclaim what was rightfully theirs.

That would have to be good enough for now.

She and the Jung had settled on leaving behind a contingent of ten Chosun to oversee the process. They'd made sure there were extremely detailed instructions of what they were supposed to do and enough provisions for a Sun or more. Unlike the flying elephants, these would not be rushed.

Contrasting the traditional cloning process, Rohta's version did not create an embryo and then grow the being from that. Instead, it created a biological map of the final expected outcome and then filled it in in stages. That shortened the overall life span of the result but not by enough to matter to her.

Although brands could live a couple of hundred Suns and some double that, humans seemed to top out around one hundred and twenty. Rohta had been doing research, which seemed to indicate those limitations could be shattered but had been unable to finish before he'd killed himself.

She'd look more into that when she had some time. Or she'd let one of the clones do it. She had some outstanding options now and intended to explore them all.

She'd decided she liked the idea of marrying her hobbies with a worthy cause. It gave her something to live for that she hadn't ever had before—a reason to help others.

Such as it was.

As far as she was concerned, genocide and rebirth were two sides of the same coin.

The three smugglers were huddled with the bridge crew. Speaking in rapid Chosun, they were looking at maps and reading reports. There was nowhere they could go that was deep enough to avoid detection. They were working on the next plan.

The Jung had shown them all the ordinance carried on each sub. Beyond the usual retinue that anyone might expect, each also carried four special torpedos, tipped with tactical nuclear warheads.

How and where those came from was never explained.

Pearl had merely laughed when she'd seen them, but now Andana was seriously suggesting using them to punch a hole through the middle of the blockade.

He was not getting much resistance.

As in none.

They would need to move fast to dive beneath the sinking

ships to escape, but they all thought they could accomplish that.

Divers swam from sub to sub relaying instructions and making sure all the chronometers were synchronized. This would be the most silent attack in history until the ocean exploded in sheets of radioactive flame, that is.

At the appointed time, the Jung signaled for full speed ahead. Just as they confirmed they'd been spotted, the three subs fired simultaneously and then dove.

The sound of the explosions echoed through the subs, and the shock waves buffeted them mercilessly. Rivets were popping, gauges were blowing out, but the crew never wavered. They stayed at their posts and guided the subs to safety.

ओम'

The mayhem on the surface was all-encompassing. Ships on the perimeter braved the fallout and raining debris to try and save as many sailors as they could. Unfortunately, there weren't any.

No one had a clue as to what had happened. Not at first anyway.

Detectors, installed by rote more than need, now began issuing warnings that had not been issued in over one thousand Suns. Horrified, the remaining ships pulled back. These explosions had been nuclear.

Not since makers had walked on Arreti had such a weapon existed. Let alone been used.

Then again, a maker did now walk Arreti, and they would have to adjust their tactics to deal with that reality.

ओम'

Messengers were hurrying through the palace of the Ice Pirates. Each of the ambassadors was trying, as best they could, to pass along factual information to their homelands. The scene was, at best, controlled pandemonium.

Navi and Asa stood, holding hands off to the side. Krark was taking care of notifying the Yelda of what had just transpired. She left out nothing that she knew. Never in her life had she wished for a mate more than now. She desperately needed a hug. Nevertheless, she kept her demeanor professional and answered the same questions over and over again, just as everyone else was doing.

Queen Lynno was sitting to the side. She looked haunted. Navi and Asa walked over to her.

"This isn't your fault," said Navi.

"Oh, I know," she sighed dejectedly, "it's just that I think we all could have seen this coming sooner. Maybe not the maker, but the strangeness in Bharat, for sure."

"And what if any of us did," he replied more calmly than he felt, "what could we have done? Declared war on it? Sent in a squad of assassins? Anything we might have tried would have died within a kay of the border, and you know it."

She nodded, patently unsatisfied.

"Well, okay," he continued, "at least we know something now that we didn't before."

"What's that?"

"The rules of engagement."

She looked at him, visibly confused.

"There aren't any."

ओम'

The three subs entered the underground pen and surfaced. All three were heavily damaged but still relatively seaworthy.

Deck crews swarmed over them as they came in and checked to see if there were any injured. They discovered there were many who were shaken and confused but found no actual injuries.

The Jung was quickly surrounded by his guards and smilingly took his leave of the smugglers and Pearl. They were escorted back to their apartments and told to call for whatever they needed.

They collapsed onto the couches, and Śūra turned the sound off on the vid. There seemed to be no way to turn off the vid itself.

Colonel Orandia got up and pulled a bottle of Sugar Pirate rum from the cabinet and poured them each a glass. Pearl didn't even try to bother asking where that came from.

She just looked hard at Andana.

"You've really raised the stakes now."

"I have done no such thing," he said defiantly, "as soon as Arreti knew a maker lived, the stakes were set. In many ways, anything we do afterwards is anticlimactic."

Six nuclear explosions was not her usual definition of the word 'anticlimactic,' but she got his gist.

"One thing's for sure," added Śūra, "sooner rather than later, they're going to throw everything they have at us. We'll need to get those designs I found built as quickly as possible."

"Where are they?" asked Pearl.

"One copy is in my duff; the other is in the hands of Yun Ku, the co-pilot from when we first landed. He was taking them to where ever it is here that they build stuff."

That seemed to be the best that could be done.

She picked up her drink and opened the door. There were no guards anymore. She guessed they were trusted now.

She walked back to the dock to see repair crews crawling over and into the subs. Welding torches could be seen in a hundred different spots. The Jung had said they could make things last longer than anyone else, and now she believed him.

She didn't hear Colonel Orandia come up behind her.

"Ya see, lass," he said dryly, "we were right. There's never a dull moment with you."

<u>The End of Kitaab Ek</u>

WELCOME TO ARRETI

NOTE: *There are two appendices here. The first pertains exclusively to the new species introduced in the Goptri series. The second is a reprint of the appendix from The Brittle Riders, which contains all the other species and societies which were previously introduced.*

All brands are human hybrids, and omnivores, except where expressly noted. They were designed to be low maintenance slave labor for a depleted human population. While many brands were designed to perform specific tasks, ranging from dangerous to tedious, others were aesthetically pleasing and created as toys or living statues.

However, all brands were designed for speech, so they don't have long snouts or beaks and, instead, have mouths that, more or less, look human.

All brands were designed with enhanced immune systems as well as the ability to create embryonic stem cells in a specially designed organ, which also provided an unending supply of Telomerase enzymes to keep their bodies in peak condition. All brands had a built-in bio-bomb that would kill them ten years after decanting so that Rohta could continue to restock the same orders over and over. Their immune systems overcame the bio-bombs, and the brands called their triggering the "ten-year flu."

APPENDIX I – THE WORLD OF THE GOPTRI

THE REGIONS

Bharat – The northern half of what used to be known as India. Many of its citizens were genetically based on Rohta's interpretations of what Hindu gods should, and should not, look like. As a general rule, the brands who live there are atheists or, at best, agnostic.

Chosun – A combination of old North and South Koreas with a little bit of Southern China added on, the Chosun are a fiercely insular race bent on world domination. They have spent their entire existence waiting for the return of the makers. They breed excessively by accepted standards but live underground, so no one can know how many of them there are.

Dravida – The southern half of the Indian continent, the country is cautious in its dealings with others but joyful and pleasant once you get to know them. One of the most genetically diverse populations outside of the ones on the continent across the ocean. They practice a ritualized version of Hinduism with an emphasis on peaceful interactions and honesty.

Ice Pirates - Settled in the lands in, around, and under the Ural Mountains, the citizens of the Ice Pirates were individually rugged and occasionally warlike, but not a threat of any scale. The discovery of maker tech, and the ability to recreate it, forced them to coalesce all of their varied tribes in one location. Their fear being, if they had it, others could too.

Lightless Lands – They live in everything but the northwest section of what was once Africa, although they tend to stay in the southwest primarily. The inhabitants tend to live in homes built into the upper branches of trees, travel via monorails, and live lives dedicated to arts and sciences. They are devout pacifists, having destroyed all weapons shortly after the gen-O-pod™ war.

Lost Gods – They occupy the upper eastern section of the continent known as Africa. They keep away from the coasts as much as possible—a collection of brands primarily made by Rohta's competitors. Unlike the known brands, some have snouts, tails instead of legs, and many other oddities. They managed to remain mostly unknown until the Chosun wars. Even then, they held back for an extended period. They practice a generic form of worship, essentially acknowledging a god, and letting people speak to it as they wish.

Nanek-Dev – Insular only in the sense they prefer to do things themselves; they are a friendly and gregarious group who enjoy the company of others, playing games, and sharing foods. They do not drink alcohol and rarely eat meat. They follow a modified form of Sikhism, emphasizing inclusion, accepting others, and living a peaceful life.

Realm of the Dragon Lords – Covering the lands of what used to be China and Mongolia, the Dragon Lords thrive in a family-based, feudal society. The dragons come in many colors, shapes, and sizes but work together for the betterment of all. Many of their cities are prosperous and well-appointed with architecture and art. Not a deeply religious society, they do keep various shrines and sacred locations in good repair.

Shin-Sen – They maintain the islands formerly known as Japan. Hierarchal to the point of nearing social atrophy, every aspect of their society has become ritualized, even down to warfare. Devout and conservative in their beliefs, they still have managed to interact with other societies and keep open trade routes. They also are the only place on Arreti where you can see a horse as it originally evolved. For reasons they keep to themselves, they managed to save them from being overrun by the genetic stock of deisteeds.

Storm Wraiths – They were the deadliest creatures ever created by Rohta, and they know it. Based on amphibian stock, there are five colors of Storm Wraiths. In order to preserve species purity, no color may mate with another. No Storm Wraith may mate with another species. Raping other species, and killing them if they become impregnated, is accepted. Due to their requirements for mating, they are not many. Seat holders rule them, one from each color, and all rules made from them are absolute. Storm Wraiths know they're destined to rule the world; they're just waiting got some of the other brands to get out of their way.

Sugar Pirates – One could say they are the last, real pirates of the Caribbean. One shouldn't, but one could—a veritable panoply of forgotten brands that have been interbreeding for too long. The majority of them are farmers or laborers in related industries. But their financial security is brought by the raids of the pirates. Feared sea folk, they are unafraid of attacking larger or better-armed vessels. Since they succeed more often than not, they are given a wide berth. Sexually, they reserve same-sex unions for their physical needs and mixed-sex unions for procreation and marriage. They practice a modified version of

Vodou.

Yelda – A gag species Rohta foisted on Eastern Europe, three-eyed Yetis with bodies covered in white fur, their minimum height of six feet made them loom over many. They were designed to be brute labor, and something Rohta's clients could laugh at. After the gen-O-pod™ war, they settled north of the Punjab and became known as fierce, but rabidly honest warriors.

THE BRANDS

Bastet – Based on the Egyptian cat god of the same name, they are an erotically feline brand meant to provide kinky pleasures to their owners. Tall, lithe, with pink noses, small mouths, soft white fur, slanted green eyes, pointed ears, and well-rounded curves, they're still viewed lustfully. They've also developed into lethal military minds which, for some, adds caution, and, others, appeal.

Bengal Tigers – Rohta took the basics of Panthera tigris tigris and turned them into a perfect killing machine. They averaged about five and a half feet in height and were born well-muscled. They were so good they were among the early troops to kill large quantities of makers. They later assumed more diplomatic, even agrarian, roles in society.

Chien-Bois – Bush dogs from the old South America were altered to be obsequious servants. After the rebellion, they relocated to the Caribbean and became integrated into the pirate culture. They proved to be capable and cunning killers.

Chosun – A custom order for a long-forgotten client. Vampire pandas with incredible strength and the ability to build anything once shown how they lack the ability to conceive anything. That was programmed on purpose. Initially shock troops for the rebellion, they were later shunned as too stupid and worthless to be of use to the new society. They took umbrage with that.

Devi Based on the Hindu god of the same name, their place in Rohta's pantheon is unclear. With four arms, blue skin, and near elastic bodies that could contort into wildly unusual forms, they could have been anything. They tended to serve in the military after the rebellion but filled many niches.

Dragon Lords – Designed to be the anti-succubi, they were meant to be arial labor and an homage to the histories of the clients who ordered them. Multi-colored and possessing various body types, they're all mighty flyers and tend to live in familial bonding units of ten or more.

Ganesh – Based on the Hindu god of the same name, they were created to be servants and sex slaves. All the males were well endowed, and the females were built with exaggerated curves to service their doms in all ways. Their noses resembled the trunks of the elephants they were based on.

Guenon – One of only four pure simian brands created by Rohta. Blue masked faces with short red fur, which feature light-colored patches around the cheeks, they have longer arms and legs than humans would and were created to be servants. After the rebellion, they fit into many niches and enjoy a reputation as a brand you can like.

Hashmallim – Based on the Old Testament creatures of the same name, they are tall, thin, with wide eyes and large wings. They aren't just white; they're translucent enough; others can watch their organs function. Despite their delicate appearance, they're capable of ripping a creature in half with their bare talons.

Ice Pirates – A bizarre adaptation of Ursus Maritimus, a/k/a Polar Bears, they were meant to serve as cheap, easily replaceable labor. Once unleashed, they had different ideas. Killing every human came easy to them. They claimed the lands near the Urals, and most other survivors were too afraid to challenge them. Territorial and violent, they are left to their own.

Kali - Based on a variant of the Hindu god of the same name, they were created to be sex slaves. Their ten arms, and hermaphroditic sex organs, were meant to allow them to service multiple makers simultaneously. Their telepathy was an unintended consequence. Given they were supposed to be short-lived, no attempt was made to correct the issue.

Lakshmi – Based on a variant of the Hindu goddess of the same name, they were created to be sex slaves. Their four arms and yellow-tinted skin set them apart. The male versions, built for middle-class clients with little money, and bland tastes, tended to be good looking but have small penises and fewer skills.

Lionine - Designed to be something beautiful to look at, and not much more, the lion/human hybrids have gorgeous manes, sculpted physiques, and developed a cunning intellect after the rebellion.

Manasa – Based on the Bengali goddess of the same name, they have seven snakes growing out of their heads, which act as emotional sensors, and organic lie detectors, and long hair, which keeps the snakes comfortable. They were designed to bring pleasure to the makers. Their snakes could sense moods and needs, and they could adjust their ministrations accordingly. They are pacifist vegetarians who have a wide variety of body types. They reside in a valley that borders the western edges of Dravida and Bharat.

Nanek-Dev – Based on silverback gorillas, the Nanek-Dev were meant to be brute labor. After the rebellion, they displayed keen intellects, a sense of whimsy, and an almost pathological desire to be self-reliant. Unlike their genetic predecessors, the Nanek-Dev have long hair on their heads, which they cover in turbans, and can grow beards.

Pangolin – A bizarre adaptation of the Asian anteater. Bred to be elite killers, many still are. Their armored bodies were enhanced with lightning-fast reflexes, superior senses, and darker shades of skin tones so they could better blend in the shadows. Their slightly smaller mouths give them all a lilting accent, which some find adorable. Usually, those they aren't about to kill.

Panther – This black-furred hybrid was built exclusively to provide sexual pleasures to the makers who purchased them. However, many makers taught them to hunt as well, so they could enjoy the feral joys of killing, albeit vicariously. After the rebellion, the panther line was so disgusted with what the makers had made them do they became founders of the Lightless Lands' pacifism movement.

Pearls – Beguiling cephalopods, the Pearls are the only parthogenic race on Arreti. Each generation carries the memories of its ancestors. The human section, the top half, of each Pearl is a clone of a woman known only as Pearl, who was the last serial killer on Earth. Rohta was able to suborn the need to kill in the clones but never could do so with Pearl. The Pearls are excellent pilots, voracious lovers, and mostly pacifists.

Pharaoh – Loosely based on the Egyptian god Mahees, the Pharaoh line is part lion, part human, part cockatrice. Like many of the Lost Gods, they were designed for military uses., and, like many of the brands who were so designed, they excelled at their tasks when they joined the rebellion. Unlike Rohta's creations, the Pharaohs have small snouts that add a rich texture to their voices.

Red Panda – based on the Ailurus fulgens line which used to inhabit China, they retained many of the base animal's attributes, their body is covered in red fur, their faces are masked with pure white, and have deep, black, eyes. Unlike many of Rohta's creations, they also have the bushy tail of their ancestor. Not much is known about why they were created, but they settled in Dravida after the rebellion.

River Gods – Named after the ancient Egyptian term for Hippopotami, this brand has a large frame, thick, gray skin, large, black eyes, and a much larger mouth than any human. This was designed so the resulting creation could have larger, squarer teeth with the upper and lower fangs of the base animal. Built for raw labor, they integrated into the Lightless Lands as cunning business brands.

Shin-Sen – Based on the Japanese Serow, they were bred to handle household staffs and not much else. They are stately to look at with white tufts under their chins, both male and female, tan to beige fur covering their bodies, and beautiful, black hooves instead of feet. They stand about five and a half feet tall and tend to pronounce words carefully and precisely.

Shiva – A four-armed variant of the Hindu god of the same name. Dark blue skin and generally muscular, the Shiva brand was built for simple labor. Like almost all brands Rohta created, he made sure to create two distinct sexual identities so maskers could have sex with them if they got bored. It was considered a perk.

Sloth Bear – A variant of the Melursus Ursinus line, Sloth Bears have long black body hair, short, prickly facial hair, deep-set black eyes, and razor-sharp talons. They were built to be a multi-purpose brand, capable of labor, military support, or even logistic support in offices. After the rebellion, they located in Dravida and melded into society as a whole.

Solenodon – Originally venomous and predatory, Rohta removed those traits but kept their slot toothed appearance. Short, with a long nose, they have long, thin arms, and powerful legs; they were bred to be miners. A task they shunned completely after the rebellion.

Sphinx – Based on the Egyptian god of the same name, the Sphinxes have four legs, powerful chests, long manes, and a powerful tail. They were built to be military shock troops and, as such, were given the ability to sustain far more damage than most other creatures.

Trachypithecus geei – These golden simians are beautiful to behold. Long, golden hair, with large tufts on their cheeks, surrounding a matte-black face, they have longer arms and legs than their human ancestors. Built entirely for the pleasure of the makers, they are powerful and cuddly. The powerful part became evident during the rebellion when they simply ripped the limbs off of makers as they went.

APPENDIX II – THE WORLD OF THE BRITTLE RIDERS

THE REGIONS

Children of the Waters – A collection of amphibian races who reside primarily on the west coast of the old United States. They also have crossed the Pacific to live on many islands. The most populous of the brand alliances, they adhere to a modified form of Buddhism. While not wholly pacifists, they go out of their way to avoid conflict.

Dwellers of the Plains – A loose collection of brands who populate the area from east of the Mississippi River to Lake Michigan and from about middle Arkansas to the Canadian border. After the gen-O-pod™ war, they renounced technology and developed an agrarian lifestyle. Each brand had its private military presence, but they had only a few disputes between brands, so they were more ornamental than useful. Some brands believe in a deity but only in a casual manner.

Eastern Warrens – A diverse collection of brands that live from the Smokey Mountains to the Atlantic Ocean. They inhabit territory as far south as Miami and as far north as Newfoundland. After the gen-O-pod™ war, they picked and chose what technologies they wished to keep. In the main, they adopted an agrarian lifestyle; they kept a standing military and armed it with weapons made by the makers or weapons adapted from those to fit particular needs. Their southern clans tend to be followers of Islam, but the rest take a more casual, slightly Gnostic approach to God.

Kalindor – A collection of reptiloid brands united under a single ruler called The Exalted. They live south of the Rio Grande to Antarctica. They want all the technology the world has to offer but had been bred in such a way that imaginative thought eludes them. Once something is explained to them, they understand it readily enough, but nothing comes to them originally. To get what they want, their Exalteds have forced them to wage war, unsuccessfully, against the realm of Lord

Südermann and the *Children of the Waters* for hundreds of suns. Their belief system is essentially neo-pagan. Their book of the five gods is part mysticism and part ecologically friendly instruction manual.

Realm of Lord Südermann – A collection of insectoid races who live in the southern Mid-West of the old United States. Their territory covers from near the Rocky Mountains to the Mississippi River. By far, the most technologically advanced brand alliance, they salvaged as much infrastructure as they could after the gen-O-pod™ war and built on it. They adhere to a modified form of Christianity. They have a defined military with an elite guard, a regular army, and one militia sworn to Lord Südermann. Until the final war with Xhaknar, their policy for dealing with trespassers was to put them to death and destroy the body.

THE BRANDS

Ant Person – Part fire ant, they averaged around 4½ feet in height and were bred to be desert espionage specialists. Unlike ants, they do not have mandibles, but they do have sensitive, silica-based body hair that they can use to propel their bodies while prone or sense changes in the atmosphere that elude others. They also have multifaceted, insect-like eyes and can see in near darkness and in multiple, simultaneous directions. After the gen-O-pod™ war, they became severe isolationists who only would work with the *Periplaneta* brand (see below). They prefer to wear full body uniforms of nondescript colors.

Athabascae Warrior – Part buffalo, they were made by the New Sons of Freedom Militia to help protect their mountain compounds before the gen-O-pod™ war. They have shaggy body hair and tend toward dark colorings. They prefer clothing made from natural materials and tend to favor buckskins. They live close to nature and are excellent healers.

BadgeBeth – Part various species of badger, they average around 5 feet in height or less. They have a mixed black and white coloring and are covered with light fur. They were designed to work exclusively with soil and were engineered to repel or attract the natural ground's basic molecular structure. They have razor-sharp talons and fear almost nothing. However, they were forced to live underground, or far from civilization, when Xhaknar attacked. They tend to favor simple clothing decorated with small pieces of jewelry.

Chaldean – Part cow, they average around 5½ feet in height. They tend to have blotchy reddish-brown colorings with no fur. They were bred to be corporate functionaries but took up an agrarian lifestyle after the gen-O-pod™ war. Even so, they do keep a small militia that serves the clan. They became followers of Allah before the gen-O-pod™ war and have retained that faith throughout, albeit with some discrepancies to take into account their genetic differences and fallacies told to them by their makers.

Columba – Part pigeon, they average a little over 5 feet in height. They are gray with touches of white. They were designed to be messengers, despite all the high-tech capabilities of the makers, and they were a popular item purchased by wealthy people who felt that they added the perfect level of secrecy to their long-distance conversations. Their heads bob when they walk, but they are almost matchless in the air.

Cudas – Part barracuda, approximately 5 ½ feet tall, a mix of mottled brown and black coloring, they have small mouths with blade-sharp teeth. They were designed to be aqua assassins and tend to be self-contained, to the point of annoyance, but are rabid believers in the ideals, if not always the practicalities, of the *Children of the Waters*.

Cyclops – Pure mutant, they average around 7 feet in height, have bright yellow skin (which is mildly phosphorescent), and just one eye. Their eye can see the complete spectrum from X-rays to Infra-Red. They were built to work in dangerous mining situations and handle heavy objects with ease. A quirk in their design gave them eidetic memories and a profoundly philosophical bend. Their philosophy includes the phrase: "Love everyone until they cross you, then kill them."

Din-La – Part rodent, probably rat, they average around 4½ feet in height and are usually portly in adulthood. They are lightly furred, typically gray, and slightly nervous. They wear a uniform of a purple jacket and yellow pants, though they've never explained why. They are excellent at keeping secrets and have a global subculture/trading network, which keeps them in the good graces of brands that would otherwise exterminate them.

Fierstan – Pure mutants, they were designed to be simple laborers. They have four powerful arms and well-muscled bodies. They average around 5½ feet in height and have bright red skin with dark patches under their eyes. Despite their intended breeding, they have keen intelligence and salvaged what technology they could after the gen-O-pod™ war. They built a powerful city within a fortress after the war and were the acknowledged leaders of the plains until Xhaknar came.

Grindle – Not an actual brand, but a creature created by Rohta for amusement. Part lizard, part bat, it has native intelligence and the ability to speak. While not intended by its makers, they developed sapience and can develop loyalties.

Haliaeetus – Part eagle, they were made by the New Sons of Freedom Militia to help protect their mountain compounds before the gen-O-pod™ war. They average around 5½ in height and are covered with white and brown feathers. They have large wings and can fly faster and farther than their genetic predecessors. They have keen eyesight and talons for fingers and toes. After the gen-O-pod™ war, they retreated to the mountains to live a primarily agrarian lifestyle.

Horun – Part falcon. They average around 3½ feet in height, are thin with agile wings. They have 200/20 eyesight and were bred to be airborne spies. They were also quite facile at micro-processing and micro-manufacturing. They have talons instead of fingernails and can use those for delicate operations. They are uniformly ebony-colored with blood-red wings and some red markings around their wrists and ankles. They have light down around their eyes, which stretch across their necks, and hides their ears. They tend to wear dark-colored clothing and prefer lighter fabrics so they can be dressed while flying.

Human – Not technically a brand; they were the creators, or "makers," of all the brands. A race that was genetic cousins to apes, and other primates, they lived on Earth and ruled over it due to their native intelligence and supposed superiority for approximately 12,000 years. When finally, aware that they were to be denied travel amongst the stars, the race began to die off. This lack of human labor combined with the need to keep up a certain lifestyle led them to create genetic hybrids to do the work and/or fighting for them. They called these hybrids gen-O-pods™ and divided them into trademarked brands.

Kgul – Pure mutant, inspired by the ancient tale of the Gollum, they are large, clay-based creatures and were designed to provide manual labor for extended periods of time. Because they were difficult to make, they were created with the ability to survive almost any injury and to be able to regenerate body parts as needed. They are smarter and more resourceful than they look and are fiercely devoted to the *Rangka* (see below).

Kleknar – Pure mutant. No one has any idea what their inspiration was. They average around 3 feet tall, are pure white, and are almost perfectly round. They were designed to get into small places in mines and can swim surprisingly well. Developed with an ability to control autism, they have keen senses that they can enhance at will and are deadly shots. If they open their senses up too much, they enter a sort of null state and need care for the rest of their lives. They also have a twisted sense of humor and can turn almost anything into an explosive.

Koi-San – Part koi, they were bred to be decorative additions to large homes with pools or fountains. They average just under 5 feet tall and are covered with translucent scales of many colors that cover pale skin. They tend to be the more thoughtful members of the *Children of the Waters*. While they did fight in the gen-O-pod™ war, they've never taken up arms again.

Kwini-Laku – Part seal, they were the first brand ever made by Edward Q. Rohta. They were designed for underwater research and to be able to go into areas that would be lethal to human divers. Averaging just over 5 feet in height, they are powerfully muscled and intelligent. After the gen-O-pod™ war, they joined the *Children of the Waters* and set up small island communities around the Pacific Ocean.

LGX-117 – Part broad-snouted caiman, they average barely five feet in height and have greenish, scaled skin with pale eyes. They were designed to survive in jungle environments and handle any task they were assigned, no matter the heat or the humidity. Physically strong, they are smart enough for many tasks but lack any originality.

Llamia– Part horse, part steer, part armadillo, they average 7 feet in height and weight around ½ a ton. They have the torso of a human, the body of a horse, with the cloven hoofs of a steer that have razor-sharp points, and armadillo-esque armor that starts in the middle of their backs and then covers their entire rear loins and rump. They were designed to be a warrior brand that could haul supplies, fight close battles, and survive harsh environments. Their skin color is as varied as the humans that were used for genetic source material, and they each have a mane that stretches down the middle of their torsos to the tip of their backs. Bred for intelligence and the ability to utilize many weapons, they were a major factor in the success of the gen-O-pod™ war. They wear clothing when they are in social situations or battle. Otherwise, they prefer to be nude.

Maker – See *Human* (above).

Mantis Warrior – Part mantis, they average over 6 feet in height but tend to be thin. They have pea-green skin and small barbs on the backs of their legs. Extremely intelligent and resourceful, they were bred to work in arid environments and handle hazardous materials. They were sold mostly to oil and gas companies. After the gen-O-pod™ war, they relocated to North America and swore allegiance to the *Periplaneta* (see below).

Mayanoren – Part gorilla, they average a little over 6 feet in height and are extremely powerful. They have no body hair and mottled, pink skin. They were designed to be infantry for a new world army by makers in competition with Rohta. In the main, they are half-witted and require extensive explanations and training to accomplish any task beyond killing. However, killing is something they do well, and with extreme gusto.

Minotaur – Part Toro Bravo, they were bred to be warriors and officers. They have deep reddish skin and powerful muscles. Averaging over 6 feet in height, they are heavy, hoofed beings who have developed a deep, spiritual side while keeping all their warrior skills. They favor simple clothing and currently live near a dormant volcano under the ground.

Named One – Smart *Mayanoren*. See "*Mayanoren*" (above) for more information.

Naradhama – *Fierstans* (see above) captured and mutated by Xhaknar into a servant class of warriors and sycophants.

Orcan – Part killer whale, they were designed to be security for several shipping companies. They never developed the real killer sense of their genetic predecessors and were scheduled for elimination around the time of the gen-O-pod™ war. Even so, they are powerful swimmers with large, finned feet and have skin coloring similar to their namesakes, as well as a developed echolocation bulb on the front of their forehead and a blowhole on the back of their neck.

Pan – Half goat, approximately 3½ to 4 feet tall, thin, and the males appear as traditional satyrs. Because Rohta enjoyed the myth so much, he ensured that all the males were well endowed. Having no template for the females, he'd simply made them voluptuous. They all have pale white and auburn hair and green eyes. Their lower body fur is thick and colored the same as the hair on their heads, and they all have a curled white tail. Designed to be sex toys primarily for wealthy Europeans, they have turned into a wildly divergent race that breeds everything from art masters to warriors.

Periplaneta – Part cockroach, they are the sole race that provides the Südermenn for the delta brands. They average 5 feet in height, have six arms and mandibles instead of mouths. They were designed to work in environments that would be lethal to humans, primarily radioactive and toxic. After the gen-O-pod™ war, they salvaged as much technology as possible and immediately set about to recreate the infrastructure necessary to run it. Highly creative and resilient, they are extraordinarily spiritual and follow an essentially Christian lifestyle. The various insectoid brands revere them.

QZD-1934 – Part chameleon, they average less than five feet in height, weigh less than 100 lbs, and have the ability to alter their skin color to blend in with their surroundings. They were designed to be spies for various corporations and militaries. After the gen-O-pod™ war, they retreated to the southern continents and waited for a ruler to emerge.

Rangka – Wizards who had their flesh removed by a military-grade virus in the first battle with Xhaknar. Much debilitated in one way, they developed even more enhanced powers over magnetism and a powerful psychic sensitivity. See *"Wizards"* (below) for more information.

RZL-274 – Part flying lizard, they average around 5 feet in height and have membranes that stretch from their wrists to their feet. They also have a stabilizing membrane between their legs. They are mottled yellow/green and have razor-sharp talons instead of fingers or toes. They were designed to work on top of the canopies in rain forests.

Se-Jeant – Pure mutant, they average around 5½ feet in height, have gray/blue skin covered with similarly colored fur, and tend to be thin. They have three-round eyes and were designed to do specialized miniature work. Their long, slender fingers, flat noses, and slits for mouths belie the fact that they are fierce warriors and cunning adversaries. They developed an affinity for colder temperatures and live further north than any other brand on the plains in a home they call The Ice Palace. While not made of ice, they do their best to keep the temperatures cool.

Snake-Man – Not a brand but a class of assassins created by Xhaknar and Yontar to act as spies. It is believed they were created through selective breeding and rude experimentation, but no records exist of the exact procedure used. They average around 3½ feet in height, have poisonous fangs, and lightly scaled skins. They serve when they feel like it and are loyal to no one. Few exist due to these facts.

Sominid – Not a brand but an alien race who encountered humans long before the gen-O-pod™ war. Over 12 feet tall, mammalian, bipedal, with bright blue skin and white hair, they came to Earth for one reason only, to party. Like good house guests anywhere, they brought their own brandy. Unlike good house guests, they destroyed the moon and killed tens of thousands of people. However, the incident was alcohol-related and not purposeful.

Succubus – Part bat, they average around 6 feet in height and are exclusively female. They have talons for toes and a spur on each heel for balance. They are partly metamorphic and can assume three primary forms; womyn, which resembles a human female except for their feet; mal, which resembles a human male except for the feet and has non-working genitalia; and their traditional form, which features large leathery wings. Their skin colorings represent all the former human races, and they have hairstyles that run the gamut from bald to lengthy locks. They prefer to be topless and wear only loincloths in the wild but can and will dress elegantly when the situation calls for it.

Super Soldier – Multiple genetic sources, they average around 7 feet in height, weighing over 300lbs. Made by the same makers who made the *Mayanoren*, they have faces that are exoskeletons and heavily muscled bodies covered in coarse, dark brown body hair. They tend to be extremely intelligent but limited in scope. Some are military tacticians, others political leaders, and so on. Nevertheless, those limitations do not lessen their deadliness.

Warters – Part warthog, they average around 5 feet in height, are rotund, and strong. They have small tusks on their lower jaw that makes speech difficult. They are dark pink in color and tend to wear robes to hide as many weapons as they can. They were originally bred to be security for a specialized company no one remembers. After the gen-O-pod™ war, they turned to banditry and are scattered across the North American continent.

White Teeth – Part Great White Shark, born to be pure warriors of the seas. Averaging around 6 feet in height with mottled white skin and a mouth that contains two sets of razor-sharp teeth, both top and bottom. They were given better eyesight than their genetic heirs and a far better sense of perception. Vicious beyond belief, they were willing to kill any who crossed them. After the gen-O-pod™ wars, they joined the *Children of the Waters* and adopted their peace-oriented philosophies as best they could.

Wizard – Pure mutants. Ranging in height from 5 feet to 6½ feet tall, they had bright blue skin and varied body types. They were designed to use the forces of magnetism for mining and related duties. To accomplish this, an average human's natural magnetic field was enhanced on a geometric scale. Their basic abilities allowed them to segregate metals from the ground, repel Earth's natural magnetism, and float a few feet above the planet. Because they were built to work in dangerous locales, they were given enhanced control over their alpha waves so they could communicate with each other, in case of danger, without the need for expensive electronic gear.

Wolfen – Part wolf, they average just under 6 feet in height. They were designed to be a forest-based, warrior brand. They have tremendous strength, an increased sense of smell, and intense curiosity, and intelligence. They tend to be covered in reddish-brown fur and have slightly scalloped ears. They can cover great distances without any artificial aid and can learn to use any weapon within seconds. They prefer to live in packs and off the land. They were forced into hiding when Xhaknar attacked.

ANIMALS

Deisteed – About 20% larger than an average horse, they were designed to be work animals. The wealthy landowners used them to show they were more in tune with nature than the robot users.

Kgum – Think an ugly cross between a cow and a water buffalo. They provide meat, wool, hides, and crude labor. They replaced domestic cows, which died off due to an inability to breed on their own.

Narkling – Approximately 8 to 10 feet tall with six legs and a segmented body covered in thick, dark fur. They have razor-sharp teeth that they can rotate inside their mouths. They will eat anything or anyone. They were designed to be mining machines but were too deadly to keep around. The makers dumped them in an abandoned forest in the Mid-West and forgot about them.

Nysteed – The only brand created exclusively by a brand. A horse-like animal, slightly larger than a deisteed, they can run vast distances at full speed and carry heavy loads if need be. They are shaggy, with dark coats, and have flames instead of eyes. Originally bred to help the Wizards explore their world, they became the plains' elite warhorses after Xhaknar came.

Pit person – Mildly humanoid, less than 2 feet tall, and thin, they are non-sapient and fearful of almost everything. They were designed to be helpers and companions for children, but they never worked out.

Quizzle bird – Think of a parrot on acid, and you get the idea. A riot of colors, averaging around 5 pounds, they are humongous and harebrained. Rohta just thought they were fun, so he made a lot of them.

Rakyeen – A six-legged creature, averaging about 6 feet in height, and around 12 feet long, they are furry mutants designed to be draft animals. They are good, if gamey, eating but do not take well to domestication.

Sna-Ahd weasel – Not a weasel, more like a long-necked rat, they were an early experiment by Rohta that escaped before he could finish their line. They were supposed to process soil like earthworms and leave it aerated and filled with nutrients. Mostly they just have sex and live underground.

Steed – About ¾ the size of an average horse, they were designed to run fast for short distances, although they could carry a rider a long distance at a comfortable trot. The makers used them to patrol their estates and impress their neighbors.

TERMS

Arreti - Earth

Brand – artificially created sentient life form

Breaklight - dawn

Clik – approximately one hour

Dark Sun – winter

Dim Sun - fall

Epi-clik – approximately one minute

Even – night

Even-fall – dusk

Even-split – Approximately midnight

Full Sun (*sometimes just Sun or Suns in the plural)*- approximately 365 turns (see below)

Goldens - money

Good Sun - summer

Kay– approximately 1.246 miles / 2.005 kilometers. Arreti has a circumference of 20,000 kays.

Maker - human

Mid-break – when the sun is highest in the sky

Pod – see Brand

Small– child

Sepi-clik – approximately one second

Turn – One planetary revolution or day

Warm Sun– spring

Youngling – pre-teen to teenaged brand

BIOGRAPHY

BILL McCORMICK is a critically acclaimed author of several novels, graphic novels, comic book series, and has appeared in numerous anthologies. He began writing professionally in 1986 for the Chicago Rocker Magazine in conjunction with his radio show on Z-95 (ABC-FM) and went on to write for several other magazines and blogs. He currently writes a twisted news & science blog at WorldNewsCenter.org. That provides source material for his weekly radio show on WBIG 1280 AM, FOX! Bill is a big fan of vodka, music, and this purple haired goddess who keeps waking up in his bed. You can find out more about him at BillMcSciFi.com.